Acclaim for Caitlin Kittredge's *Nocturne City* series

"*Pure Blood* pounds along hard on the heels of *Night Life,* and is every bit as much fun as the first in the series. With a gutsy, likable protagonist and a well-made fantasy world, *Pure Blood* is real enough to make you think twice about locking your doors at night. A swiftly paced plot, a growing cast of solid supporting characters, and a lead character you can actually care about—Kittredge is a winner."

—Jim Butcher

"I loved the mystery and t ..."

... *ork Times*

... *by Shadow*

"A nonstop thr ... usly deadly menace. Count on Kittre ... never say die!"

—*Romantic Times*

"Kittredge takes readers on a dark adventure complete with thrills, chills, and a touch of romance. Well written…and impossible to set down." —*Darque Reviews*

"Fast-paced, sexy, and witty with many more interesting characters than I have time to mention. I'm looking forward to reading more stories in the exciting Nocturne City series." —*Fresh Fiction*

"Wow, I am still thinking about this book. The last time I reacted to a book this way, it was the first Mercy Thompson book by Patricia Briggs. If you are looking for

MORE…

a book that seamlessly blends a police procedural with a paranormal, go out and get this book."

—*Night Owl Reviews*

"A tense, gritty urban fantasy that grips the audience from the onset."

—*The Mystery Gazette*

"Caitlin Kittredge just keeps honing her craft with each new book. *Second Skin* has some pretty creepy elements and page-turning action. Readers who enjoy good solid urban fantasy will enjoy this installment."

—*A Romance Review*

"*Night Life* dove right into the action, and carried me along for the ride...If the following books are written with the same care and interest as *Night Life*, they will be a welcome addition to this fantasy genre."

—*Armchair Interviews*

"Kittredge's amazing writing ability shines through in this wonderful tale of murder, magic, and mayhem...The intriguing plot grips you from the very first page and takes you on a roller-coaster thrill ride with an ending that will leave you gasping for more."

—*Romance Junkies*

"Hot, hip, and fast-paced, I couldn't put it down. Don't go to bed with this book—it will keep you up all night. It's that good."

—Lilith Saintcrow,
national bestselling author of *Working for the Devil*

"Luna is tough, smart, and fierce, hiding a conflicted and insecure nature behind her drive for justice and independence, without falling into cliché. It's also just a lot of fun to read."

—Kat Richardson,
national bestselling author of *Poltergeist*

St. Martin's Paperbacks Titles by
Caitlin Kittredge

Night Life

Pure Blood

Second Skin

Street Magic

Witch Craft

Witch Craft

A Nocturne City Novel

Caitlin Kittredge

St. Martin's Paperbacks

This is a work of fiction. All of the characters, organizations, and events portrayed in this novel are either products of the author's imagination or are used fictitiously.

WITCH CRAFT

For information address St. Martin's Press, 175 Fifth Avenue, New York, NY 10010.

ISBN: 0-312-94362-2

Printed in the United States of America

St. Martin's Paperbacks edition / September 2009

St. Martin's Paperbacks are published by St. Martin's Press, 175 Fifth Avenue, New York, NY 10010.

10 9 8 7 6 5 4 3 2

For all my readers—you know who you are

Acknowledgments

Rachel Vater and Rose Hilliard, agent and editor supreme.

All of Team Seattle, and their insistence that sometimes, I have to leave my office and have a life.

Agent Heidi Wallace of the ATF, whose unparalleled knowledge and fantastic stories of her job ensured that I had to include an ATF agent in the novel.

Lastly, and most of all—thank you to my readers. You helped bring Luna's world to life and here we are four books later, still going strong.

Witch Craft

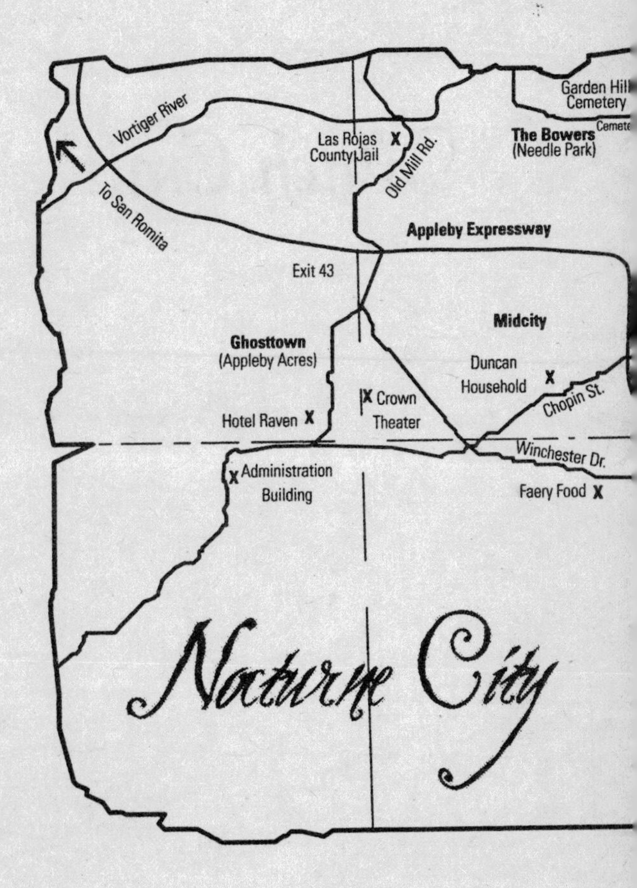
Garden Hill Cemetery
Vortiger River
Las Rojas County Jail
Old Mill Rd.
The Bowers
(Needle Park)
To San Romita
Appleby Expressway
Exit 43
Midcity
Ghosttown
(Appleby Acres)
Duncan Household
Chopin St.
Crown Theater
Hotel Raven
Winchester Dr.
Administration Building
Faery Food
Nocturne City

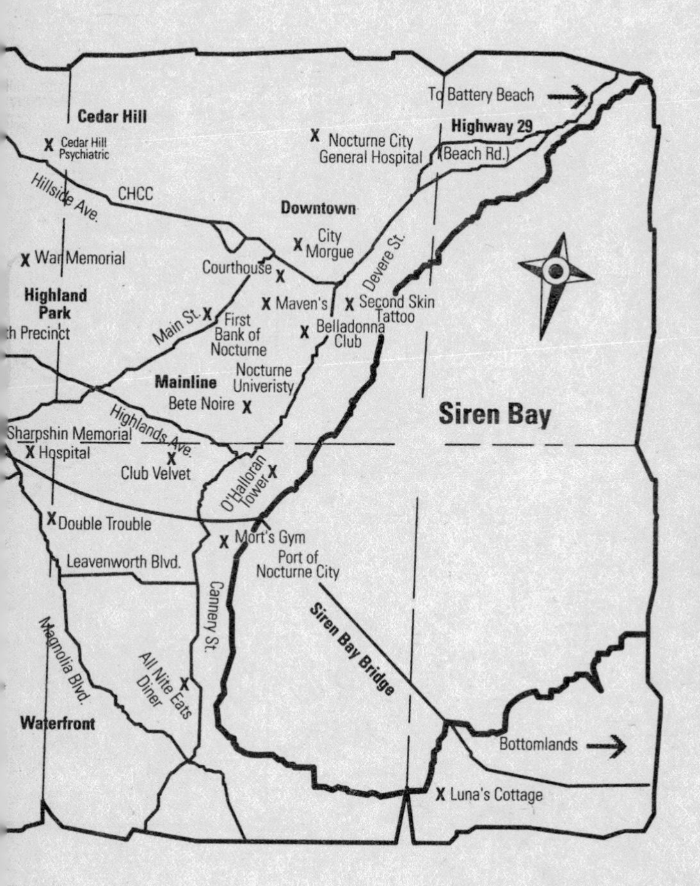
To Battery Beach
Cedar Hill
Highway 29
Cedar Hill Psychiatric
Nocturne City General Hospital
(Beach Rd.)
Hillside Ave.
CHCC
Downtown
City Morgue
War Memorial
Courthouse
Devere St.
Highland Park
Maven's
Second Skin Tattoo
Main St.
First Bank of Nocturne
Belladonna Club
th Precinct
Nocturne Univeristy
Mainline
Bete Noire
Siren Bay
Highlands Ave.
Sharpshin Memorial Hospital
Club Velvet
O'Halloran Tower
Double Trouble
Mort's Gym
Port of Nocturne City
Leavenworth Blvd.
Cannery St.
Siren Bay Bridge
Magnolia Blvd.
All Nite Eats Diner
Waterfront
Bottomlands
Luna's Cottage

One

Chaos crept up on me like someone had tossed a stone into a pond. I was sitting in a window booth at the Devere Diner, shoving a double bacon cheeseburger into my mouth, while across the expanse of red formica table Detective David Bryson did the same with a grilled chicken club.

"Cholesterol," he explained around a mouthful of lettuce and dead bird. "Doc said I'm going to keel over if I don't cut back on the carbs or calories or what have you. Put me on one of that whatchacallit—Long Beach Diet."

"South Beach," I corrected him, taking a pull at my diet soda. Just because I have a werewolf metabolism doesn't mean I need to abuse it.

"However you call it," Bryson said. "All I know is that in a week, I get to maybe eat a burger once in a while." He regarded his sandwich the way most people regarded a dead pigeon on the sidewalk.

"My sympathies," I said, and signaled the waitress for a slice of pie. Bryson glared at me. The waitress finished writing an order for two uniformed cops at the counter and sashayed over. Bryson checked her out. She checked him out.

I cleared my throat. "I'd like a slice of key lime, when you two are done."

"Krystal," said Bryson, reading the name tag. "You ever get down to my part of the city, cutie?"

"Depends what part we're talking about, honey," she said, batting her heavy fake eyelashes at him.

I kicked Bryson on the ankle. "Pie. Key lime. Essential to my continued good health and temperament."

A fire engine roared down Devere, sirens going full blast, and drowned me out. The waitress cupped her ear. "Huh?"

"Key lime!"

A pair of patrol cars followed, their lights revolving heartbeat quick, tires laying black rubber streaks as they took the turn onto Hillside Avenue at top speed.

"Say that one more time, honey." The waitress was still smiling at Bryson. She was brassy-skinned from a spray-on tan and had a red bouffant piled on top of her head. She and Bryson, who was a bull-necked man with powerful arms, a greasy pompadour, and small bright blue eyes, would make a cute couple. You know, if you were into that sort of thing.

"Key lime," I said, rubbing the back of my neck. I could still hear the sirens, even though they were long gone into the crisp October air. Were hearing is sensitive. I could hear Bryson's heartbeat, too, how it quickened when Krystal looked at him.

It was five days before Halloween. The leaves were falling and paper pumpkins and ghosts were everywhere. Halloween made everything seem benign. You could almost forget that the real monsters might be sharing a subway car or a cubicle with you.

The patrolmen at the counter jumped as their radios

crackled. The dispatcher burbled their call numbers and then squawked out, "Eleven-seventy-one in progress at One-oh-seven Hillside Avenue. Fire and rescue en route. All units respond."

To give the cops credit, they were a well-oiled machine. One dug out a twenty and threw it on the counter while the other grabbed his car keys off the counter and ran out the door to start their prowl car. "Dispatch, Ten-ninety-seven is en route," the second cop bit off into his clip mic, before he followed his partner.

The ripples spread out from the stone fall, and a beat after the door slammed shut after the two uniformed cops, my BlackBerry went off. Bryson's pager followed it a moment later.

I tore it off my belt and looked at the text message. *107 Hillside. ASAP.* That had to be Annemarie. Only she would dare *ASAP* the boss. Bryson looked at me, blinked once. "One-oh-seven Hillside?" he asked. I nodded.

Bryson snapped his fingers at the waitress. "Krystal, doll? We're gonna need that pie to go."

I smelled the smoke before I saw it—my nose is my best feature, and I'm not just talking about it complementing my pretty face. Weres can smell a lot, which normally is a mixed blessing. Do you have any idea how a hobo smells to a werewolf? You're better off not knowing.

A black cloud stained the faded-denim blue of the sky, boiling up from the crest of the hill. I pushed my foot down on the accelerator of the Ford LTD that I'd gotten from the motor pool a few months previously, and was rewarded with a groan from the transmission and no discernable increase in speed.

I hit the steering wheel. "Piece of crap car." My previous ride, a 1969 Ford Fairlane, had blown up when I drove it into an open chasm with a pissed-off Wendigo spirit clinging to the hood. Both the spirit and the car were crispy now, and I was back to driving the Cop Standard model, stale upholstery, dubious brakes, and all.

"Jesus Christ, that's a big fire," said Bryson. "Somebody's McMansion is McToasted, for sure."

We were in the exclusive section of the Cedar Hill neighborhood now, Victorian stately homes sitting shoulder to shoulder with large modern monstrosities shoved wherever the developers could find a spare greenbelt. They were uniformly hideous. "How much you wanna bet me it's the fucking ELF or PETA or one of those fucking hippie groups that set their armpit hair on fire to save the whales?" Bryson said.

"I think we wouldn't have gotten paged," I murmured as I rolled up on the scene. Three ladder trucks were hosing down a blaze that was giving off enough heat to break a sweat down my spine and curl my hair, even from twenty yards away. A token ambulance and a phalanx of patrol cars had the street blocked off, and neighbors were staring.

We crossed the street to the cordon and I found the fire chief on scene, a barrel-chested man named Charlie Egan. "I'm Lieutenant Wilder," I said, flashing my badge. It was still new enough that the shine hadn't come off the bronze crescent-moon seal.

Egan grunted. "So?"

"With the Supernatural Crimes Squad," I elaborated, and waited for the inevitable wisecrack, sigh, or meltdown that followed with most city personnel.

The big fire chief just grunted again. "We don't need you."

That tone carried so much more than the words would imply. *We don't need the freak squad reminding the plain humans that there are things in Nocturne City that will bite their faces off with a smile.*

"Someone paged us," I said. "You mind filling me in, since I left a perfectly good lunch for you?"

"No," Egan said. "In case you hadn't noticed, we got a situation here."

A month or two ago I probably would have grabbed him by his polyester tie and made him do what I wanted, but instead I shielded my eyes from the smoke and stepped back. Letting Egan know he was in control, that his manly manliness was secure. "When you've got the fire under control, Chief, you and I will talk again." *And when we do, it will be for a royal dressing-down on your part, mister.*

He didn't pick up on my nuances. Men are like that.

I recrossed the street to find Bryson scooping the last of my key lime pie out of the box with his fingers. "Dammit, David!" I yelled. "What happened to your diet?"

"Hey, I got job stress." He shrugged. "My therapist said I'm a emotional eater."

I turned my back on him and leaned on the hood of the car, watching the blaze. The house wasn't a McMansion—it was one of the old ones, a timber-frame place with too much scrollwork, now a nightmare of gingerbread and burning shingles that made me cough.

Egan strode around looking important until he realized he wasn't doing any more good than Bryson and me, and stomped over to us. "Guy that lives here is named

Howard Corley," he snapped, like he was giving me an order. "Deals in antiques. Works from home."

He paused to let that sink it. I winced as I looked at the smoke and the flames, which had started to recede, barely. "You think he was in there."

"Car's in the garage," said Egan. "Gas tank blew, almost took the scalps off a couple of my men. No reason to think he's not."

I wasn't any closer to understanding why Annemarie had paged me, but I smiled at Egan anyway. "I appreciate it, Chief."

"Yeah, well. Keep your spook squad out of the way if it comes to that."

Then again . . . I sighed and kicked at the concrete, forgetting for a moment I was wearing classy Prada flats instead of my usual combat boots. "Shit," I sighed. The wardrobe that went with being lieutenant of the most-hated task force in the Nocturne PD was massively expensive, the headaches even larger.

"I have better things to do than stand around a crime scene that isn't even ours. Or a crime scene, yet," I complained loudly to Bryson, hoping Egan heard me.

"Well, here comes Hotlanta. Why don't you ask her?"

Hotlanta was Bryson's personal nickname for Annemarie Marceaux, a firecracker-redhead who hailed from Louisiana . . . one of the northern parts, with some tongue-twister French name. She was tiny and slender and efficient, a near-constant *bless her heart* smile in place. A new hire in the department, she'd been shunted to the SCS and taken the news pretty well, at least outwardly.

"Sorry I'm late, ma'am," she hollered at me. "Damn traffic cops wouldn't let me through!"

She was also profane, funny, and a hell of a lot nicer

than an ex-special victims detective had a right to be. I liked Annemarie. Bryson snorted, low. "Here she is, Scarlett O'Hara."

"Hello there, David," she said brightly. "You're looking slender today."

Bryson turned about eight shades of red, and wiped the sweat away from his forehead. "Hiya, Annie."

"Lieutenant," she said breathlessly. "I'm sorry for the cryptic message, but I was in the area and I saw the blaze start. There's something here for us, believe me."

"Okay," I said. "Spill it." The firefighters had finally gotten the flames under control, and new smells were creeping in: char. Cooked electrical circuits. Burnt meat.

Egan had been right about someone being at home.

"I saw the fire start, ma'am," Annemarie said.

I focused on her, and tried to block out the smell. "You don't say."

"Yes," said Annemarie, stepping out into the street and gesturing at the traffic cameras, a few at the intersection. "I think those picked it up, too. It wasn't like anything I'd ever seen, Lieutenant. It caught all at once, from all points. An inferno."

"And you just happened to be driving by?" I cocked my hip and glared at Annemarie. Her cheeks were flushed from the fire and she seemed almost happy. I don't know too many people who get happy about fire and death, except weirdos, and I had enough of those in my life already.

"Oh, I was visiting a friend who lives on the other side of the hill," she said. "Going to clock in when I saw the fire. I called it in and paged you, ma'am."

"Detective Marceaux, if you don't stop calling me ma'am I'm going to slap you right in the head, got it?"

She nodded, going even redder. "Sorry, ma'—Lieutenant."

" 'Luna' would be just fine, Annemarie. Go find out when we can walk the scene, and call the rest of the squad."

After she walked back to her own car, Bryson snorted. "Time was, I only had to put up with you. Now there's another one running around, like some kind of tiny, evil doppelgänger."

"David, did you actually just use the word 'doppelgänger'?"

He spread his hands. "I watch a lot of horror movies. So what?"

I shook my head, hiding a smile. "Never mind."

Two

The sun had nearly set by the time the wreckage was cool enough to be examined, but it gave the rest of the Supernatural Crimes Squad time to get to the scene.

Pete Anderson, our resident CSU tech, stood in what had once been the home's foyer, and shook his head. "There's nothing overtly hinky here, Lieutenant Wilder. Even burn patterns, no accelerants used to the naked eye, no smells you wouldn't expect in a burned-out hulk."

"Then how do you explain what Annemarie saw?"

Pete spread his hands. He had an angelic face, chocolatey skin, and close-cropped hair, both flawless even in the ash and the ovenlike heat of the burnt house. Sweaty, sooty, and unkempt as I was, I sort of hated him.

"Maybe Annemarie made a mistake."

I looked over at her petite frame, as she picked carefully through the wreckage with Javier Batista. Next to Sergeant Batista's ex-SWAT bulk, she seemed even slighter. "Has Annemarie ever made a mistake in the time you've known her?"

Pete's mouth crimped. "Nope."

"So walk the scene and see what jumps out at you," I said.

The medical examiner's staff appeared, somber and silent in their blue jumpsuits, and unfolded a body bag in what was once a study. Ash from paper and books drifted around them as they rolled the corpse of Howard Corley into the bag, zipped and tagged it, and carried it between them back to the van. Corley didn't look anything like a man now. He was raw and featureless, just flesh.

Before the morgue attendants got their cargo shut away, a black Mustang roared to a stop behind the cordon, and disgorged a lanky figure in a black suit.

I checked out the car before I checked out the driver. It was glossy, unmarred, so shiny I could have fixed my makeup in it, had I been wearing any. Red leather bucket seats and a matching detail on the steering wheel. Chrome reflecting the dying sun. Maybe a '67 or a '68. The driver cared about the car, to the point of obsession. And he had flashy taste and probably a glove box full of speeding tickets.

The driver argued with the uniform for a minute and then did an abrupt left turn and stopped the morgue attendants, making them set down the body bag and open it. He took out a penlight and bent over Corley.

I held up my finger to Pete. "Excuse me." I covered the distance to the stranger and the corpse in about two seconds flat. Another benefit of the were, to counteract all the hassles it gives me.

"Excuse me!" I said, loudly.

The stranger looked up at me, tilting square black fifties-style sunglasses down his nose. One inky eye regarded me. "Yes?"

"Why are you poking my corpse?"

He stood, brushing at his knees. His black suit was wool, a custom-tailored job, and the shirt was crisp linen the color of virgin snow. A skinny black tie and cuff links completed the look, along with a swath of burnished blond hair swept back from a high forehead. Mid-Century Hipster with overtones of G-Man.

"I'm sorry. I didn't know it belonged to you."

I crossed my arms, wrinkling my suit jacket. It already had soot and sweat on it—a few wrinkles wouldn't hurt. "Cut the smart-ass act and let's see some ID."

He blinked. "I'll show you mine if you show me yours."

I stared at him, at a loss, which is rare for me. He stared back, one eyebrow cocked, until his jaw twitched and he broke into a grin. "I'm sorry. I'm just messing with you." He stuck out a hand. "Will Fagin, Alcohol, Tobacco and Firearms."

"Lieutenant Luna Wilder." I took the offered hand, shook, and gripped it hard enough so that he couldn't let go. Bones creaked. Fagin yelped.

I reached into his inside jacket pocket with my opposite hand—brushing a silk lining, no nylon for the G-man—and drew out his ID wallet. Sure enough, he was staring back at me from the corner of his ATF laminate. I heaved a sigh. "What the hell are the feds doing at this crime scene?"

Fagin grinned weakly. "You mind letting go of my hand, She-Ra? It's hard to formulate a witty response when I'm worried about my metacarpals."

I released him. "And I ask again: Why are you here?"

Fagin gestured at the burnt husk. "I'm a silent E."

"What?" Was everyone at ATF crazy, or just this guy?

"ATF also covers explosions and explosives, especially since 9/11. We call ourselves the silent E in 'ATF.' You know, because it's not in the acronym. . . ." He trailed off and shoved a hand through his hair. "And I see the little anecdote that works so well on girls in bars is not working on you, is it?"

"Signs point to 'no.' "

That grin swam up again, dazzling me. "Can I at least have my ID back, Lieutenant Wilder?"

I slapped the wallet against his chest. "Take it. And while you're at it, take yourself back to that penis replacement you call a car and get out of my crime scene. I'm not giving the feds jurisdiction without a good Hexed reason, and your skinny ass isn't it."

I expected the requisite pissing contest to follow, but Fagin just lifted one bony shoulder and nodded, putting his sunglasses back on. "I'll see you around, doll. Watch for me."

"Very intimidating, coming from a guy who's dressed like a reject from *Reservoir Dogs*."

Fagin gave me a mock salute, and loped back to his car. I watched him leave. "Jackass."

Bryson came over to me, looking even more hangdog than usual. "I'm gonna clock off and go get supper, boss. I'm gonna pass out otherwise."

"Go," I said. "We're done here."

I made sure Pete would follow the body to the city morgue and collect trace evidence, and then satisfied that we'd done everything we could for a crime scene that we didn't even belong at, I signed out and went back to the SCS's squad room to end another shift no better than when I'd started it.

Frustration was my life, since I'd been promoted to lieutenant in August and given the task of heading the SCS and all its associated baggage. The city had created the task force because they couldn't ignore the monsters anymore, not after a Wendigo named Lucas Kennuka had raised a hunger god in the center of the city. Couldn't ignore Wendigo, couldn't ignore witches running most of the infrastructure from the shadows, daemons rising in the slums. Couldn't ignore the were in me—who was already the were face of the department, thanks to a propensity for people trying to kill me, right out where everyone could see.

And I couldn't ignore or forget Lucas, who'd stabbed me in the gut with a silver knife while he was possessed by his hunger god, and later had saved my life. I'd let Lucas go when the department wanted to lock him up, and I'd sworn I'd never see or speak to him again.

It had to be that way, no matter how much I might want it different. Lucas was a fugitive and I was a cop, a cop who was on thin ice as it was with my history.

I steeled myself as I pulled into the Justice Plaza, the former courthouse that now held the administrative staff and all of the major-crimes task forces—Narcotics, Vice, Special Victims, Fraud, SWAT. The nice, normal folks got sprawling floors of the turn-of-the-century building all to themselves.

The SCS was in the basement.

I successfully avoided everyone's eyes in the lobby, and took the elevator down, watching the storage level and the parking level tick by before the light finally announced "B." Bowels of Hell: supernatural crimes, occult occurrences, dumping ground for problem cops.

"Lieutenant Wilder!"

I flinched. Norris had spotted me. Norris Obermann was the department secretary—or administrative assistant, as he'd be quick to correct you. He was a civilian, old as the hills, and hated everyone. In his spare time, I imagine he hit things with a cane and hollered at kids to get off his lawn.

"Yes, Norris?" I said, turning around with a brilliant fake smile on my face. Norris was so old-school that he didn't even know he was supposed to be an asshole to me because I was female. He was simply perplexed at how "nice girls" like Annemarie and me had come to be in a line of work that involved gun toting and arresting people.

"You have messages," he said, like that was a grave failing on my part. "I've forwarded them to your mailbox. And I tried several times to raise you on your cellular telephone, but you did not answer. Was there a reason for this? Department protocol states—"

I cut him off. "My phone was silenced."

"Department protocol states a ranking officer must be reachable at all times during an assigned shift," he scolded, crossing his wiry little arms. Norris proper came up to my neck, and his shock of gray hair came up to my chin. His sweater-vest and checkered shirt were, respectively, brown and yellow today, and his tie was green paisley.

"I'm sorry," I said. "I must have forgotten department protocol while I was dealing with a corpse that had been burned over ninety percent of its flesh."

Norris swallowed, two blossoms of color springing to life in his cheeks. He hated any discussion of dead things.

"You know when you burn a sausage?" I continued, moving in closer. "And then you cut it open and the insides are all . . . squashy?"

Norris swayed, swallowing so hard I thought his Adam's apple would pop out of his skin. "I . . . yes. I . . ."

I dropped him a wink. "Thanks for taking my messages, Norris. You have a nice night."

He grabbed his coat and satchel and scurried to the elevator. I smiled for the first time since I'd gotten to the fire scene.

My messages weren't anything I didn't expect—one from the chief of detectives, asking me again for a progress report on my three months of running the SCS, which he'd forget about as soon as he got to the cigar club tonight, one from Pete letting me know that he was going to stop at the trace lab and process the evidence from the body, and one from my cousin Sunny.

"I'm going to stop by and make dinner for you. Grandma is driving me insane. You better not be working late." She hung up without a good-bye, but it was all right.

Sunny lived with my grandmother and viewed any defection to spend time with me as some sort of volley in the territorial war we'd been playing out since I was a teenager. I smiled again when I thought about the old bat sitting alone watching TV and thinking up ways to get back at me. The rift between my grandmother and me is simple—she and Sunny and practically everyone else in my family are witches. I'm not, and a shape-shifter to boot. It makes for awkward family holidays, to say the least.

I poked at my computer for a few minutes, before the quiet got to me and I went out into the bullpen. Two detectives were working late—Andy Zacharias, a wide-eyed, vacant-brained rookie who had been in uniform until a few months ago, and Hunter Kelly, a washout from Narcotics who had more suspensions than I had pairs of designer shoes.

"Gentlemen," I said, passing between the empty desks

to the charge board. It was pathetically empty, only three open cases, two of which were simple assaults where one or both of the participants happened to be a witch or a were. Annemarie had made Zacharias write in the fire—his pained scrawl read *suspisious death.* I rubbed out the *s* and changed it before moving to an empty slot on the board.

"Hi, Lieutenant Wilder," said Zacharias, and then spilled his coffee all over whatever he was writing on.

Kelly just grunted. If Bryson was burly, Kelly was simply a grizzly bear wearing a cheap suit. He was younger than me by a few years, taller by almost six inches, and wide enough that he overflowed his desk in all of his pro-wrestler glory.

"Don't strain yourself," I told him. The sole reason Kelly was still on the force was the number of busts he pulled in, in a division where force and little else actually got results from time to time. Then, when Internal Affairs had had enough of him, they washed him out to me.

Kelly gave me the evil eye. I gave it right back, daring him to stand up and finally say something with more than two syllables. I would love for Kelly to take a swing at me so I could get rid of him. Weres are strong, and tough, and I wondered if he knew that I could bounce him off the ceiling.

Zacharias watched us both like a small child when Mommy and Daddy are fighting. I pointedly turned my back on Kelly and wrote *Squad Briefing—10 A.M.* Anything before ten was asking Bryson to show up hungover and cranky, and Kelly not to show up at all. My squad. I was so proud.

Three

Sunny was in my cottage when the LTD grumbled to a stop in the driveway and I extricated myself from its vast interior like Indiana Jones fleeing the rolling rock ball. Sunny had recently gotten a new car, a bubble-topped hybrid that she adored. Everyone except me had a car that didn't suck. Especially Fagin. Damn him. If I ever saw that guy again I was going to kick him in the shins, just because.

I unlocked the front door, stripped off my suit jacket and my shoulder holster, letting it hang from the coat tree with the butt of my new service weapon displayed. In a fit of extreme retail therapy just after my promotion, I had decided that as long as I had a new rank and a new office, I needed a new gun, and traded in my Glock for a Sig Sauer P226. It was very sexy, a TV cop's gun. I'd never actually had to use it.

"In the kitchen," Sunny called. I kicked off the decidedly *un*-sexy Pradas and padded toward her voice. She was cooking macaroni and cheese, the sharp tang of the cheddar tickling my nostrils. Sunny was a vegetarian, but she made mac 'n' cheese like nobody else.

"Thanks for cooking this . . . ," I started, and then stopped, staring at my cousin.

Sunny crossed her arms and glared at me. "What?"

"Nothing," I managed. Her caramel hair was swept up and off her face, secured with a silver clip. She was wearing makeup—actual makeup—and a green velvet blazer with jeans that would have cost me easily a few days' pay, plus my lunch money.

"Is there something going on I don't know about?" I said, trying to discreetly rub the soot out of my shirt. "Is this an intervention?"

"Why?" said Sunny, as the oven timer went off. "Have you done something?"

"What are you wearing?" I demanded. "You look like . . . well. Normal."

Sunny rolled her eyes and pulled out the casserole dish. "Gee. Outpouring of approval. Thanks."

Normally given to peasant tops, loose skirts, or T-shirts exhorting me to *Visualize World Peace*, natural hair and skin that never saw a dab of cosmetics, Sunny looked fantastic. She was prettier than me anyway, but usually I could ignore that by telling myself she looked like the deranged hippie child of Keira Knightley and Buffy the Vampire Slayer.

"I'm sorry," I said, grabbing flatware and place mats to apologize. "You look really good. Is that my blazer?"

"It will be fine," said Sunny, knowing how jealously I guard most of my vintage finds. "I'm just going to a late movie. Nowhere with a water hazard or messy food."

Shock all over again. "You have a date?"

She nodded, a flush creeping into her cheeks. "Who with?" I demanded.

Sunny chewed on her lip while I grabbed a soda from the fridge and served myself casserole and salad. "Troy McAllister."

I promptly choked on my first bite. *"Mac?"*

"Yes," said Sunny, straightening her spine. "That's what I said. Troy."

Just as I was about to lay into her for forgetting to mention the small fact of dating my old lieutenant from Homicide, my ears picked up a sound outside the back door of the cottage. It wasn't much of a sound, really, just a sliding of skin along sand. My rental overlooks the beach, and it wouldn't be the first couple I'd rousted from a blanket and a bottle of wine.

"Wait here," I commanded Sunny. "Don't think we aren't going to discuss this."

She just flapped her hand at me. I ran to the door and grabbed my gun in its holster. Never hurts to be ready.

I shut the door silently behind me and killed the outside light. I didn't need it to see, and whoever was down there trespassing didn't need to see me until I was ready.

The wind bit into me. It was cold, during the night. Gooseflesh blossomed up and down my arms.

Again, that sound. The hiss of something slick and wet over sand, and along with it this time a low burbling of voices in a language that sounded like rocks scraped by waves.

I wasn't dumb enough to call out, not with some of the things I'd encountered during my time in Nocturne City. Blood witches sacrificing to their particular spirits, the daemons who roamed the mists between worlds, Wendigo feeding on the hearts of the living, and enough nasty werewolves to form my own country club.

The moon was half-full, and it tugged on my mind as I crested the dune and started down the rotten steps to the beach. I was in the shadows, and whatever was down there was exposed. Point to me.

The Sig was sweaty in my grip, despite the chill, as I scanned the sand, noticing tracks that came out of the water and crossed the tide line.

They weren't human tracks. They weren't like anything I'd seen before.

Burbling talk came again, and I crept along in the shadow of the dune, lifting my nose to scent the wind. Salt, a lot of it, something rotten from the ocean floor, and that particular singed scent I associated with magick. Not the good happy kind.

I saw them then—three shapes, hunched and crawling along the sand, their rounded heads gleaming under a half-moon, still damp with salt water. Their flippers were the source of the odd tracks, and the sound, I realized as I watched the closest throw its head back, was laughter.

They were seals. Sentient, giggling seals. Just when you think life can't possibly get any stranger . . .

A big piece of driftwood was between me and the seals, and I crouched, watching. They didn't smell right, seals or not, and I wasn't about to let some weird ritual take place fifty yards from where I slept.

The trio circled for a moment, and then one of them paused and, with a groan and a shift, shrugged out of its skin. A human form unfolded from the sealskin, a female form with long tangled hair.

Wind picked up, and I shivered again, realizing my teeth were chattering. The second pair followed their sister, becoming human before my eyes, their skin still gleaming an unearthly deep green. "Holy crap," I muttered, watching the seal women bury their skins and turn toward the water. Their eyes were inky black with no pupil or iris, like most things that didn't come from this part of the world, and their hair was long, dreadlocked with seaweed and sea glass.

The air shifted, and as one they turned and looked in my direction. Lips curled back to show sharp abalone teeth.

They smell you.

"Shit," I said out loud as the three women began to advance, deliberately and with a delicate step, in my direction. The beads and shells in their hair clacked in the breeze.

I had about three seconds before they found me, and less time than that to make a decision. Every sensible bit of me dictated that I should just hide and hope it wasn't me they were smelling. But I'm not famous for being sensible about anything, from my shoes to my boyfriends.

So I stood up, aiming the Sig. "That's far enough."

They hissed at me, and kept coming, the one in front reaching for me with hands that ended in sharp, gleaming obsidian nails.

Okay, so first instincts aren't always right. I started backing up, fast, my finger itching to lay on the trigger of my gun. But they hadn't actually *done* anything yet except creep me the hell out. I had never killed someone who didn't have it coming, and I wasn't about to start now.

The seal woman screeched something at me that made my ears ring and set my teeth on edge, and then she leapt and sprang, fluid as if she were still in the water.

I threw myself to one side, landed hard in the sand, lost my gun, grabbed it again, and decided, *Hex this right to the seven hells.* I ran for the house. Behind me the three seal women gave chase, and I felt cold air on my neck as one set of claws barely missed my skin.

I cleared the steps two at a time, and saw the lights from the cottage. "Sunny!" I bellowed. "Get your ass out here and help me!"

There was a sick crack, like an old bone snapping, and pain sank teeth into my leg. I lost my balance and fell, the Sig skittering away across the crushed shell of the drive.

My foot had gone clean through the rotten steps, and jagged wood drew blood from my ankle that gleamed in the low light.

Fantastic. Not only had I marked myself as a threat to those things, but I'd put my blood into the wind. Could I be asking *Please eat me* any louder?

"*Sunny!*" I hollered. I'm fine in a close-in fight with just about anything this side of the netherworld, but there was no way in the seven hells I was getting close to those things if I could help it. I needed long-range magick.

The three stopped at the foot of the dune, and at some signal from their leader all three of them sprang, loping up the sand on all fours like they were still in the deepest ocean.

"Fuck," I snarled, low, tugging at my leg. There was a rip, and my suit pants came free. There went three hundred dollars straight down the tubes. My actual leg was another matter, still shackled by rotten wood. The pain caused bright flashbulbs to explode in my vision, but my desire to survive was stronger.

I resumed yanking, tears springing involuntarily to my eyes as I felt skin and wood grate, slicked with my blood. I could smell it—heavy, metal, dank with fear. My stomach lurched. I can deal with decomp and stinky gym socks and other weres, but my own blood? Not so much. It's a thing with me.

The lead predator was on me, and she landed, spraying

sand into my face. Noises like stones in a brook burbled from her mouth. She was laughing at me.

Just as I started thinking I was Hexed, my skin prickled as the air around me changed, electrified. A small strong hand closed around my shoulder and tugged hard, Sunny's familiar scent and the sting of her magick wrapping around me.

She met the seal woman's eyes, and Sunny's were snapping with power as she pulled it out of the aether. "Back off of my cousin, bitch."

Sunny's caster was in her other hand, the wooden disc she used to focus her power wreathed in energy. I felt my skin begin to siphon off Sunny's power, pulling the magick through my body to augment my were DNA to heal me and help me. Being a Path, able to absorb the power of others, the magick I got from the were who turned me—that's also a Thing with me.

The pain in my ankle lessened marginally, and I jerked it free with a cracking of wood and a spray of blood. Sunny yanked me over the lip of the dune, and I thought we were home-free as I felt the crunch of the driveway under my butt.

Then a hand latched around my ankle, digging into the wounds and making me yelp all over again. The seal woman snarled, and even though I didn't understand any of what she was spouting, I've been cursed out enough to know it when I hear it.

"Let go!" Sunny cried. "I swear to everything Hexed and holy I'll fry you!"

I whipped my head to the left. My Sig was still out of reach, but that didn't mean I was defenseless.

"Should have listened to her," I told the seal woman, and flexed my hand. With a sting, my were claws sprouted from my fingers, and I felt my monster explode into the forefront of my mind. I raked my claws across the seal woman's face, digging deep and leaving bloody furrows from forehead to cheek. Being bloody, terrified, and pissed off is prime time for your were to come out, and I was all of the above.

The seal woman squealed and fell backward, clapping her hands over her face. She and her sisters retreated, staying just out of my reach like a pack of hyenas.

That was exactly what they were—hungry, hunting predators. I rolled over, grabbed my gun, and fired three shots into the air. The seal women fled back down the beach and grabbed up their skins, slipping back to flippered, hunched shapes as they took to the waves and disappeared.

Sunny helped me up and we hobbled awkwardly back to the cottage, me leaving little dribbles of blood that looked black under the moonlight across the shells.

"What the *hell* were they?" I demanded, as if Sunny should know everything just by virtue of being a witch.

"You're asking me?" She transferred my weight to the doorjamb and nudged open the front entry, helping me in and dropping me on the sofa. "Lift your leg up," she ordered. "Don't bleed everywhere."

"You don't live here anymore," I reminded her, crabby. "And I'm already healing up, anyway."

That was a lie, but by morning I'd be good as new. Between the speedy regeneration given by the bite and the energy I'd Pathed from Sunny, which kicked all of my were side into overdrive, you'd swear nothing had ever happened to me in forty-eight hours. It's a good thing I don't scar, because otherwise I'd look like Frankenstein.

Well, I didn't scar anymore. The worst of the scars was

still there, itching even now against my trapezius muscle on my right shoulder. The bite would never go away. I shoved a finger under my collar and scratched at it, feeling the four round rough patches in my skin.

Silver also doesn't go away. I had two of those, one from a daemon armed with silver rounds in his big-ass gun and one from a Wendigo's silver knife, whom I let too close because I was a big-ass idiot.

Sunny came back and interrupted my mental catalog of scars. "Here. Towel, bandages, antiseptic." She'd done this enough times to know what I needed. "You going to be okay?"

I blinked. "Yeah, sure. I've had a lot worse."

"Good, because I'm late for my date."

I'd forgotten all about that. "You and *Troy* behave yourselves. No sneaking off to make out."

The towel whapped me in the face. "Grow up, Luna." She flounced out the door, not a hair out of place even after she'd rescued me.

I cleaned the blood off of myself and bandaged up the cut, which was deep. I felt lucky—an inch lower and it would have punched into my Achilles tendon.

Maybe it was just a random attack, and maybe I wasn't as lucky as I thought. Briefly, I scrolled through the list of people who had the juice to send three supernatural hunters after me. It was a short list, these days. Alistair Duncan, a blood witch whom I'd killed, had no more followers who were loyal, and besides, the Big Daddy of Nocturne City's blood witches owed me a favor. No blood magick user would dare.

The Warwolves, whose pack counsel I'd sent to Death Row at Los Altos for murder, could care less about me. I was an Insoli, a packless were, and rated next to nothing.

The Wendigo who had stabbed me was long gone, and had been possessed by a Wendigo hunger spirit when he pigstuck me, anyway. When he'd been himself, he'd saved my life and I'd saved him from the cops. We may not be best friends, but we were even.

There was one person—if you could call him that—whom I hadn't heard from lately, who might want something from me. This could just be his sick way of getting my attention, after the last time we'd parted, when I'd ended up owing him a favor.

"Asmodeus?" I whispered, experimentally. The daemon had a habit of showing up, demanding things, and vanishing again back into whatever world he called his. He was, ostensibly, among the last of his kind. They called him the Wanderer between the worlds, the only daemon to escape being cast out of our dimension by caster witches, with golden eyes that could look into your soul. I'd met him for the first time when an insane blood witch had summoned him, only to have Asmodeus turn. He was inhuman in the coldest, most alien way possible, and he scared the hell out of me.

Nothing happened, except for the whining of the wind under the eaves. The power flickered as a particularly strong gust rattled my windows, and the waves sent subtle vibrations through the floor as they pounded the beach. I hoisted myself off the sofa and skip-hopped over to the stairs, up to my bedroom.

At least up there, it was a little less creepy.

Four

The day did not dawn bright and early. As I drove across the Siren Bay Bridge toward downtown, it was wrapped in mist, fingerlets of moisture curling across the LTD's dirty windshield. It was like driving through the netherworld, or what I imagined the netherworld looked like.

I stopped at Java Jones, the cutesy chain coffee place where all the baristas wore precious yellow aprons and visors with cheap plastic sunglasses wired to them, in a nod to Jones, the fictional founder of the place. His visage graced their logo, a fisherman's hat and huge shades overshadowing a moustache. He looked like a cartoon Hunter S. Thompson with overtones of seventies porn star.

After I poured a double mocha into myself, I felt marginally more alive, and even greeted Norris with a smile when I stepped off the elevator. He thrust a sticklike arm at me, pink sheets clutched in his fingers. "Messages."

Not *Messages, ma'am*, or *Messages, Lieutenant*, or *Yo, dude, you got some messages.* I accepted the slips from him and leaned on his desk. He completely ignored me, and swiveled back to his workstation with a snap. When Terminators from the future took over, Norris would fit right in.

"Why didn't you send these to voice mail, Norris?" I asked, gently as I could.

"Phones are down. This entire place is going to shit." Bryson stomped by, pastry crumbs adorning his violet shirt and matching tie.

"Internet, too," Annemarie said, following him. "He's just pissed because he can't get online and quest for the Holy Grail, or some nonsense."

"It's not the Holy Grail!" Bryson yelled. "For the last time, I'm a paladin and I'm trying to find the cup of rejuvenation! I need it to level up!" He slammed the conference room door after him. Annemarie shook her head and gave me a *can you stand him?* smile.

"I guess it's better than surfing for Japanese porn," I sighed.

"Who's surfing for porn?" Zacharias had a look of absolute terror on his face as he scuttled past us. "It wasn't me! Kelly must have used my workstation!"

I rolled my eyes. "Relax, Andy. It was a joke."

"Come on, honey," said Annemarie, taking him by the arm. "Let's get you some decaf before the meeting starts. You look a little high-strung."

She led Zacharias away, and I was left to go into the bullpen and find Kelly. I dropped my shoulder bag in my office on the way, noting the sad blinking light on my modem that told me it was out of service.

"Electrical surge."

I jumped about a foot in the air. "Hex my mother, Kelly! Don't sneak up on me!"

His flat ugly face split into a grin. "Sorry, ma'am. I didn't know you spooked so easy."

I breathed in, out, trying to get my kill instinct back under control. The were doesn't have time for figuring out *who* is behind you; it just wants to gut them from crotch to throat before they do the same to you.

"Back up," I told Kelly tightly. He raised his hands and backed away from me. He had gotten behind me, almost touched me, and I hadn't smelled or heard a thing.

I filed that one in the mental in-box for later, after I calmed down enough not to tear pieces of Kelly off and throw them across the room.

"Like I said . . . there was an electrical surge last night. Knocked out service to the whole Plaza. They don't know when we'll be back up."

"Be that as it may, there's still a staff meeting and you're late for it," I said, sharply enough to stab something. "Get your ass in the briefing room."

"Sure, LT. Whatever you say." Kelly turned, fluid for such a big guy, and strolled toward the conference room. I leaned against the door for a second and let my heart drum itself out, sinking back to a normal rhythm. My palms and spine were sweaty, and I felt pain in my jaw and hands from an imminent phase, triggered by my scare.

Kelly was going to get himself castrated if he didn't stop testing me. I had no patience for macho assholes who decided to turn their insecurities on me because I was pretty and female. I'd put up with enough of that shit in Homicide. Not in my squad.

I rubbed my hands over my face, and put a smile on it before I stepped into the briefing room.

"You get lost, Wilder?" Bryson asked me. "I know it's confusing, what with the three whole rooms they gave us and all."

"Coming from someone who once got lost in his own apartment, David, that's funny," I returned. It was a weak rebound, but it got everyone smiling, or, in Pete Anderson's case, giggling. Pete was still young enough to giggle. I let him.

Everyone was accounted for—Annemarie sitting just to my right, where she always did, Bryson slouched next to her because he always attached himself to the prettiest woman in the room, at least until she Maced him, Batista and Zacharias sitting like a study in contrasts: All-American Dweeb, meet Latino SWAT Badass. Kelly crouched in a corner, away from the table, rocking back and forth in his chair. He looked like that kid who always sleeps through class, and his posture clearly telegraphed he had far better things to be doing.

I kicked his chair as I walked to the front of the room. "Listen up." Kelly jumped, and I was gratified.

"We have to face facts, guys. Nobody in this city likes the SCS. Nobody thinks we're effective. Nobody wants us doing our jobs."

Batista gave me a thumbs-up. "Way to boost morale, jefe."

"If you'll let me finish? Because of this, we are going to work this case Annemarie got us as hard as we can. Even if it's not an SCS case, we're going to make it one. And we're going to close it, airtight, and we're going to do it flashy and public. Everyone got me?"

There was general nodding and muttering around the table. Annemarie swelled up with pride, as much as a tiny 110-pound woman could.

"Okay," I said, clapping my hands like a leader would. "What have we got?" I didn't feel like one. Only with these people did I even get a semblance of respect. Everyone else in the department probably thought I slept my way into the job.

Annemarie held up a folder. "I did some research on Howard Corley, and I discovered he's a person of interest."

"Oh?" I sat, glad to have all of the eyes off me.

"Yes, ma'am. He was suspected of dealing with a black-market fence by the name of Milton Manners."

Bryson gave a snort.

"Manners has some small-time convictions for pushing articles without proper provenance, stolen goods, but his real talent is in magickal artifacts and rare tomes of spells."

"And you know this how?" Batista asked.

Annemarie shot him a dirty look. "I have informants the same as you do, Javier. The SCS's job *is* to keep tabs on the supernatural community, right?"

"Right," I agreed. "So you're thinking that Corley and Manners got into something that was above their pay grade?"

Annemarie nodded. "And Corley was incinerated for his trouble."

I turned on Pete. "Speaking of the crispy Mr. Corley, where are we on the arson investigation?"

"Chief Egan is keeping me briefed on what they find," said Pete. He had that expression on his face, cagey and excited, that let me know he wasn't finished. "But I got to thinking . . . maybe someone besides Annemarie saw something. Or something saw something, I could say."

"You don't make any gods-damned sense," Bryson complained.

Pete rolled his eyes. "I had Traffic pull the footage from the speed camera at the intersection near Corley's house," he said, waving a DVD. "It's worth looking at."

"Go for it," I said.

Pete booted up the DVD player and TV in the corner and slid the disc home. The screen fizzed, and then, absolutely nothing played. I was looking at gray fog, the same as what had enveloped me during my drive in.

"Well, this is scintillating," said Bryson.

"Is something blocking the camera?" Zacharias asked, his first speech of the meeting. He immediately blushed and slid down in his seat when Pete looked at him.

"No, no physical obstruction, and furthermore, Traffic's computers swear the camera was operating normally during the entire five-minute stretch that's blacked out."

"Someone doesn't want us to see what's going on at that intersection," I said softly.

Pete hit fast-forward and the gray fog slithered away, revealing the edge of Corley's blazing house.

"That all happened in under five minutes," he said. "Fires don't burn that hot and fast without a hell of a lot of accelerant—which the fire crew found no evidence of."

"Could be an incendiary working," I said, thinking of the magickal car bomb that had nearly killed me while I was in Homicide.

"Nope," said Pete. "For that, you need a circle, and a circle around a house that size would take a lot longer than five minutes to cast and set."

"Plus, you'd see the remains," Kelly spoke up, surprising the hell out of me. "The burn mark from where the victim crossed and set the working."

"Okay," I said. "So not a witch's working, but definitely unnatural in origin."

"You got it," said Pete.

"Good call, Annemarie," I told her. She smiled. "We're all working this unless the world suddenly ends," I said. "Bryson and Annemarie, we're going to go check out

Manners. Zacharias and Batista, pull everything you can about Corley—financials, permits, everything. Find out who might have wanted to set him on fire. Pete and Kelly . . . figure out how this fire got started. Go back to the scene."

Kelly grunted at Pete, who just gave me a mock salute and headed out the door, his CSU windbreaker flapping. Kelly lumbered after him, once he'd given me the requisite poisonous look.

I just smiled, because I was starting to feel good about myself for the first time since the promotion. We had a case—a real case, not bullshit—and we were going to crack it fast and I was going to be able to hold my head up again.

I let myself think that until we got to Milton Manners's antique shop, downtown.

The shop, called Echoes of Yesteryear, was nestled into a brick storefront on Main Street, before it turns into Devere, in the tony part of Downtown. "Tony" here meaning, "the part without crackheads sleeping on the sidewalk vents." It was a cozy block, nevertheless, with window boxes and street lamps that worked and no graffiti on the walls.

Gentrification was creeping up, slowly but surely, on my city. Highland Park, my old precinct, had been the first to clean up, and the area around Nocturne University was getting pricey and snooty. Even the Devere Diner, my favorite hole-in-the-wall, was getting a face-lift. They'd been closed for renovations for two weeks not so long ago. My stomach rumbled with the want of a bacon cheeseburger, even though it was barely 11 A.M.

This block of shops and flats was the first volley for Downtown, which was mainly famous for being dirty and housing the city morgue. I'd be sad to see the atmosphere flee in the wake of condo developers and yuppies, truth be told. I came from a broken-down resort town with a population that could fit into one block of Nocturne, and if the city was dirty and dangerous, it was still mine.

Annemarie led the way into the store, which greeted us with a perfectly retro door chime. Bryson glowered at his surroundings, the mellow woods and delicate glass at odds with his blocky frame.

"You break it, you buy it," I whispered to him, and then called aloud, "Hello? Mr. Manners?"

The shop was silent, and layered with hundreds of years of dust and must. My nose started to twitch and I willed myself not to sneeze. The weak October sunlight did little to illuminate shelves stuffed with rare books and floor space crammed with furniture. I wound my way through the mess, looking for anything out of place, anything overtly magickal. There was nothing, just a bunch of low-end antiques. Smart little fence, was Milton Manners.

"Hello, sir," Annemarie called in her syrupy accent. She could lay it on thick when she wanted. "We're here to speak with you about a matter of some importance."

There was something in the shop that wasn't right, even if no contraband was in sight. I walked up to the counter—a repurposed bar from some Art Deco club that went a little bit crazy with the gilt—and checked the antique register. It was locked up tight. "Milton?" I said again, dropping a hand to my waist and unclipping my radio. "Dispatch, this is Seventy-six."

"Go ahead, Lieutenant," a dispatcher said after a moment.

"Has there been a silent alarm triggered at Eighteen-ten Main Street today?"

My radio hissed for a moment and then the dispatcher said, "Negative, Seventy-six. No alarms triggered."

"Could have been knocked out in that surge," Annemarie muttered.

"Thanks, Dispatch," I said, shooting Annemarie a glare. I was already jumpy from Kelly. I didn't need her doomsaying just then.

Slipping around the counter, I rattled the office door, the pristine frosted glass just as it must have appeared in the 1940s, the gold filigree lettering still reading *Manners & Son Fine Antiquities, Office.*

The iron knob turned in my hands, and I drew my weapon, holding it down at my side. Bryson moved in on the right and I gestured at him to open the door and cover me.

On an internal count of three, Bryson stuck out his hand and shoved the door open. As the space inside opened up, I realized why I was on edge.

I smelled blood. Dead blood.

The door banged the wall and I went in, gun first. Milton Manners lay on his stomach, one arm reaching toward a desk that had been ripped apart, as if by gale-force winds. Papers, ledgers, and office supplies were scattered to the four corners of the small room.

Everything was covered in blood. Liberal lines of low-velocity spray coated the desk, the carpet, the walls, even the blacked-out window that looked at the alley behind the shop. Manners had been shredded. It wasn't hyperbole—his clothes were in tatters and the skin beneath was flayed open so that I could see gristle and muscle and bone.

"*Jee*-sus." Bryson stood in the doorway, one hand over his mouth. "Poor bastard."

I shut my eyes for a second, the blood scent and the sticky feeling on my skin making me want to scream—or howl.

Get a grip, Wilder. Get it fast.

Okay. I took two steps back, putting myself outside the crime scene. There was still blood on my shoes. "Crap," I muttered.

"My lord." Annemarie took one look at the body and the blood-painted office and retreated. I heard her calling for backup and radioing Pete to come down and assist the CSU team.

Bryson put a pudgy hand on my shoulder. "You okay, Wilder?"

I looked at him. "Not really, David," I said.

He grinned. "Because of that little old dead body? Come on. I've seen worse at the butcher's shop."

"No," I murmured. "Because I think someone tried to kill me."

Five

I got the duty of standing by the crime scene, making sure no one disturbed it, while we waited for Pete and a CSU team. Annemarie barely stayed in the store, and Bryson hovered where he didn't have to look at the body.

"What d'you mean, someone's trying to kill you?" Bryson hollered from his vantage point.

I waved him off. "Forget it, David. It's not important right now."

He looked like he wanted to say more—Bryson is a gossipy old woman at heart—but the CSU team arrived, all somber navy windbreakers, silent figures who went about their duties with an air of resignation.

Pete came over to me. "I called the medical examiner from day shift, but he kicked it to Dr. Kronen, because they're swamped from the weekend. I didn't complain."

"Fine," I murmured.

The tech with the camera did the requisite headshake and muttered, "Hex me." I took note of that. She might be a friendly, if this was the sort of thing that put people on opposite sides of the supernatural/plain human fence.

Pete did his job smoothly and efficiently, and I was

proud of him. He had his own camera and a slew of evidence bags, and he bagged Milton Manners's hands and photographed every corner of the room. Anything that might be trace, including the blood-spattered laptop and ledgers on the desk, got bagged and tagged.

Bryson yelled again. "Sawbones is here, Wilder!"

Bart Kronen gave him a distasteful look, lips pulled tight like a purse. "So good to see you again, Detective." Sarcasm dripped off his words like venom, but he smiled when he saw me. "Lieutenant Wilder. Congratulations are in order."

"Appreciate it, Bart," I said. "But save it for when I haven't just discovered a hacked-up body, maybe?"

He shrugged. "As you wish." The dead never bothered Bart. He pulled their secrets free as easily as I interrogated a live suspect. Bending over Manners, Bart didn't even flinch as he peeled back the shirt shreds and shone his penlight into the wounds.

"Well, I can already spot your fallacy, Lieutenant," he said.

I didn't want to walk into that room again. The smell was overpowering, and looking at the red, ripe meat was making me think all sorts of nonhuman thoughts.

But I did, because I was better than my were. I had a job to do, and the day I freaked out in front of Kronen, the gods, and everybody was the day I retired for something less taxing, like mall security.

"Okay," I said to Bart. "What did I do wrong?"

"Aside from put your footprints in the crime scene?" His eyes twinkled with amusement. This was Bart's version of comradely chatter. "This body was not hacked." He showed me the furrow in Manners's back, ragged along all the edges. "I can see how you made the presumption. Something like a machete would make these long cuts. But this was a short sharp instrument, dragged with great force, almost as if this poor soul were raked over."

I knew what was coming and excuses were already in my throat.

"These marks were most likely made by claws," said Bart.

"It wasn't a were," I shot back. "I would have smelled him. Her. Point is, it couldn't have been a shape-shifter." Both were and Wendigo smell pretty distinctive, and they weren't here. Just blood, and the cloying smell of imminent decomposition.

"Be that as it may," said Bart gently. "There are a great number of scent markers in this room. Are you sure you did not become confused?"

"I don't get *confused*," I snapped. "It was not a were. I'm not turning this into a witch hunt, Bart."

He stood up, careful not to get any of the spatter on him. Better than I'd managed it. My skin crawled and I wanted nothing more than to douse myself under a hot shower.

"As you wish, Lieutenant," said Bart. "But until you can show me the talons of the creature that did this, I will be forced to record my initial impressions when I retrieve this man for an autopsy."

He turned to sign out with the uniformed officer at the door, and I had a brain wave. "Bart, wait!"

I caught him by the shoulder. "Could the weapon have been anything like this?"

This was going to suck, both for me and for my reputation in the department. Who was I kidding? I had none left, except as *Wilder, that crazy bitch in the basement.*

Bart eyed me. "I'm waiting, Lieutenant."

I sucked in a breath and let the phase come, drawn in by the smell of Manners's blood. My claws came out again, my eyes changed from gray to gold, and I felt my teeth start to grow.

"Holy crap," Bryson said, from far away. I held up my hand to Bart. The claws were clean, the blood from the seal woman erased.

"Could they be something like this?"

Bart never blinked. He took my hand and examined my claws, running his thumb along the edge like you would a high-quality kitchen knife. "No," he said shortly. "These are too small and narrow." He released me. "It appears you were right, Luna. A were is not the culprit here."

I didn't tell him that I wasn't as sure as I seemed. Every were pack is different—different magick, different abilities, different physiology. I already lived with enough twitchy fear in my hindbrain because of what the general public thought of us. I wasn't giving Bart any more reasons.

"Hey, Wilder." Bryson's voice broke through my fog. I spun on him, snarling. To his credit, he only flinched. "You can put it away now," he said. "Uh . . . everyone's sorta looking."

My instincts warred for just a second before I clamped down on the were. I've had fifteen years of practice, and only when I get truly enraged do I have trouble keeping my monster under wraps. Slowly, I felt stings in my eyes and jaw and hands as the phase receded.

"What are you all looking at?" I snapped at the slack-jawed evidence techs. "The department doesn't pay you to stand around picking your teeth. Get back to work!" The force of my voice shook them out of their stillness, and they flew back to their tasks.

Bryson shook his head. "You gotta prepare me for that shit, Wilder. Otherwise I'm gonna be reaching for the silver bullets."

"You don't have silver bullets," I snarled, childish and cranky. The phase was a lot like PMS—it played havoc with your emotions and never left you in the best of moods.

"I do."

The voice from over my shoulder had an amused tinge, which was the only reason I didn't spin around and immediately punch the owner in the face.

Will Fagin stood just behind me, way too close for comfort, his sunglasses in place. The suit was slate-blue today, with a red tie and shiny black shoes. Very Rat Pack. "What are you doing at my crime scene, Lieutenant Wilder?"

Maybe it wasn't too late to punch him in the face.

I pasted a wide smile on my face instead. "I'm so sorry, Agent Fagin. I wasn't aware that your name was on this particular crime scene. That seems to be an issue with the two of us."

Okay, that was kindergarten, but the guy was so smug he could drive a Buddhist monk to sarcasm.

Fagin got even closer to me, tilting his shades down. His eyes, up close, were the color of India ink, with tones of deep blue like sunlight trying to reach the bottom of the ocean. "Look, Ms. Wilder, I don't want to get into a jurisdictional pissing contest here, but if that's what you want, I'm telling you now—I'm the best in this town, and you'll lose to me."

Bryson and Annemarie had clustered behind me, and

Annemarie gasped at what, to her ears, was foul language. Bryson just looked like he wanted to clean the floor with Fagin. I gripped the agent by the elbow. "Can I speak to you outside for a moment?"

"I don't think we really—ow! Hey!"

Were strength has its benefits, for sure. I grabbed Fagin by his upper arm—solid, lean muscle under my grip—and dragged him out the front door and onto the sidewalk.

"Bloody hell!" he snapped. "You almost dislocated my shoulder."

"Yeah, well, man up," I suggested. "Mr. Big Tough Federal Agent."

"I never claimed I was tough," Fagin said. "Just the best. Now, what? What's so important?" The corners of his mouth were twitching. I amused him. Christ, he really was looking for a beating.

"Why the Hex are you here?" I demanded. "This guy was a small-time fence for stolen goods, which, last time I checked, was not the provenance of ATF. So either come up with a damn good reason for being here, or step off."

Fagin looked at his shoes. Probably checking his reflection. Not a hair was out of place, and in the sun he was very blond and very good-looking. Not that I was checking him out or anything. Police officers notice everyone, pretty or not.

What? We do.

"I can't tell you that," he sighed finally. "It's a confidential investigation by the Bureau."

"No interdepartmental cooperation, no crime scene," I said. "Get moving, Fagin."

He sighed. "You're really throwing me out? Me? I class up the joint."

"Try to get a court order, if you want," I suggested.

"Or show me some proof that this is an ATF case. Your choice."

Fagin paced a few steps away, and then back. He was out of control now, and I liked it. People are easier to read when they're off balance. "You're a real hard-ass, you know that?"

"Thank you," I said with a grim smile. "I've worked at it. Mostly because of cocky bastards like you."

"Me?" He poked his vintage jacket, affronted. "Doll, *I* simply acknowledge that I have a certain skill set. It's everyone else who's cocky."

Doll? I contented myself with rolling my eyes. "You going to 'fess up, or are you going to hit the road, Agent?"

"Fine." He heaved a sigh. "But I'll need access to the office."

"Fine," I agreed. "Let's go."

We wound back through the dusty shop, putting on paper booties this time to protect our shoes from the blood. Fagin snapped on gloves, stepped over the body like it was a box of crackers, and beelined for a cheap oil painting on the wall. A pastoral scene, cows and all. He took the ugly thing off the hook and there, set into the plaster like a fresh wound, was a safe.

"None of you thought to look for this?" I demanded to the CSU crew and my detectives. Annemarie spread her hands. Bryson had the grace to look embarrassed.

"My fault," said Pete shortly. "I didn't search the room thoroughly. I'm sorry, Lieutenant." He was glaring at Fagin like he wanted to melt him in a microwave.

"Forget it, Pete," I said, loud enough for all to hear. "Fortunately, we have Agent Fagin to show us the error of our ways."

Every single eye in the room lasered into the agent's

back. There. See how smug he was with my entire squad and tech team turned against him.

"Thanks," Fagin said, examining the safe. There was a keypad combination lock. "Really. Can't tell you how much I love dealing with hostile locals."

"Payback for the whole pissing-contest thing," I said, pleasant as if I were in church, chatting with the vicar. Not that I've ever actually been to church, voluntarily.

"You know, I was wrong about you," said Fagin.

"Oh?"

"Yes. Not only are you a hard-ass, but I think you're as nasty and underhanded as I am." He punched a code into the keypad and the safe unlocked.

I edged up to him until we were touching, front-to-back. "I don't know what universe you're living in," I murmured into his ear. He got very still, every bit of him tense, hand resting on the safe handle. "But in case you didn't know, women work in law enforcement now. And occasionally, we're even good at it. Call me a cute nickname again and I will castrate you in public. And then I'll laugh. You're right: I am nasty. That's exactly the kind of nasty thing I'd do."

I punctuated the last with a soft growl that stood every hair on Fagin's neck straight up. He turned around, ever so slowly, until we were separated by maybe half an inch, sharing body heat.

"Wow," he said, taking off his sunglasses. His eyes were shining. Both of us were shaking a little, me from being pissed the hell off, Fagin from . . . I scented him.

"Do you want to go out to dinner sometime?" he asked, a grin splitting his face.

I closed my eyes and forced myself not to bang my head into the wall. He smelled cool and sweet, with an undercurrent of that man smell that they get when they're, well . . . use your imagination. "Gods," I muttered.

"I'm sorry," Fagin said. He dropped his gaze from mine. "I'm just . . . I'm used to dealing with dumb cops. It's been that way in every posting I've had. No one wants to deal with the feds, and they stonewall us, and they're rude. But you—you're not rude."

"What am I?" I asked, not backing up. I had the upper hand, it seemed, what with my chest pushed into his, and I was going to abuse it. "Tell me, Fagin—what else could you possibly say about me?"

"You . . . you are something approaching terrifying," he said, and laughed. "Now, Lieutenant Wilder, do you want to see why I'm interested in poor old Milt down there? Really?"

Kronen's morgue team had arrived, and rolled Manners into a body bag. The screech of the zipper bespoke finality. It was over now. We could return to our lives.

I backed away from Fagin, who still had that evil grin on his face. "Yeah. Show me."

Fagin twirled a combination and jerked the safe open with a *ker-chunk*. I expected cash, drugs, maybe some gold bars from Nazi Germany. I didn't expect guns.

They lay in neat rows, eight of them, four pistols and four small-caliber machine guns. Fagin swept his hand over his bounty. "We got word of high-end guns coming into Nocturne via antiques shipped from Eastern Europe and Asia. Seems that Milt wasn't happy with fencing Grandma's jewels any longer and went after the big bucks."

"Holy crap," said Bryson. Inwardly, I was thinking pretty much the same thing.

"So," Fagin said. "You ready to admit that I belong here now?" He snapped open his phone and put in a call to his agency to collect the guns before I could say one way or the other.

I didn't put up a fuss. I was looking for something non-human that had ripped Manners apart, and I was inclined to think it probably wasn't because of his gunrunning.

"Look," I said. "I'm willing to let you in on the investigation, on a *cooperative* basis. 'Cooperative' here means that I'm in charge."

He nodded. "I can live with that."

I cocked my eyebrow. "Coming from someone with an ego the size of Downtown, I find that hard to believe."

"I'm not an egomaniac," Fagin said. He leaned on a banquette upholstered in dusty blue velvet. "And I'm not adverse to a woman in authority. I'm just an equal-opportunity asshole."

"Oh, really."

"Yep. It's one of my more charming traits."

"Is your continued health and safety enough of a reason to knock it off?"

He shook his head, ruffling those golden locks just a smidge. "No. But you yourself are, dollface." He stuck out his hand. "You have my full cooperation."

"Good," I said, not shaking. "And the Corley fire—we're investigating that as an SCS crime. You'll back off?"

"As long as we're sharing information, why not let me help you?" Fagin said. "ATF has resources that your department doesn't. And there's, you know, my continued presence and its associated cachet."

"The SCS needs this case," I told him, in a bout of all-too-frequent honesty. I have a hard time keeping my mouth shut. It's served to get me into a whole lot of trouble, but sometimes it works out in my favor, because the people I'm talking to are so stunned they let me grab the upper hand.

"Did I say anything about taking credit?" said Fagin. "I don't need some podunk arson case to make my career. It's made, doll. I am the golden boy of the Nocturne City office." He rubbed the back of his neck when I didn't immediately swoon. "But it's still an interesting fire and I want to help. Or is that more than your pride will allow?"

He grinned again, showing his teeth. Daring me to go one more round.

"You know something, you sell yourself short," I told him. "You are the king of all the assholes I've ever met."

"Can't say I didn't warn you," he said, as I turned to walk away. We were done here. Manners was tagged and bagged, and Pete had all of his evidence for analysis. We'd find the killer—who- or whatever it was.

"Hey, sweetheart," Fagin called. "You never answered my question."

I turned around, feeling the pink creep up my face. "What are you talking about?"

"Dinner. You and me. Yes?"

"Yes," I said.

Fagin relaxed into that too-cool pose I was starting to recognize as his triumphant posture.

"When all seven of the hells freeze over," I added, and strolled out the door.

Bryson was sitting on the hood of the car with a chili dog halfway down his gullet. Annemarie looked on like she was watching pigs at the county fair. "Let's go," I told them. "Back to the house." Two cases in one day, after three months of drought. Either I was lucky, or I was cursed.

"I'll drive." Bryson inhaled his chili dog and bolted for

the driver's side door. I let him. I was tired already and my thoughts were in a muddle. Plus, my ankle still hurt.

"Did you get rid of that awful man from ATF?" Annemarie asked.

"No," I said. "He's going to be working with us for a while longer."

"Well, shoot," Annemarie muttered.

"Asshole," Bryson said around his mouthful, jerking us out into traffic.

"He's not disagreeing," I murmured, and stared out of the window at the passing skyscrapers, many of their upper floors vacant and gray with the reflection of the sky. A black shadow passed overhead, something that flicked in and out of vision faster than a breath.

I leaned over and looked out again, between the stone canyons that made up my city. It flicked by again, a black blot on the paler-than-pale sky. I thought it had wings—couldn't be sure.

We turned and I watched, my breath still and my heart pounding in my chest.

It came again, lower. Following the car. Following me.

"Bryson," I said urgently. "Take your next right."

"Huh?" he said. "That's the Downtown Passage, Wilder."

"So?"

"So, it's lunch hour. It'll be packed."

The shadow came again, closer. "Take it!" I thundered at Bryson as the light went green. He cut a lane of traffic with tires squealing and merged onto the underpass, a section of Wagon Way that cut under the old central district, before Mainline went up in the middle of the last century. It was theoretically the fastest way back to the

Justice Plaza, but it was, as Bryson had threatened, packed.

We ground to a halt, Annemarie's small frame snapping against her seat belt, at the edge of a sea of red taillights.

From outside the tunnel, I caught a faint cry on the wind, and a pumping of great, heavy wings as whatever-it-was flew away, robbed of prey.

Six

It took Bryson nearly fifteen minutes to cover the two miles back to the Plaza, and he complained every inch of the way.

I floated for a bit after we returned, waved off Batista's offer of lunch, and shut myself in my office, staring at myself in my dark monitor.

What the Hex was going on in this city? Magick fires, critters that flew, all of the above after me?

Well, I reasoned, they didn't *have* to be after me. I tended to get paranoid about things like that, because I've had enough people try to kill me to justify it. But two partners in crime, dying hours apart—that was solid. That, I could sink my teeth into.

So quit being self-involved, Wilder, and work your case. I'd find whoever had burned Corley and shredded Manners, and I'd put them behind bars, publicly. I'd redeem the SCS. This little fantasy propelled me out of my chair and into a much better mood, at least for the moment. I was even able to forget about how Fagin smelled, up close.

I stuck my head out of my office. "Hey, Javier—you still on for lunch?"

"Sure thing," he said, grabbing his wallet, badge, and keys off of his desk. "You doing okay, Wilder? You look a little spooked."

"Hex me, is it that obvious?" I found my own wallet in the depths of my bag and shoved it into my suit jacket—this one was an old Valentino dinner suit from the seventies that I'd repurposed into something for the daytime by adding a severe red blouse and my trusty combat boots peeking out from under the wide hems of the pants. At the rate I was going through clothes, I was going to have to start shopping at T.J. Maxx. The thought filled me with no small amount of horror.

"A little bit, yeah," said Batista. "But you hide it well." He winked.

"I am," I admitted. "Spooked." I could tell Javier that much. Batista was a good guy—he kept secrets like nobody's business. "I ran into these . . . things at the cottage last night. Spooked me."

Batista cocked his head. "What things? Like, weres? Somebody messing with you?" Batista is a very good loomer, and he loomed just then, his eyes murderous.

"No, these were women. Women who turned into seals. Three of them."

"Selkies," said Zacharias, setting a precarious stack of folders on the desks he and Batista shared. We both stared at him, which made him turn interesting colors.

"Excuse me, Andy?"

He swallowed, his skinny Adam's apple poking against his throat. "Seal women are selkies, ma'am. Water-going shape-shifters, most often found in Ireland and the outlying islands."

"With a hunger for were flesh?" I guessed.

Zacharias shrugged. "They're considered foragers, but

they are predators, much as seals are predators in the open sea," he said.

"Andy, how do you know this shit?" Batista demanded.

Zacharias drew a nervous breath. "I read." He dropped the folders and scuttled back down the hall to the elevator. Batista shook his head.

"Three months we sit together and he doesn't say boo to me, and now he's freaking Monsterpedia."

I hid a smile. Maybe Andy would make it in the SCS yet. "Let's eat," I told Batista. At least I was hungry again.

The elevator doors rolled back as we approached, and a scarecrow shadow stepped out, topped by dark hair going gray around the edges and the too-familiar tired eyes.

"Mac." I blinked at him. "What brings you to my little corner of Hell?"

He cracked a smile, his long lean face lightening, but his eyes were still somber as a gravedigger's. "Good to see you, too, Luna. There some place we can talk?"

"I'll get yours to go," Batista said, stepping away. Nobody wants to be around when the big kids fight. "You still like it with extra cheese and chilies?"

I shot him a smile. "Thanks, Javier. And get Bryson something that agrees with his diet, will you?"

Mac and I stepped back into the elevator, and I pressed the R button to take us to the top of the Plaza. We rode in silence, Mac watching the lights tick past on the old-fashioned dial above the door, me watching Mac. I took a second look at him, after five years of working together. I tried to figure out what Sunny was seeing.

The elevator chimed and let us off into a small breezeway that led out to the roof. Up this high, clouds were scudding in from over the bay and the air smelled like cold, smoky rain.

"Hell of a view." Mac leaned on the railing, the wind whipping back his hair and tie.

"Hell of a surprise to see you in my squad room," I returned, leaning my back against the rail so I could look east, toward the mountains. They wore crowns of ice, the forests below so deep and green I felt like I could sink my hands into them. "What's wrong, Mac?"

"SCS is not proceeding like the brass hoped it would," he said. "As department liaison, it's my job to tell you that if you don't close the Corley case, they're going to shut you down."

I knew that SCS had no friends in the department, but I felt the cold ball drop into my stomach all the same. "Mac . . . that's insane. We haven't been given a chance yet—"

"Three months," said Mac. "The same chance any task force gets. And what's this I hear about you getting on ATF's shit list?"

I groaned and pressed the heels of my hands over my eyes. "If we're on the subject of rumors, there's the one about you dating my cousin."

Mac looked startled when I took my hands away. "She told you?"

"Of course she told me! Hex it, Mac, what are you doing with her?"

His knobby hands curled around the railing. Good—I'd successfully diverted the subject from Fagin and from my squad being disbanded.

"I'm enjoying the company of a brilliant, beautiful woman who for some strange reason agreed to go out with taciturn, middle-aged me. What happened with ATF, Luna?"

Dammit.

"Mac, they can't shut us down. I'm on to something here. The agent from ATF thinks it's a gun case, but I know it's more than that. Corley and Manners were into some bad mojo and now they're dead."

"Evidence?" Mac fished in his jacket pocket and brought out a crumpled pack of nicotine gum, shoving three pieces into his mouth. "Sunny," he explained. "She wants me to quit."

"Watch out—she'll have you doing yoga and eating tofu before you can say 'Kansas City rib eye.'" I sighed. "There's no evidence yet. Just one burnt body, some claw marks, and a distinctly bad feeling."

"Far be it from me to rain on your parade, Luna," Mac said, "but I'm here to give the official word. Thirty days with no closures and you're shut down. Your squad will be reassigned. You, too." He blew a bubble. "Do me a favor."

"What, throw myself off the roof?" I slumped, the mountain and sun and clouds mocking me with their serenity.

"Prove them wrong," said Mac. "Because if anyone can, you can. Take care of yourself, Luna." He walked back to the elevator, Jack Skellington come to life, and disappeared behind the worn brass doors.

I stayed up on the roof a while longer, wondering just how the fuck I was going to do what he asked.

Pete Anderson and a beef burrito were waiting for me when I got back to my office. "I got something!" Pete announced, waving a file over his head like it was a Dead Sea Scroll.

I tore the wrapper off of my burrito and bit into it. Extra cheese and chilies. Batista was a good man. "Go ahead," I announced around my mouthful. Pete, Batista, and everyone else currently eating or working in the small basement room would never know what Mac and I had spoken about. They didn't deserve it, and it wasn't going to happen.

I hoped.

"All right, what we have here is the report on the fire from Egan's arson investigator," said Pete. He spread out a bunch of readings and photos on my desk, knocking paper and empty fast-food containers aside. "Egan's team found that no accelerants were used, as I suspected, but most important . . ." He ran his hand across the swath of photos. They were burn patterns, fans and arcs of phantom flame against the bones of Corley's home. "No point of origin."

"It had to start somewhere," I said. "They missed it."

"Nope," said Pete. "The lead investigator swears up and down by her findings. The fire started everywhere at once—and it started hot. Poor Mr. Corley never had a chance in any hell."

"Let's reserve the 'poor' part until we figure out *why* someone wanted to set him on fire," I said. "What else?"

"It resembles nothing so much as controlled burn," said Pete. "Except instead of a forest, it was a house. A man."

"Okay," I said, pushing back and shoving the last of my burrito in my mouth. "Good work, Pete."

"I mean, it *has* to be supernatural, right?" he asked, eyes alight. "Fires don't just spring up perfectly formed, in a finite area. Notice how even though it was hot and fast, it never spread and the fire crew had no problem getting it under control."

"It did its job," I murmured. I banged open my door. "Batista. Where are we on Corley's background?"

"Still digging," said Batista. "There's precious little there."

"Well, find something," I said. "Pete, how soon can you get to work on Manners's computer?"

"Already done," he said. "I have Technical Services pulling the information on the hard drive. Shouldn't be more than a few hours."

"All right," I said. "Page me when you have it. I'm going out."

"Where?" Batista called, but I didn't turn around to answer. I didn't feel like explaining, anyway.

I skipped the sucky motor-pool car when I hit the main lobby of the Plaza and walked the ten blocks to the federal building on the corner of Devere and Highlands. FBI, DEA, and ATF shared an alphabet soup in a grim gray building with grim gray men and women scurrying back and forth beneath its frowning edifice. I made it to ATF's floor on my own and caught a passing suit by the arm. "Will Fagin. Is he in?"

The suit jerked a thumb toward the back of the cube farm, looking me over like he thought I might be a salesperson. Or a hooker. Who knew with somebody like Fagin?

Following his admittedly vague lead, I wended my way to the back wall and found Fagin sprawled in his chair, his feet on the desk and puffy sound-blocking headphones atop his scalp. They were mussing his hipster hair.

He was watching information from the ATF database scroll by, fingers tapping his desk in time with the music. I tuned my ear and caught snatches of bass and a pack-a-day woman's voice. Peggy Lee.

"How retro," I muttered. I snuck a glance at Fagin's

screen, since he hadn't noticed me yet. Milton Manners gave me a hangdog look from behind a mug slate, with all of his vital stats displayed.

I dropped a hand to Fagin's shoulder. "I think now is an excellent time to begin sharing information."

How it happened I still don't have clear in my head, but one moment I was leaning down to talk to Fagin, and the next I was on my back staring into the ugly fluorescent tubes that flew low across the office ceiling, my view partially blocked by Fagin and the business end of his service weapon. All of my air went out of me with a *whump.*

"Jesus," Fagin breathed, ripping off his headphones and tucking his gun back into its holster. "You should know better, Lieutenant."

"Apparently," I snarled, knocking away his proffered hand. Heat started in the place where my shame lives and spread to my face. "What the hell was that, *The Matrix*?"

"No, that was me being snuck up on when I wasn't expecting it," said Fagin.

I dragged myself to my feet. I was winded and startled as hell, but intact. Mainly I was humiliated. It takes heavy-duty reflexes to be faster than a were. "Yeah, well, your technique sucks. You could have broken your own wrist trying to do that move sitting down."

"That's what this is about? A critique of my manly prowess?" Fagin twitched his cuffs back into place. I got a glimpse of brass cuff links, dice stamped with three pips on the left and four on the right.

"Lucky seven," I said.

Fagin blinked. "You're the only person who's ever noticed that."

"What, that you have appalling fashion sense as well as appalling manners?"

He smiled at that, thin and sharp as a razor. "Oh, Lieutenant, we've done the snarky banter, don't you remember? We decided it was beneath you. Now, did you want something, or do you just like to give men heart attacks?"

I opened my mouth to shoot out something else juvenile and pissy, but instead, I stepped into Fagin, forcing him to drop into his chair. I put my hands on the armrests and rolled him back to the desk, hitting with a bang. We were close again, trading breath, my lips an inch from his and my breasts brushing the immaculate fold of the red silk handkerchief in his pocket. I could hear his pulse and smell his sweat, and I slowly ran my tongue across my teeth. "Fagin, if I wanted to give you a heart attack . . . you'd be flatlining about now."

Just as fast, I stood up, stepped back, and stuck my hands in my pockets, relaxing and giving him a perky smile. "Now, let's hear everything you've got on Milton Manners."

Fagin lost his cool for just a second, his eyes darkening and his lips parting. He leaned forward, like he wanted to say something, and then he also snapped back into his pose. "Not a lot to tell. Started as a fence, ended as a wannabe gun smuggler hacked to death by critters unknown."

"Then read it off the screen," I purred. "Even you should be able to read, Will."

He flushed, but he gritted out, "July 1977, possession of stolen property. September 1981, possession of stolen property. May 1987, receiving stolen goods. June 1987, he got two years in the state pen for the same." He opened his mouth again and I cut him off, leaning over his shoulder.

"On second thought, let's just read to ourselves."

Milton Manners's sad and largely wasted life scrolled by, his arrests getting fewer and far between, his bank account shrinking.

"Wait," I said, as a line of text flashed past. "What's that?"

"'November 2003,'" Fagin read. "'Possession of a controlled substance.'"

I raised my eyebrows. "Does that seem like it fits in with a small-time fence to you?"

He opened the file and read, "'Suspect was detained crossing the border in Tijuana. Suspect was found to be in possession of a large amount of unprescribed pharmaceutical medication, purchased illegally in Mexico.'"

"What the hell . . . ?" I read on. "He was crossing the border with *Viagra*?"

"Shitty off-brand Mexican Viagra," Fagin agreed. "Hell of a party." He caught my look and swallowed. "So I've heard."

"Why did someone like Manners need Viagra?" I muttered.

"You've seen the guy. Why *didn't* he is the better question." Fagin closed out the file with a swish of the mouse. "And on the subject of questions: Why did you really come over here?"

"Excuse me?" I gave him a glare. Men questioning my motives is never my favorite thing.

"You could have dug up Manners's sheet in your own office. Why'd you come over here and bother me for it?"

"I . . . we're supposed to be sharing information," I said. "This is your case, too."

Fagin regarded me steadily, with dark animal eyes, unblinking. "Okay," he said finally. "If that's how you want to play it for now. This is me, sharing my information like a good boy."

"Thank you," I said, backing out of the cube.

Fagin caught my wrist. His fingers were corded and cool, not rough in the least. "I'll get the truth out of you, Wilder. One way or another."

I smiled, showing my teeth. "You threatening me, Fagin?"

"Not at all," he purred. "Just assuring you that I'm going to figure out what's going on behind that pretty face."

A connection clicked in my brain. Swirling shadows hiding simple clear facts. "Can you tell me who bailed out Manners on the drug bust?" I said.

Fagin let go of me. "Sure. Good thinking." He brought up the sheet, and ran his finger down the lines. "Some woman named Grace Hartley. No priors. She put up her house as collateral. Fifteen-fifteen Bonaventure Drive, here in town."

"Thank you," I said. My BlackBerry shrilled on my hip and I looked at the incoming call. It was Bryson. "David, no. For the last time, no. Pie does not count as a fruit. Stay on your diet."

"Wilder, what are you jabbering about?" Bryson said.

I sighed and wheeled away from Fagin. "This better be something earth-shattering."

"Close to it. There's another fire."

My heart leapt up into my ears, the blood roaring. "Give me the address."

"Warehouse in Waterfront, the old wrecks behind the port of Nocturne City. Just drive down Cannery . . . you'll see the smoke."

I jabbed the call off. "Shit."

Fagin perked up like a dog sensing blood. "Something come up?"

I pointed at him. "I need your car. Cannery Street. Fast as you can."

Seven

The Mustang was lightning on wheels, never mind what reasons Fagin had for keeping a car like that. We sped down the waterfront to the port, following the plume of black smoke that echoed the Corley fire down to the sick flutter in my stomach.

Fagin laid a sideways stop next to the cordon the fire department had set up across Cannery, black tracks springing to life behind us on the pavement. He waggled his eyebrows at me like I was supposed to wave pom-poms at the effort.

“I see Hutch,” I said, “but where’s Starsky?”

“For your information, Starsky and Hutch drove a Torino.” Fagin grinned, and hopped out of the car, a skinny jackrabbit on springs.

I followed, catching the slouchy rotund figure of Chief Egan beyond the cordon.

“If it isn’t the freak squad,” he greeted us. “What did I do to deserve this?”

I jerked my thumb at Fagin. He was irritating, sure, but he had his uses. “You got yourself a big-ass explosion. I’m just tagging along.”

“Warehouse full of hazardous material?” Fagin said.

"Not the first time a firebug has picked that as a spot to test out a new incendiary device."

"No," said Egan. He rubbed a hand over his thinning hair, bald pate shiny with sweat. "No, this warehouse and the other two on the block were all owned by a fellow named Brad Morgan. This one," he swept his arm to indicate the blazing warehouse, "was a community center for underprivileged kids or some crap."

"*The* Brad Morgan?" I asked. "The news anchor?"

"Yeah, why? You know him?"

"Shit, Egan, I watch the news same as everyone else." Everyone in Nocturne City could put a face to Brad Morgan. He was dark-eyed, hero-chinned, and dulcet-toned. Perfect gravitas, perfect hair.

"He's big into charity work," said Fagin. "Does the pledge drive every year for the community centers around the city. I see those ads fifty fucking times a night when I'm trying to get baseball scores."

"Tell me about it," Egan grumbled. "The wife gave two hundred dollars last year. 'It's a tax write-off, Charlie.' "

"Was anyone inside?" I cut through Egan's screed.

He lifted one shoulder. "School just let out about twenty minutes ago. Most of the kids are back there behind the tape—can't get a straight story out of 'em about any of their friends being inside."

I looked in the direction of his chubby finger. A cluster of elementary school–age children were standing behind the tape, corralled by three patrol officers, several of the children's anxious faces streaky with tears.

"Somebody should call Brad Morgan and get him down here," Fagin said. "Chief, you want to take care of that? It's your scene."

Egan nodded and backed away, pulling a cell phone. Distracted from the freak squad, at least for the moment.

"Smooth," I told Fagin. Before he could answer me, one of the children began to holler, trying to rush the cordon. A uniform lunged and held him back, chubby legs kicking.

"Hey, hey." I jogged over. "What's the problem, kid? It's dangerous in here."

"Mister Nick!" the kid hiccupped. "Mister Nick is inside!"

Oh, Hex me. "And Mister Nick is?"

"He's our counselor. You gotta get him out!"

The kid resumed kicking, and the officer holding him grunted, "That's enough, kid!"

"Shut up," I told the officer, because a sound had come to me over the blatting of ladder trucks and the clamor of the onlookers behind the cordon. It was high and thin like a mosquito in my ear. Screaming.

I would be the only one who could hear it.

Fagin looked at me askance as I skidded to a stop next to him and Egan. "There's somebody in there."

Egan's face sagged. "Ah, fuck."

"Get back in there and get him out!" I demanded.

"Much as I wish we could, there's no way in hell my crew is going back in," said Egan. "It's so hot in there it would melt the skin off of your little bones, Lieutenant. And in big boxy old places like this, there's always the chance of flashover. I'm not risking my men."

I grabbed him by the shoulder of his scratchy fire-chief shirt. "Someone is *alive* in there, asshole!"

"And he's as good as dead, has been since we got here!" Egan yelled back, his face going florid. "Now, I'm not turning one dead body into five!"

The screaming wavered, bent by the force of the heat rolling out from the burning warehouse.

I snarled at Egan, "Fine." Turning, I made a run for the closest truck.

Fagin followed me, planting himself in my way when I grabbed an oxygen tank and mask, and a heavy protective jacket and fireproof gloves. "The Hex do you think you're doing?"

I shrugged into the jacket and snapped the mask over my face. "Going in there." The words echoed loud in my ears.

"Oh no, you're not," said Fagin. He put out his arms to stop me and I growled, fangs sprouting with no urging from me.

"I can hear him screaming, Will."

He made no more moves to stop me as I ran toward the blaze. The heat closed over me like a diving bell, sweat breaking on all of my exposed skin and curling my hair like straw around my face.

I cut right, around the worst of the blaze bursting through the shattered windows at the front of the warehouse, following the thin, pitiful sound of Nick's voice.

There was an alley between the warehouse and the one next door, filled to my ankles with dirty brown water from the firefighters' hoses. I sloshed through as ash fell around me like nuclear snow, catching in my hair and eyelashes and sticking to my cheeks.

The air here was thick and visible, and it stung my eyes, causing tears to sprout and mingle with the sweat. I could smell the overwhelming stench of a thousand burning things, even through the cool scentless oxygen flowing up my nostrils from the tank.

I turned the corner and saw a fire escape, smoke roiling out of the window at the top. But no flames, and no heat.

The screams were much closer now.

I took the steps up the fire escape two at a time, the warm metal shuddering under my weight. The window at the top was shattered, jagged glass mouths snapping at me.

My foot broke away the mullions on the tall old-fashioned casement, and I stepped into the smoke, yelling, "Nick! Where are you?"

"Help me!" he screamed. "I'm in the office!"

Great. That could be anywhere.

I couldn't breathe, even with the mask, and I dropped down to a crouch, where the air was marginally clearer. I still couldn't see more than an arm span in front of my face, and punctuated the fact by running into a soot-covered desk.

"Fuck." That smarted.

"Where are you?" Nick screeched. "I can't get out!"

"I'm coming!" I hollered, getting down on my hands and knees and feeling along the wall until I got to a door. It wasn't any hotter than the rest of the wall, so I opened it.

The corridor in front of me was like the nightmares I had about the night I got the bite. Smoke curled down from the ceiling, long white fingers exploring the contours of my body. Far away, orange flames leapt, and the entire corridor was stifling and dreamlike, my vision blurring.

Peripherally, in my animal brain, I realized it was from a lack of oxygen, and took a deep hit off the mask.

I crawled again, past smoldering doors and overturned pieces of furniture, toward the orange haze at the end of my vision. I could feel the bone-melting heat of the fire, and the sound of it, the snapping roar, began to overtake the sound of my own rushing blood in my ears.

"Nick!" I bellowed.

"In here!" he shouted. "The door's stuck!" I batted aside the smoke and saw a door in front of me. I also saw the problem—the door was wreathed in flames and a large piece of burning timber had fallen across, barring it shut.

"Shit," I muttered. "Nick!"

"Yeah?"

"You're trapped by debris. . . . I'm going to try and move it, but *do not* open the door. You understand me?" I knew enough from the arson investigation class we all took at the academy to know that a bubble of oxygen suddenly exposed to an inferno would equal bad news for everyone.

"Why not?" His voice notched up into hysteria. "I want out of here!"

"Me, too, dude, but that's not going to happen unless you stay calm and do as I say." The fire spit hot air and sparks at me as it ate through the electrical wiring in the wall, the hissing and the smell of burnt elements making me gag.

The roof beam that had fallen in was still burning, white and ashy and far too hot to touch.

I slipped my arms from the fire-retardant jacket, keeping it around me like a cape, and stripped off my suit coat with a sigh, leaving me in a white tuxedo blouse soaked with sweat. Farewell, wardrobe.

Exerting my were strength, I ripped the Valentino down the back seam, using the two halves to pad my hands underneath the gloves. I tugged on the beam, my shoulder screaming at me.

I felt the flames licking at my exposed skin, above the neck of my protective gear, as the beam shifted with a groan. It fell away, smashing through the rough wood beneath and allowing a gout of flame from the floors below.

"Is it shifted?" Nick's voice was shrouded in wet hacking coughs.

"Yeah," I panted. How the Hex we were going to get out of here was another question. The flames had eaten away the walls around me, and they were spreading fast. Could we get back to the fire escape in time?

"I'm coming out!" Nick said.

"*No,*" I growled. "Don't open the—"

I caught just a flash of Nick's face as the cheap particleboard door swung back. Young, tan, floppy black hair left over from college, terror and soot trailing down his hawkish features.

Then, with a great slap of air, the fire was sucked inward, blossoming all across the ceiling and down the wall and over the assemble-it-yourself Target furniture that made up the office.

Bright paintings of families and outer space and dinosaurs curled up and disintegrated under the flames.

Whump. I was on the ground, the flashover blowing a furnace into my face, and the screaming had started again.

Nick writhed on his stomach, flames coursing along his back and neck and even in his hair, which popped as it burned away.

"Shit," I panted. "Shit, shit, shit."

I shucked my protective coat and threw it over Nick, tamping some flames out but not all of them. "It hurts," he sobbed. "Oh, Jesus, it hurts. . . ."

"I know," I said. "But right now we got bigger problems." Like the orange corona that wreathed the hallway, a gauntlet made of heat between us and the way out.

"Can you stand up?" I asked Nick. He just sobbed, the scent of overcooked meat in the air, even with the smoke. Okay, that was a resounding *No*.

I grabbed Nick by the belt and his collar and started to drag him, feeling heat on my own back. Bad enough with the fire gear—now I felt as if my sweat had started to sizzle, like my back was a frying pan. The metal snap on my bra dug into me like a branding iron.

Nick was deadweight, and the beast in me commanded me to leave him, abandon him as the weakest of the pack, and run before I burned.

I ordered my monster to be silent, and put my back into dragging Nick down the hallway. There was a groan from above and I snapped my head up, eyes full of ash, to see the roof beams at the crux of the warehouse tremble as the fire roiled over them, not hot and urgent and consuming, but nearly gentle, like fingers in a caress.

"You so owe me," I informed Nick. Would we make it before the roof came down on us?

I hoped so. Prayed a little, as I dragged Nick and myself through the fire, toward the broken window, the smoke replaced now by pure shimmering heat.

Nick wrapped his fingers around my wrist. "Don't leave me," he wheezed.

"I'm not," I managed. The heat was stealing air from me, moisture. Soon I'd pass out, and cause some poor morgue newbie to vomit when he showed up to collect my charbroiled corpse.

The roof beams groaned again, and a piece of half-melted sheet metal crashed to the floor in front of us.

"That's it," I said to Nick. "We gotta run for it." Not that he could respond to me. I wasn't even sure if he was breathing, but that I was going to find out outside, with paramedics, not here, in this version of my own private hell.

I gave one last heave, and reached the window with Nick's body. I ducked through the glass, putting one foot on the fire escape. It showed me the error of my ways by giving a screech and giving way from the brick, clattering into the alley below.

Well. Wasn't that just fan-fucking-tastic.

Nick moaned feebly and I looked at the ground twenty feet below. "You so better live through this," I told Nick, and then wrapped my arms around him in a lifesaving hold. I slid my butt across the sill and leaned out, into open space, feeling the cool air sting my skin like plunging a burn into ice water.

I let gravity take me, me and Nick's deadweight, downward to meet the earth.

We fell split-second quick, and the ground rushed up at me like a hammer. I felt two ribs crack on impact, something separate in my shoulder, my neck whipsawing like a carnival ride. Nick's body flopped off of me like I was a trampoline, landing in the water. I gasped, the pain taking any words I may have had and smashing them. But it was all right. I'd heal. Nick wouldn't have been so lucky.

"Luna?" Fagin's voice cut through my long, blurry tunnel, staring straight up at the smoke-clouded sky. "Oh, jeez," he breathed. "Hey! Get the medics back here!"

Fagin fell to his knees beside me. "Luna, can you hear me?"

I coughed and then grimaced, because every breath stabs you anew when ribs are broken. It hurt so bad I couldn't see straight, could just see Fagin's narrow face as he checked my pulse and my pupils and then grabbed my hand between his two bony palms. I Pathed a spark from him, barely a flicker, but it spread warmth in my gut and straightened me out enough to rasp a few words. "I'm fine. Check Nick."

Fagin withdrew and after a moment floated back into my line of sight. "Doesn't look good, doll. I'm gonna give him CPR. You don't move. That was one hell of a hit."

Paramedics came running, got both Nick and me onto backboards, carried us clear of the fire with the staccato code they use amongst themselves to keep from their charges how bad things might really be. Someone jabbed me with a fat syringe full of painkiller, and I stopped feeling much of anything.

I heard a few snatches of radio talk as they bundled Nick into an ambulance, me beside him. "Smoke inhalation . . . third-degree burns . . . cardiac arrest . . ."

Fagin hopped the tailgate of the ambulance just before the doors slammed. "I'm riding with her," he told the paramedic when she opened her mouth to object.

She shrugged at him, and, as we pulled away, leaned over me to start an IV. "Lights-out, Officer."

"I'm a lieutenant," I slurred, but the morphine took hold, and I don't remember anything else between the blackout in the ambulance and the rude awakening in a hospital bed.

Eight

The pain was ten times worse when I woke up. Weres heal fast, but we also shake off painkillers like end-stage junkies. "Fuck me," I groaned, throwing a hand over my eyes to block the fluorescent lights.

"How you feeling, slugger?" Fagin said. He was sitting in the chair next to my bed, reading a magazine.

"Like hammered crap," I said.

"Well, you'll be gratified to know nothing is broken except the ribs. Doc says you can go home once you're walking again."

I felt around for my clothes, or what was left of them, folded neatly at the foot of my bed. I was dressed up in one of those oh-so-charming paper gowns with no ties in the back.

"It's a good look on you," Fagin said, nodding to my state of undress.

"Get out and let me change," I snarled.

He stood up, long and lazy. "You in that big of a hurry to go home? Stick around. I hear the pudding is to die for."

"I'm not going home," I said. "I'm going back to work."

Fagin tilted his head. "After what you just did? They're gonna put you on psych leave, doll."

"Trust me, the department has seen worse," I said. "And in case you missed it, someone is setting things on fire in my city, and now people are being hurt."

"No doubt," said Fagin. "But don't you think you should, I don't know, rest for twenty-four hours?"

"In twenty-four hours I'll look like none of this ever happened," I said, throwing back my blankets and standing gingerly. Ice raced up and down my spine and neck.

A nurse busted in, like there was some kind of alarm attached to pigheaded patients. "Miss Wilder! You can't be out of bed yet. You're still heavily sedated."

"Sounds like a party," I mumbled. Grabbing up my clothes, I turned on Fagin. "Get out, unless you want to see my sooty naked body."

"That supposed to be some kind of incentive to *leave*?" Fagin said, that smart-ass, incredulous lilt to his voice.

I threw a shoe at him. "Out!"

"Fine. Hexed temperamental woman." He threw me a wink and ambled out.

The nurse remained, glowering at me. "Miss Wilder . . ."

"Lady, I'm leaving. If you want to try to stop me, I swear to everything Hexed and holy that I will stab you with this IV, because I am in that rotten of a mood." My morphine hangover wasn't doing anything to improve my outlook, and combined with the pain it made for a potent Bitch Cocktail.

Her face curled like a sour pug dog. "Fine. The hospital is not responsible."

"Yeah, I'll be sure to sue you if I drop dead," I told her. She huffed and moved to leave.

"Wait," I said. "I'm sorry—well, not really—but the man who came in with me, the burn victim. Is he . . . ?"

"He's been taken to ICU," said the nurse brusquely. "His condition is critical." She swung her broad hips around and waddled out, leaving me with a stone of anger in my stomach.

"All that, and you couldn't even fucking fight," I told Nick, or the spirits, whichever.

I caught a look in the mirror opposite the bed after I tore the gown off and winced. I had bruises the color of grape Kool-Aid all over my side and back, and red blisters and scorching everywhere else. The ends of my hair were singed and my face was crimson, like I'd overdosed on a sunlamp. Gorgeous.

I managed my lingerie with minor aches, my bra lumpy over the elastic bandages holding my ribs in place, but getting into my shirt defeated me. I rooted around in the closet and found an oversized hoodie sweatshirt, managing to slide it on with minimal agony. I banged open the door and found Fagin dozing against the opposite wall.

"Let's get back to the SCS," I said shortly. "We've got work to do."

Fagin reached out to steady me, and I caught the flutter again, my magick reacting to something in him. This time it wasn't a spark; it was like someone had clubbed me in the knees. I lost my balance and fell on my ass, sprawled in the hallway as nurses and patients and for all I know the gods themselves looked on.

I glowered at his hand when he offered it. "What the Hex are you?"

Fagin spread his hands. "I don't understand."

Scrambling up hurt a lot, and I hissed between clenched teeth, "I touched you and I felt something. I Path magick from witches—it's my pack talent." Not technically true:

I was born of the Serpent Eye pack, who had no unique talent. But Fagin didn't need to know that being a Path was my own personal freak show. "I Pathed something from you," I continued. "So I'll ask you once more, nicely, before I get pissed—what are you?"

Fagin crossed his arms. "I'm a man, Luna. That's all, and that's all I've ever been. Maybe I have an ambient talent, but I'm pretty happy being an ATF agent. And I do my job with such flair, it would be selfish to have two natural talents on top of my good looks and charm."

Liar. Liars always protest too much.

"Maybe your special snowflake talent is broken," said Fagin. "Get a fairy godmother in to service it is my advice."

I'd been wrong—liar *and* jackass.

"Whatever you are, I've had enough of you," I said, his arrogance pushing me into a growl. I turned and limped away, with as much dignity as I could muster.

"Hey," Fagin called. "What about the SCS?"

"I changed my mind," I snapped. "I'm going home. Alone."

Riding in a cab with cracked ribs is no picnic, but I made it home and to my front door, fumbling with keys and bag.

As my door key slid home, I noticed scratches around the lock, small enough to be almost invisible. It could be tarnish, but it wasn't. I ran my finger over the rough spots on the latch plate. I'd made enough of them honing my own skills at the academy.

Someone had picked my fucking lock.

My bag hit the ground and my Sig came out, down

and away from my body. I twisted the key with my free hand and shoved the door inward.

I'd had enough unsavory types, both human and worse, break in over the years to expect the worst, but something whispered at the back of my brain that this wasn't something from the netherworld. Did daemons pick locks? Did selkies have to skulk around?

"I'm armed!" I called before I shoved the door open with my shoulder and went in.

It felt so wrong to be making a dynamic entry into my own cottage. And it had happened too many times already. "Anyone in here, get the fuck out now! I'm not in the mood!"

Nothing appeared. No one jumped on me from the shadows; nothing exploded. There was only the faintest scent of another person, faded and long gone. I felt my heart beating along all of my bruises. The barrel of the Sig dipped, and I slid it back into its holster with a sigh. Whoever had broken in, they weren't here now.

The front room was in shadow and I twitched the curtains aside to let in the afternoon sunlight. It wasn't even sunset yet, and I felt like I'd crammed a hundred years into the day. I flopped onto the sofa and shut my gritty eyes, tilting my head back to the ceiling.

When I lowered my chin, I saw it. It was nailed to the wall in the center of a symbol opposite the sofa. Dead, and had been for some time, judging by the entrails from its split stomach and the bulge in its small black eyes.

I stared, for a full five seconds, unable to comprehend what I was seeing. Then I rocketed off the sofa and called Bryson, and my cousin.

While I waited for them to show up I grabbed my pocket camera and snapped pictures of the symbol, which dripped black down my walls. I knew things that had black blood, and feared the worst, but a sniff test confirmed it was paint. Thank the gods for small favors.

Sunny's hybrid skidded to a stop in the drive, closely followed by Bryson's grimy Taurus. She jumped out and ran inside, stopping short when she saw the thing on my wall. "Oh, gods. What *is* that?"

Bryson ambled in at a more leisurely pace, making a face like he'd just stepped in roadkill. "Hex. Is that a sparrow?"

"Was," I corrected. "It's a pretty fucking ex-sparrow now."

Sunny grabbed my arm. "Who would do this to you?"

"The same person who tried to kill me on the beach, and who's been following me," I muttered. "What I need to know is, what are they doing in my *house*?"

Bryson walked around and examined the sign from all angles, shaking his head. "This is some freaky crap, Wilder. No lie."

The symbol wasn't like the blood witch sigils or the daemonic summon marks, but it was unsettling nonetheless, a square made out of glyphs that described eyes, and thorns, and bleeding hearts. The dead bird in the center pushed it from Disturbing to Oh, Dear God, What Is That?

"Is it vaudaun?" I asked Sunny. "Some weird animal sacrifice?"

"No," said Sunny. "A vaudaun priest would use a *veve*, the signature of his patron spirit, and this is something else. I've never seen it before. But . . ." She stretched out her hand and almost touched the symbol, then curled her fist and drew it away. "It's meticulous. Correct. The symbol is built for power."

Bryson looked at her askance. "It's, you know, safe to be standing here all near it and shit, right?"

"David, don't be an idiot," I said. "If they were after anyone, they were after me, not some burned-out detective with low blood sugar."

"I never thought I'd be saying this, but Bryson may be right," Sunny said. "Luna, whoever put this here—they were trying to curse you."

"Trying?" Prickles of nerve ran up and down my back, the baser instincts of my monster putting me on high alert.

"Yes . . . the spell didn't take," she said. "Like I said, the symbol is a perfect curse, but there's no magick charge behind it. The working is incomplete. They called the corners and used a psychopomp—a harbinger of death—with that poor sparrow." She rubbed her arms. "You're damn lucky whoever did this wasn't a witch. I suggest you get what you need for evidence and then let me wash it off, before it has a chance to do anything to you."

I looked over the eyes, huge and unblinking writ in the stark black against my wall. My landlord was going to have a fit. I'd already paid to patch bullet holes, sand blood out of the hardwood floors, replace a wall cracked from Lucas, possessed, tossing me into it, and a thousand other small mistakes from my own hand, when the phase got the better of me.

"I'll document it," I said, "and then I need some sleep, because this day has been, to put it mildly, insanely craptastic."

"Heard about you and the fire brigade," Bryson said. He was keeping his distance from the grisly offering on my wall, practically in the kitchen. "You're still crazy, Wilder."

I felt Sunny's gaze latch onto me. "What about a fire?"

"Nothing," I said, shooting Bryson a *shut up* look that could have drawn blood. My cousin likes to pretend my job is all kittens and rainbows.

"Fine, I'll just get it from Troy later on," she said sweetly. "David, be a dear and grab the bucket and cleanser from under the sink, please?"

Bryson meekly did as she asked, and when water rushed into the sink I spoke to Sunny, low. "Should I be worried? Could it work next time?"

She spread her hands. "Someone wants you dead, Luna. If they come back with a friend who can pull down power . . ."

I sighed. "I'm not taking leave from the force. I'm in enough hot water with the commissioner as it is."

"Then at least find another place to stay until you figure out *who* is doing this and *why*," Sunny said. "You can come to Grandma's."

"Oh yeah," I snorted. "Me and Grandma, under the same roof. That'll be a laugh and a half." The last time I'd lived with my grandmother, I'd been young enough to still hide pot under my mattress, which she promptly found and evicted me for. That, and there was the werewolf thing, which to a prissy witch like her was as bad as coming home engaged to an unemployed drummer named Snake.

"Well, there's nowhere else you can go," Sunny said, folding her arms. "Troy lives in a one-bedroom condo and Dmitri is gone."

She just had to bring up the ex-boyfriend, the werewolf whom I'd told good-bye a few months before I got promoted. It wasn't a clean break; it was one of the messy ones, with deep wounds and recriminations on both sides.

I put the image of Dmitri's eyes—green when he was human, black when he let the daemon blood that rode his monster's back control him—out of my head. Hopefully, after almost six months, for good.

"That's none of your—you've seen where Mac lives?"

"What, you thought he curled up under his desk at night?" Sunny smirked.

"I'm not going anywhere," I said, mimicking her posture. "It takes a lot more than eviscerated fowl to chase me out of my own home."

Bryson plopped a bucket full of sudsy water down at Sunny's feet. "I'll make sure Batista, Hunter, and I take shifts tonight watching your place, Wilder."

"Make sure Zacharias helps, too," I said absently. "He needs the time in the field."

"Hell, Raggedy Andy is about as useful as a rubber gun loaded with Jell-O bullets," Bryson sniffed. "We'll take care of it."

I wasn't 100-percent sure that Kelly would raise a finger if I were being ritualistically murdered, but I smiled gamely at Bryson. "I appreciate it, David."

"Don't take it all personal," he grumbled. "I'd do anything not to push paper in Homicide again."

Sunny found a rag to go with the bucket and started washing the symbol off the wall, until it was a faint shadow. I had a feeling I'd seen the eyes somewhere before, much larger and much more faded. I blinked to clear my vision and went over to the window that looked down on the beach, turning my back on the grisly scene until Sunny had scrubbed the wall and Bryson had put the sparrow into a trash bag and tossed it into the outside can. "I'll make a report," he said when he came back in, washing his hands at the sink with the concentration of someone who's just been licked by a leper. "And you sit tight tonight."

"I'm not a victim," I reminded him, testy.

"Someone broke into your house, Wilder, and scribbled freak hoodoo all over your walls. That makes you the victim of something."

Bryson was more right than he knew, though I didn't reply to him, didn't dignify his "victim" designation with a comment. I hated that label, had hated it ever since I'd been attacked and bitten by the were who made me, fifteen years past. *Victim* was stationary, broken, hollow. The bite had gotten me up and out of my dead-ended life, and put me on the path to today. So it was a bad name for me.

I wasn't broken yet.

Nine

I was in my office by 7 A.M., because sleep was an elusive monster. When I did pass out, my subconscious decided that Luna's Past Mistakes were prime fodder for nightmares and I was treated to a parade of everyone who'd ever harmed me, so it seemed—Joshua Mackelroy, Alistair Duncan, the man I'd shot my first year as a detective, and Lucas, his eyes as he stabbed me and left me for dead. His skin on mine as he kissed me . . .

At least he didn't stab me in the back. Then my life really would be a sad country song.

Batista rolled in a few minutes after me, bags under his eyes, his normally granite-hard face drawn. "Luna, you mind if I clock out and sleep for a few hours? I've been up since two on your protective detail and Marisol is fit to be tied that I had to go out in the middle of the night. You'd be doing me a solid."

"Sure thing," I said, waving him away. "Hey, what did we find out about Corley and Manners?"

"Ask Andy," Batista said, masking a yawn with his broad hand. "He's been working at it like a grad student on speed. He's got spreadsheets."

"Thanks," I said, hiding my own yawn inside a large swallow from a very large mocha. If I couldn't be doped up, I might as well be caffeinated. My ribs still groaned every time I tried to draw breath.

Zacharias flew in like a skinny omen of ill fate, throwing down his briefcase and an onion bagel with lox. My nose twitched and my stomach followed. I took half of Andy's bagel and bit down, chewing and swallowing before my body could tell me different.

"Good morning, ma'am," Zacharias said meekly.

"Gods, Andy." I finished my half of the bagel. "It's okay to get pissed with me, you know."

He cocked his head. "I don't understand, ma'am."

"I just stole your food without asking, Zacharias. It's all right to relax that rod in your butt a centimeter once in a while."

He dropped his eyes to the floor and gave me a jerky nod. "Okay, Lieutenant."

"Good. Now, what did you find out about Corley?"

Zacharias looked like he would piss his pants with relief at the change of subject. "Corley was an established antique dealer as well as manager of a high-end auction house here in town. His financials are clean, as are his backers."

"Backers?" Another swig of coffee.

"Yes, ma'am."

"Andy . . ."

"I mean Lieutenant. Sorry. He had three investors in his business as of six months ago. He expanded into import/export, and the licensing fees alone will kill you."

A sheet listing out the backers and their invested amounts appeared in my free hand, detailed in meticulous columns. OCD—not just for weird old men anymore.

The first two names meant nothing to me, but the third jumped. "Grace Hartley?"

Zacharias perked. "Yes. Does that mean something to you, ma'am?"

"It might," I said, folding the paper into quarters and shoving it into my back pocket.

"You need an address, ma'am?" Andy asked, sitting down at his computer like an eager student.

"Taken care of," I said, as the elevator dinged. I expected Kelly or Annemarie, the only two members of the squad who kept remotely punctual hours, but instead it was Bryson, leading a tall, dark, and handsome stranger with a pink visitor pass dangling from his chest.

"Well, crap," I said, setting down my coffee on Andy's desk and hurrying to intercept them before Bryson opened his big yap.

"David. Don't you turn into a pumpkin if you rise before nine A.M.?"

"Morning, Lieutenant," he greeted me, his jaw twitching. I dropped my smile at his cue. Bryson slid his eyes toward the visitor, and I recognized him, in tight shot, close as I'd be to my TV screen at home.

Brad Morgan had come to my squad room.

"Mr. Morgan." I pasted a wide bullshit smile onto my face, the same one he gave me every night at five and eleven from the nightly news. "Welcome. I was so sorry to hear about the loss of the community center."

"It was a terrible blow," he said, extending a hand with nails buffed and shined. When I shook, his grip was firm, with just a tad too much pressure. Letting me know I wasn't as strong as he was.

Fine, he could go ahead and think that. "What can the SCS do for you today, Mr. Morgan?"

He jerked his thumb at Bryson. "I heard about what happened to Nick Alaqui, my supervisor at the center, and I took the liberty of calling the chief of detectives. We golf. At any rate, he referred me to Mr. Bryson and I called him at home early this morning."

"Early," Bryson echoed, pulling a face behind Morgan's back. The circles under his eyes stood out even more against his four-hours-sleep sallow skin.

I sort of felt bad for him. Sort of. But more than that, I felt rising irritation with Brad Morgan. "Well, sir, I appreciate you coming in. Is there something specific you were hoping to accomplish?" *Just keep smiling and wait for the inevitable shit to hit the fan.*

"I'm just here to be a good citizen, miss. I want to help in any way that I can." He looked back at Bryson. "Is there somewhere that we could talk? I assume you need background information on me and on the property, to rule out a revenge attack?"

"Andy!" Bryson barked. "Show Mr. Morgan to the interview room."

Zacharias took charge of Morgan, and Bryson turned back to me, rolling his eyes to high heaven.

"Not only a macho ass but a cop groupie," I said. "Must be your lucky day, David. You should ask him if he wants to hold your gun."

"Look," he said. "Morgan calling in the dead of night isn't the only reason I'm here."

"Oh?"

Bryson looked back and forth, as if ninjas were waiting in the corners to record our conversation. "I did some work last night after we got the call about you and the burn-unit sausage. Did you know Narco had a watch on those warehouses?"

Maybe this day wouldn't be all ass-kissing and bad coffee. "Really. They think Brad Morgan is a drug smuggler as well as a jerk-off?"

"Not him, but his employees at the center," said Bryson. "Been getting a lot of traffic from the port. Cargo. Not enough for a search warrant—just surveillance."

I tapped my teeth. "Can you get Narco to give us what they have?"

"Doubtful," said Bryson. "They hate you just as much as the rest of the department."

I flashed him a thumbs-up. "Way to go, David. Need I remind you that your fat ass sits at a desk in this den of iniquity, same as me?"

"Shit, Wilder. I'm just being honest."

"Then allow me to do the same: Get me those goddamn surveillance tapes before I slap you in the head."

Bryson grumbled his way back onto the elevator, and I downed the last of my coffee and went to interview Brad Morgan.

He stood up again when I walked into the interview room, pressing his hands together in the movie-actor version of contrite. "Is there any chance I could get one of those lattes?"

I gave him my granite glare. "No." I took the high-backed leather chair at the head of the table, forcing Morgan into one of the 1970s-vintage plastic and metal contraptions designed specifically to numb someone's ass.

"Listen, I want to help," said Morgan. "Nick was one of my success stories—he came to the center as a very troubled high school sophomore and now he's a teaching assistant at Nocturne University, after completing a psych major. He wants to get into social work."

"Mr. Morgan," I said, leaning across the table, mimicking the posture he used to interview unsuspecting victims on his news show, "why would our Narcotics squad have your warehouse under observation?"

I was taking a huge risk, and no doubt Captain Hollings from Narcotics would call me up and scream his choice slurs at me until he had another heart attack, but I was tired of games. I'd been through fire, not to mention ineptly cursed and attacked by carnivorous seals. This case was getting on my last nerve, and if Brad Morgan showed his stomach to me I was going to sink my teeth into it.

Morgan, for his part, recoiled, shock springing into his eyes. "Drugs? Nick was not a drug smuggler, nor were any of my employees."

"Fine. Your delinquents aren't dealing to their emo-kid pals, but what about the other two warehouses?"

"I . . . I lease them," Morgan said numbly. "I have no idea what goes on apart from collecting the rent and doing credit checks on the leaser."

His eyes dipped, and his right ring finger had started up a tapping that I was sure he didn't notice. I did, because they're two of the textbook hallmarks of a fibber. I scented Morgan, and got sweat underneath his botanical body wash and tony aftershave. The interview room was cool. My arms had gooseflesh.

"You want to tell me the truth now, Mr. Morgan? You're a bad liar, so just come clean and stop wasting my fucking time."

He flinched. Obviously, this wasn't playing out like his favorite episode of *CSI*.

I tapped my wristwatch, a 1940s army officer's model that I'd treated myself to on my thirtieth birthday. If I had to watch time pass me by, at least it would be aesthetically pleasing. "I'm waiting, Mr. Morgan. Or should I call you Brad?"

His jaw twitched. "I don't know anything."

I shoved back the rolling chair so it hit the whiteboard mounted at the front of the room, and grabbed Morgan by the elbow. "Let's take a walk."

At the elevators I turned us left and pushed through the old door sprayed with the symbol for a fallout shelter. It was supposed to be locked, but I'd learned that some long-ago janitor had jammed the lock open during my time on SWAT.

The old tunnels lead a quarter of a mile down the road to the Nocturne City morgue, spitting halogen lights and exposed pipes creating slices of light and dark. Every few hundred feet, a cage used for bunks or supplies leered out at us with rusted metal mesh for teeth. Instead of cans of supplies for the post-apocalyptic Nocturne City, the cages now held old files, ruined mouse-chewed furniture, and the detritus of thirty years of police work.

Morgan eyed his surroundings like he was the star of a slasher film and I was the hockey-mask killer. "This is . . . unusual, Lieutenant."

"You have no idea," I muttered, shoving open the red door marked EMERGENCY. We came face-to-face with a surprised morgue attendant, but he waved us on when I showed him my shield.

Dr. Cordova was on duty, slicing up a fat retiree with the purple, swollen face of a heart attack victim in the autopsy bay. Cordova's pug face wrinkled up even further when he saw me. "What do *you* want?"

He and I go way back, all the way to the Holly Street

shootings, where Cordova had done his best to paint my shooting of a suspect as a bad one.

"Doc, someone might think you weren't happy to see me," I said. Cordova never stopped working on the old man. Next to me, Brad Morgan blanched.

"Spit it out, Wilder," Cordova grunted.

"What drawer is Howard Corley in?" I asked.

"Fifteen," he snapped, and yanked the mask back over his face. I dragged Morgan over to the alcove that held a bank of freezers, each stamped with a number and labeled by hand with the name and case number of the corpse within.

I yanked drawer fifteen open with a clang, cold and sharp in the hard-walled room. Corley was covered by a plain paper sheet, and I jerked it off.

Morgan clapped eyes on the body, and his face went slack. "Dear gods!"

"This is what happened to someone else who got caught up in whatever you're lying to me about," I said. "This is what's going to happen to another person if you don't come clean with me right now."

Morgan's throat worked, and I could tell from the waxy color of his face that he was trying heroically not to vomit. I didn't blame him—Corley was stiff and brittle, his skin boiled into a carapace by the fire, lips pulled rigid over blackened teeth.

"So," I said softly. "Are you going to tell me what was really going on at your property? Or do you need some alone time with Mr. Corley?"

Morgan buried his face in his hands, his fingers leaving purple indents on his forehead as he let out a shuddering sigh. "I'm a witch."

"Pardon?"

"A witch!" he bellowed, loud enough to bounce his voice off the tiles that lined the freezer alcove. "I have the blood!"

"That explains why you're twitchy—sort of—but what got your warehouse burned?" I said.

"They told me it was for the cause," said Morgan. "That I just had to look the other way for one night."

"They?" I covered Corley back up and shut the freezer, mostly so I didn't have to smell him anymore.

Morgan slumped down on the rolling stool next to the freezers. "I'm mixed race, Lieutenant. My father is Afro-Cuban and my mother is Irish. Morgan is just some bullshit name I took when I got on my university radio station. Ditched the accent, wore white-guy suits, and here I am, fifteen years later, and no one except my wife knows."

"Are you blood or caster?" I asked, rubbing the point between my eyes.

"Neither," said Brad. "I'm a shaman. From both sides . . . my *abeula* was an old hoodoo witch and my mother was a shaman from the Old Traditions."

I raised an eyebrow. "Never met a shaman before."

"There's more to the blood than just casters and black magick," said Morgan, almost testy.

"Yeah, okay, whatever," I said. "You're a shaman. What cause were you contributing to by lighting your own volunteer on fire?"

"Someone contacted me a month ago. They knew everything about me, and the price for not sending proof to Channel One was that I look the other way while a shipment from the port came in to one of my rental properties."

I drew in a breath. This was getting better by the second. "You have anything more specific than someone?"

Morgan rubbed his forehead. "The man I met with was named Milton. That was all I got."

"Well, you can rest easy," I said, tapping on the drawer labeled *MANNERS* in crooked Sharpie printing. "He's number twenty-two."

Ten

Brad Morgan was silent and waxen-faced as a mannequin while we walked back to the SCS offices. He and I parted ways with me shoving a business card into his hand with my home number scribbled on the back, and knowing I'd never see him again except from my TV screen after the doors rolled shut on the elevator.

Bryson stuck his head out of the bullpen. "Wilder. Nick Alaqui died. Just got a call from the hospital."

I'd done so well, all day, for Fagin and for Brad Morgan. Holding it in. Being the professional. Running my squad like a lieutenant, not a were.

I turned around and punched the wall next to the elevator.

A few chips of brick rattled to the floor and pain blazed to life across my knuckles. "Hex it," I said plainly, then turned and walked back to my office, measured. Bleeding knuckles leeched all of the rage from me, and now I just felt like a rag doll.

Bryson appeared a minute later with a roll of gauze and some peroxide. He set them on the corner of my desk. "You wanna put some ointment on that, or it'll hurt like hell."

"It already hurts like hell," I muttered, taking the peroxide and holding my hand over the wastebasket. The bathrooms were two floors up, and I wasn't about to risk running into someone who would want to know what happened.

The peroxide sizzled as it hit my gashed hand, and I hissed, clamping my teeth together. Bryson shut the door behind him as I wrapped my hand and shuffled from one foot to the other. "Wilder, you gotta do something. We're sitting around playing grab-ass while the feds walk all over us and a witch with a pyro fetish runs around the city like motherfucking Godzilla."

I pushed my chair back. "I am doing something," I said. My stomach was dancing, but Bryson was right. Nothing was going to happen while I sat around bleeding and feeling sorry for myself. I picked up the phone with my good hand and debated, then punched in the number.

"Fagin," I said when he answered. "I'm going to speak to Grace Hartley. If you want to be there when I do, drive fast." I hung up and jerked my chin at Bryson. "Come on."

"Does the fed have to come?" Bryson complained as we went to the car. "That kid is so slick that if you put a condom over him you could—"

"I'm gonna stop you there," I said with a grimace. My hand stung when I gripped the wheel and put the LTD in gear. The bandages were already red across the knuckles. I'd heal up, but now I just felt foolish. There had been a time when I barreled around hitting walls and people and snapping at anyone who got in my way, and it was, indeed, my way. But that was before I'd lost Dmitri to a daemon bite. Before I'd ended it because he needed a pack to survive with the daemon inside him and no pack would accept an Insoli as his mate.

If I could live through that, I could leash the were. Every time I held on to my human side instead of my monster, I felt something inside me wither a little bit.

But it was for the good of everyone, I reminded myself as my gut clenched again. The old Luna destroyed what she touched. The new Luna protected, and she did it by being a person and not a werewolf.

"You okay, Wilder?" Bryson said after a time, as we drove toward Bonaventure Drive. "Usually you're yakking my ear off."

"Fine," I said shortly, and turned up the volume on the dispatch radio. Robberies and traffic accidents and domestic disturbances filled the space around me, their cadence far better than the heavy nothing that I felt on my skin.

"Alaqui's funeral is on Saturday," Bryson said, opening my glove compartment and taking out a granola bar I had stashed. "The mosque on Tenth, and a memorial afterward." He bit into the bar without further comment and then made a face. "This tastes like moose crap."

I pulled to the curb in front of Grace Hartley's house and shut the engine off, staring straight and not really seeing the street ahead. Orange and brown and blood-rust leaves danced across my field of vision from the oaks along the curb, and I breathed for a second before I looked at Bryson and past him to the house. "Thank you, David."

Bryson shrugged. "Yeah. We gonna talk to this gal or what?"

Fagin's Mustang pulled in behind me, and I got out of my car, putting on a pair of aviator shades as an afterthought. The October sun wasn't strong enough to warrant them, but I wanted answers and I wanted them fast, and if I had to intimidate the crap out of Grace Hartley to do it, then I could play Bad Cop for a few minutes.

Fagin looked me over when we met on the sidewalk. "I like it. Very Dirty Harry meets *Charlie's Angels*. All you need are the bell bottoms."

Bryson made a sound under his breath, and Fagin grinned. "Detective, haven't you heard? All real men can talk fashion nowadays."

"Fuck you," Bryson said clearly. "I'm not a twenty-year-old titty-bar waitress, so you can stow the charm shit."

"It's a shame," said Fagin. "I think you missed your career calling with that one, David."

"Both of you shut the Hex up," I said loudly, when Bryson made a move toward Fagin. I pressed my hand into Fagin's chest, aware of how he'd tossed me on my ass earlier. This time I'd be ready.

Fagin put up his hands. His smile never wavered. I was starting to think Agent Will Fagin, ATF, was a little bit crazy.

"Bryson, let it go," I ordered again, still seeing murder in his eyes. "At least pretend to be a professional, if you can."

After a moment Bryson rolled his shoulders and turned his back on Fagin. Whatever else Bryson had to say was lost to the wind.

Fagin started up the walk and I followed, my palm still warm from where it had touched his chest. He was built spare, but solid enough to stop bullets from what I'd felt. I let myself think, just for a second, what might be under the expensive suit and the slick smirk, and decided it probably wouldn't be all that unpleasant.

Then I decided I also had a job to do, and should stop

behaving like one of Fagin's twenty-year-old waitresses. If I was ready to start dating again, it wouldn't be with anyone as smug as Will Fagin.

"Christ on a cracker," said Fagin, gesturing at the house. "Could this place be any more perfect for the lair of a sinister old lady?"

The Hartley manse was an expansive old firetrap, cobbled together from a variety of architectural periods and materials, all of it topped off with black slate tiles, gingerbread, and a turret like a tall crooked finger against the sky.

"Feels like I came through the woods to Grandma's house," Fagin muttered, mounting the sagging steps and pressing the bell. Piles of newspapers drifted around us, and porch furniture covered liberally with rust crouched sadly at the other end of the veranda. "Guess that makes me the Big Bad Wolf."

"There's only one Big Bad Wolf here," I told him. "And I'm pretty sure it isn't you."

The curtains behind the stained-glass rosettes in the door twitched, and then it opened a crack. An honest-to-god maid peered out, uniform and all, complete with a little cap over her wispy bun of hair. "Yes?" Her accent was strong Eastern European, maybe Romanian. It wasn't the slightly nasal twang of Dmitri's native country, but the girl's big eyes and thin mouth would have made her model pretty, if she didn't look so depressed.

Bryson, Fagin, and I flashed our various IDs. "Police," I said. "We're here to speak with Grace Hartley."

The maid bobbed her head and opened the door all of the way. "Please come in. I will inform Mrs. Hartley of your presence." She talked like she'd been coached, badly, and heaved a resigned sigh as she disappeared down the hallway into the back of the house.

"Not bad," said Bryson, of the girl's retreating rear end. "Needs a little meat, though."

"You're a class act," Fagin informed him.

Bryson's comments had become so much white noise during my time with him that I didn't even bother with a return. Me personally, I checked out the house. The dilapidated outside was a world away from the inside, which was like the sets of those period dramas that Sunny sometimes forced me to sit through. I expected Mr. Darcy or Heathcliff to pop out at any second.

A library sat through a pair of rolling doors carved with frolicking nymphs and satyrs, the shelves heavy with the sort of books that people actually read. I peered in the crack and saw a pair of leather chairs flanking a fireplace and mantel heavy with memorabilia.

"Where are you going?" Fagin hissed as I rolled the doors open just wide enough to pass through and stepped in.

"She didn't tell us to wait here," I said with a shrug. Fagin shoved his hands in his pockets and looked over his shoulder as if Grace Hartley might appear and rap him on the knuckles.

I explored the library, my feet silenced on the thick Persian rug. Everything in the room was heavy and real, left over from a time when homes were stately and women wore corsets. Books on the shelf were leather-bound, plenty of volumes on spiritualism and the occult, by Gerald Gardner and Aleister Crowley and all of the rock stars of witchcraft.

The photographs on the mantel went as far back as sepia,

well-dressed men and women playing croquet and sitting stiffly at formal dinners, and one posed portrait in long black robes. The picture was grainy, but the robes each bore a small symbol over the left breast and the background was a blank stone wall, hardly the sort of place where a rich society woman would hang around.

Before I could exercise my larcenous talents and get the thing out of the frame for a closer look, someone spoke up behind me. "Please don't touch that."

I jerked my hand away like the guilty teenager shoplifting cigarettes that I once was. "Sorry. Just trying to take a good look."

Grace Hartley glided into the library, and I say "glided" because she had one of those Miss America walks, hips swaying and feet that never seemed to leave the ground. She was twice my age if she was a day, but the expensive clothes combined with the frosted hair and flawless makeup made me feel like a housewife who'd decided to say, *Hex it*, and gone out in pajama pants and her husband's sweater.

"I trust you're still young enough to get a good look without putting your hands on other people's property," she said, and then turned on a megawatt smile and extended her hand. "Grace Hartley."

"Lieutenant Luna Wilder," I said, and squeezed her hand a lot harder than I really had to.

She flinched, but the smile never did. "How can I help you, Lieutenant?" When our hands parted, a prickle of magick went from her palm to mine. Grace Hartley had the blood. It was my freakin' day for witches.

"This is Agent Fagin with ATF," I said, indicating Will. "We'd like to ask you a few questions."

Hartley made a show of checking the hands of the Tag Heuer paperweight on her wrist. "I have some pressing appointments today, Miss Wilder. Can we conduct this quickly, or at a later date?"

"What's your relationship to Milton Manners?" I said bluntly. "We know that you bailed him out after his drug-trafficking arrest, so don't bother lying to us. You're not a very good actress anyway."

Bryson snorted, and two blooms of color appeared in Hartley's cheeks. "Milton is a friend of the family."

"Were the two of you close?" I watched Hartley carefully. She was staring everywhere except my face, and her eyes kept darting to that damn picture.

"Not at all. Milton was eternally in flux, a crisis case who only asked for money to finance his latest schemes. He had nothing but that wretched antique shop and he saw not a penny from it."

"And yet you bailed him out," said Fagin. "You must have held some fondness for him. As a friend."

"I have a fondness for not seeing my family's good name splashed across the police blotter in the *Nocturne Inquirer*," Hartley sniffed. "Milton had a fondness for spilling nasty secrets when he didn't get his way. Why are you pestering me about my relationship with him?"

"Because he was found dead," said Fagin. "Yesterday. It was not natural causes."

Hartley sank into one of the leather chairs, pressing a hand to her mouth. She shut her eyes for a moment and then composed herself.

She still wasn't a very good actress.

"I always knew that Milton would bring himself to a bad end," she sighed. "Poor boy. So troubled, always. His mother . . . she was a common thief and gold-digger, you know, but my dear father saw some hope for the boy, so I endeavored to be charitable."

"Where's your bathroom?" I said abruptly. If I had to listen to one more second of this, I was going to reach over there and slap her across her nipped and tucked face.

"I . . . it's down the hall, on your right. The last door." Hartley gestured. I gave Fagin the eye, and he glared at me. Oh well. I couldn't care less what he thought about me lying to nice old ladies.

I ventured down the hall, which held the same entombed elegance as the library, and was self-consciously sprinkled with memorabilia on small tables and alcoves in the wood paneling. A curved dagger with a blood groove and daemon sigils carved into the handle. A dog's skull with the teeth painted black and the *veve* of a *loa* spirit painted in some dark tarry substance across the crown. An iron caster, probably as old as the house. I brushed my finger over it. It was dead and cold, the witch who had owned it dust by now.

Whatever kind of craft Grace Hartley practiced, she sure kept a lot of creepy shit around to do it with.

The bathroom was right where she told me it would be, but I ignored it and stepped through a pair of double doors into a large kitchen. It was a kitchen, normal, and a quick look in the cabinets and pantry didn't turn up anything except pricey organic food and dust.

I stepped onto the rear porch, which looked at a backyard overrun with weeds and browned plants swaying in the breeze.

Even though they were dead, I recognized a few of the blooms—nightshade, vervain, rosemary. Witch's herbs. The porch was rotted and the roof creaked in the wind, but I spotted the remains of a shipping crate in the brown grass beyond, shattered wood and packing straw strewn like someone was in a hurry.

I stepped off the stoop and into the grass, dead and crinkling under my feet with the sound of something burning. The box was stamped in black with Cyrillic and English lettering, too obliterated to understand except for CROATIA as the country of origin.

Bending down to pick up the shattered pieces of wood and try to make sense of them, I felt something slip over my foot, like a snake across my ankle.

I lurched backward, but it was too late. The binding grabbed me and sucked me down to my knees and then onto my side, my cheek pressed into the dead grass. The working circle hidden under the flora snapped closed around me and I felt it on my skin, all over my face and hands like a thousand venomous spiders.

The back door of the Hartley house banged open and a long shadow fell over me as someone approached. "Fucking cops," the voice sighed. "You people always go where you're not wanted."

She was taller than I was, and from my vantage the first thing I saw was her boots—Nixon-era Doc Martens, the kind self-conscious kids trying to look punk wear. Skinny legs in skinny jeans, and an impressive chest topped by a glaring face.

"Oh, man, did you fuck up," I told her, even though the binding was tight and bit liked barbed wire against my exposed skin. I'd been held in a binding once before and it was exactly like being paralyzed. Your mind goes into overdrive to compensate for your body being numb and still, and you can hear your heart pounding furiously.

"Yeah?" she said, taking out a pocketknife and picking

at her fingernails. "Tell me exactly how I fucked up, Detective."

"It's Lieutenant," I snapped. "And you are?"

"Talon," she said, with a porn-star pout. "Like it matters."

"Well, *Talon,* my two partners are in there talking to Mrs. Hartley. Let me out of this goddamn binding and maybe I won't knock your teeth in when they get here."

She tossed her hair over her shoulder—it was the plasticky red of extensions—and I saw the four circular scars on her neck. The mark of the Serpent Eye were pack, four fangs. The same four fangs that had given me the bite.

I started to agree with Talon, the smallest bit, that I might just be fucked.

"Make me," she said, in a startling display of originality.

I wriggled some more against the binding. I was lying on my SIG and my backup .38 revolver was on my ankle, as far as if it had been locked in my desk at the Plaza. Shooting the bitch in the head was out. That sucked.

The binding itself cut cold and sharp, not like any magick I'd felt before. Usually it was warm and a loss of feeling on my skin, like a bad case of hypothermia. This just hurt, raw and powerful as if someone had wrapped me in barbed wire.

Talon paced carefully around the circle, which was important. It meant that the witch who'd cast the binding circle wasn't choosy about who it locked down.

"I think we'll just wait here until the Maiden comes back," Talon said, crossing her arms over her impressive chest. "She'll know what to do with you."

"I can't tell you how much I enjoy it when you people

give each other silly names," I grunted. "It makes me feel like James Bond. Is Jaws going to come with her?"

My chattering was just a front for what I was doing with my hands, digging through the grass and the earth, trying to find the actual circle cut into the clay beneath. For my Pathing to work, I have to touch something physical.

Not that I thought Pathing this particular brand of iron-cold magick was the greatest idea I'd ever had, but I didn't have a lot of options. If Fagin and Bryson came looking for me, all three of us would be stuck, bound with a pissy fashion-victim were looking down on us. Better it was just me.

"You probably think you're really fucking witty, huh?" Talon inquired. "That's so lame. People are just being nice to you, sweetie."

The tips of my fingers hit earth, felt the *pop* of magick as my were blood connected with the witch's power that held the binding. I let it come, let it flow into me and make me stronger and better and faster and, if I wasn't careful, much crazier.

My eyes burned from the sudden overload of light and color, staring straight into the sky, and I bunched myself and tugged against the binding. It felt so much like something was cutting me I swore lines of blood broke all over my skin, but I kept Pathing, draining the working and making myself stronger.

Talon stepped closer, curious. "What do you think you're doing?"

The binding snapped with a sting of ice across my face and I rolled over, grabbing her legs in a scissors hold and jerking with my new strength. As I rolled out of the working circle, Talon fell in, and screamed as the magick caught her. I saw it shimmer above the girl's prone body, black knots like the legs of a phantom spider twining the air itself into a net to hold its newest prey.

I leaned over Talon, careful not to slide my foot over the edge of the circle. "*This* is where I say something witty." I straightened and brushed dead grass off of myself, my hands shaking. "But I'm fresh out. Have fun explaining to the Maiden how you got yourself tangled in that, bitch." I opened the rickety gate and went to the car, sitting on the hood and putting my hands on my knees.

There, in the open street, where I knew I was safe, I let myself finally break down. The shuddering consumed my whole body and I felt blood trickle from my nose as the magick worked its way out of my system. Too much and I could have fried myself into a permanent vegetable. Too late and Talon could have done whatever she wanted to me. All of the what-ifs scrolled past, ugly and gruesome, and I pressed the heels of my hands into my eyes to stop stress tears.

It's the same when you have to shoot someone, or get shot at. You start seeing paths not taken whether you want to or not and wondering, *Why am I still here?*

"Luna." Fagin and Bryson came out the front door, watched by Grace Hartley and the maid. Once he'd blocked their view with his back, Fagin reached out his hand for me, and I let him touch my shoulder. "Where did you get off to?"

"You don't want to know," I muttered. "You really don't want to know."

Eleven

Fagin and Bryson got the story out of me by the time we were back in the SCS offices.

"We have to be able to run that Hartley bitch in for something," said Bryson. "Obstruction?"

"She wasn't hiding the shipping crate," I reminded him. "It was right there, in plain sight."

"Inside a working circle that almost killed you," Fagin reminded me. "Like bait in a cop trap."

"That's a tad overdramatic," I said. "Look, aside from hiring were goons and having a snooty attitude, Grace Hartley's done nothing wrong that any court will hold her for."

"Maybe we can dig something up on the were bitch," Bryson said, and then flinched, looking at me. "No offense, Wilder."

"I can try," said Fagin. "Someone moonlighting as muscle, chances are they've got an odd assault charge or two."

"There was something else," I said, thinking back to Talon's calm face. She'd known I was a cop from the moment we clapped eyes, that she could go away for assaulting me, and yet she'd been utterly calm, right up until she found out I was a Path.

"What?" Fagin said. "What is it?"

"She talked about someone else, a third person." I chewed on my lip for a second. "Called her *the Maiden*, like we're all in Avalon or some crap."

Bryson snorted, but Fagin's face went hard and gray, set in stone. "Did she say anything else?" he ground out.

"Not about that specifically, no. The conversation was not the most stimulating I've ever had."

Fagin stood up, paced rapidly back and forth, and shoved a hand through his hair. Blond strands dropped into his eyes. "You're *sure*. Nothing else?"

"No," I said again, frowning at him. "Something the matter?"

Fagin grabbed me by the upper arms. "You've got to think, Luna. Think of what else that she said or did that could tell you anything."

"You're hurting me," I said quietly, as his thin fingers dug into my biceps. "Don't make me turn this into a scene in front of my guys."

Zacharias and Annemarie were at their desks, watching us with large eyes. Fagin darted his gaze to them and then locked back on me. His eyes were terrifying, dark and intent as a predator's.

"The Maiden is here? She said it just like that?" he demanded, from between clenched teeth.

"So I gathered," I said, in the same tone. "Now. *Let go of me.*"

Fagin held on to me for another second. It was the third time I'd been close to him, and the only time he'd made my heart beat faster. My were commanded me to close the distance and put my lips on his and my hands on his skin.

I told it to shut up.

"I'm sorry," he breathed finally, letting go of me and stepping back. "Sorry. . . . I'll . . . I'll see you later." He turned and practically smashed into Batista before making his escape.

"Fuckin' weirdo," Bryson said, straightening his forest-green polyester jacket over his weapon. "Thought I was going to have to get all noble and pop a cap in him for you, Wilder."

"The women you date find that charming, do they?" I murmured, with no real bite behind the words. I was looking at the spot where Fagin had stood, thinking about his eyes. He was spooked, no question. "The Maiden" meant a hell of a lot more to him than it did to me.

Deciding to focus on what I could actually solve, I walked over to Annemarie. "Grace Hartley had a shipping crate on her property from Croatia. If it came into the warehouse Brad Morgan owned, like he said, there's no record, but there should be an outgoing manifest."

Annemarie smiled. "I'll get right on tracking down the original, Lieutenant."

"That's fine," I said. "Thanks, Annemarie."

My phone buzzed, and I ran for my office, picking it up as the last ring died.

"Yeah?"

"Luna, you sound out of breath," Sunny scolded. "What's wrong?"

"Not everything is an emergency, Sunny," I told her. "I was outside getting some information."

"I just wanted to tell you that I'm meeting Troy for an early dinner and the two of us would like you to come."

Great. Spend the evening watching my cousin make kissy faces at my ex-boss. Where was my cyanide capsule?

"Luna?"

"I'll think about it, Sunny, okay? I'm not entirely comfortable with your and Mac's epic love just yet."

"Maybe if you got out a little bit more, you wouldn't have such an issue with me dating Troy," said Sunny placidly. "It has been almost six months. . . ."

I was about to swear at her and hang up, but I remembered Fagin's face. I'd had enough boiling-over rage for the day. "Sunny, does the designation the Maiden mean anything to you?"

"Sounds vaguely familiar," she said after a second. "I have a hair appointment, so I have to go, but I'll look it up for you in Grandma's books."

"You told me hair and makeup were tools of the patriarchy."

"We're having dinner at Mikado. The patriarchy has nothing to do with me wanting to look presentable."

Fantastic—now I'd not only have to endure Mac and Sunny playing footsies; I'd have to do it in a dress and heels.

"Eight o'clock," she said. "Be there, Luna. This is important to me."

"Fine, fine. See you and Captain Wonderful at eight."

"He's a lieutenant, like you," she reminded me before she hung up. Smart-ass.

Pete Anderson stuck his head into my office. "Wow, it's messy in here."

I cast an eye on my papers and piles of files, overflowing trash can, and spare raincoat hanging from a corner of the closet door. "Thank you, Pete. Very astute. Are you shooting a special for the home and garden channel, or was there something you wanted?"

"I finished running through Milton Manners's computer hard drive," he said. "There's something you'll want to see."

"Finally," I said. "Something that isn't about dating or magick."

"Don't be too sure," said Pete. He led me into his office, where Manners's laptop was hooked up to an array of cables and external drives. "Whoever killed him wiped the hard drive," said Pete, "but I was able to recover his e-mail from the last few months and a few fragments of data. Here it is. . . ." He popped up a box on the screen. "Manners and Corley were pen pals."

The text was partially corrupted, just lines of wingdings, but the bottom half of the e-mail was visible.

. . . found what you asked for in Croatia. Dead witch's estate. Expensive to get out of the country—bribes, shipping, secure rec'ing warehouse. Can she cover it?

Manner's reply was succinct, and uncorrupted.

You know she can. How soon?

The message was dated eighteen days ago. Two days ago, whatever it was had arrived in Nocturne City. I rubbed my forehead and looked at Pete. "Somehow, I don't think they're talking about collectible *Star Trek* plates."

Pete nodded. "The drive shows a large wire transfer, but I can only get the bank, not the originating account number. They did a pretty thorough job of wiping this thing down. Not cheap to get your hands on that kind of equipment—mostly used by intelligence agencies."

I cocked my eyebrow. "Are you saying that we have to deal with spies now, in addition to witches and the goddamn ATF?"

"Nope," said Pete. "Just someone who's rich and smart."

Like Grace Hartley. The woman with the working circle and the werewolf in her backyard.

Tomorrow, I'd find out who Grace Hartley really was and rattle her cage. Now, I had to go get ready for dinner with my cousin and her new boyfriend.

Joy.

Mikado was a fusion Japanese place done entirely in white and gray, at the top of an old office building in the part of downtown where Jaguars and Mercedes slumbered at the curb like sleek racehorses and every door had a doorman in full livery.

I let one help me through the revolving door in the lobby and another push the elevator button for the penthouse. In my Dolce&Gabbana dress and matching red satin pumps, I looked like one of the six diners sharing the car with me. Just another idiot with too much free time and money.

The woman closest was wearing too much of a perfume with some kind of animal gland base, and I sneezed. She curled her delicate Botoxed lips and moved away from me. I put my head down and fled across the restaurant to where Mac and Sunny were sharing a window table.

"Give me something with booze in it," I told the waiter when he approached, bowing. He was tall to be Japanese, at least four inches taller than me, and built like the evil henchmen from a karate film, but he gave me a dazzling smile. It didn't do anything to change the fact that I was in a royally bad mood.

Sunny cocked her eyebrow at my lushly ways. "Rough day at the office?" She had done her makeup, and her hair was sporting new golden highlights, swept up and off her face. Mac had found a suit without wrinkles at the elbows and knees. Wonders never cease.

"I don't want to talk about it," I muttered as the waiter set a jar of hot sake and a cup in front of me.

Mac helped himself. "Let's just enjoy dinner, Sun. Cops don't like to take their work outside the office. Especially not when they're paying this much for the privilege of chewing on raw fish and sea life." He nudged Sunny and she broke into a smile.

"This was all your idea, and you know it, Troy McAllister."

I waved the bottle at the waiter. "Sumimasen. This is not going to be anywhere near enough for me."

"Luna." Sunny reached across the table and took my hand. "I want you to be okay with this. It's important to me and it's important to Troy."

"Gods!" I exploded. "Date whoever you want, Sunflower. I couldn't give a crap. I just want to know why someone cursed me, and who's setting fires and killing people. Okay? Is that what you wanted? Can I go across the street and get a cheeseburger now?"

I shoved back my chair and threw my napkin across my empty plate, while Sunny watched me with tears brimming in the corners of her eyes. I pressed my hands over my face, willing myself to be somewhere else.

"Luna, you need to apologize," said Mac. "Your cousin is upset."

"I'm sorry," I said. "I really am. This was just not the right night for this. Good luck, to the both of you." I turned before I made things any worse and walked toward the door. The woman overloaded with perfume glared at me. I snarled at her, showing fang. "See something you like, bitch?" She dropped her eyes to her plate.

I strode for the door, tangling my heel in the gaps of the tatami mats and almost falling into the arms of one of the silent, white-kimonoed waiters. He was white, and when he grabbed me I felt something sharp dig into my arm.

"Hey," I growled. "Watch it."

The waiter stared at me, his eyes glassy, like looking into the eyes of a particularly lifelike statue. "Excuse me," he murmured, at length.

I pushed away from him, felt wetness on my arm where he'd touched me. I looked down and saw a long bead of blood from a scratch in my forearm, welling a truer crimson than my dress.

The waiter's lips peeled back to reveal a row of teeth that belonged behind the counter chopping sushi, not in the mouth of a person. "So sorry," he intoned in the same voice made of dust. "I seem to have slipped."

His eyes changed, the pupils shrinking down to nothing, and I felt myself unable to move as a gray forked tongue rolled from his mouth. I wanted to scream, but I just stood there like a stone.

It was like someone had dosed my sake with GHB. I could see, but I couldn't speak as the waiter's eyes irised and became the eyes of a serpent.

I dug down deep, past the paralyzing fear that rushed up at me out of nowhere, to the beast within me. My claws and teeth grew, and I dug my fingers into the wound in my arm. The pain ran up my arm and into my heart like a flash flood, slamming me back into reality.

People all around me were screaming, dishes crashed from the kitchen, and the bitch from the elevator nearly bowled me over as she made a run for the door.

The waiter shoved me aside and grabbed her. I went down hard, my ankle twisting under me. Last time I wore three-inch heels in public.

Elevator Lady froze, choking, and then went rigid. Her face grew soft and dreamy, her skin turning from Tanorexia Orange to Goth Alabaster, her veins popping black. The skin on her face started to flake, like she was decomposing, and the waiter shuddered, releasing her with a satisfied post-orgasmic grimace. Elevator Lady toppled backward. One of her arms snapped off and rolled over to rest against my leg.

"Oh, *hell* no," I snarled, kicking off my shoes and scrambling away from the thing wearing the waiter's uniform. There were three of them, hissing and snatching at the patrons of Mikado. I fought my way through the tide back to our table. "Mac!" I bellowed. "Sunny!"

Mac had his arm thrown over my cousin, his sidearm in his free hand. "Luna, what the fuck is this? Does trouble just follow you like a stray dog?"

"We have to get these people out of here," I said as a fat middle-aged guy fell over, like a badly made statue from an amateur ceramics class.

"Great thought," said Mac. "Not so clear on the execution."

I eyeballed the distance from our table to the swinging door of the kitchen. "Give me two minutes and then get people ready to run for the fire stairs," I told Mac. I wish I could say I had some daring plan in mind, worthy of the best spy movie, but in reality, I was closer to John McClane in *Die Hard*—crashing the party without a goddamn clue.

The kitchen was empty, the chef and sous-chefs gone. There were plenty of blades lying around, knives, and hot burners, but I wasn't a circus performer.

I spun, looking for any sort of weapon, and let out a scream. A chef in a plain black uniform was standing behind me, a cleaver clutched in his fist. "Sorry," he said. "I thought you were one of them."

A hiss like skin on sandpaper sounded from the dining room, and the waiter's lip curled back over an impressive set of fangs. I blinked.

"And you are?"

"Akira," he said shortly. His ears, underneath his shaggy mane of hair, were pointed, and a hint of burnished red tattoos crept out of the mandarin collar of his uniform.

"I'm Luna," I said. "Don't take this the wrong way, but what the Hex are you supposed to be?"

He growled under his breath, big shoulders hunching. "*Oni*."

"Werewolf," I said, tapping my chest. "Nice to meet you."

"I smelled those beasts this afternoon, when I came to my shift," he said. "But I couldn't pinpoint them until they showed their faces. What do we do?"

"Get the diners down the fire stairs and don't make eye contact?" I suggested.

Akira raised his cleaver. "I can make a path."

"Wait!" I lunged for the fire extinguisher hanging next to the range. "Let me go out first."

Fire extinguishers are great for impromptu weapons.

When I was on patrol, I cleaned up more bar fights than I could count where some slap-happy biker got his hands on the fire-safety equipment at his watering hole of choice.

I kicked open the kitchen door and one of the waiters launched himself at me, toadlike, his long forked tongue lolling from his toothy mouth. I pulled the pin and let loose, giving him a face full of stinging foam.

"Hey!" I bellowed at the other two. They both turned, the cold reptile intelligence in their faces making my stomach quiver. But I kept talking. "That's right. Come on over here and make me pay for my mistakes. Give me a look at those big, pretty eyes."

"You're crazy," said Akira as the two remaining waiters bounded toward us, down on all fours now like some sort of bizarre carnival attraction. "Really fucking crazy."

"Thanks," I said. The extinguisher sputtered, useless as it ran out of foam, so I spun it in my grasp and hit the second waiter in the face. His nose crushed inward and he lost a couple of those oversized teeth, but he kept coming. "*Mac*," I bellowed. "Go!"

Sunny shoved open the fire door and an alarm began to whine. Good. The fire department would come, and backup would come with them.

I fended off another swipe from the second waiter, smashing the butt of the extinguisher down on his hand. Knuckles crunched, and he howled. Akira whipped a smaller knife out of his apron and pinned the critter's limb to the floor. The last one landed on his back, digging its teeth into the *oni*'s meaty shoulder. The fabric of his uniform tore and I saw more of the tattoo, demons and dragons and smoke, all done in red.

A bottle of sake sat on the nearest table, one of the pricey ones that the waiters had hand-carried and fussed over before they started eating people. I grabbed it and smashed it across the waiter's skull, then picked up the lit paper lantern from the same table and tore it open, touching the bare flame within to the swath of alcohol.

Blue flames went up with a whoosh, shooting toward the ceiling. I gagged on the scent of burning hair. The waiter lost his grip on Akira, and the chef gripped his cleaver and drove it between the waiter's beady lizard eyes with a *crunch* of skull.

"We should go," I said when Akira turned back, chest heaving. "That fire might spread."

"You come to Mikado often?" Akira asked as we trailed the group of traumatized diners down the fire stairs.

"I'm more of a bacon cheeseburger kind of girl," I said. "And tonight hasn't really done a whole lot to change that."

"I just like working with food," said Akira, easy as if we were strolling along the sidewalk, rather than finishing a fight with a trio of flesh-hungry, stone-gazed monsters. "I'd be happy in a diner. It's why I came to this country, to go to culinary school."

"Good for you," I said. "You're not, I dunno, freaked out that we almost got killed horribly during the aperitif?"

"I'm an *oni*," said Akira. "In my country, plain humans would spit on me. Here, no one looks twice. I can deal with the occasional upset."

I kept my thought to myself, that if he thought Nocturne City was so great, his corner of Japan must really suck. A ladder truck and a pair of ambulances greeted us when we reached the street. I found Sunny and Mac, Akira trailing me.

"You're bleeding," Sunny said. She was unhurt, just shaking.

Mac put his suit jacket around her. "What the *Hex* were those things, Luna?"

"Basilisks," Sunny answered for me. "I've read about them, but I didn't think there were any in this country. In Europe, they're practically extinct. They come from the daemon realm and interbreed with human women. They birth stone eggs and set their spawn on humans to feed."

"Filthy, unnatural things," Akira said. "I'm glad that we killed them." He hissed when he saw the cut the basilisk had left on my forearm. "Do you need to get that looked at?"

The wound was long but not deep, and I pulled away. "I'll be fine. It's already healing."

"One of the benefits of your species?"

I gave a curt nod. I really wasn't up to discussing biology with a six-foot-four Japanese fairy-tale creature.

"How long have you been a werewolf?" he asked. "Were you born this way?"

"No," I said shortly. "How long have you been in Nocturne City?"

"Five years."

"Ever seen anything like what happened tonight?" I said, looking at the revolving lights of the fire trucks reflected in the coffee shop window.

"No," Akira said. "Never."

"Thank you," I said, sincerely. "If you need anything . . . anything at all . . ." I felt for a card in the pocket of my dress.

"Maybe a cup of tea," said Akira. I looked to Mac and Sunny.

"I'll take her home," said Mac. "Once we give our statements."

I spotted the coffee shop across the street and touched Akira on the arm. "It's on me."

After I got a tall black coffee to go and Akira a hot tea, I unlocked the car and sat behind the wheel for a minute, letting myself come down from what had happened in the restaurant. My hands were shaking. It was the third time I'd almost died in as many days.

I could go home, but home was vulnerable, held the memory of the curse working and the selkies on the beach. I drove to the office instead, and instead of going into my private space, I turned on the lights in the briefing area and kicked off my heels to do some thinking.

A black marker lay abandoned on the table from my rousing speech about the Corley case. I picked it up and wrote *selkies* on the board, and added *basilisks* and a big question mark for the thing that had killed Milton Manners. The two fires went on the board, the deaths of Corley, Manners, and Nick Alaqui. Fagin's gunrunning investigation, the Narcotics watch on the warehouse.

When I was done, it looked like chaos writ small. My arm hurt and I could feel exhaustion creeping around the edges of my vision. I was no closer to finding anything out about my case, anything real, other than that three people were dead and someone had tried to both kill me and curse me.

"Crap," I sighed, and went into my office to catch up on paperwork. If someone was going to shut us down, our records would at least be meticulous.

I'm not sure when I dozed off, but all I dreamed of was fire.

Twelve

A persistent beeping from the bullpen woke me, the direct line of one of my detectives sounding in the empty bullpen. I unfolded myself from my ergonomic chair and padded across the office on bare feet. Annemarie's phone was beeping. I scooped it up. "Detective Marceaux's desk."

"This is Commandant Ivanović with the Croatian customs office. I would speak to Detective Marceaux."

"Annemarie isn't in right now," I said. "This is Lieutenant Wilder, her commanding officer. Can I take the message?"

"I require only to inform you that fax of information you requested is coming," said Ivanović. "Have a nice day."

The connection clicked off, and the fax machine whirred to life behind me. I turned toward it and let out a shriek as I nearly plowed into Hunter Kelly's barrel chest. He laughed, low in his throat.

"Overdressed a little bit today, ma'am."

"Hex *me*," I shouted, thumping Kelly's pectoral with the back of my knuckles. "Stop sneaking around like that!"

I stepped around him to the fax machine, aware of his

eyes on my back. "What are you doing here so early, Kelly?"

"I'm a morning person, ma'am."

"Then why don't you make yourself useful and get us both a coffee?" I said, pulling the cover sheet and the twice-copied, blurred Croatian forms off the fax tray.

"All due respect, ma'am," said Kelly. "I'm your detective, not your cabana boy."

"All due respect, Kelly," I said, looking to the last page, which had a low-quality photo of the crate I'd seen dismantled at Grace Hartley's home, "I don't like you much and if you don't get me some caffeine I'm going to come over there and beat your head against the desk to vent my frustration." Smile, after you threaten someone. It's very important because it keeps the someone, particularly someone bigger and badder than you, off balance if you don't show fear.

I gave Kelly a wide grin. "I take two sugars in the morning."

The air between us got thick, and not in the metaphorical way. My exposed skin crawled with magick as Kelly glared at me, his big flat face not at all hiding the fact that he wanted to smack me across the room. My Path ability picked up on the power surge and my heartbeat got loud in my ears as all of my body's were parts came awake.

Then, everything went away and it was back to silence except for the whir of the HVAC and the click of the computers in the bullpen. "You gonna be wanting a pastry?" Kelly growled.

"No thanks," I said absently, still staring at the photo from the customs office. "But you're a big strapping boy, Kelly. You should eat."

He stomped off toward the elevator, and I went back into my office. I'd have to keep an eye on Kelly. If he was a trained witch and he kept it from me, we might have a problem when his anger management issues finally blew up all over the SCS.

For now, though, I had something more pressing. I turned on my desk lamp and held the photo under it. The crate was open and the thing nested within was plain gray stone, oval and slightly off of symmetrical. It was the carvings I was interested in. They were blood witch lettering—something I'd seen enough of investigating the Skull of Mathias, another blood witch artifact, to know on sight. They meant that whatever Grace Hartley was messing with would get bigger and uglier and meaner, until the whole city burned.

Danger I recognized from long experience, but I still had no clue what the fuck I was looking at. I looked at the time and called Sunny's cell.

"Hello?" she mumbled. "Luna?"

"You're still asleep?" I said in astonishment. It was nearly six-thirty and Sunny was usually up with the sunrise.

"You're awake?" she returned.

"Hey, I was night shift for almost three years. This is my prime time."

"Yes, and since you got the cushy desk job the end-times themselves wouldn't rouse you before eight. What do you need, Luna?"

"Well, to make sure you're all right, for starters," I said, defensive without my coffee.

"Turn off the light," said a male voice from Sunny's end. "It's too goddamn early."

"Sorry," Sunny said sweetly. "It's my cousin."

"Who else would it be at six in the freaking morning?" Mac grumbled. "She always did have great Hexed timing."

I put my forehead on my desk and fought the urge to bang it repeatedly into the wood. "Sunny, I need your help with something. Can you come down to the office?"

"What sort of help?" she said. "I'll be honest, it's feeling like a lazy day at *casa* Swann."

"Okay, I'm going to ignore the fact that you go stupid the minute you have a little sex, and just say that I think we may be dealing with a blood witch artifact and I'd like to have some idea of what it is before any more of your dates get ended by an attack of man-eating lizard people."

"Crap," Sunny said. "Give me an hour. I need to shower and get dressed."

"Fine by me," I said.

"Good-bye, Luna," Mac said into the speaker, and the line went dead.

"That's just gross and unnatural," I told my empty office. Kelly appeared again, and slammed down a paper cup full of coffee at my elbow. "Don't get emotional on me, now," I told him as he stalked back to his desk; then I picked up the phone and called Batista, Annemarie, Zacharias, Pete, and Bryson.

After assorted grumbling and some colorful cursing on Bryson's part, I got them all to come in at the same time as Sunny.

My office closet held a few pairs of jeans and spare blouses for days when the weather turned while I was in the field. Or days when I got blood spatter on me. I pulled the shades and changed out of my sadly wrinkled dress, shoving it into a dry-cleaning bag for later, and downed my coffee while I waited for the team.

I took one last look at the photo from Commandant Ivanović's fax as Norris and Annemarie came in, laughing and talking like grandfather and granddaughter. Annemarie just had that effect on people. I wished for a second that it was that easy for me.

"Hey." I stuck my head out. "Just be a minute."

"Hey yourself, lady," said Annemarie. "You look rode hard and put up wet. Long night?"

"Nothing a spa day and about fifty hours of sleep wouldn't fix," I said. "Can you get everyone into the briefing room when they show up?"

"Sure thing," said Annemarie. Norris just looked at my tangled hair and the circles under my eyes and gave a small snort.

Sunny came from the elevator, looking refreshed and wholesome as a milk ad. I growled under my breath. "Where's the artifact?" she demanded, slinging her purse into my spare office chair. "I brought some things to cast a protective working."

"See, that's a problem," I said. "I don't know exactly where it is. Hell, I don't know *what* it is." I held out the photo to her. Sunny squinted at it, chewing on her lip.

"This is it?" she said.

"Yeah, that was faxed to us direct from the customs office that cleared it," I said. "And thanks to a certain anchorman, we have no idea where it went once it came into the country."

"This is bad," Sunny said, and she wasn't looking quite so refreshed anymore.

"On a scale of one to Armageddon . . . ?"

"Well, I wouldn't start any long-term home renovation

projects," Sunny said. Annemarie appeared in the door and gestured to the conference room. I touched Sunny on the arm.

"I need you to brief the team. Let's go." I followed her in, trying to ignore the sinking feeling in my gut that said we were all Hexed.

"Everyone knows my cousin, I take it," I said to the assembled cops. They were in various states of alertness, from bright-eyed Annemarie to Andy hiding his yawns behind his hand. Bryson was outright nodding in the corner chair that Kelly usually took. I picked up a dry eraser and threw it at Bryson. He came awake with a start.

"I put the trash out, Annie!"

Kelly and Batista snickered, and even Annemarie bit the inside of her cheek. Bryson flushed and smoothed his tie down. "What, like your wife never gets on your case, Javier?"

"Yeah, but she ain't my ex-wife yet," Batista said with an easy smile.

"Enough," I said. Most mornings I'd be happy to let them go at it—happy cops are snarky cops, after all—but my sense of humor had fled somewhere between the basilisks and sleeping at my desk. "We have a picture of what was shipped to Brad Morgan's warehouse, went to one Grace Hartley, and from there . . . we have no idea."

I gestured at Sunny.

"I was wondering what all that scribbling was," Zacharias said. "Looks important. You think the Hartley broad is involved in this?"

Hearing Andy use the word "broad" without irony was

almost enough to restore my sense of humor, but Sunny spoke up.

"What we're looking for is known as a heartstone." She worried the picture in her hands. "It's an archaic blood witch artifact, predating later advances in workings that allowed for only a circle and blood to be used to call down power."

" 'Heartstone' doesn't sound real worrisome, you want my honest opinion," said Annemarie.

"Ditto," said Andy.

"What mojo does this thing work?" Batista said.

"While they're not used much any longer, they're still very bad news," Sunny said. She stood up. "Imagine five personal computers wired together. More powerful than an individual, but limited. That's a blood witch cast—the limit on their energy draw is their own bodies. Now . . . ," she bit her lip, "imagine those same five computers hard-wired into a mainframe that could single-handedly run this entire city."

"Dios mío," said Batista. Andy looked pale, and Annemarie muttered something, stroking the Saint Michael's medal she wore at her throat.

"The heartstone is capable of channeling five hundred times the power of an individual witch's body," said Sunny. "And the results have ended in disaster before. We weren't meant to control that much magick. No one was."

"And now this thing is somewhere, loose?" Kelly spoke up for the first time. His big face was furrowed, shadows of anger hiding the color of his eyes as he glared. "There's not a fucking thing we can do about that, I take it?"

"Sunny," I said, pointedly ignoring Kelly. "What can these be used for?"

"That's just it," she said. "They were phased out by new casting methods—easier, safer methods—but they can be used for any sort of working."

"This is enough for a warrant for Grace Hartley," I said, tapping my finger on my chin. "Bryson, get that worked up. And while you're at it, get one for Brad Morgan's house and car as well."

Bryson blinked. "I don't understand."

"Whatever his reasons were, he let this thing into the city," I said. "And he's a weak link. I need something to lean on him with and hope he snaps before whatever dastardly black plan these freaks have is put in motion."

"What should we do?" Zacharias asked.

"Get ready to serve the warrants and find out everything you can about heartstones," I said. "Sunny, thank you. Sorry I had to drag you down here."

She stopped me as we were filing out of the conference room. "That other thing you asked me about, the Maiden? I'm still working on it. 'Maiden' is endemic to Gardnerian Wicca and hundreds of older sects before it, so the exact context of the term would be helpful."

I remember how unconcerned Talon had seemed when I'd been lying there under her not-so-tender mercy. "It was definitely a person," I said. "And somebody who was a hell of a lot scarier than me, in Talon's mind." The calm on her face was the same type I'd seen on mob hit men confident their bosses would bail them out of a jam with the police. The ease of the untouchable.

"I'll ask Grandma," said Sunny. "She won't like that I'm helping you, especially after what happened last night."

I leaned against the wall. My arm was itching as it healed and I didn't want to add more problems with our intractable, disapproving grandmother to the mix. "This is getting so big," I said aloud.

Sunny gave me a wan smile. "This world was always big, Luna," she said. "Blood witches and caster witches aren't the only things out there. There's a lot more waiting—back in the shadows where they're hard to see—but the visible magick of the world is only the tip of something much larger."

I'd never cared to know much about magick before I discovered I was a Path, and I cared even less after I found out. I was a were, but the part of the darker world that Sunny walked in terrified me. Every experience with witches I'd had firsthand had ended in blood, pain, and terror. I didn't care how many sects and types and factions there were. All that mattered was that most were bad news and held no love for weres.

Since I don't like admitting when something scares me, I let out a growl instead. Sunny wasn't fooled, but at least she didn't say anything except, "Take care of yourself, Luna."

Bryson waved at me from his desk. "I got Judge Spencer to sign off on those warrants, Chief. Which one you wanna hit first?"

"Let's go see Brad Morgan and kick his tires a bit," I said. "Annemarie, you come with me. Bryson, have the rest of the squad standing by to serve the search warrant on Grace Hartley once I'm done with Morgan."

Sunny was gone when I looked back, and I was glad. I didn't need someone who knew me that well around right then.

Annemarie checked her gun and shoved it into its holster. She wore it on her hip, cowboy style, her one nod to the fact that she was a petite, attractive woman in a dangerous job. I preferred to wear mine in the small of my back. Easier to surprise somebody that way.

"We ready to rock and roll, Chief?" she asked me, slipping on her trim dark blue jacket.

"One thing first," I said, after a moment of internal debate. It wasn't his case, but knowing him, he'd show up anyway, and it was better if I invited him. It was a control game with Fagin, and I needed this round to go to me.

I picked up Annemarie's desk phone and told him to meet us at the Morgan residence.

Thirteen

He was idling in the driveway when Annemarie and I pulled up, his head tilted back, fingers tapping his steering wheel in time with the car radio. I glared at him from the curb.

"Sure is a cutie," Annemarie said, under her breath. "What do you think, Lieutenant?"

"I think the cuteness is offset by the attitude," I told her.

The Morgan residence was not small, the broad front steps designed to make anyone mounting them feel insignificant. I don't like people who put on an offensive front and I jabbed the doorbell harder than necessary.

"If Morgan isn't a player in the gun case, why am I here?" Fagin said, leaning against the frame and peering in the opaque glass panes in the door.

"You're here to flash your fed badge and act scary," I told him. "I think Brad Morgan knows more than he's telling us about Manners getting hacked and I'm through playing around."

"Fair enough," said Fagin. I rang the bell again.

"Door's open," Annemarie said, pushing on it with the flat of her hand. It swung inward, showing a darkened hallway.

"Mr. Morgan?" I called, pushing my jacket aside to touch the grip of my Sig. The plastic was cold under my hand, as was the air breathing in my face from the interior of the house.

Annemarie put herself out of my fire zone, slightly back and to the left, and motioned me forward. Her own gun, a ladylike Heckler & Koch nine millimeter, was down at her side in a stance straight out of the police academy. She gave me a thumbs-up to show she had me covered. Fagin had drawn his weapon, too, his mouth set.

"Go ahead," he told me, barely more than a rumble in his chest.

Wishing mightily that I'd put on Kevlar, I put a foot over the threshold, my footstep muffled in the thick entry runner. No one likes making primary entry. The first person through the door always takes the bullet, or trips the bomb, or—

Stop it, Wilder. Get your head in the game.

"Brad Morgan," I called out again. "It's the police."

Like that ever stopped anyone with a gun bent on using it. The inside of the Morgan house was expensive and sleek, but airless, like a museum where no one actually lived. Tiny cracks in the façade were showing, though—a picture on the wood and glass entry table was facedown, a snowfall of glass trailing across the carpet like spent, frozen tears.

I picked it up. It was a family portrait—Brad Morgan, his stiffly smiling wife, and a grinning brunette kid in a Spider-Man shirt. The glass pricked my palm and I dropped the frame.

"Oh, that's not a bad sign," Fagin murmured. "Not at all."

"Brad?" I called, taking my penlight out of my pocket.

All of the shades were drawn in the room we entered, a sitting room frozen in shop-window perfection. Static fizzed on the expansive plasma-screen TV mounted to the wall. The remote was crushed at my feet, as if some giant had attempted to change the channel.

The cold was worse here, and I saw a small hallway leading us toward the back of the house, the carpet runner wrinkled and a smear of something dark on the wall.

"Oh, good lord," Annemarie whispered. "Is that what I think it is?"

I drew a deep sniff of the biting cold air. Pungent, dead, but not human. "It's animal blood." Thank the gods. The blood was arranged in smears that looked random at first, but I saw the squares and shapes of a crude cuneiform writing trailing along the pale yellow paint, probably a color named Harvest Sun or Lemon Fantasy.

"If this is some Satanic shit, you can count me out right now," Fagin said from behind me. "I'm not with that whole cat-sacrificing, goat-worshiping gig."

"Shut up," I hissed. "There are things a whole hell of a lot worse than Satanism, trust me."

"This isn't right," Annemarie murmured. "We shouldn't be here."

Just what I needed—my team cracking up the minute they saw a little haunted-house action. "Brad?" I shouted, coming around the corner and finding myself in a laundry room.

"Go away," Brad Morgan whispered. He was naked, squeezed into the space between his clothes dryer and the wall. The blood writing spilled down the wall and formed a shield around him, one that breathed ice and magick across my face.

"Brad," I said. "Whatever it is, we can talk about it."

He let out a sob, pulling himself tighter against the wall. "I tried to send her away, but I can't. I tried to call it for protection, but . . ." He started to shiver uncontrollably.

"Who?" I said, crouching near him. "Who did you send away? Who is here with us?"

"I should never have come to you," he sobbed. "I hear her inside my head every minute, every *second*, since I betrayed her. She's traveling, along that black plain and coming right for me. I just wanted it to stop, and now . . ."

His palms were streaked with drying blood and he began to claw at his face, swatting as if ants were crawling out of his skin.

"Brad. Brad!" I reached out to stop him, and something cold and black latched itself onto my arm. I saw a swirl of magick come out of the blood on the floor, like choking carbon fog with teeth, and wrap itself around my hand, covering my skin and sending row upon row of pain, like the magick was run through barbed wire.

I let out a scream, jerking backward and into Fagin, who had stepped in to cover Morgan. We both fell against the laundry sink, the thing attached to me snarling and growing, more and more of it pouring from the blood.

"What the Hex is it?" Fagin bellowed in my ear. Through the pain in my arm I started to see details—eyes, flaring nostrils, and teeth, long and curved like a prehistoric beast. The eyes locked onto mine, and red flames danced in their depths.

"I don't know," I ground back. "But I'm going to get rid of it. Stand back."

"Kinda hard when you're sitting on me," Fagin grunted.

"Fagin," I gritted. "It's not the time to be picky." I shut my eyes and opened myself, Pathing the magick of the thing that had sprung from Brad's blood ritual. I braced myself for pain ten times worse than the thing currently sunk into my aura.

Nothing happened. The shadow dog gave a snarl and shook my arm, trying to wrench it from the socket. It was latched onto me physically, but that wasn't what hurt. I saw a blossoming of silver and white from around its jaws, a slow-motion aural blood spray as it disrupted the magick that clung to my spirit, what made me a were, what made me *me*.

I snarled back and put my foot into it, meeting something solid in the mass of writhing energy. It gave a yelp, and its grip on me loosened a fraction. Behind me, Fagin grunted as I slammed into him again from the impact.

"Morgan, call it off!" I bellowed. "I'm trying to help your sorry ass!"

"I . . . I can't," he quavered. "I called it and it . . . got away from me. But it's no worse than what she'll do to me, if she gets through. . . ."

He thrashed, convulsing with a scream as the dog redoubled its size and leapt at me, taking me to ground. It was real now, had paws and claws and obsidian teeth that grazed my shoulder as it went for the throat. Brad Morgan gave a sigh and a shudder, limbs twitching uselessly as his magick chewed him up and spit him out.

Watching a witch lose control of a working is never pretty, but I had more pressing things on my mind. I grabbed a box of fabric softener and shoved it between the beast's wide jaws, cuffing it in the side of the head with my closed fist. It spit out the box in a shower of powder and lunged at me again.

I caught it in the throat this time, with my elbow, heard

a crunch as the airway closed. The black dog gave a strangled yelp, some of the malignant life draining from its fire eyes.

"No . . . ," Morgan moaned. "No . . . she'll find me."

"Who?" I demanded, struggling with the dog as it snapped feebly at me. "Who is she, Brad?"

"She walks," he whispered. "She is the Maiden, eternal. She is—"

He screamed, and I felt his working slip its bonds and swell, fat on the blood of his psyche. The magick flow from the markings on the floor grew and ballooned until my head was a screaming knot of feedback.

A cacophony of thunder stopped it cold, leaving my ears ringing but my other senses clear. Annemarie lowered her gun, a little smoke curling up to join the dissipating magick in the low light.

The black dog gave a howl and shrank back, into the blood marks, until it was nothing but a dense coating of bad magick on my skin. I slumped, legs akimbo, against the wall of the laundry room. "Hex me."

"Morgan, too," said Fagin, putting away his sidearm. "He doesn't look good."

Brad Morgan still curled against the wall, his arms limp now and three tightly clustered holes in his torso leaching his life onto the pure white tile floor.

"Oh, crap," I whispered, scrambling over to him. My hands and knees smeared the blood markings with no repercussion now. Without the shaman behind them, they were just blood. "Brad." I shook him. "Come on; stay with me. Call a bus!" I snapped at Annemarie.

She nodded, her blue eyes wide as dollars. "Dispatch, this is One-eight-two requesting an ambulance at . . ."

Her voice faded out as I focused on Brad Morgan. He coughed, black arterial blood coming up from his lungs.

"Stay with me," I told him. "Don't you go dying. It's no kind of day for that."

"Hate . . . to disagree with you," Morgan sighed. "Day . . . isn't the problem."

He shuddered again, not the desperate convulsion of a body trying to contain too much magick but the last, shocky attempts of a nervous system to save itself. Brad Morgan was dying, and doing it fast.

"Morgan," I said. "Who brought the heartstone here? Where is it now?"

He rolled his eyes over to me, filmy with the last glimpse of the living world. "Grace Hartley," he said. "She has it. In her basement. Took it and never left."

Fuck. It had been right under my nose and I'd backed off, let Hartley slip it past me. "Morgan," I said, gripping his shoulders, "who is the Maiden?"

His head lolled against my hand, startlingly warm after the chill of the working and the sudden, sharp shock of a death.

"No joy," said Fagin, bending down next to me. "Deader than the proverbial doornail at an undertakers' convention."

I snapped my head around and growled at him, a full were snarl. "Do you have to turn everything into a joke?"

Fagin raised his hands. "Sorry, Luna . . . but he did try to kill all of us."

"He was scared . . . ," I started, and then stood up. I couldn't be near the body for another second. "You know what, forget it. Just get out of my way." I brushed past Fagin, who for once looked at a loss, and stumbled down the hallway, through the TV room, and out into the early-afternoon sun without seeing any of it. I just needed to get out of that tiny space, away from the blood smell and the fear and the rag-doll body that had until recently been Brad Morgan. Alive, scared, and begging for my help.

A lot of good I'd done him.

"Luna?" Annemarie came over to me from where she'd been standing with her cell phone. I looked at her. Usually it was *ma'am* or *Lieutenant*, the southern upbringing always in place. Now she sounded like she was falling and asking someone to catch her.

"What is it, Annemarie?"

"I'm sorry about . . . in there. That man was gonna kill you. I had to do it. I'm so sorry."

I reached out and clapped a hand on her bony shoulder. "It was a good shooting, Detective. You don't have anything to be sorry for."

She swallowed, and I saw her willowy frame barely containing the shakes. "First time?" I said. I vomited after my first officer-involved shooting, right into the bathtub of the lousy tenement bathroom where the suspect's body lay, spreading his brainpan across the pitted tile. The evidence tech at the scene gave me hell for it.

Annemarie nodded, her face screwed up, her cheeks crimson. "I've drawn my gun before, but I never fired it on duty. Never. And now I killed a man."

"Listen," I said. "They're going to get Internal Affairs down here, and there's going to be a review, and you're going to have to talk to a shrink. Beyond all of that, the one thing you need to know?"

Annemarie put her hands over her mouth, the fingers pale and white as bone. I grabbed her shoulders and made her look at me. "The one thing, Detective Marceaux, that you need to remember is that you did what you had to do and what you were *supposed* to do. You protected Agent Fagin and me from a dangerous, armed suspect."

"Why'd he have to do it?" Annemarie murmured. "What was that thing?"

"He was scared," I said. "Shamans, like Morgan—they can call guides, I think. Spirit guardians. I think he tried to call it to protect himself, and it got away from him."

While Annemarie got hold of herself I tried, temporarily at least, to block out the image of the teeth and the flaming red eyes, the closest thing to a hellhound I'd ever seen.

In a small voice, finally, she said, "What do you think he was scared of, ma'am?"

The Maiden. "Something a lot badder than that dog of his," I said. Morgan's dying words. *Grace Hartley. . . . Took it and never left.*

"Annemarie," I said, as the wail of a patrol car's siren cut the crisp air. "I need you to wait here for those officers and help them secure the scene. Agent Fagin and I have something we need to do."

"The room is secure," said Fagin, stepping out. "And fuck me, could I ever use a cigarette." He paused. "Dare I ask what it is you and I need to be doing?"

I was already pulling out my cell to scramble the rest of the SCS. "We need to get to Grace Hartley."

Fourteen

Fagin broke a lot of traffic laws getting to Grace Hartley's pile, once I told him what the heartstone was and what Sunny thought it could do. Bryson, Kelly, Andy, and Javier were waiting for us. Pete was behind them in a CSU Jeep.

"Wait here," I told him. "I'm sure there will be plenty of stuff for you to swab once we're finished."

"So how is this playing?" Fagin asked as I stomped up the walkway, trailed by my four detectives. "Hard entry? Polite knocking?"

I slammed my fist into Mrs. Hartley's ornate front door, hard enough to rattle the leaded panes. "Open the door, Grace!" I bellowed. "I know you're in there."

After a long second a face swam up in the glass and the same maid opened the door. She was wearing jeans and a hoodie this time, clearly on her off day, and her wide face went blank with fear. "INS?" she said.

"So far from it you don't even know," I said. "Where's Mrs. Hartley?"

The maid's eyes twitched between me, Fagin, the spread of cops behind us. "You will have to try again later," she said. "Mrs. Hartley is very busy—"

I gripped her by the shoulder and moved her aside like

I'd push a swinging door—firmly, but not forcefully. It wasn't her fault that she was trying to keep her crappy illegal job.

"Grace Hartley!" I bellowed. "We have a warrant to search your house and we're doing it with or without you!"

"There's no need to shout so," she said, appearing from the kitchen. It was casual day at the mansion, apparently. Grace was decked out in a matching sweat suit, black with gold embroidery, like the oldest schoolgirl in existence.

"Finally," I snapped back. "David, give her the warrant." Bryson stepped forward and pressed the green-jacketed copy into Grace's stiff fingers.

"What *is* this mess?" she demanded.

"That gives us permission to search your home," I said. Grace's lips nearly disappeared as she compressed them into a glare that could have stripped flesh from bone.

"You have no right," she hissed. "I've done nothing."

"Oh no," I agreed. "Except for bring a heartstone into my city. Terrify Brad Morgan to the point of insanity and have Milton Manners blackmail him to be part of your filthy blood witch plan." I closed the distance between us. "I know what you're doing, and if you think I'm going to sit by and let it happen, you're sadly mistaken."

Grace Hartley bored into me for a moment, and I into her. Her eyes were green, flecked with gold, and they were placid as pools. I didn't scare her, and that got my back up.

"Lieutenant Wilder," she finally sighed. "I have no idea what you're talking about, but go ahead and search for whatever-it-was. Satisfy your curiosity so this harassment by your department can end."

Just the right amount of bored frustration verging on anger in her tone. I didn't bite. "Where's your basement?"

"Through the kitchen and down the stairs," she said, tonelessly.

I jerked my head at Andy. "Watch her."

"Yes, ma'am," said Zacharias nervously, stepping in front of Grace Hartley like she might sprout wings and fly away. I wouldn't put it past an old witch like her, honestly.

"Bryson, Batista, search the upstairs," I said. "Kelly, see what you can find down here. Agent Fagin and I will check the basement." And find the heartstone, and bring the whole mess to a close.

The basement was one of those endemic to old houses—low ceiling hung with cobwebs, beams with nails sticking every which way, waiting to catch someone tall as I was in the forehead. I found an old-fashioned round light switch and flicked it experimentally. A string of weak, flickering bulbs struggled to life, showing me stone walls, an antique washing machine and hand-crank dryer, and a small archway leading farther into the subterranean depths. Deep rust-bleeding bolt-holes ran around the rim, as if something had been fixed there long enough to rot, and then summarily ripped away.

I looked at Fagin, then at the archway. He nodded, and took out his gun.

The room beyond the arch was dark, and I snapped my light on, sweeping it over the dirt floor and the curved brick walls, barely large enough for me to stand straight in. Water had worn the bricks smooth and rounded, like rotted teeth, and moss pushed between the cracks.

"It's a sewer tunnel," I said to Fagin. "For the original plumbing, looks like." I shone my light into the darkness, trying to see how far the tunnel went.

Something gray and about the size of a large suitcase,

sitting on a crude scaffold of boards, jumped under the light's beam. "Hex me," I breathed. The swirl of blood witch lettering was familiar and sickening to me now as it had been the first time I'd seen it, on the Skull.

The heartstone sat in front of me, innocuous and smaller than I'd imagined. There wasn't even any magick curling around it, like most objects of power I'd encountered.

"That's it?" said Fagin from behind me.

"Expecting something guarded by sinister robed witches and stained with the blood of the innocent?" I said.

He holstered his weapon and stepped closer to it, reaching out a hand. "Something like that, yeah."

I closed my fingers around his wrist and jerked it back to his side. Fagin grunted in surprise.

"Best not to touch it," I said. "Trust me."

I pulled out my radio. "Guys, we found it. Pete, get ready to come down here and process the artifact. Andy, arrest Grace Hartley."

Only a fizz of static came back to me. I looked down at the radio's display screen and saw that I had no bars, just a blinking antenna. "Shit. Fagin, go upstairs and get the rest of the team down here."

Compared to what might have happened, no reception underground was the least of my worries. The heartstone was here. No one else had died.

So why was my heart still thudding as if a pack of blood witches on brooms were chasing me?

I looked back at the heartstone, battered and chipped at the edges from centuries of wear. It should have been so much harder to find it, to touch it. Instead it was under my hands with no resistance. I shivered at the proximity of the thing, and felt dampness on my face. It was cold in the tunnel, too cold to be sweating, and in the recesses of my hindbrain the were snarled a warning that this had been way too easy.

"Fagin," I said as he started back into the basement. "Wait a second."

The moisture hung in the air all around us, chill against my hands and face. I knew the feeling of the cold, oily mist—I'd felt it before, as I lay on my back in a filthy alleyway waiting to die from the knife wound in my stomach.

A Wendigo.

"What is it?" Fagin said, his brows drawing together as I took out my weapon and aimed it into the darkness. "You see something?"

"Get out of here," I hissed at him. "Get out and get out fast."

Fagin took a step back, still staring into the shadows. "Luna, what in the hells—"

The gunshot split my head, a flash and a boom like a grenade in the enclosed space. The muzzle flash blinded me for a split second and I saw Fagin jerk backward like he was on a string, an explosion of brick erupting behind him, carving a hole the size of a fist into the tunnel wall.

Whoever was in the tunnel fired again, five shots, fast and high. It was suppressing fire, not intended to do anything except make us duck and cover.

I dropped behind the heartstone and rolled over to rest next to Fagin. He was still, facedown.

"Fuck," I hissed, shoving my finger against his neck and groping for a pulse. Nothing.

After Brad Morgan, it deadened me like a blow to the chest. Fagin couldn't be dead. Couldn't be.

The tunnel lit up with another burst of gunfire and I heard the clink of an empty chamber after the last shot.

If I was lucky, I'd have five seconds before the person in the tunnel reloaded—if "person" was even the right word for what was waiting down there.

I tucked my legs under me and sprang up, jumping over the heartstone and rattling it on its base, aiming myself for where the muzzle flash had come from.

The figure hunched before me slid the clip home in his gun, the silvery mist swirling around him thickening as he looked up, black eyes meeting mine.

I froze. I had expected to see a Wendigo, nightmarish silver flesh and teeth, out for my blood, but I'd never expected to see him.

"Lucas?"

Lucas Kennuka snapped the slide closed on his pistol and held it up to my face. "Luna Wilder. Wish I could say it was good to see you."

My gun was at my hip. I'd relied on strength and surprise to carry me through and I'd miscalculated.

Now I was going to die at the hands of a man who'd already nearly killed me once before. Fantastic.

"Don't move," Lucas said. "It's not personal, but don't you move. I know you're tricky." His eyes bled to silver and back to black, and his tongue flicked over his lips. Lucas had delicate features, almost pretty, and it was easy to forget that there was a monster, a real one, hiding under his skin. He was a bloodthirsty shape-changer, and while we weren't enemies, he hadn't been happy with me the last time we'd met. Well, he'd been unconscious and nearly dead the last time I'd seen him, but the words we'd had before that hadn't exactly been tender loving endearments.

"What are you even doing here?" I said. "Why did you shoot at me?"

"I heard voices, voices that don't belong to anyone who has business down here, and I shot at a trespasser," said Lucas in that maddeningly calm way he had about him. "Like I said—not personal. But I forget everything's personal with you." He had a soldier's cool, the dead calm of a special operative who was most at ease in a hot zone.

"Like hell you shot a trespasser!" I exploded. "That's a federal agent that you gunned down!"

Lucas flexed his grip on his pistol. "Sorry. Humans all sort of look alike."

I knew he didn't really need the gun—he could change at will into a Wendigo, made of little more than smoke, teeth and hunger. He was just pointing the cannon in my face to get a rise out of me.

It worked, too—I cut left and grabbed the gun, clamping my hand over the slide so Lucas couldn't fire. Twisting the weapon backward, I heard a pop as his trigger finger dislocated. Lucas let out a snarl, showing his sharp incisors as his lips curled back. The pistol went skittering away across the dirt floor of the tunnel and I wrapped my hand around Lucas's throat, squeezing hard enough to cut off the air.

"I don't want to hurt you, but you bring out the worst in me," I snarled at him. "Don't give me an excuse."

Lucas just smiled. "What makes you think I won't shift and eat you whole, Luna?"

He had a point there. I squeezed, and he just kept smiling. "What makes you think you have any hope of stopping me leaving here?" Lucas tsked.

"This," said Fagin. His gun came into my narrow field of vision, kissing Lucas's temple with an oily print. "Want to bet I can put one in your brain before you shift? You want the long odds or the smart money?"

Startled as I was, I didn't slacken my grip on Lucas in the slightest. "We're even, Kennuka. I don't want to see you again."

Lucas looked at me, looked at Fagin. "Your new knight, riding to the rescue? I never thought you were the type, Luna. The were I knew didn't need any human man."

"You do not know who I am, Lucas, and you suck at pretending that you do," I snarled, pushing harder against his throat. "Got any more insights before I arrest you?"

He sighed and relaxed under my grip. "I give up, Luna. Take me in."

I grabbed him by the front of his T-shirt and turned him around, putting on handcuffs, for all the good they'd do if he decided to shift, and reading him his Miranda rights.

"Nice work," said Fagin. "Guess it helps when you know the bad guys on a first-name basis."

"Don't even start with *that*," I said. "You need to be checked, even if you were wearing a vest." He had to be wearing a vest. I'd seen the shot, and it was true to the chest. Lucas was a cool head and a dead shot. When he aimed to kill, he killed.

"Wilder?" Bryson and Batista came skidding into the tunnel, closely followed by Kelly, before I could articulate to Fagin that he shouldn't still be walking around.

"We heard shots," said Batista. "Everything good?"

"Take him upstairs," I said, shoving Lucas at Bryson. "Kelly, Batista—get Pete down here to process evidence and then get this stone back to the SCS office."

"I'll just go and file my report," said Fagin, starting to step away. I grabbed him by the lapel of his coat.

"We are not anywhere *close* to finished," I told him. "Get your ass moving."

We mounted the stairs, Fagin ahead of me with a pathetic and confused expression on his face. I wasn't fooled.

Andy was still standing with Grace Hartley, who favored me with an unbearably obnoxious smile. "Did you find what you were looking for, Miss Wilder?"

"Yes," I said with a smile of my own. "No thanks to your hired muscle and his .45. Andy, I thought I told you to arrest her."

"Uh . . . for what?" he called as I marched Fagin across the foyer to the front door.

"Oh, let's start with obstruction of justice and take it from there," I told him.

Grace was still smiling. "You have nothing to hold me on. Magickal artifacts are not considered contraband under U.S. criminal codes. I'll be out within the hour."

"Believe me, witch," I said, banging the door open. "You are welcome to go ahead and try my patience again. I am going to hand you your wrinkly ass on a silver platter."

I shoved Fagin ahead of me onto the porch and slammed the door, jabbing my finger into his chest. "You have a lot of fucking explaining to do."

He shook his head, all of his usual easy arrogance run out of him. "I don't know what you're talking about, Luna."

"I *saw* you take that bullet," I whispered, my hand resting where I was sure the round had gone into him. There was warm skin and muscle under my hand. No vest.

"You don't know what you saw," Fagin said quietly. "It was dark. You were confused."

"I reached down and felt your pulse and you had no heartbeat," I said in the same low tone, only mine had a snarl behind it. "So don't tell me what I imagined and don't tell me I was confused. You were dead, Will. Dead and cold on the ground. And yeah, when you got right back up I was admittedly startled, but I know what I saw. You don't have body armor. . . . What do you have?"

Fagin turned away from me and paced toward the end of the porch. The sun was bright and crisp, filtered through high clouds like cotton balls, and it turned his hair and his skinny frame into a stark ghost shadow in the shaft of light.

"You're not normal," I whispered, "are you?"

"No," Fagin sighed, rubbing the back of his neck. "I'm not."

I came over to him and leaned on the railing, looking out into the wilderness of Grace Hartley's side yard. A few stubborn sunflowers poked out of the tangle of dead grass and nettles. "Then what are you, Will?"

He pressed his hands over his face, and leaned on the rail next to me. "I'm cursed."

I stared at his profile for a second and then all of the compounded events of the day piled up on me. I started to snicker, and it bubbled into an outright laugh.

Fagin drew back, wounded. "Well, don't act so concerned. You're going to smother me at this rate."

"I'm sorry," I managed, getting myself under control. "It's just so . . . melodramatic. *I'm cursed.* Someone cursed me a few days ago, you know. I wish mine came with fewer dead birds and more awesome superpowers, honestly. I'm thinking I got a raw deal."

"Walk with me," Fagin said. He jumped the steps and started at an easy lope down the sidewalk, polished shoes sending a pile of leaves flying. I jogged to catch up with him and we settled into a pace down the broad street. Bonaventure Drive was stately, shabby elegance in the intricate latticework and stained glass of the houses. The pumpkins and fake foam gravestones in the front yards added a touch of the macabre, like strolling through a disused cemetery.

"It was 1560," said Fagin. "England. I was a trader—silk and dye, with the East. I traveled and I saw a lot of strange things."

"You expect me to believe you're over four hundred years old?" I said. "And British?"

"I fell in with a circle of witches," he continued, as if I hadn't spoken. "One in particular. Her name was Esme, then. I let myself grow close to her, before I realized how mad she was. The magick she used had corrupted her mind to the point that she saw conspiracies and deception around every corner. When she started to believe I'd strayed from her . . ." One side of his mouth curved up. "You can probably guess."

"She made with the cursing?" I said.

Fagin nodded. "She and her sisters drugged me and they cursed me to, as she put it with a gleam in her eye, *wander the earth, forever and alone*." He stopped walking, looking at a particularly garish Halloween display with an electric skeleton that jiggled and howled when we got close. "I can't die. Not until I come back to her. She cursed me with a heartstone. The most powerful magick there is."

"So some psycho ex-girlfriend cursed you to come back to her four hundred years later? That's insane, Will. Totally off the reservation."

He looked down at me, his eyes in shadow as a cloud passed over the sun. "You think that's bad? After she cursed me, she turned me over to the Inquisition. I can't die." He gave a small shiver, which I don't think he was even aware of. "Eight years in their dungeons. They tortured me until I begged to die, over and over. And they killed me, over and over. After I escaped, I tried it myself, dozens of times. Each time, I'd wake up and I'd still be here, in this world."

Will started walking again. "A few hundred years later, after I got tired of hanging around Lord Byron and the two of us bemoaning our sad lot in life, I decided that I would break the curse. I've been waiting since then to find her."

I stopped him with a hand on his elbow. "You can't think Esme is still alive."

"A heartstone gave me life," said Fagin. "You think that Esme couldn't do the same thing to herself? I've chased her across most of the world, and she's changed her name and her face, I'm sure, but one thing is always the same."

"What's that?" I said. I was still touching him, but Will didn't pull away.

"The Maiden," he said. "That name. It follows her. Esme was the Maiden to her sisters and she's the Maiden always. This is the closest I've ever been." He turned his hand and gripped my arm in turn. "Luna, I'm begging you, now. Please don't let her get away from me again."

"Breaking the curse," I said. "What does that entail?"

Fagin's lip curled. "I find Esme and I plant a blade in her heart, and a few rounds in her head for good measure. Workings can't sustain when the witch who cast them is dead. You know that."

I let go. "Here's the deal. I need your help to figure out what these witches are using the heartstone for. When and if we find the Maiden, you can make her lift the curse. But you will not kill her, Will. There is no vigilante justice in my city."

He put a finger under my chin. "You're so very young, Luna. You still think people can be saved. It's not true. I hope you learn that before it gets you killed."

I reared back and slapped him, hard enough to snap his head around. "Hex you," I said. "You may be older than dirt, but you know shit about me."

"I'm going to find her, eventually," he said, rubbing his jaw.

"Not in the middle of my case," I said. "And not with my team and my family in your way."

Turning my back on Fagin, I left him on the sidewalk and stalked back to the Hartley house. I had a scene to process and a case to close, and there was no room in it to think about Will.

Fifteen

SCS was buzzing like a shaken hive when I got back, Hartley's maid sobbing by Annemarie's desk, Annemarie herself talking intently to two suits from Internal Affairs, Bryson and Batista helping Pete carry in boxes of evidence from the Hartley house, and Zacharias and Kelly sitting with the woman herself, who was handcuffed to a chair at Andy's desk.

"Sorry they're not Tiffany silver," I said as I passed. "Short notice. You understand."

"You go ahead and keep gloating, Lieutenant," said Hartley. "My lawyer is going to pulverize you. You'll be working mall security."

"I like the mall," I said. "The gyros at the food court are amazing. And you don't scare me, so why don't you hop back on your broom and do a lap?" I rounded on Kelly. "Why isn't she in a holding cell?"

"Her lawyer is coming," he grunted. "It's fine if she waits here."

"Oh really. I'm so glad that I have you to make executive decisions for me, Hunter. I really don't know what I'd do without you."

He turned colors, and Grace Hartley snorted. "It's always so fascinating to see the inner workings of our city's finest."

I pressed my thumb against the bridge of my nose. "Why don't you just tell me what you're doing with the heartstone and how you're setting these fires, and oh, while we're at it, why you tried to *fucking kill me*, you crazy old bat."

I was yelling and I didn't particularly care. Grace Hartley leaned back a bit, as if I'd dropped my finger sandwich at her tea party and made a mess on the carpet.

"You certainly have a thorny set of problems, Miss Wilder," she murmured. "However, they are not mine and I maintain my innocence of anything except perhaps an unwise purchase of objet d'art for my home."

I would have hauled off and smacked her if it wasn't for Kelly's and Andy's eyes on me. The were clawed up in my throat as I chafed under Hartley's hard granite gaze, wanting to break something, to hurt something.

"Mom?" A voice broke the battle inside me. I turned and saw a tall teenage girl, willowy like Grace Hartley must have been, once, before she ran to old-woman stockiness, the same eyes and the same blond hair. Huh. Guess it really was natural.

"Sophia," said Hartley, extending her free hand. "Come here, my dear. How I hate for you to see me like this."

"Mom," she said again, staring at Andy, Kelly, and me like we were standing around poking Grace with sharp sticks. "What the Hex is going on?"

"Language, Sophia," Grace admonished her. "Just because we're in this situation, there's no reason to—"

"Your mother has been arrested," I said. "She's going to be held for a bail hearing, and you can see her then.

We're still taking a statement, so I'm going to have to ask you to wait in the visitors' area."

Sophia winced at the word "arrested." "What's she done? She has a lawyer. You can't just keep her here."

"Andy," I sighed. "Can you please take Miss Hartley back to the front until we're finished with her mother?"

"Sure thing, ma'am," he said, jumping up and managing to knock over his desk chair. Sophia followed him to the front with a hangdog look on her face.

"It will be all right, dear," Grace called after her. "I'll be out of here in two shakes."

"Yeah, don't bet on that," Kelly said dourly.

Grace Hartley sneered. "You have quite the brain trust here, Miss Wilder. Especially this one. He stinks of the blood."

"You shut up, lady," Kelly warned, and I saw a flash of life in his dull-edged face.

I held up my hand. "Is Lucas Kennuka in the holding cells?"

"Who?" Kelly said.

"The guy that shot at Agent Fagin and me."

Kelly nodded. "Took him over holding myself. Him and the bitch."

I raised my eyebrows. "And which bitch would that be?"

"The were hellcat Bryson and Batista found hiding in one of the upstairs bedrooms. This one has all kinds of freaks on her payroll."

"You're one to talk," Hartley snarled.

"I'm not the one in handcuffs, lady. I'll talk all I want."

"Shut up, the both of you," I said. "You're giving me a headache." I left them and headed for the holding cells, two floors up. So Bryson and Batista had found Talon.

Good. I was looking forward to talking with her. Right after I figured out what to do about Lucas.

The cells had old-style prison bars, controlled by an antique switch system and a single guard. He waved me through after I dropped anything that could be used as a weapon in the basket at his desk.

I stepped through the outer gate as the buzzer rang off the whitewashed brick walls. Most of the Justice Plaza had been reclaimed into sleek, boring modern office space, but not here. Here it was all hard time like a Johnny Cash song, scuffed linoleum floors and windows barred with mesh that cut the sun into diamonds against the wall.

Lucas was in the last cell, sitting still as a dead man on his unmade cot. Only his fingers moved, the black nails tapping against the knuckles of his opposite hand like a bird's heartbeat. Talon, the were, was in the cell across from him, pacing back and forth. She flipped me off when I looked at her.

"Your parents must be so proud," I said.

"What brings you down this way with the rest of the bad seeds, Luna?" Lucas whispered to me. His voice was like steam in cold morning air. It was one of the things I'd liked about him, before I'd found out what he had inside him. Before the hunger god riding his spirit made him stab me and leave me for dead.

"Grace Hartley?" I asked him. "Really? You went from a heavy for weres to a purse holder for blood witches—that's slumming, even for you."

He let out a laugh. "Grace Hartley isn't a blood witch. You're getting blind, Luna."

I stepped closer to the bars. "What the hell is that supposed to mean, Lucas?"

Lucas flowed to his feet, coming to the bars and wrapping his hands around them, leaving maybe a foot between us. I shivered. His body gave off cold, a notch more chill than the air around it. "Think about it, Luna. The thing you wanted most in the world, just lying there in front of you? The bad guys all locked up tight? Grace Hartley uses magick, but you and I both know she's not operating with blood witch workings. And she's not in charge."

"Then who is?" I demanded. Lucas shook his head and paced away from me. I grabbed the bars in turn. "Gods damn you, Lucas, tell me! I saved you from going to prison once. You owe me."

He stood still again, staring at the wall. Ignoring me. I lowered my voice. "After this . . ." I pulled my shirt aside to showcase the long sliver of scar. "It's the least you could do."

Lucas shook his head. "You do know how to work a person's conscience, Lieutenant."

"It's a gift."

He came back to me, scratching the back of his head. "Hartley is who I dealt with, but she has a lot of meetings I wasn't allowed into and she is not calling the shots. You can tell by the fear that crawls into her whenever you bring up payment, or what exactly these people are up to and what magick they're using."

He sat himself on the cot again and crossed his arms, tapping his toes to the beat of an invisible melody. "That's all I know. Debt is paid. How much longer am I going to have to pretend that this cell can hold me?"

"As long as it takes," I snapped. "You shot at me, Lucas."

His mouth quirked. "Some women I've known would consider that foreplay."

"You're a little twisted," I informed him. "Possessed or not."

He flinched. "I was always sorry about that."

"Oh, save it," I said. "Possession is an excuse that can only take you so far."

"I'm not who you think I am," Lucas murmured. "And I'm not going to cry and plead for you to see that I'm a changed man, but . . ." He gave me a slow smile. "Someday, I'd like the chance to show you."

I caught a flash of fang, and backed up from his cell fast. "Just keep it in your pants, cannibal boy, all right?"

"Will do," said Lucas. "Might want to say something to her, though."

Before I could ask him what the Hex he was talking about, I felt a skinny arm slide across my throat and jerk my head against the bars hard enough to shake stars loose over my vision.

"I've got you now," Talon hissed in my ear. Her free hand searched my waist and armpit for a gun.

"I left it outside the cell block," I said. "Sorry to put a crimp in your daring escape plan."

She let out a snarl and squeezed harder. Blackness started to creep around the edges of my eyesight. You can lose consciousness in as little as thirty seconds in a properly applied sleeper hold. Faster if you struggle. I went limp, bargaining for air in the thin space left to my throat between her arm and the cell bars.

"Whatever you think you're doing, Talon, it's not working out." Stupid. I was so stupid. The first rule of containment—don't turn yourself into a hostage. I'd let Lucas distract me and now I was the key to Talon's cell.

"You get me out of here," she hissed, "or I swear to all the gods I will paint you with your own blood." Her other hand abandoned its search and came up to dig claws into my carotid artery.

"You dumb bitch," I said. "What were you in for before this little turn of events, a class-D felony? You just made the A-team, baby. Hard time for assaulting a cop. They're gonna love your pretty face at Mountain Valley Correctional."

"Hey!" Talon bellowed toward the cell guard. "I got your girl down here! You open up or she's going to puff up like a blowfish when I wring her Hexed neck!"

"Not the most eloquent threat I've ever heard," I croaked. My vision was spinning. I clawed at Talon's arm, but she was strong as I was, and she held on tight.

"Open it!" Talon bellowed as the guard's lanky frame shadowed the cell gate.

"Don't you fucking touch that switch," I shouted at him with the last of my air.

"Fuck this," Talon hissed as the guard took out his radio to call for backup. She closed her claws around my throat. My vision spiraled, arching toward unconsciousness, and I had the small comfort that at least I'd be unconscious before I bled out on the cell block floor.

The last thing I saw was Lucas stand up and come to the bars, his black eyes rolling back in his head to show pure mercury silver. His body elongated and hunched, flowing from human to Wendigo in the space of my fading heartbeat.

Little more than a hulking mist-shape with eyes and teeth, Lucas reared back and flew at me through the bars, mouth opening like a wide pit.

Talon screamed and her grip lost purchase on my neck. I fell to the floor, coughing, nausea threatening to overtake my gag reflex.

Lucas shifted back to human, pulling the mist back into himself, and knelt down beside me. "You okay?"

My throat felt like I'd swallowed a ream of sandpaper. I gagged. "Yeah. I'll live."

Lucas looked over at the guard, who was still watching us from the gate. "Then I'll be seeing you, Luna. Don't be a stranger." He stood up and began to run, shifting on the fly into mist. The guard watched, gape-jawed as Lucas loped toward him, passed through the bars of the gate, and slipped down the hallway, leaving a sheen of moisture behind.

I rolled to my feet, even though I was still seeing spinning wheels. "Fucking stop him!" I screamed at the guard. He just stared helplessly as Lucas turned the corner and bounded out of sight.

"Nice work, pig lady," said Talon. "You almost get killed by one and you let the other get away. My faith in the police is restored."

I raised my voice. "Open on Seven!"

The flummoxed guard buzzed the cell door open and I stepped inside, cocked my fist back, and hit Talon in the jaw. Her head snapped around and she sat down hard on her ass.

"You should learn your place," I said, shaking out my fist. I met her eyes and pushed against her willpower with my own, dominating her as a superior predator. I smiled as her defiant, too-sharp face crumpled and a tear of frustration slid down her cheek. "It's right about there," I told her. "Stay."

I backed out of the cell and the door rolled closed with a death knell. "Good girl," I told Talon, and managed to keep my smile in place until I got to the women's room down the corridor.

Sixteen

After my mini-breakdown, I washed my face and took the fire stairs back to the SCS. Norris jumped out at me as soon as I stepped out of the stairwell.

"Grace Hartley's lawyer is here. He's demanding to speak with the detective in charge."

"Cut her loose," I sighed.

Norris's prune face squished even tighter. "Excuse me?"

"Tell Kelly to cut her loose," I repeated. "And while you're at it, put out a BOLO on Lucas Kennuka. He just escaped from the cells upstairs."

"Nice work," Norris said under his breath.

"What was that?"

He jumped as if the blades in my tone had cut him. "I'll do that immediately, Lieutenant."

"Do. And make sure that when Pete is done with the heartstone he secures it in the storage cage. I don't want anyone except the SCS anywhere near that thing." *And maybe not even all of them.* I remembered what Grace Hartley had said about Kelly. She could be crazy, but she could also be right.

Norris looked like the thought of carrying out my orders

gave him acid reflux, but he snapped his fingers at Andy. "Take that *thing* into the storage cage and lock it up."

I gave Andy a silent smile of thanks.

"Ma'am," Annemarie called to me. "Your cousin left you a message. She said she'd found the information you wanted and she'd meet you at your cottage when you got off shift."

"Thanks," I said, passing a hand over my face. My limbs were heavy with fatigue, even though it was barely mid-afternoon. Fagin, Lucas, the heartstone. "Annemarie," I said. "How are you holding up?"

"All right, I guess," she said. "To tell you the truth, I could really do with a mojito and a hot bath after this morning, ma'am."

"Clock out and go home," I said. "I'm going to do the same. If I don't sleep soon I'm going to fall down."

I turned on my BlackBerry so it would catch any forwarded calls and took my radio for emergencies, and drove home through the fading sunlight. Traffic was terrible, the first ripple of rush hour, and by the time I got off the expressway I was ready to strangle someone.

The smoke drifted across the road when I was about a mile from the cottage, whiter than the mist that had shrouded Lucas's Wendigo form. I searched for the source, my nose crinkling at the smell of burning roof shingles and insulation.

My foot slipped off the gas pedal as I saw the white billow of smoke in the direction of my turnoff.

My cottage was the only thing on that road.

"Oh, shit," I breathed, stomping on the LTD's accelerator. The car gave a pathetic jerk and fishtailed on the gravel road leading to my house. My burning house. I could see the flames now, leaping and dancing along the bowed roofline that had greeted me every day when I got off of work, a familiar workhorse shape surrounded by weathered shingles and sheathed in climbing roses. They were ash now, and fire danced behind every window as I skidded to a stop in the drive and fell over my own feet trying to get out of the car faster, fast enough to stop the flames, to beat them back from destroying my life. . . .

I fumbled my radio off my belt, the heat from the blaze beating down on me like an ocean wave, stealing all the moisture from my skin and singeing the ends of my hair. "This is Seventy-six. I need fire and rescue at Nineteen Shell Drive. There's a house fire. . . ."

I couldn't speak anymore. I choked on smoke and my eyes watered from the heat.

"Ten-four, Seventy-six," said the dispatcher. "Any persons inside the residence?"

"No, I . . ." Annemarie's smiling face swam up in my memory. *She said . . . she'd meet you at your cottage.*

The radio fell from my hands and landed on the drive. The back splintered and the battery fell out, cutting off the squawk of the dispatcher.

"Sunny . . ." It came out small, lost against the scream and hiss of the fire eating everything that was mine.

"*Sunny*!" I screamed, my abused throat closing, pain stabbing me deep in the neck. I started toward the fire at a run, seeing nothing except the firelight, smelling nothing except the char, knowing that somewhere within the inferno, the cold, all-consuming fire, was my cousin's body.

The propane tank in the kitchen exploded when I'd only gone steps, throwing a wave of flame and heat outward, shattering windows and sending shrapnel arching toward me. A dagger of glass sliced across my biceps.

Smaller fragments peppered my face, and over the stink of the fire I smelled my own blood.

I didn't care. I had to find Sunny, had to save her if I could. I couldn't leave her to be turned into nothing but ash and bone.

"Sunny!" I tried again, but only a tired croak came out. My voice was gone. I threw my arm up to protect my face and ran at the fire again, feeling it suck air from my lungs when I came within striking distance. I was blacking out. I couldn't see, couldn't hear. I wanted nothing more than to lie down and surrender to the flames, but Sunny was in there, Sunny. . . .

"Luna!" Hands grabbed me by the collar and pulled me away from the flames. I tried to tell the rescue crew to leave me, that I had to get to my cousin, but the smoke cleared and I saw the face of the person holding me. "What the *hell* are you doing?" Sunny shouted, shaking me. "What's so important you had to go in there?"

I couldn't answer, so I wrapped my arms around Sunny instead, my eyes stinging from the smoke. I told myself the moisture on my cheeks was sweat, but I was a liar. I sobbed into her shoulder, clinging to her like I'd cling to the last piece of driftwood in a shipwreck.

"Luna," she said. "Luna. I'm all right."

I let go of her and swiped my sooty hands across my face. "How did you . . . how did you get out?"

"I went for a walk on the beach," she said. "You were late. I got bored waiting for you."

Sirens shrieked from the main road as two fire trucks and an ambulance turned off and bumped along the rutted lane toward us. Sunny watched them, mute and shell-shocked as I was. "Your house . . . ," she murmured. "Luna, what's happening?"

"I wish I knew," I whispered.

The firefighters did their job, training hoses on the blaze, making Sunny and me back off to the foot of the driveway, behind the perimeter. It was far too late for them to do anything except soak the blackened frame of the cottage and watch the contents smoke and smolder as the fire went out, little by little, taking everything I owned with it.

"All your clothes," Sunny murmured. "Your beautiful dresses. Your shoes . . ."

I put my hand on hers and squeezed. "I don't care. At least, I'm still too numb for it to be sinking in. I'm sure in a day or two I'll be a lot more upset about sixty-seven pairs of designer footwear reduced to a shoebox full of rubble." I coughed. "Right now, I'm just glad you weren't in there with it."

"I've never had someone try to kill me before," Sunny mused. "I always thought I'd be more upset by it. Rattled. Jumping at shadows and stuff. But I feel . . ." She shrugged. "Normal."

"That's the shock," I told her. "Soon enough I'll be crying over my burnt-up Balenciaga and you'll be freaking out over someone setting this fire. Although if it's any comfort, I think they were probably trying to kill me."

Sunny led me over to the ambulance and I let her, without protest. After a paramedic got me breathing into an oxygen mask, Sunny said, "I found them, you know."

"The Maiden," I said. "Annemarie told me that you called, before all of this happened."

I put the mask aside and walked back to my car. The windshield was covered with ash and I leaned in and hit the wipers. My Alexander McQueen bag was on the passenger seat, and it struck me that everything I had in the world now was my silly designer purse and the shitty motor pool LTD. "Who did this?" I demanded. "Tell me their name."

"Luna . . . ," Sunny said. I looked down at my hands, resting flat on the roof of the car, and saw claws there. I knew my eyes were gold and my teeth were starting to fang out. I slammed my fists into the metal and left twin dents in the LTD's roof.

"Tell me."

"Thelema," Sunny said, taking a judicious step backward, out of arm's reach. She really did know me well.

I slumped, all the fight knocked out of me. "What the fuck is Thelema?"

"It's an ancient discipline, predating most everything except blood magick," said Sunny. "Caster workings, shamanism, *brujeria* all share basic principles with Thelema. Their ancient symbol was the Maiden, the female symbolizing the fountainhead of life through magick." She rubbed her forehead. "Aleister Crowley triggered a revival in the early part of the 1900s and then his teachings were largely absorbed into caster witch tradition. It's why we spell 'magick' with a *k*, why we set a circle, and," she pressed her lips together, "why we don't deal with daemons. Crowley had a nasty experience with one himself, late in life."

"And someone is using Thelemic spells to set the fires," I said.

"It's the only explanation," Sunny said. "Thelema doesn't require a circle, only an act of will from a talented witch versed in the tradition. It's nasty, dark magick at the core, and the power it gives someone . . . well . . ." She sighed. "There's a reason there aren't many practicing Thelemites. Magick whispering in your ear all the time drives you insane pretty efficiently."

"So . . . ," I said, ticking off on my fingers. "We have a super-powered, magickal, possibly insane arsonist. Hell, Sunny. I feel better already."

"There's more," Sunny sighed. "Have you given any thought to what a Thelemite would want with a heart-stone?"

I stared at her. "Gods above. You think Grace Hart-ley's a Thelemite?"

"Well, do you think the fires and the heartstone are connected?"

I did; I just didn't know how yet. I was saved from ad-mitting ignorance by the arrival of Bryson, who took a look at the wreckage of the cottage and let out a whistle.

"Crap on a cracker, Wilder, this sucks."

"Gee, really?" I said. "I hadn't noticed yet." I'm very good at hiding behind snark when things get too unman-ageable. I put on a smile, just for good measure. "You gotta admit, David, I throw one hell of a barbeque."

He frowned. "It looks fried, all right. You think these were the same bastards that burned the warehouse and the Corley place?"

"I do," I said. "David, get everyone back to the SCS in two hours. We're going to have a briefing."

"Excuse me?" said Sunny. "No, no. You are going to go to a hotel and get some rest. You can brief tomorrow."

"Sunny . . . ," I warned. Before she could start to argue, I heard the rumble of a familiar engine and watched Fagin's Mustang arrive in a cloud of dust. "Oh, great," I said. "A visitation from the Highlander."

"Luna!" Fagin jumped out of his car and jogged over to me. "I heard the call come in on the rescue frequency for your address."

"You know my address?" I raised my eyebrow.

"I check out people that I'm interested in," Fagin replied. He looked at my house, shook his head. "Everyone all right?"

"I'm fine," I said shortly. "Thanks."

"She's not fine," said Sunny. "Where is she going to *live*?"

"She can stay with me," Fagin said. "My loft has plenty of extra room. Near some nice shops so she can get new clothes, and there's this trendy little Greek bistro . . . if she likes Greek?"

"*She* can make her own gods-damned decisions, and if you don't stop talking about her like *she* is deaf, *she* is going to punch someone right in the face," I said, pressing my hands over my eyes. I had work to do—finding a place to live was the least of my concerns. I could sense something moving just under the surface of all the scattered bits of the case, and it was dark, and I needed to focus, get it into sight. . . .

"Luna, you need to go to the hospital," said Sunny. "Let them at least check you out."

"No," I cut her off. "I'll get a hotel room. Sunny, you can lend me some clothes and I'll eat at the Plaza cafeteria, unappetizing as that sounds."

"You can stay with me," Bryson piped up. "It's not a problem."

I just stared at him, like a prize idiot. "Excuse me?" Bryson forming whole sentences was an accomplishment, but behaving like a human being? Better check his head for wires.

"I have a house," he said. "My aunt Louise left it to me—well, she will, when she croaks. Old bat is hanging on tighter than a virgin in a Navy bar."

I massaged my forehead hard. "I appreciate the offer, David—"

"No trouble," he grunted. "Place is so damn drafty, anyway. Ghost of my uncle Henry hangs around in there."

"Really?" Sunny said.

"Yeah," said Bryson. "We think Aunt Louise killed him."

"Charming as this is, in a *Beauty and the Beast* sort of way," said Fagin, "I think Luna would be more comfortable with someone of her own species."

"Oh, and you think that's you, G-man?" Bryson scoffed. "Take off your goddamn sunglasses for a minute and get a grip. She ain't interested in you."

Fagin's smile changed into something cold. "I think Luna's very interested in me. I think I'm a man of mystery, actually. What do you say, Luna?"

I rolled my eyes at Fagin. "David, I'd be happy to stay with you. Thank you for the kind offer."

Fagin's mouth curled with amusement. "And *you*," I hissed at him, grabbing his arm. "Don't think just because we shared deep dark secrets means I'm going to put up with your arrogant little power plays for another second. I'm past it, Will. Way, way past it."

His smile turned down. "Fair enough. You need to be the dominant one—I never had a problem with being the bottom."

Only the fact that Sunny and Bryson were watching kept me from hauling off and kicking him square in the groin. Will Fagin was one of the most irritating men I'd ever met—and coming from me, that was really saying something.

I settled for giving Will a snarl. "I'm warning you now.

I don't deal well with guys who always have to be in control."

"What are you so afraid of?" Fagin whispered back, in the same raspy tone. "Are you afraid you might like letting go? Of losing control?"

I leaned in to him, letting my lips touch the warm skin of his earlobe. "The last man who saw me lose control ended up dead, Will. So the one who should be afraid here—it's you."

"I like fear," he said. "It gets my blood pumping."

I stepped back from him, and ended the game, much as my were wanted to continue it. Fagin dropped me a wink and stepped away as well, putting the distance back at professional.

He disconcerted me, and I didn't like that. Men who disconcerted me inevitably led to danger, to complications, and the potential for hurt. It was always the way, with me.

So I turned my back on Fagin and gave Sunny a reassuring and entirely fake smile. "I'll be fine with Bryson. I want you to go home and stick close to Grandma, all right? Anything happens, I'm sure the old bat will scare them away when she makes her angry face."

Sunny grabbed my arm. "Not until you tell me what's going on. Curse markings, Luna? Arson? What have you *done*?"

I sighed. "First of all, why do you automatically assume this is my fault? Second of all, someone is trying to kill me." Saying it out in the open like that sobered me, made it all real—my destroyed home and things, the curse, the selkies on the beach.

Before, the people who wanted me dead at least had the gall to come out in the open. Now, I had no idea who

I'd pissed off or why. Grace Hartley had been in the SCS office when the fire started; Talon was behind bars; Lucas . . .

I shut my eyes. Lucas would at least have the grace to come do the job himself, face-to-face. He was a warrior at heart, and besides, he didn't have the magick to do something like this.

At least, I really hoped not.

"You got any ideas?" Fagin said, on cue.

"No," I said.

"You sure?" He crossed his arms. "No enemies, ex-cons, ex-boyfriends?"

"No one who has a grudge against me is in the wind. I haven't picked up any tails since this case started. The only people who know where I *live* are the nut job who sent the selkies after me and my squad. . . ."

I trailed off and Sunny's eyes widened. "What? What is it?"

Bryson caught my gaze and his face slackened. He knew where my train of thought was heading at break-neck speed. I didn't want it to stop there, with every fiber of me, but it was the simple conclusion. The logical one. I felt a little sick.

"Oh, fuck me," Fagin said. "You have got to be joking."

"Will somebody *please* tell me what is going on?" Sunny said loudly.

My words came out small, for such an important bit of information, one that had the potential to blow up my entire life. "The people who tried to kill me had to get their information from somewhere. I think there's a dirty cop in the SCS."

Seventeen

Bryson's house rested on the last lot of a dead-end street—somehow appropriate for him.

"Seven-seven-one Mulberry Way," he said. "Home sweet fuckin' home."

I gazed out the windshield of his Taurus. The house was nondescript, a boxy two-story with blue asbestos shingles and planter boxes on the windows. Some late-blooming flowers were still in evidence.

"Well, come on," Bryson grunted. "I ain't getting any younger."

"Could you just give me a minute?" I said. "Go ahead and put potpourri in the guest bathroom or something."

"Fix us both a drink is more like it," Bryson muttered. "You take Scotch?"

"Double," I murmured. "No ice."

After Bryson stumped inside I got out of his car and walked around his little yard, gnomes peeking at me from behind overgrown shrubbery with accusing ceramic eyes.

Of course I'd known dirty cops—this was Nocturne City, after all. Narcotics detectives were notorious for their "overtime bonuses," a hundred or two hundred here and there for looking the other way while street dealers did business. There was a bathroom on the third floor of the Eighteenth Precinct that was a favorite spot of vice cops and their complimentary hookers. Nolan Dexter, a burnout homicide cop who'd been around my first year wearing a shield, took a fifteen-grand payout from a husband who beat his wife to death with a piece of his home gym in their Cedar Hill mansion.

Dexter never forgot the crime scene photos, and eventually that woman's red, pulpy face and her blood-darkened eyes came to him in his sleep, while he drank his morning coffee, over and over again until he took an overdose of Percodan. He didn't even have the panache to eat his gun.

I'd never liked dirty cops and I'd never considered being one myself. There was something fundamentally weak about crawling into bed with the people we were supposed to be keeping off the streets, something two-faced and parasitic about the whole situation.

And now someone under me, someone I trusted with my life every time we went into the streets, was working with the Thelemites.

I felt like I was going to vomit on one of Bryson's tacky gnomes.

Instead, I went inside, up the cracked front steps, past the bank of junk mail in Bryson's box, and into a small hallway wallpapered with yellow flowers and shepherd girls in green dresses.

The front room was crammed with overstuffed pink furniture done in thick shag, a console TV, and a mountain of laundry taller than I was.

"This isn't the Hilton," said Bryson, coming down the stairs and rattling the faded photographs on the wall. One of them was of a much younger and less muscular Bryson in a blue and white satin tuxedo—which I would have expected from him—standing next to a pretty round-cheeked woman in a wedding dress.

"It's fine . . . ," I said. "Is that your wife?"

"*Ex*, in the big time," said Bryson. "That's Annie. We got married in Las Vegas."

"I'm shocked."

Bryson took me by the elbow and pulled me away from the row of photographs. "Your room's in the back, up the kitchen stairs." The kitchen was as old lady as the rest of the house, giant yellow enamel stove and fridge humming away like two sleeping, contented beasts and more wallpaper, this time with a windmill-and-tulip motif.

"Your aunt Louise has questionable taste," I told Bryson.

He snorted. "Beggars can't be choosers, Wilder."

The room itself was under the eaves, a twin bed made up with a quilt, and none of the stuffiness of downstairs. I sank down on the bed, hugging an embroidered throw pillow to myself.

"Okay?" Bryson asked anxiously. I flopped backward and stared at the cobweb-strewn roof beams, the dead spider silk drifting back and forth in the draft.

"It's fine," I said. "It's more than fine."

Bryson stood, breathing, and stuffed his hands in his pockets like he was waiting in line at the DMV.

"I'll be better after I've had a few hours' sleep and gotten some clothes," I said. "You don't have to babysit me."

"Wilder, do you really think there's a bent cop in the SCS?" he blurted.

I sat up, still hugging my pillow to my chest. It smelled like cinnamon cookies and mellow dust. "Yes," I told him. "There's no other explanation for how they knew I would be home in the middle of the day, and the address of my cottage."

"Maybe those Thelema freaks read your mind or something, or looked in a crystal ball. . . ."

"No, David," I said. "Someone gave one of those freaks the information, and someone cursed me, and someone has been trying to make me deceased for a while now."

"That blows," he said flatly. "It's someone I eat lunch with every day."

"Me, too," I said. "We've had a drink with them, probably sang 'Happy Birthday' and eaten a piece of that crappy cake Norris buys from the day-old bakery."

"It's not me," said Bryson flatly. "I may not be in line for a commendation, but I'm not bent. I wouldn't do that to you, Wilder."

I threw the pillow at him. "I know that, you dumb bastard. You think I'd be staying in your house if I thought you were the one passing information about the unit?"

He turned the pillow in his hands. "I guess not. Hey, you hungry? I got some meat loaf. Meat loaf sandwiches?"

"Easy on the mayo," I said. Bryson backed out of the room and I heard him rattling around in the kitchen. I went back to staring at the ceiling and wondering what the Hex I was going to do.

After I ate two meat loaf sandwiches, a bag of barbeque chips, and downed more than a few fingers of Scotch, I fell asleep in my clothes on the bed, only stopping to kick off my shoes. I checked in with Norris before I dozed off and told him I was at a motel downtown that was a well-known crash pad for cops going through house painting or divorces.

I gave him a nonexistent room number and hung up. Everyone except Bryson was suspect at this point.

Gods, what would I do if it was Batista or Pete? People I'd considered friends. Because it could be them. It could be someone in HR. It could be someone on the commission who had a bigger problem with the SCS existing than Mac realized.

Anyone. Anyone who had met my eyes in the department in the seven years I'd worked there.

Paranoia feels like a spider on your neck, light and fleeting, enough to send shock waves down your spine.

I jerked out of a dead sleep, certain that someone was standing over my bed, someone or something, waiting to choke the life out of me.

"Jumpy," Lucas said from the rocking chair in the corner. I bolted up and smacked my head on the eave.

"Daemons below, Lucas! What the Hex are you doing here? How did you find me?"

"I followed your scent," he said. "Your blood. Weres are distinctive. Much easier to track than humans."

"Did you come here to take another shot at me?" I snapped, rubbing the lump on my forehead. "Still Hartley's good little lap Wendigo?"

"There's no contract on you that I've heard of," Lucas said, standing. "And my job with Hartley was over the minute she got arrested. Those are my terms." He switched on the bedside lamp even though we could both see reasonably well in the dark. He was unshaven and wearing a different set of clothes, but he looked as much at ease here as if it were his own bedroom and I belonged in it, instead of the other way around. His dark hair was shorter than when we'd last been together, and it curled at his neck, brushed his high forehead and his dark, melting eyes. Lucas radiated lust, hunger; his thin nose and full lips and large hands made for tactile sensations. Made to consume. I shivered, and got ahold of myself.

"Well, somebody sure as shit wants me in a freezer down at the morgue," I said. "They burned down my house earlier today."

Lucas inhaled sharply. "Thought I smelled smoke."

"Do you know who it is?" I said.

He shook his head. "I only hear about paid contracts, hits and bodyguard jobs and run-of-the-mill stuff. What you got after you is someone doing it on faith."

"Then why did you come here?" I demanded. "I get really cranky when I don't get my full eight hours, Lucas."

"I came to apologize for this morning," he said. "I know I probably caused a lot of trouble for you by running. Are you suspended?" He sounded almost anxious.

"No," I said. "They don't suspend lieutenants; they just fire us." I stretched, popping my neck. "Not to bruise your male ego or anything, Lucas, but you running off is the least of my worries right now."

He sat on the edge of the bed, suddenly close, like a shadow in a dark room. "So you're not going to be chasing me, Lieutenant Wilder?"

"Depends on how far you run," I said. "Now get out of my room and let me get back to not sleeping."

Lucas snaked his hand out and put it on the back of my neck, fingers closing with gentle pressure. I grabbed his wrist, just as fast.

"Stop it," I said.

He didn't stop. He leaned close and pressed his lips against mine. It was a high school kiss, dry and sweet and soft, the way that shy boys would have kissed me, if I had kissed any that were shy. Or still boys.

I grabbed Lucas's neck in turn, my fingers sliding through his raggedy black hair, and pushed back, opening his lips with my tongue. I could tell him later that the were had overtaken me and consumed me with lust, or some crap, but it would be just that—crap. I wanted to kiss Lucas, and his no-strings-attached closeness was something I needed and hadn't even realized until now.

A light flicked on downstairs, and I heard Bryson grumble to himself as he opened the refrigerator. A second later a bottle opener clacked and a beer opened with a hiss.

Lucas pulled away from me just enough to speak. "Take care of yourself, Luna."

I pulled him back down when he started to rise. "Listen. Don't you dare pull some lone wolf/mercenary disappearing act on me. You come back."

Lucas laughed, just a vibration in his throat. "Well, when you put it that way . . ." He flowed to his feet. "See you soon, beautiful." He shifted to mist, and flowed around the cracks in the small casement window above the bed, disappearing into the moonless night.

Eighteen

"You know what we need?" Bryson said the next morning around a mouthful of bear claw. I'd gone and gotten donuts as a protest against both his cooking skills and the rapidly advancing age of most of the food in his icebox.

"What?" I grunted from where I sat with my forehead on the table. Even a double-tall latte that I'd procured along with the donuts couldn't rouse me.

Lucas may be a fantastic kisser, but he had lousy fucking timing. As if I didn't have enough to worry about without wanted fugitives sneaking into my bedroom. Lucas still had outstanding warrants from the swath he'd cut through Nocturne when he was possessed, plus the flight from the jail.

And I had let him into my bedroom and made out with him like I was a fucking teenager. Every time I saw Lucas, I screwed up. I forgot I was a cop, and became wholly a were. I liked what he did to me.

That made him too dangerous to even consider.

"We need an outsider," said Bryson, snapping me back to the real. "I been giving this a lot of thought."

"That never bodes well."

He gave me the finger and continued. "Someone who

ain't attached to the department, who can help us figure out who the mole is. They do it on TV sometimes."

I pinched the bridge of my nose. "Yeah, since real police work so often mirrors what all the hot TV cops are doing."

"Hey," said Bryson, brushing crumbs off the front of his Nocturne University T-shirt. "You can sit there and be bitchy all morning or you can admit that what I've got is a solid plan."

"No, a solid plan would be figure out what the Thelemites want the heartstone for, why they set the fires, and what they were planning to do to my city," I snapped. "And I have none of the tools to do that, so please just eat your pastry and shut the Hex up."

"My therapist is gonna be very unhappy with you," said Bryson. "You're an enabler, is what you are. A perpetrator of diet sabotage."

"If I give credence to your idea will you *be quiet*?" I snarled, feeling my teeth fang out.

Bryson shivered. "Always gives me the creeps when you do that. Anyway, yes. An outsider with the skills to help us take down the rat on the inside, like Tom Berenger in *The Substitute*."

"Fagin," I said, putting a hand over my eyes.

"Now you're thinking," Bryson said. "He's federal and he ain't native to the city. Plus, he's a dick and that always helps when you're dealing with scum like dirty cops. He's got that killer look in his eye, if you can get past the stupid Dean Martin getup."

I groaned. "He will *love* me crawling back to him and asking him for help."

"Don't see that we have much of a choice," Bryson said.

I downed the rest of my coffee and dug my BlackBerry out of my purse. "Me, either. He's going to love that, too."

Fagin's office phone went to voice mail, so I tried his cell number and got a muffled, "Hello," after a dozen rings.

"Where are you?" I said. "You sound like you're in someone's trunk. Did that big mouth finally get you in trouble?"

"You think about my mouth often, Lieutenant? Tell me more."

I held the BlackBerry away from my ear and gave Bryson a murderous glare. "Where are you?" I asked Will again.

"In my car," he said. "I'm sitting on the Hartley place."

"What?" I said. "Will, what are you up to?" I really hoped his next words wouldn't be *And I have a gun sitting in my lap to shoot the immortal witch who cursed me.* Then I'd have to go running outside with my hair tangled and in yesterday's clothes. I really hate that.

"You had to let her go, but I'm sure I can think up some illegal-weapons charges if pressed," Will said. "I'm not losing the Maiden, Luna. I won't. I'm so close."

"Will . . ." I stood up and paced away from Bryson, into the front room. A small boy with red hair was riding a tricycle in concentric circles in the street in front of the house. "We are not doing this again," I growled. "I told you, if you want to stay in my city then we're going to do things my way."

"Your threats work most of the time, don't they?" Will sighed. "But not on me. You have your case and I have my project, and never the twain shall meet. I *will* find her, Luna, and I *will* break the curse."

He was right, and my cheeks went warm under the

plastic of the BlackBerry. Threats were my preferred method of making people do what I wanted—you had the control that way, the upper hand. But I needed Fagin, and I couldn't have him pushing the Thelemites into something worse than setting fires.

"Listen, Will," I said, letting my voice soften. "I'm going to trust you. I *need* to trust you."

"Oh?" He sounded marginally less hostile, so I pressed on.

"There's a crooked cop in my division, someone who is passing information to the Thelemites, and I can't trust anyone in the SCS. I need allies. I need to find this person and use them to figure out what the Thelemites are doing, because . . ." A calculated pause, a tremor into my voice. "I think it's bigger than me, Will. I'm scared for what it means for the city."

He breathed into his phone for a minute. "Where should I meet you?"

"After Dark bowling alley," I said. "Make it an hour."

"Will do," Fagin said, and rang off.

Bryson came into the front room. He'd added a Hawaiian shirt to his ensemble. I cocked an eyebrow.

"I'm pretty sure it's not theme day at the office, David."

"Office?" He snorted. "With everything that happened, I sort of figured today was an off day, Wilder."

"Oh no," I said. "You're going to work and you're going to behave like everything is normal. Tell them that I'm taking a personal day to meet with the insurance adjuster after the fire. Tell them that I'm fine—better than fine. The mole needs to know that they can't get to me that easily."

Bryson rocked back and forth on the balls of his feet.

"Problem?" I inquired.

He heaved a sigh. "What if the mole goes after me next?"

I let out a short bark of laughter, curbing myself when Bryson looked offended. "David, I think you're safe. But I need you to be there. If we're both out of the office the informant will know something's up, and I can't have that. Not yet. So do this for me, all right, Detective?"

"I'm going in wearing this," Bryson informed me sulkily.

"Just go," I said.

"Wilder," Bryson said slowly. "Why do you want them to know you're alive? Shouldn't we be—I dunno—not rubbing their faces in the fact you survived?"

"We should because I want them to try again," I said. "Mistakes make people angry. Anger makes people sloppy. If they know I'm laughing at them they'll be inclined to go after me again and we'll figure out who's passing information from the SCS. Simple."

"Kind of stupid, too," Bryson muttered.

I locked onto him with my worst stare, guaranteed to make a perp piss himself. "What was that?"

"Nothing," Bryson squeaked. "I'm late." He scuttled out of the sitting room, and I went to get my wallet and go find some clothes to meet Fagin in.

The After Dark lanes were in the heart of the rot of Waterfront, a loud, noisy, steamy stretch of road and tenement that housed bums, junkies, weres, and combinations of all of the above. Two weres lounging outside the entrance to the lanes scented me, and showed their teeth.

I slowed, my new sneakers scuffing the debris on the sidewalk. "Get within arm's reach and do that again, flea licker," I told him.

"Not smart for an Insoli bitch to talk like that," he told me. He was skinny, with bad skin—he had drugs pumping through him as well as were blood. Once, Waterfront had been Redback territory. Dmitri's own crumbling kingdom. I didn't know what pack this guy was from, but I was in no mood.

I jerked my new shirt aside and let him see the butt of my Sig. "Ooh," he said, waving his hands at me like a cheap stage magician. "Careful. She's packing heat and looking for trouble."

"Fuck off," I said plainly. After a few seconds of staring, he shrugged and nudged his companion. They ambled across the street and took up residence in front of a pawnshop. "Jackasses," I muttered, pulling the fabric of my shirt back over the gun. I had bought jeans and a purple baseball jersey at the big-box stores near Bryson's place. The jeans rode too low on my ass and the snug shirt wasn't designed for someone with actual breasts, but I made do.

After another check of the street to make sure no one had followed me, I pushed open the doors and stepped inside.

The interior of the alley was like something out of Lewis Carroll's nightmares, a riot of neon and murals painted in reactive colors that glowed under the ministrations of ultraviolet tubes recessed in the ceiling. Giant playing cards grinned at me from the walls, wizards and goblins skulking in the cracks, and grinning Cheshire Cat mouths encircled the end of each lane, devouring balls and pins underneath glittering, pulsating light.

I spotted Fagin standing by the shoe rental desk, looking distinctly twitchy and out of place in his black suit and thin tie. His shirt glowed a serene violet under the black light.

"You look confused," I said to him over the pulse of remixed disco favorites pumping from substandard speakers.

"As to why I'm here? Yes," Fagin said. "Did you have the sudden urge to bowl a few frames? And perhaps drop acid while you do it?"

"As a matter of fact . . . ," I said, passing two twenties to the guy behind the desk. "Size eight and a half and size . . ." I tilted my head at Fagin.

"Twelve," he sighed, when he saw I couldn't be swayed.

We got our shoes and I carried them over to a free lane, one lit with green and pink psychedelic flower patterns.

"You don't fool me, you know," Fagin said, unlacing his pointy patent-leather shoes and trading them for bright red bowling kicks.

"Oh?" I said, slipping off my overpriced pink sneakers.

"That little act on the phone," he said. "You're good. You may have missed your calling. Do any drama at the community college?"

"I hate that you can just press a button and find out everything about me," I said.

Fagin laughed. "Fair's fair. You manipulated me into meeting you. . . ."

"You're here, aren't you?" I said with a smile, picking up a ball and giving it a heft.

Fagin returned the smile. "I guess I am. Why *here* remains a mystery."

"Look at this place," I said, going to the line and bowling a strike. "Busy, noisy, impossible to listen in on with magick or without it. This is where I feel safe meeting at the moment, so you're just gonna have to deal with it."

Fagin grabbed up a ball as I stepped back and bowled into the gutter. He blew out a sigh of frustration. "This sucks."

"You sure do," I said, giving him a nudge as he selected a fresh ball. He took the time to stick a thin cigarette in his mouth and light it.

"Watch it. You may be cute, but there's a limit to what I can take." He bowled two more gutter balls.

"Four hundred years and you can't even bowl straight," I said. "Tsk, tsk, Agent Fagin." I was flirting with him to take my mind off of Lucas and how screwed up the whole thing was.

"You actually want to talk, or did you drag me down here to Tackyville to bat your eyes and wiggle your cute ass at me all afternoon?" Will said.

I threw another strike and straightened up. My neck popped where Talon had grabbed me. Fagin was right. I was avoiding the whole sordid mess that I'd made of my career. Assassins, dirty cops, and witches. It really couldn't be better.

Fagin was watching me. "Well?"

Dammit, Wilder, swallow your pride and admit this is bigger than you can handle. "I need help, Will," I rushed out. "And I don't say that a lot. Someone in my unit is passing information to the Thelemites and I have no fucking idea what they're doing with it, beyond trying to kill me. Hells, I don't even know why they're trying to do *that*."

"Aside from your charm and winning personality?" Fagin said, and ducked as I swiped at him. "In all seriousness . . . Thelema is a dodgy business," he said.

"It's unpredictable and its acolytes are usually a pack of crazy bastards." He sat in the conversation pit at the end of the lane and gestured for me to do the same. "I'd be very, very careful messing with them, if I were you."

I stayed standing, rolling a ball between my palms. I needed to be up, moving. Ever since I'd come home to flame and smoke I'd felt eyes on my back, felt the thin cold finger that told me how lucky I'd been that the arsonists hadn't checked too hard to be sure I was home. "But you're not me, and they made this personal," I said. "So now I'm going to return the favor any way I can."

Will spread his hands. "Then I'll help in any way I can, on one condition."

I tensed. "My answer to your crusade against your psycho ex is the same. No executions. No vendettas."

"I want to die." He stood up and took the ball out of my hands, replacing it with his own two palms. They were hard, warm, and strong—fighter's hands, with scarred knuckles and palms. "I don't mean crash my car into an abutment or shoot myself in the face. I mean live, age, and die. Like a human being. I was supposed to have that and she took it from me. I want to lift the curse, Luna, and I want to die. If we find her, you let me make her take this magick off of my spirit and I'll let her go."

I searched Will's face for duplicity, the smell of him for deception, but there was nothing except the low, dark scent that clung to him because of the curse, and a hard gleam to his eyes, the driven rage of a man denied.

"Okay," I said, squeezing his hands and letting go. "You got yourself a deal."

"Good," Will said, and he was back to his old self, easy and relaxed in spite of everything. "Now, let's hear what you've got. Information sharing is essential for any law enforcement partnership. Any partnership you'd care to have, actually—"

"There are the fires," I cut him off. "There's the heartstone, and there's a group of Thelemites connected to Grace Hartley. Something I just can't see yet crouched behind them, just waiting to open its jaws. I don't like that at all, Will. It's the same feeling you probably get when you find out a nut in Nevada has stockpiled five hundred assault rifles in his underground bunker."

"So what do we know?" Fagin handed me my ball.

"It's safe to assume the Thelemites got the heartstone to enable them to work a large spell, something their will couldn't sustain alone," I said. "But I have no earthly idea what, and I'm really starting to hate that."

"Bet you good money it has something to do with the fires," said Fagin. "Smart domestic terrorists always test their devices before the actual attack. Maybe they were just seeing how well the heartstone worked."

"You really believe that?" I asked.

Fagin sighed. "I don't pretend to understand witches, Luna."

"Those fires definitely weren't random, and Milton Manners was killed by something else entirely," I said. "Casting from a remote location could explain how they didn't know I hadn't gotten home yet, how they took out the traffic camera at Corley's place."

I pulled my BlackBerry out of my hip pocket. If I called him, it might get back to the rat in the SCS, but if I didn't, I'd be no better than I was now.

"CSU special branch," Pete Anderson said into the phone.

" 'Special branch'?" I asked him.

"Hey, it worked for the Brits," he said. "And 'guardian of all shit freakish and strange' is too much of a mouthful. What can I do you for, LT?"

"I need to talk to you about the fires," I said. "Can you bring all of Egan's findings and meet me?"

"I . . . suppose," he said. "There some reason we can't do this in the office?"

"Yes."

"Okay," he said. "Where?"

"The After Dark lanes. I'm sorry I can't tell you more."

A voice burbled on Pete's end and he said, "No, I don't have that . . . it would have been signed back out when we let her go."

"Pete?"

"Sorry. Detective Kelly's here."

"Hang up the phone," I told Pete. "Don't say who you were talking to, get the fire investigation jackets, and meet me at the bowling alley, fast as you can."

"Can I ask what this is about?"

"No," I said, and pressed the disconnect on my BlackBerry. I *did* trust Pete—he'd gotten himself arrested and threatened for me once, and he didn't have the agenda a cop did: close the big cases, get the headlines, get the promotion and the desk job where meth junkies don't routinely try to stab you. Sure, you may have met some bleeding hearts or bullshit artists who told you they were in it to help people. Ninety percent of them are fucking liars.

CSU, on the other hand, are usually in it for the science, and for the truth in the science. They're removed from the dirt and the blood on the streets, more objective. Usually. I hoped I hadn't made the worst mistake of my life trusting Pete. I didn't want him to be the rat, but what I wanted was getting precious little regard these days.

I returned my bowling shoes and moved into the diner attached to the lanes, ordering a bacon cheeseburger with chili fries. Fagin abstained, taking a black coffee.

"You're no fun," I said.

"I'm immortal, but I can still gain weight," said Fagin. "There were a few years there in the 1940s when I was . . . shall we say . . . pleasantly plump. How do you put that stuff away?"

"Were metabolism," I said around a mouthful of fries. "I burn hot."

"I bet you do," Fagin said.

I spotted Pete at the door of the diner when I was half-way through my meal and waved to him. He came over and slid into the booth next to me, taking a stack of folders out of his messenger bag. "This is everything the arson investigator gave me. It looks legit. You think something's hinky besides the way the fires started?"

"Looking that way," I said softly. "Tell me everything about fires. Pretend I'm dumb," I said. I paged through the reports, the photographs of the eviscerated interiors making my stomach turn. I had almost been a blackened, split-open corpse like Corley.

"You have your basic insurance-fraud arsonist, the sick freak who lights fires, and the efficient type who knows that fire can hide a multitude of sins," Pete said. "I think what we got here is the third type."

I scattered the photographs on the table in front of me. "Corley sold antiques, right? Magickal artifacts? And Milton Manners was a fence who would have the connections to get a suspect crate into a country. Brad Morgan had a warehouse off the grid, one that Customs wouldn't come knocking at."

"It's a cover-up," Fagin said before I could go further

with my musing, dropping his spoon into his coffee. "They tried to cover up the heartstone coming into the country. Jesus. Who thought it could be so simple?"

"Not that simple," I said. "They're still after *me*. They got rid of everyone who could spill the beans about the heartstone—they burned Corley, they hacked up Milton, they scared Brad Morgan so badly that Annemarie had to shoot him, and they burned the warehouse and probably the person who received the crate with it, since Nick Alaqui is dead. But they're still coming after me. There's something else going on here."

Pete collected the photographs and reports, swishing them back into a neat pile. "Damned if I can see what from the evidence, LT."

I put down some money for my food and stood. "Let's go back to your office. Lucas was right—Grace Hartley isn't at the top of the Thelemites and we need to figure out who is."

"*Lucas* told you this? The jerkwad who shot me? There's a source," Will snorted.

"It's not just him; it's common sense. Magick users insulate themselves like the mob. You don't see the big boss out in the open because it makes them vulnerable."

"If you cut off the head of the snake, the body is pretty well fucked," Fagin acceded. "All right, you can have a look at ATF's data banks, but I can't have you hiding out in my cubicle like some low-rent version of *The Fugitive*."

"Don't worry," I said. "After today, I have a feeling it won't matter much where I go."

Nineteen

Fagin's co-workers barely glanced at me when I came in. One of the clerical staff, a petite woman with a sharp pinup-girl bob, gave me a dirty look, but that was about it.

"I get the feeling I'm not the first woman you've brought to the office," I told Fagin.

He pulled up an extra chair for me. "Maybe, maybe not. I don't kiss and tell."

"Chivalry is alive and well in you," I said, rolling my eyes.

"That, and being with a federal agent gets some women hot," he said, lacing his fingers behind his head like he expected a cookie for his cleverness.

"I'm not one of them," I informed him. I rolled his chair out of the way with my foot and pulled up to his computer. Fagin grunted as his chair hit the cubicle wall.

"You're a wee bit of a bring-down, you know that, Luna? Most women like it when I flirt."

"I don't," I said flatly. "It's artificial and condescending, and backs women into a corner, and if the twits you usually hang around with giggle and blush when you pull out the cowboy routine, that's not my problem."

Fagin grinned at me. "You are so smart. Feisty, too."

"Probably too smart for you," I said. "Now you want me out of here fast? Shut up and let me work."

"Me-ow," he said, and then yelped when I reached out and clipped him in the side of the head with my knuckles.

"Enough," I said. "I know you're not really this big of an asshole. The act doesn't suit you."

"It becomes a habit after a few hundred years," Fagin muttered, but I pretended not to hear him.

Grace Hartley had all the right pedigrees on paper—she donated to charity; she belonged to the Boosters and the Rotary; she had one dead husband and one divorce in her past, the daughter, Sophia, attending an East Coast school, and no financial hanky-panky.

"She's so clean she squeaks," I said, and fought off the urge to hit the keyboard.

"You know what that means," Fagin said, sitting forward with interest lighting his eyes.

"That I want to drive to her house and smack her all over again?" I said.

"She's faking it," said Fagin. "Number-one mistake of false identities—making them too nice. You want someone to leave you alone, throw in a few DUIs or a gambling problem."

"I guess you'd know," I said. "How many names have you had? *Is* this your real name?"

"No, it isn't," Fagin said, and didn't elaborate. He took the mouse and ran a search. "Here it is—Grace Hartley, born November 1973."

"Damn," I said. "And here I thought she looked good for her age."

"Died January 1974," said Fagin. "She got a new birth certificate in her twenties, looks like. Anyone's guess who she was before that."

"She lied," I said, feeling ridiculously vindicated. "She lied about everything." Something fell into place in my head. "But she bailed Milton Manners out when he got busted."

"So?" said Fagin.

"So, someone who's trying so desperately to lead a clean life doesn't get involved with the legal system unless she has to," I said. "How much you want to bet me Manners knew her before she got a whole new life? 'Friend of the family,' my ass."

Fagin leaned over and kissed me on the cheek. "I love the way your big brain thinks, woman."

I pulled back, just a reflex when someone gets too close. Fagin's mouth turned down. "I get it. Sorry." He turned back to the computer as if nothing had happened.

"Aha," he said after a moment. "Look at this."

Birth records for Macon County, Georgia, stared back at me. Milton Manners was a Gemini, born in 1947.

His sister was an Aquarius, and four years younger.

"Hex me," I said. "She's his sister."

"Blood is thicker," Fagin said. "She must have kept tabs on him her whole life."

"That is so creepy," I muttered. "Imagine holiday dinners with that family. . . ."

"Parents died when Grace was eight," said Fagin. "Massive coronaries in both cases."

"Gee, what are the odds of that?" I said.

Fagin looked at me. "You thinking she had something to do with it?"

"Wouldn't be the first time a talented witch lost control

when they were young," I said. "Sunny had some issues in that area when we were kids."

"She ever whack anyone with her evil brain powers?" said Fagin.

"Not that I know of," I said. "Pull up Hartley's financials and let's try to figure out who else is in bed with her."

Fagin jabbed at the computer and then sat back. "Mostly clean. Trust from her dead husband, alimony from the live one, a few expenses here and there . . ."

I pointed at her bank statement. "What's this?"

"She made a donation every six months to the Center for Mind-Body Awareness, here in Nocturne," Fagin said, expanding the transaction. "Same amount. Never took a tax deduction."

"Address?" I said. A donation with no deduction from someone in Hartley's income bracket wasn't a charity; it was a front.

"Cedar Hill," said Fagin. "Where all the ex-hippie rich folk go to expand their minds."

I pushed back from the desk and picked up Fagin's car keys. "Feel like taking it for a spin?"

He raised his eyebrow. "Let's go."

The Mustang had enough power under the hood to press my spine into the bucket seat, and I pushed it through the gears like it was an old friend. Fagin hung on to the door handle, looking like we were in danger of imminent fiery death.

"You know, I took the same driving courses as you did," I said. "I even got to visit Quantico when I was on SWAT and drive the FBI cars. I am not going to dent, ding, grind, or otherwise harm your baby, so stop looking like I'm gonna get girl cooties all over the steering wheel."

I came up on a stop sign and popped the emergency brake just to be mean about it. Fagin winced.

The long climb to Cedar Hill is like the climb out of the pits on a distant, dystopian planet—going from the grime and desperation of downtown to the tiers of wood-frame houses in cotton-candy colors set into the hillside, their napkin-sized yards a riot of late-fall flowers and pumpkins, and finally the drives get longer and homes larger, the tall cedar trees hiding the iron gates and the slate rooftops of the mansions that industry, smuggling, timber, and greed built in the nineteenth century.

The Center for Mind-Body Awareness was not in keeping with the rest of Cedar Hill. The house was a sprawling mid-century wreck, adobe walls and angular glass windows, all covered with a thin scrim of moss and mold. Needles covered the driveway and the few cars parked to one side, and the sign advertising what lay within was crooked.

"They don't even try to hide the fact that it's a front," I said. "Time was, criminals had a little bit of self-respect."

"What is the world coming to?" Fagin agreed. He popped the passenger door and stepped out. I followed, checking for security cameras. None were trained on the front lot, but the door had a pin camera next to the bell as well as heavy-duty locks and an alarm system that would make a drug lord feel at ease.

"Come on," I said, starting down the side path between drooping Japanese pines that looked like they belonged in a late-night samurai film.

"Wait!" Fagin jogged after me. "We don't have a warrant. We also don't know how these people take to trespassers."

"You don't need a warrant to investigate a suspicious dwelling," I said. Pulling the law out of my ass usually worked, for a little while. If we did get caught, I'd probably get screamed at by a lawyer in a cheap tie and that would be the end of it. "And if they do take exception to us looking around, I'm an armed werewolf and you can't die."

"Yet," Fagin said darkly.

"Well, if you gotta be all *Dark Shadows* about it—"

Fagin stopped me with a hand on my shoulder. "Look."

The back of the house was as decrepit as the front, moss and weeds growing from a cracked driveway, with garbage piled high at both sides of a sagging garage door. The shaggy berm we were standing on overlooked the drive, which resembled some horrific sacrificial pit from my vantage.

"They should fire their landscaper," I said, with great disappointment.

"Let's get out of here," said Fagin. "There's nothing."

My ears pricked to an encroaching noise, and I grabbed Fagin's arm. "Wait just a second." An engine with a shrieking fan belt grumbled down the backstreet behind the house and Fagin grunted as I jerked him down behind the overgrown berm and out of sight.

A windowless van creaked into the drive, and a sleazy little guy with a combover who couldn't have looked more like a pimp if he walked out of a seventies B movie hopped from the driver's seat. He rolled back the doors, ushering out five girls in various stages of teased, painted, and junkie. One extinguished her cigarette under the cork wedge of her cheap shoe, and glared at the house.

"I thought you said this was a nice place, Lenny."

"Shut up," Lenny said. "You're not getting paid by the word." He snapped his fingers at the women. "Listen up. These clients are paying you a flat grand each for the weekend, so do what they say when they say it and no shooting up in the house." He stalked over to the garage and buzzed the bell. "Spit out that gum," he told the youngest, skinniest girl. She flipped him off, and he slapped her.

It was Fagin's turn to jerk me back down as I started upward. "You go down there now and we're blown."

"I don't go down there and those girls get taken in by the Thelemites," I hissed.

"Yeah," Fagin said.

I turned to look at him. "Are you insane? You'd knowingly let innocent women walk into that place, after what we've seen?"

"I think that we're not getting in there . . . ," he said, as the garage door rolled up and the girls filed in, slump-shouldered and in a line like a chain gang. "And they are. So, what does that tell us?"

"That we should call Vice and order a raid?"

Fagin stood up and dusted off his suit, helping me to my feet. "No. That's our way in. You want to find out who's at the top of this, then we're going to have to give them what they want." He looked me up and down.

I glared. "I am not dressing up as a hooker. That's for amateurs."

"You'll put on a short skirt, I'll put on a silk tie and too much pomade, and bada-boom. We're in."

I pushed past him and went back to the car. We were driving away before I spoke again. "If this is going to work, we're going to need someone else. You look more like a priest than you do a pimp—at least one from *this* century."

"Met your share on the force, I take it?" Fagin said.

"My ex-boyfriend," I said. "Before I knew him." I dared Fagin with my silence to make a comment.

"Maybe I don't know everything about you," he said finally.

"Trust me, you don't," I snapped. The ATF building loomed on the left and I jerked the Mustang into the garage.

"So tell me who we need," Fagin said. "Since you seem so intimately versed with that section of the world."

"Like you never spent any time with a whore or two," I said. "Mr. English Lord."

"I did my time in the brothels and the alehouses, true," Fagin said, "but then I devoted my time to helping people, not knocking all sense and dignity out of them."

"You know what I realized that I hate today?" I said, stabbing the button for the elevator.

"What?" he said.

"Preachy immortals who think that talking down to us human beings somehow makes their pathetic lives less of a sad, gray road that goes on and on with no exits. I hate that."

The elevator arrived and I stepped in, hitting the button for the lobby. Fagin made to follow, but I held up my hand. "You can wait for the next one. You've got the time."

Twenty

I walked up the hill to Bryson's neighborhood from the federal offices, my footsteps in angry time with my heartbeat. Maybe Will was right about the prostitutes. We needed a way into the house, and I didn't have a better idea than the short skirt. But not with Fagin. He'd blown his chance.

I sat down on Bryson's front steps, wishing I had a double-dipped chocolate cone from the Devere Diner. Or a stiff drink. Or both.

"Long day?"

I rocketed off the steps, pulling my gun. "Hex it, Lucas, you cannot keep showing up here!"

"You look upset," he said, stepping from the shadow of the locust tree in Bryson's yard.

"That's because I am," I said. "I've had a really shitty day and I had a fight with someone I may actually sort of like, when he's not being an insufferable jackwad."

"These nonjackwad periods are few and far between is the problem?" Lucas said. He sat on the steps and looked expectantly at me.

"No," I said. "We're not sitting here like we're waiting

for the ice-cream truck. What if someone recognizes you and calls my team?"

"I'll run fast," he said, taking my wrist and tugging at me until I sat down next to him.

"Hex it," I moaned. "I'm tired of sitting around, and I'm tired of these Thelemite bastards being ahead of me." I looked at Lucas. "You work for Hartley."

"Did," he corrected. "Incarceration sorta voids my contract."

"Well, you're going to pretend for one more night," I said. "Because I need your help."

Lucas slung his arm around my shoulder. "I thought you'd never ask."

"Get off," I warned. "It's not that kind of help."

He moved his arm, a smile playing at the corners of his mouth. "Tell me the plan. Why do I already have the feeling it will be risky and full of people who want us dead?"

"I need to get inside the house the Thelemites are using as their central collection point," I said. "They got an order of five hookers earlier today—gods know why—so I'm going to be the bonus round and you're going to be my, well . . ."

"I don't have any bling, FYI," Lucas said. "I tend to stay low-profile. And gold teeth are right out. Sensitive gums."

"I just need you to stand around looking like you sell sex for a living," I said. "And we've got to go soon. A too-large gap in time and they'll get suspicious and probably peel our skin off with pliers."

"Your team must have great morale," said Lucas. "Because I sure feel inspired."

"Just wait in the kitchen while I get changed," I said, opening Bryson's front door. "And if Bryson comes home early, shift out through the wall and wait for me in the alley."

"Risky and dangerous," Lucas muttered, following me. "Just like I said."

I got him one of Bryson's cheap beers and left him in the kitchen, praying that this flimsy plan would pay off. Sometimes they did, and sometimes they self-destructed.

When they did, it usually tended to be spectacular and life-threatening. Nobody ever said that my job was easy or particularly good for my health. If it were, I would have retired a long time ago. A desk job was not the world for me, not the dead-end life both of my parents had been consigned to. I liked the threat of fire, the knife's edge. Sometimes I just wished I didn't dance it quite so often.

I went into Bryson's room and searched through the closet, hoping he was the kind of guy I thought he was, one who liked his girlfriends to dress trashy on occasion.

The closet yielded a multitude of tacky—shredded denim miniskirts, cheap nylon halters, a bustier for someone both rounder and more bountifully endowed than I, lace leggings, a few pairs of spike-heeled shoes. There was even a French maid outfit.

"Gross, David," I muttered, shoving it to the back of the rack. I chose a pair of fishnet leggings, platform sandals in pink patent leather, and a black vinyl tank top that laced at the sides with strategic holes. I dressed and messed up my hair with a comb and spray, and then painted the new makeup I'd bought after the fire on thick enough to look like it had been done in a hurry, in a half-lit gas station bathroom.

The trick to undercover is not trying too hard—

costume yourself up and the bad guys will smell you coming a mile away, sometimes literally. You want to change yourself just enough to be unrecognizable to strangers but not to yourself. Pull a character around you like a cocoon, but keep yourself inside. If you slip on an undercover investigation, it usually means that the medical examiner is digging your body out of the gutter the next day. If they find you at all.

"Louella," I said, making my crooked lips into a pout. I added a touch of East Coast whine to my voice and the lilt to my body that suggested pharmacy whore. My sloe-eyed pill popper might not pass muster on a Vice bust on the mean streets, but for a nest of magick users I thought it would do fine.

I tottered down the narrow stairs in the high shoes and tapped Lucas on the shoulder. He nearly spit out his mouthful of beer. "Holy shit, Luna, Halloween's tomorrow."

"You're funny," I said. "Louella likes funny guys. Want a date?"

Lucas frowned. "That's creepy. My mother would have said you were letting a *ujuk*, a bad spirit, talk out of your mouth and that you were letting yourself in for trouble."

"Your mother sounds like a piece of work," I said.

"She was that," said Lucas. "She wouldn't have approved of you at all."

"I get that a lot from mothers," I said. The keys for the LTD were at the bottom of my purse and I realized that the stupid car was actually going to do me a service for once—it was the perfect generic beater. The Mustang and my dearly departed Fairlane would have stood out like hammered thumbs.

"You drive," I said. "Girls like Louella don't drive."

"Got it," said Lucas. "You, uh . . . you gonna tell anyone what we're up to? Even I like to have a backup plan."

"Someone knows," I said, gritting my teeth. Fagin and his high-handedness could go Hex themselves. I shoved my BlackBerry deep into my purse. If anyone spotted the designer, I'd tell them it was a knockoff, insulting as that was to my inner fashionista. "We'll have backup if we need it."

Lucas jangled the car keys. "Day's not getting any longer. If I'm going to do my killer pimp impression I'd prefer to get it over with."

The drive back to the Thelemite compound seemed disproportionately long, the shadows along the road nightmarish, with teeth. The were in me was on edge, every sound and passing scent a cause for alarm, for battle.

Lucas fiddled with the radio, his lanky frame slung back over the seat as he drove with one hand. "Nervous?" he said.

"Not really," I lied.

"Sure you are," he said. "I always get nervous before a job. Must be worse for you, with the were inside. Pacing back and forth always."

"You don't have that?" I asked. "That feeling of something clawing at your skin?"

"I'm at peace with what I am," said Lucas. "I am Wendigo, and that's a fine thing to be. The hunger in me is the same as the spirit in me. It's nothing to be ashamed of. Or afraid of."

I leaned over and patted him on the knee. "You have it easy, Lucas."

"I suppose I do," he said. "No one ever pressured me to be a human being."

"Being human isn't as bad as you might think," I told him. "There are some definite benefits."

"I don't wear a mask," Lucas said. "And you shouldn't, either."

"Lucas?"

"Hm?"

"If you spend enough time around me, you'll learn the hard way I don't like being told what to do, so since I like you I'm giving you the advice for free."

The LTD groaned in protest as we climbed the driveway to the compound. Lucas stayed quiet and I did the same. I was 0 for 2 with interpersonal relations today.

"Park here," I said, and he pulled the LTD into the last spot before the driveway spilled into the street. No way to block us in if we had to run for it.

The front of the house, when I got close, was even more like a stitched-over wound than it seemed from afar, broken shades pulled over windows with security mesh bolted to the frames, rusted and weeping down the sides of the adobe.

I rang the bell and stepped back behind Lucas, letting him be the first thing they saw.

The door cracked and an eye and sliver of face appeared, washed out and suspicious. "What do you want?"

"Hear you got a delivery earlier," said Lucas. "Thought maybe you'd like some real quality goods."

The scent of someone else behind the door filtered to me, coffee and cigarettes, like the inside of a diner just before closing, and I nudged Lucas in the back. "Two of them," I murmured in his ear. His muscles tightened and his skin got cold.

"Just a minute," said the face, and the door slammed. I

pricked my ears and got snatches of conversation, the gist of which was, *"Fucking Lenny."*

The door swung wide again and I got a good look at the body that belonged to the face. Another anorexic, over-tanned specimen of Nocturne City's top income bracket, her tightly pinched face in a frown. The guy next to her was big and blocky in that ex-military way, too many muscles crammed onto a frame that bowed under its own weight. A crew cut did nothing to dispel the notion that he was made out of stone.

"We don't want what you're selling," said the woman. "We get our order from Lenny."

"Wait a minute, now," said the man. "One more can't hurt."

"You tell that worthless piece of street trash that the next time he divulges a private business transaction to his *colleagues*," said with the same tone and sneer you'd apply to *disease-ridden snuff porn enthusiasts*, "that he can kiss our arrangement good-bye."

The bodyguard rolled his eyes. "Come on in," he said. "We pay a grand for the weekend, and there are no limits. Your girl isn't delicate, I hope."

"Healthy as a horse," said Lucas, slapping me on the ass. "Ain't that right, sweetie?"

Oh, I was going to get him for that later. I just smiled and simpered, keeping my boozy just-popped-an-Oxy stance in place. "Whatever you gotta do, man," I said to Bodyguard.

"I'm going to have to clear this," said the woman.

The bodyguard snapped his fingers. "Get back into the ritual room. You aren't supposed to be wandering around."

Interesting. The woman stank of magick, the guard

read as mundane, but the Thelemite wasn't the one in charge.

She retreated, and the guard counted out a roll of bills to Lucas, who pocketed the cash and shoved me forward. "I'll just make myself comfortable."

"You can come back Monday morning and collect her," said the guard. "Medical attention is your responsibility."

"All due respect," said Lucas, "but I don't leave my product unattended. That'd make me a bad businessman. I'm sure you understand."

"Are we gonna have a problem?" Bodyguard asked. Lucas lifted one shoulder. They were doing some kind of masculine stare-down that I didn't understand, despite my all-too-frequent struggles for dominance with pack weres.

"Only if you try to mess with my business." Lucas was better at this than he realized. He altered his voice and his posture, made himself look droopy and sleazy instead of straight arrow and dangerous.

"Fine," the guard finally grunted. "If the snatch means that much to you, be my guest." He gestured at a threadbare sofa in the waiting area, which bore a token handful of pamphlets on things like Reiki and crystal healing, some battered furniture, and little else. "You," he said, grabbing onto my arm like I was a runaway dog, "come with me."

"You're cute," I purred as he dragged me down the hall. "What's your name?"

"Bud," he said shortly. "You can call me Bud."

"Bud," I said, and added a giggle. "Like the beer." A nickname was better than no name at all. I could run a search for him, based on his description and name.

"That's it," he said, not a smidge of human emotion in his face. I bet Bud was the type whom they sent in to execute civilians. He looked like it would bother him less than cutting back a plant.

The hall took a sharp left and led down a flight of stairs to a steel security door at the bottom, the subterranean level of the house.

I looked back once at the sliver of light coming from the hallway, where Lucas was. Then I turned around and put the dopey grin back on my face. I couldn't be relying on a lifeline. I was on my own.

Bud keyed a code into the door, blocking it with his body. Not as stupid as he looked, then. I filed that in the animal brain, for when and if I had to get primal.

"Get in there and get yourself ready," he said. "Then go through the door into the altar space and wait. No talking. No lip. You understand?"

Deep in my bag, my BlackBerry went off. I jumped and hoped Bud attributed it to my strung-out state. I should have silenced the fucking thing before I came in.

Bud just glared at me. "I asked you if you understand. I'm not a dumb john, you strung-out piece of meat with legs. You answer me when I talk to you."

"Sure, cutie," I said. "Whatever you say."

He bored into me for another second and then opened the door. "You remember that."

The door revealed a space that was the direct antithesis of the rest of the house. The furniture was sleek and plush, the walls were done in dark purple silk, the lighting was mellow and indirect, and the entire place stank of blood.

The were howled at me not to step across the threshold, but I gritted my teeth, breathed through my mouth, and went in. The door slammed behind me with the finality of a coffin.

"Oh, look," said one of the girls I'd seen going into the house. "Competition. I thought this here was a private party."

"Shaniqua, shut up," said another. "They're paying all of us, no matter what."

Shaniqua brushed past me, slamming me hard with her shoulder. I grunted and swayed to the side. Fine, let her think she had the upper hand. People aren't nearly as tough when they think you can't hurt them.

Shaniqua curled her lip. "Guess one skinny-ass white bitch don't make a difference."

"Is there a bathroom in here?" I sighed. "I gotta pee."

"Through there," said the second girl. She had a strong face, underneath the cheap makeup, like a hard-bitten Lucy Liu. A small black door led away from the plush room that smelled like blood, and I practically fell through it.

The bathroom was utilitarian, black tile and white countertop, a mirror surrounded by harsh bulbs. There was a linen closet full of bloodred towels and a door at the opposite end of the small space held shut by a heavy padlock.

"Hello there," I muttered, taking the clip out of my hair. I was good with a set of lock picks, but I didn't want to risk my police set being found if they searched me. Most padlocks can be broken with simple tools, and I fiddled with the cheap one on the door until it popped. They didn't expect anyone to penetrate their inner sanctum, and they didn't take the measures they did on the outside.

I drew back the hasp and eased the door open, reaching back to flush the toilet with the toe of one shoe. That would buy me five minutes. I silenced my BlackBerry and stepped out, shutting the door behind me.

The hallway beyond was depressingly normal, plain walls and carpet, devoid of any markings. The low fluorescent lights led on through a series of turns, doors with locks scented of nothing except stored-up dust.

I sensed I'd made a full circuit of the basement when I came to the door beyond and found another lock, a good one this time.

Putting my ear to the door, I listened and heard the low rise and fall of voices within. Some kind of chant, or meditation—my fingers came away pricked with magick, like the door was covered over with nettles.

My BlackBerry vibrated again and I almost fell off the ridiculous shoes. I jerked it out of the bag and saw *Pete Anderson* blinking on the screen. I jabbed the call button. "What, Pete? What?"

"I got that list of artifacts you wanted," he said hesitantly. "Um, is this a bad time?"

"Couldn't be worse," I whispered. "Anything red-flagged in there?"

"One thing," he said. "A codex of Thelemite daemons written in the nineteenth century. Basically just a phone directory, but in the right hands your cousin said a decent Thelema witch could summon with the daemon's name alone."

"You talked to Sunny?" I hissed.

"Well, yeah," said Pete. "She is my go-to woman for that sort of thing. I like your cousin. She's chatty."

"Pete?"

"Yes, Lieutenant?"

"Is there reason to believe that the Thelemites have this codex?"

"It came through Corley's antique business and disappeared after it cleared Customs, just like the heartstone. I think it's safe to assume they have it."

"Fantastic," I muttered. "Thanks, Pete. I have to go now."

"Take it easy, ma'am."

I hung up and turned back toward the waiting room, to sit with the rest of the girls.

A codex was bad news. Daemons were bad news, period. If I never saw another daemon, another being from the shadows between worlds where they hid and skulked, it would be too soon.

Lucas and I had to get out of here. If the Thelemites were calling daemons, it wasn't anywhere we needed to be.

I slipped back through the bathroom, relocked the door, and stepped back into the red light and blood smell, working over a plan to get out of the house before the summoning and screaming and dying happened.

When my eyes adjusted to the low light, I saw I was already too late. The girls were clustered in a corner, naked except for the few scraps of underwear they'd been lucky enough to put on, an eye painted on each of their foreheads in red pigment. Open and staring. I slowed, suddenly having the irrational longing for my gun that accompanies walking into a bad situation that has just gotten worse.

"Sorry, Luna," Lucas said, and my stomach dropped through the floor. *Shit.*

Lucas and Bud stood on the other side of the room. Lucas had his hands behind his head. Bud had a sawed-off shotgun. "Just FYI, that dopey act wouldn't pass on *American Idol*, never mind in the field," he rumbled.

"Sorry, Louella," Lucas said. "Looks like we've been made."

"Your name," said Bud. "Your real name, or I kill him right here."

I shut my eyes. *Crap.* And it had all been going so well. "I don't have to tell you shit."

Lucas met my eyes, and dropped me a wink. I forced myself to keep looking scared rather than irritated with Lucas, which I was. He could have dropped Bud as easily as he breathed. He was just playing along, letting me see how my grand plan had gone wrong. He didn't know about the codex, about the horrible danger we'd stumbled into.

Fine. I could play it cool, too.

"Yo, I didn't sign on for any snuff shit," Shaniqua spoke up.

"Shut your trap, whore," Bud growled.

"Hey," I said. "Don't talk to her like that. At least her living is honest and doesn't hurt anyone."

"You," Bud said, jerking the shotgun at me, "didn't answer my question."

"Luna Wilder," I said, meeting his eyes and letting my own flame gold. "Lieutenant, Nocturne City police."

He started to laugh, which wasn't the reaction I was used to getting from letting my monster out to play. "You think we didn't know what you are? We felt your filth from the minute you came in the door."

Shoving Lucas ahead of him, Bud stepped up to the door of the altar room and pounded with the flat of his fist. "Open up. I got a real treat for you out here."

The door swung open and I saw three Thelemite women, one of them with red paint on the tips of her fingers. They were draped in diaphanous purple robes that didn't leave much of anything to the imagination.

I memorized the faces behind the veils, those red eyes

staring back at me, tattooed into their foreheads instead of merely painted.

"What is this?" one demanded. I had expected husky voices, foreign accents, ancient tongues, but she sounded like she was from somewhere around LA that existed in a valley.

"Spies," said Bud. "They say they're police, but do you really care?"

The three stared at us for a moment. "No," said the lead woman. "Bring them in."

Bud shoved me ahead of him, and I stumbled into Lucas in turn. "Shift as soon as they're all in," I whispered into his ear. "They have a daemon codex. We need to get the Hex out of here."

"Codex?" Lucas hissed. I rolled my eyes.

"Long story."

"This is a great motherfucking plan," Lucas whispered. "Really."

I didn't have a comeback. He was right—this was hasty and the worst possible outcome that could have happened from my confronting the Thelemites.

The girls filed in after us, and Bud slammed and locked the door, staying outside. He looked relieved. That worried me.

"One by one, you will step to the circle, kneel, and prepare to receive the bounty of our gifts," said the tall Thelemite. "We are Myra, Kendra, and Pauline. You do as we say and you do it when we say it. As for you two . . ." Myra smirked at us. "You stay put. We've got something just for you."

The altar at the center of the room wasn't much, just a wooden box with a lid inlaid with the same eye symbol, a painted working circle on the floor, and that same stifling smell of blood.

Kendra lifted the lid of the box and drew out a long-handled black knife and a book, bound in leather, with the smell of dust clinging to it.

"Now," I said to Lucas. "Shift."

I stepped up to Kendra and grabbed the book out of her hands. She gave a shriek and lifted the knife, and I felt her magick clamp down around me.

Falling, like I'd stepped off the side of a building, while all the air whistled out of my lungs. Kendra hit me again and it was like taking a two-by-four across the chest.

"Lucas," I wheezed. "Shift!" I rolled over to look at him, fighting off Kendra feebly as she snatched the codex back from me.

Lucas stood stock-still, sweat beading on his forehead. "I'm trying," he gritted. "It's not working."

"Don't worry," said Pauline, knocking on the door. Bud opened it and passed her a pair of plastic riot handcuffs. "It happens to lots of guys."

Lucas backed up, his fists coming up. "You stay away from me, lady."

Kendra pressed her knife to my throat. "Calm down. Unless you want her to get cut because of your carelessness."

Pauline narrowed her eyes, and Lucas slammed back against the wall, hands whipping behind him. It was disturbing to watch, like a puppet writ large. Pauline pulled the handcuffs tight while I lay still and tried to breathe, and thought of fifty creative ways to kill Kendra when I got out of this mess.

Assuming a daemon hadn't chewed my head off by then.

Pauline strapped the second set of handcuffs to my wrists, tight enough to draw blood, and then tossed me into the corner with Lucas. He sighed.

"I don't like it when things don't go my way, Luna."

"Join the club," I muttered.

The Thelemites laid the open codex atop the box and stood around the edges of the circle. Their chanting was low and deliberate, and I felt the power in the room rise, like humidity on my skin. I couldn't Path it—it didn't touch me like a normal working would. I just felt it inside my head, dense and painful like a dark mass on a CAT scan.

"We call upon the one who is named in these pages Cerberus," said Myra. "We call him to his feasting place, and offer him his spoils."

She and the other Thelemite women joined hands, and their working shimmered against the air, while Lucas and I watched. This was a practiced maneuver, which meant it wasn't the first time they'd tried to call a daemon. This was bad.

"What the hell do we do now?" Lucas whispered.

"I can't Path, you can't shift, and they're calling a daemon," I said. "What do you think we're gonna do? We're gonna sit here and wait for them to get bored with us. Then they might get sloppy while they're feeding us to some creature from the pit."

Lucas snorted. "Cerberus? Even I know that's not real. He's a myth, straight out of a gods-damned storybook."

"You might be surprised," I said faintly, as a shadow started to gather on the pages of the codex, to grow and shape itself, a narrow serpent body topped with the triplet head and shoulders of a huge, snarling wolf's head.

"Welcome," said Myra. "Feast and be whole, and walk in this world as if it were your own."

Cerberus swung its still-spectral head from side to side, scenting the air with nostrils that could enclose my fist.

"This is so not good," I muttered to Lucas. "We are so Hexed."'

"Duh," he whispered back.

I fell silent. There had to be some way out of these cuffs, out of this room, while the Thelemites were feeding their new pet dog.

I strained against the plastic and got blinding pain for my trouble. The person who realized the thin plastic strips were mighty effective for subduing big crowds of people wasn't stupid. The harder you pulled, the tighter they got.

My usual strength had deserted me, and the same negative effect on shifting descended on me—I couldn't even get my claws to grow to try to saw through the cuffs.

Some were you are, I thought. *Brought down by some naked chicks and a strip of plastic.*

Lucas nudged me with his shoulder. "I don't want to alarm you, but that thing is getting pretty solid."

The figure of Cerberus was no longer shimmering and translucent, like the daemons I'd seen before. It looked real, and only slightly out of focus, like we were looking at a projection rather than a solid object. The hard, smooth, powerful magick of the Thelemites had pulled the thing through the realms faster than I would have believed possible, even with a blood sacrifice.

This was seven kinds of not good.

"We are honored to hold your presence here," said Kendra. "Please eat of what we offer, and return our offering with your favor until we require it no more."

This was not like any daemon summoning I'd seen—admittedly, I'd only seen one and that guy was insane, but

I'd learned a few things since then, and I knew that the Thelemites were off-book.

Cerberus flowed off the sad little altar, its serpent tail trailing it, powerful front legs pulling the flaccid body along like a dead thing dragged across the burying ground. "*Our hunger is prodigious*," it spoke. A high, thin voice, at odds with its huge, many-fanged heads, ragged ears, and lolling tongues. *"And we will sate our lust on your altar."*

"I really don't like the sound of that," Lucas said.

Cerberus turned on us with a snarl, and its nostrils twitched. *"And what of you, shape-changers, skin-slippers? Do you taste sweet?"*

"I'm a bag of bones," I said, snarling at the thing reflexively. The heads were like those of a giant wolf, and my were saw challenge in its pure black eyes. "But you're welcome to come get a taste of me."

Cerberus let out a wet, hacking sound and it took me a moment to realize it was laughing. *"Away with them. They can do nothing to my hungers."*

Pauline bit her lip. "Are you . . . are you displeased?"

"I came when you spoke my name aloud, did I not?" Cerberus demanded. Hex me, was that all it took with Thelemic skills behind you? I'd be in a crapload of trouble if that was really the case. More than I was now, even.

"Get them out of here!" Myra hissed at Pauline and Kendra. "They are insulting to our guest!"

The women hauled us up, and once again I was shoved like a cheap shopping cart through the double doors to the ridiculous anteroom. I looked back. Cerberus approached the girls, paws and tongue passing over and through each one of them, its incorporeal state allowing it to reach into the faint pink halo that surrounded each girl, their auras visible in the high energy around the altar. Each girl in turn shuddered like she was in the throes of an orgasm, a smile lighting her face and her own hands rising to touch her sweat-sheened body.

Cerberus met my eyes and curled its lips back. *"Good parting, to one who is marked by the sign of Asmodeus."*

The doors slammed shut and I was left staring at them, listening to the moans of the girls and the primal grunting of the daemon. I didn't even feel Kendra tugging at me; all I heard was that voice, terrible and soft like the skin of a drowned man.

One who is marked by the sign of Asmodeus. Cerberus had spared me because I was already another daemon's property. *Marked. Marked by Asmodeus.* It was the only explanation, and the one I positively could not stomach. Of course.

"Move," Kendra said, shoving me. Bud watched us impassively from his spot beside the door, shotgun dangling loosely from his arms. I shut my eyes, allowing the were to creep into the forefront of my mind. They stung, and when I opened them again Kendra's gasp told me they were gold.

I could phase again. Thank the gods for small favors.

I ripped my wrists free of the plastic cuffs, starting blood afresh, and shoved Kendra away from me and into Lucas, who shifted on the fly and caught her up in his skeletal Wendigo arms, sinking his talons into her chest. He was nearly my height, like a prehistoric wolf made of bones and molten silver, graceful as the wind and cold as the grave.

Pauline screamed, running for the door, and I let her go. Bud was the more pressing problem, as he raised his shotgun and drew down on Lucas.

I caught Bud in the midsection with a knee, and knocked the shotgun toward the ceiling. It went off, louder than thunder in the enclosed space, and rained plaster down on my head as I wrestled with Bud.

"Were bitch," he managed. "Get the hell off of me!"

I was getting tired of struggling with guys who slung insults about my DNA, so I lunged forward and knocked my forehead against Bud's nose. He folded like a dirty suit, and I picked up the shotgun.

Lucas released Kendra, who twitched feebly on the floor, bleeding from the five thin wounds in her chest where Lucas had drunk her heart's blood down into his Wendigo shape, fed it, so that all of his veins turned black under his translucent skin. Lucas shifted down to his human form bit by bit, and Kendra slid to the floor.

He was flushed and covered in moisture from his shift, while Kendra was pale and still, not breathing. I stared, silent. A Wendigo feeding is not something you ever really get used to.

"I had to feed on her," said Lucas. "I'm sorry—I saw what she did to you in there and I couldn't think of another way."

"Never mind that," I said. I tossed him my purse. "Go outside, get the car running, and don't lose that bag. It cost me four hundred dollars on the Internet."

Lucas flashed me a smile. "I like a woman with priorities."

"You're damn right you do," I muttered, turning to pound on the door. A second later Myra's face appeared.

"Did you get rid of—"

"I think it's safe to say that's a no," I said. Beyond her purple-clad body the girls lay on the floor, limbs akimbo, sweat and blood coating their bodies, but breathing to a woman. None of them looked particularly upset. In fact, they looked like they'd just had a full weekend of fantastic sex, possibly with Brad Pitt.

Cerberus hovered over them, grown twice in size, his feet leaving deep scratches in the floor. Solid. Corporeal. Swollen on the girls' energy.

"Crap," I whispered.

Myra's face went pale. "You can't kill me. I'm a person. It would be wrong."

"Lady, if I had a dollar for every time some two-bit witch said that to me." I pressed the shotgun barrel against her clavicle. "Try another working like what your friend did to me and I guarantee that I'll turn you into a sieve before I drop this thing."

Sometimes old-fashioned threats work better than any magick or trickery ever will. Myra's lips tightened, but she put up her hands and backed away from me. I reached out and snatched her by the shoulder of her wrap.

"You stay out here. I think you've had enough fun for one night."

"I can do no more," said Myra. "You are foolish, and you don't know a thing about us. Your fear and ignorance blind you to the truth of all things."

"Not this," I said, shoving her onto the sofa. "I know what that daemon is. I get that you're feeding him with some kind of sex magick. Gross and wrong as that is. All I need now is the real name of the Maiden."

Myra's face darkened. "You know a lot for a bitch-in-heat werewolf."

"Thanks," I said. "Tell me who she is."

Myra raised her chin. "Never."'

"I don't have time for this," I warned her.

Myra smirked. "Do I look like I care about your problems, were?"

So she wasn't afraid of me. Fortunately, I wasn't the scariest thing in the room. I grabbed Myra's arm, shoving her back into the altar room.

Cerberus gave a growl and rose onto his front legs, two of his three heads swinging toward us. I'd seen drawings of the dog at the gates of Tartarus before, but seeing him in front of me, smelling the rank charred odor that preceded daemons, was so horrifying I struggled to keep myself from screaming aloud.

I shoved Myra toward him and she collided with his enormous barrel chest, falling to the floor with a yelp. Cerberus caressed her cheeks and shoulders with his three tongues.

"She's all yours," I told the daemon. "Unless she tells me who the Maiden is and what they're trying to do."

"I don't know!" Myra's voice rose into a panicked shriek. "Only Grace and Pauline know the inner sisters who surround the Maiden. We're just acolytes! I came from Ohio two months ago. Please. Please."

And I'd let Pauline get away in the chaos surrounding Cerberus. Fantastic.

"What are the Thelemites doing in my city?" I said, as Cerberus scented Myra through his giant nostrils. "What do they need the heartstone and that codex for?"

"I just do what I'm ordered," Myra sobbed. "They found me. I was like those girls, but the Maiden's benevolence shone on me and I was saved. I just do what they tell me to do. I just say the names and let the power through my vessel."

Cerberus's serpent tail wrapped around Myra's bare leg, traveling up and up, and she let out a shriek.

"It doesn't seem so wonderful when it's you, does it?" I said. "One last thing—how is Grace Hartley getting information from inside the SCS?"

"I don't know! *I don't know!* Make him stop!" She was beyond coherency, screaming and rocking, trying to draw herself into a ball under the daemon's ministrations.

"Enough," I told Cerberus.

He raised his heads. *"And who are you to speak to me as equal, skin-changer?"*

"You said it," I told him, bringing the shotgun to bear on the largest of the heads. "I'm the one with the mark of Asmodeus." I'd figure out what that meant and what awful repercussions came with such a title later.

"You believe I owe alliegiance or fear to Asmodeus?"

"I think you would have already sucked me dry if you didn't," I said.

Cerberus inclined his heads. *"There is a code of courtesy among the Abandoned, skin-changer. Be fleet. I will not extend such courtesy again."*

He stepped over Myra's prone, shaking body and ambled out the door, mounting the stairs and vanishing in a streak of magick and smoke.

I picked up the codex and left Myra on the floor, sobbing. "You may want to reevaluate the life choices you've made," I told her. "Ohio is very pleasant this time of year, and I don't think they make you wear that ridiculous outfit to serve donuts at the Krispy Kreme."

"The Thelemites will kill me," she whispered. "Their kindness is infinite. . . ."

"You tell me what I want to know and I'll protect you," I said.

Myra laughed, cold and dry. "You can't protect yourself. How can you help me against their kind of power?"

Well, I tried. "Best of luck to you. And do something about that tattoo." I nodded at the eye emblazoned on her forehead. "It's way over-the-top."

I hobbled up the stairs on feet that were starting to ache from the damn cheap shoes, and walked out the front door with the codex under my arm. Lucas was waiting in the LTD, tapping his fingers impatiently on the top of the steering wheel.

"Let's get the fuck out of here," I said, sliding in and slamming the door.

Lucas looked at the house. "I can't believe I'm about to say this, but shouldn't we call in the body?"

"We will," I said, leaning my forehead against the glass. "From a pay phone, when we're away from the house. That informant is still in the wind, and after what I just went through I don't feel like dying today."

Cerberus was out there, in the darkness sliding past the window. I thought of the thing's flat, pure black eyes, like a road slick from the rain, and shivered. I had seen daemons, talked to them, even willingly summoned Asmodeus once before, but to see something that was never supposed to exist in this world, solid and real as Lucas and as close to me, triggered every instinct I had, to run and bare my teeth and aim for the throat.

"Take the expressway north," I told Lucas. "There's someone I have to talk to." The codex sat on my lap, far from the forbidding leather-bound tome I'd first thought, and more like an old ledger with pages falling out, handwriting cramped and running off into the margins, pages stained with moisture rings and dabs of dark, dried blood.

We sped along in the dusk, me holding the thing on my lap and Lucas keeping his eyes straight ahead. "Thanks for trying to help me," I said after the lines of the highway smoothed out, Lucas pushing the car to top speed. "I'm sorry it turned out . . . well . . . it was FUBAR."

"Don't mention it," he said. "I owe you."

"You don't . . . ," I started.

"You didn't turn me in when you could have. I owe you," he said again. I stayed quiet, and didn't tell him that I didn't like owing or being owed anything.

It seemed to be the safest thing, for now.

Twenty-one

My grandmother and Sunny lived in a cottage that overlooked the water, waves the same color as the gray rock they washed pounding away at the bottom of the cliff, slowly eroding. In another fifteen years the cottage would be in the ocean.

I tripped up the steps, skinning my knee because of the shoes, and fell against the front door. "Fuck!"

The latch clicked and the door drew back just as Lucas was helping me to my feet. My grandmother stood there silently, stern and silver-haired as she'd been my whole life, her stony eyes narrowed. "Luna. To what do we owe the pleasure?"

"That smarts," I muttered, rubbing my knee.

"Luna," my grandmother snapped, putting one hand on her hip.

"Lucas Kennuka, ma'am," Lucas said, stepping forward and extending his hand. "Are you Luna's mother?"

She looked at the hand like it was made out of maggoty steaks. "Hardly. I am her maternal grandmother. Rhoda Swann."

"Good meeting you," said Lucas. "Luna's told me a lot

about you." Bald-faced lie, but I was amazed to see my grandmother's face soften.

"Has she? Odd. She usually gives the impression to strangers that she sprang fully formed from the foreheads of the gods."

"I'm hardly a stranger," said Lucas. "Your granddaughter and I go back quite a bit."

Rhoda looked him up and down, and I felt the energy crackle around us as she pushed on Lucas to see what manner of creature he was. "As far as boyfriends go," she told me, "I'm frightened to say that this one is an improvement over that were you brought around."

"Thanks, Grandma," I said. "Really. You want to whip out the baby pictures while we're at it? Go for maximum collateral damage?" I brushed myself off. "Are you going to let us in or not?"

"Of course I am," she sniffed. "I was raised in a civilized household and mine is the same. Come in, Lucas. Luna."

We stepped over the threshold, the familiar shiver of my grandmother's ward marks slipping over my bare skin. Lucas looked around the neat living room with its hooked rug and blue denim furniture. "Cozy," he said.

My grandmother was squinting at me. "What on earth are you wearing? It's a bit trashy even for you, Luna. Aren't you bitter cold showing so much skin?"

"Hex you, Grandma. Seriously."

Sunny came down the stairs from the small second floor and saved us from hair-pulling and biting. Lucas just watched us like we were a particularly salacious episode of *Maury*. "What are you doing here? What is *that*?" Sunny pointed at the codex.

"It's the thing that Pete spoke to you about earlier," I

said, sliding a look at my grandmother. I didn't know how much Sunny had told her about our little arrangement with her know-how and the SCS's cases.

Rhoda glared at me, and stepped forward. "Let me see that book."

"Hey, I hate to trouble you, but could I get a cup of coffee?" Lucas stood and beamed at her, his thin face innocent and open as could be.

Rhoda pulled her hand back to her side. "Of course you can, Lucas. Luna, where are your manners? Go make your boyfriend some coffee. And Sunny and I will have tea."

"He's not my boyfriend," I said. "He's just a friend."

"I'll help," Sunny said quickly, pulling me toward the kitchen.

Lucas stepped over to my grandmother and took her elbow, guiding her to the sofa. "Rhoda, what can you tell me about the house? It's so well cared for. I'd be interested to know how old it is."

I mouthed, *Thank you*, over my shoulder as Lucas took the bullet, sitting my grandmother down on the sofa. I just hoped he didn't get so annoyed that he ate her. My grandmother has that effect on people.

"I can't believe you stole that thing," said Sunny.

"I didn't so much steal it as jack it," I said. "There was a shotgun and a lot of yelling involved. I wasn't real sneaky about my intentions."

She sat down at the table in the eating nook and paged through the book, shaking her head. "I recognize sections of this—it's from caster witch texts. Some blood witch workings as well. Thelema is the thrift store of disciplines. If it works, they can cast it." She pursed her lips, rifling the pages. "Sometimes I think my life would have been a lot easier if I was a Thelemite."

I remembered the women, the daemon standing over them, the crushing feeling of their power. "Don't be too sure about that," I murmured.

Sunny stopped reading through the codex. "What's wrong?"

"They called a daemon," I said. "Cerberus. It's loose, Sunny. *I* let it out."

"What? Luna, what are you saying?"

"It fed off the energy of these girls, these prostitutes . . . and it was *real.* It *talked* to me." I pressed my hands over my face. The gravity of the night was finally dragging me down.

Sunny held up her palms. "Whoa. A daemon actually manifested fully, and then it talked to you?"

"I should have helped those girls," I murmured. "What it did to them . . ."

"Sex magick," said Sunny. "It's sort of a hallmark of Thelema."

At least now I knew why Milton Manners had needed all of that Viagra. "It talked to me," I told Sunny again.

She put her hand over mine. "I believe you. What did he say?"

"Well, it sure wasn't *Luke, I am your father.*"

"Cerberus is a gateway guardian," Sunny said. "A totem spirit that guards waypoints between the daemon and human realm."

"Somebody's going to be late for work today," I muttered.

Sunny bent her head back to the codex. "This means something. If they summoned him instead of one of the other names in here, they must need him for something. He's not particularly powerful on his own. More like a watchdog that barks but doesn't bite."

"We are talking about a daemon here, Sunny. The same thing that almost destroyed part of the city, that requires blood sacrifice, that . . ." *That has marked me with something.*

"Daemons are like people, Luna," she said. "Dangerous and unpredictable, but there are many kinds and many species. Caster witches are forbidden from them for exactly that reason—meet one with a lesser power and the control you have over it can be seductive. Then you meet something stronger than you are and—" She snapped her fingers. "Poof."

"You sure know a lot about them," I grumbled.

Sunny lifted her shoulder. "There are a lot of things I know about that I'm not supposed to, Luna. I don't tell Grandma about what you did when we were kids, and you won't tell her about what I read. All right?"

"Yeah, yeah, your weird secret is safe with me," I sighed. I pushed back from the table, feeling cold in all of my limbs. "I need to go upstairs for a minute. Do you think you can figure out what the Thelemites are doing with Cerberus, a heartstone, and that codex?"

"Maybe," Sunny said. "I can certainly extrapolate some scenarios from the workings in here." She eyed me suspiciously. "What are you doing?"

"I just need a minute to myself," I said, backing out of the kitchen. I crept past Lucas and Rhoda, and up the stairs into Sunny's room. It was painfully neat, purple velvet bed covering and matching curtains without a speck of dust, no clothes or makeup cluttering the dresser, books lined up by height in the bookshelves. Witches tended to be a little bit OCD.

In this case it was in my favor, as I opened Sunny's desk drawer and found all of her casting supplies laid out neatly before me. Her caster was there, in its velvet bag, and her oils, herb bags, and chalk for emergency circles. I took out the chalk, kicked out of my shoes, and pulled her carpet back, revealing the blond wood floor beneath. Wood was the best thing for a circle—alive, suspended, with magick still coursing through it.

I drew a simple circle on the floor and stepped in. I hadn't even bothered with this formality last time, and he'd come. This time was no different. I let his name fall from my mind, through the layers of magick around me, the crackling ambient energy that made me a were, the higher-than-usual magick in the room because of Sunny's ghostly presence, and the ripples in the atmosphere that I could feel sometimes, when my Path ability reached out from the beastly part of my mind.

Asmodeus.

A drop in temperature, a breath of ice on my face, told me that he'd come, just like a faithful dog.

"You called, Insoli?"

I opened my eyes and looked at his face, that human face with the serpent eyes descending to a lion's body. The gold light that ringed Asmodeus gave him an angelic appearance, something that couldn't be further from the truth. There were benevolent daemons, and mischevious daemons, and evil daemons. I was pretty sure Asmodeus was the third.

"You marked me," I said.

His eyes danced with firelight. *"Who has told you this?"*

"Cerberus," I said, jutting out my chin.

"Yes, the dog who begs for scraps and feeds on carnality. I am sure he is a fine source of information, Insoli."

I didn't know that daemons grasped the concept of sarcasm, but Asmodeus's lips curled upward in definite amusement.

"It doesn't matter who the tip comes from," I said. "It matters that I think it's true." Good advice for daemons as well as confidential informants.

Asmodeus let out a sigh and the curtains in the room rippled. I could almost see through him, like looking through a glass filled with amber liquid. Everything around him twisted and distorted as his presence worried the ambient magick in the room.

"I aided you, Insoli, and this insolence is how you repay me? I thought you wished never to speak with me again."

"You helped me," I said. "You saved my life. And I also recall that you said I owed you something for that, when you agreed to it."

Asmodeus tilted his head. *"So I did."* He wasn't smiling anymore.

"Then why don't you remember that it was a straight-up deal between us, helping me protect myself from Seamus O'Halloran, before you get all high-and-mighty?" O'Halloran, the witch who had attempted to break down the barriers between blood magick and casting, was in the ground and I was alive.

But that didn't mean I owned the daemon a damn thing.

"Very well," Asmodeus said. *"What is it you wish of me?"*

"Cerberus said you marked me," I said. "What does that mean? What did you do to me when you saved me from O'Halloran?"

"Those afflicted with certain maladies never quit of

them," he said. "*They carry the strain in their blood until their dying day. You can see it in them, the poison, the corruption. Those who touch daemons do the same. You made your bargain, Insoli, and you did not ask me for the particulars. This is one.*"

"You son of a bitch," I whispered, feeling involuntary tears start on my cheeks. "You're in me now? You're *part* of me?"

"*Indeed,*" he whispered, drifting closer as if the wind pushed him. I held up my hand, shaking and hating myself for the display of weakness.

"You stay the fuck away from me."

"*Insoli.*" For the first time, the insult sounded like an endearment rather than his condescension toward me, the small and frail living thing. "*Those who are touched by my kind are not corrupted, not anywhere except in the minds of those who are small and shortsighted. You and I have unfinished business. This is my reminder. That is all.*"

"What do you want from me?" I whispered. "Let me pay you back and get rid of you. I don't want to see any more daemons. I just want my world to be normal, even for five seconds."

"*What I will take from you is not ripe, not ready. Not yet. I can give you this wisdom, however: cease your dealings with the whores of Thelema. They bring nothing but sorrow.*"

I glared at him. "No. You may hold our bargain over me, but you do not tell me how to live my life."

His face hardened. "*Have a care, Insoli, about how you speak to me. I am still the debt holder in this pairing.*"

"I don't want your mark," I said again. "I'll do what I have to in order to get rid of it."

Asmodeus let out a chuckle, which managed to be both obscene and terrifying. *"I know that you will. And in time, you and I will speak again."* He rolled his shoulders, his lion tail switching back and forth. *"Now I grow weary of this place. Good night, Insoli."*

In a burst of char and a *pop* of air, Asmodeus was gone.

"Thanks a bunch," I said to the empty room. "That was a big fucking help."

Twenty-two

I found a sweat suit in Sunny's closet and changed into it. It was too short for me at the wrists and ankles, but it beat the hooker getup by a mile. Lucas stood up when I came downstairs, looking me over appreciatively.

"Stop that," I said, when his gaze lingered too long.

"Sorry," he said. "Can't help it. You look like you again. It's sort of a relief."

"You're a strange one," I said. Lucas gave me a crooked smile.

"Same to you. Maybe we're more right for each other than you think."

I raised my eyebrows. "You're really hitting on me. Here, now. In my grandmother's house."

Rhoda snorted softly on the sofa. I ignored her and looked Lucas in the eye. He shrugged.

"Seizing the moment." He stepped closer and leaned in, and I backed up, almost mowing Sunny over.

"Luna . . . are those my clothes?"

"Definitely," I said. "I don't own things that are baby-blue velour."

She glared at me, but I pointed at the codex, tucked under her arm. "What did you find?"

"Not much," she said. "This book is maybe a hundred and twenty years old at the most, amateurish, without any sort of indexing system, and, aside from the names, pretty much utterly worthless." She shoved it back at me. "It also smells funny."

I looked at the dog-eared pages, the smeared ink, and the tattered clothbound cover. "You didn't find *anything*?" It was something of a letdown. . . . I was used to imminent disaster when I got my hands on magickal artifacts.

"Only a few interesting workings, nothing that's going to blow up *zee vurld*," Sunny said. "Here." She took the book back gingerly and settled on the sofa next to Rhoda. I took the far cushion, and my grandmother and I traded the requisite dirty looks before Lucas perched on the arm of the sofa and looked over my shoulder.

"Do you have to be so close?" I muttered.

"Yes," he said. "Because you get a cute little blush when you're uncomfortable."

"You're an ass," I said, loudly.

Sunny thwapped me on the shoulder. "Could the two of you either make out or grow up? It's really no fun for the rest of us."

"Sunflower!" my grandmother snapped.

Sunny shrugged. "What? It's true."

"Could you please just tell us what you found?" I said. "Please?" Before Lucas decided that my entire family belonged in a zoo.

Crap. It was bad that I cared what he thought. I only cared with people I liked. And Lucas was so wrong for me it wasn't even worth mentioning.

"Well, I did find reference to the things that attacked you," said Sunny. "The selkies, as well as the basilisks and a bunch of other daemon-born monsters. Harpies, trollkin, wyrms. All things that humanity hasn't seen in, well, centuries. Ever since casting overtook Thelema and the hedge disciplines. Made it safer."

"Harpies," I said, tapping the drawing. A bare-breasted woman, winged and with the talons of a bird. "Milton Manners was hacked up with something that looks a lot like those claws."

"Well, I hate to tell you this, but I doubt these are what killed him," said Sunny. "To allow these creatures from the daemon realm into ours is almost impossible. . . ."

"But not completely," Rhoda spoke up. Everyone stared at her. She stood up with difficulty, and stalked over to the window. "Sunflower, what was the first thing I taught you when you came to me as an apprentice?"

Sunny stared at her hands, stricken. "Never bring food into the working circle?"

"That nothing is impossible in magick, Sunflower. That's what I taught you." She folded her arms. "Somewhere in that book you'll find a working designed to open a devil's doorway."

"And that would be?" I said, as heat crept up Sunny's face. I knew all too well the bite my grandmother's words could have. They were usually directed at me, while Sunny was immune. There had been a time I resented Sunny for that, but it wasn't now.

"Sunflower, can you at least explain the devil's doorway?"

She flinched, and I got to my feet, grabbing the codex. "No. You do it, since apparently you're today's fount of wisdom. Explain it all to us, Grandma. Thrill us with your superior knowledge and make us feel three feet tall, just like you always do."

Her thin lips curled. "Well. Quite the outburst, Luna.

Have you been practicing in front of the mirror, telling me what a horrible person I am?"

"You," I said, "are a shriveled, bitter old woman who can't accept that I made something good out of my life, and even when you have Sunny, who is ten times the person I will ever be, you can't be happy because I am. But you know what, right now? I don't give a shit. Tell me what you know, Grandma, and do it now, because as of this moment I no longer have time for your bullshit."

We stood, staring at each other, for a long time. Neither of us would turn away; that much I knew. I get my intractability from my grandmother, and she was as cold as they came.

Sunny made a small noise on the sofa. It may have been, "Oh, Hex me."

Lucas just watched us, his face composed into serious lines. I knew him well enough to know that he wouldn't get in between Rhoda and me like Dmitri would have. Lucas believed in fighting your own battles.

"Fine," said my grandmother tightly. "You've made your opinion clear."

"Better late than never," I said, under my breath.

"A devil's doorway is a gap between the daemon realm and this one that is open for a short time through an enormous effort of will. It could allow something free, such as these harpies and the basilisks which Sunflower told me about." She passed her hand over her forehead. Her practical iron-gray hair ruffled like we were standing in a wind. "The Thelemites must have released these creatures. Who understands a mad mind?" She glared at me, and I got the feeling we were no longer speaking about the Thelemites.

"See, was that so hard?" I said.

"I don't see what good it will do you," said my grandmother. "You have a worthless codex, a fathomless series of events, and nothing to connect them. You are no better than when you started." She left me standing there and went into the kitchen.

"Always has to get the last word," Sunny said.

"I'm done," I said, spreading my hands. "I'm done with the case and I'm done with my career. I can't close this, and that's all the excuse the commission needs to shut us down."

"Stop it," said Sunny. "You have the codex and you have the heartstone. You have all the aces the Thelemites did."

And no Hexed clue how to use them to my advantage. I was in a library full of all the world's knowledge, and I couldn't read a damn word. The only person who might be able to shed some light was the SCS rat, and to entrap them . . . "The heartstone," I said, sitting up.

Sunny looked at me in alarm. "What about it?"

"We have it," I said. "And I bet the Thelemites want it back."

"I am totally lost," Sunny said.

I grabbed my purse, digging out my BlackBerry. I called Bryson at home and gave him a simple, "Get over here," and Sunny's address. Then I called Fagin.

"Just about to walk out of the office for the day," he said, crisp and dry as a glacier. "What can I help you with?"

"I'm sorry," I said, deciding to take the direct route. Maybe if I said the two words I hated more than any others in my native tongue, that would be sufficient karmic payback.

"You are?"

"You don't have to sound so surprised." I turned my

back on Sunny and Lucas. "Look, I need your help with something."

Fagin sounded suspicious. "What? Is it a felony?"

"Not unless you want it to be. Meet me at my cousin's place, okay?"

I gave him the address and Fagin sighed. "I'm not coming unless you tell me what this is about."

"I figured out how we can catch the informant in the SCS," I told him, and hung up.

Lucas stood. "If they're coming, I better be going. I'll see you around, Luna."

Before I could stop him, he kissed me on the cheek and then in a swirl of mist, he was gone.

Bryson showed up in under fifteen minutes, disheveled and still in his workshirt stained with chili from his lunch. "Don't judge me," he said. "I can't keep lying to everyone about where you are and not stress-eat."

"It's fine, David," I said absently, watching Fagin's Mustang nose into the driveway.

"Oh, great," Bryson said. "It's Agent Douche Bag."

"Mature," I said, giving him a thumbs-up. "Be nice, David. He's here to help us."

Fagin knocked on the door and I let Sunny invite him in. He did all of the right things, smiling and shaking hands, but his eyes locked onto me and they were cold, angry.

"Let's sit down," I said. I put the codex on the coffee table, in front of all of us. Bryson wrinkled his nose. "That thing smells like a hobo's armpit."

"I know how to get to the informant," I said. I told them about the Center, the Thelemite women, Cerberus, all of it. By the end, Bryson looked as if he'd just heard a scary story and Fagin looked distinctly unimpressed. "Why haven't the Thelemites just stormed your evidence locker and taken the heartstone back?"

Bryson snorted. "Because they'd have to march through a building full of cops and show Luna and the rest of us who they really are? No one risks that unless they're bat-shit insane, and these people are smart, even if they are a little wacked in the head."

"How do you plan to find out how the information is being passed?" Fagin asked. "Either everyone who knows is beyond sanity or we can't get to them."

I tapped my finger against my chin, and gave Bryson a thin, wicked smile. "Talon spent an awful lot of time with Grace Hartley. She's still in custody. What say we go have a chat?"

Walking out, I spotted Lucas standing under a tree at the edge of the yard. He raised a hand to me, and then faded back into the shadows.

I turned away, feeling the familiar clench of stress in my gut. How much longer could I keep this up? Lucas was a wanted fugitive—if Bryson and Will found out I'd been with him, my job would be the least of my worries, once I got out of jail for harboring a felon.

"Everything okay?" Fagin put his hand on my shoulder.

I gave him a wide, guilty smile. "Peachy. You?"

"Better," he said. "For some reason, fighting with you didn't agree with me, at all."

"Me, either," I blurted, and then flushed.

"That's strange," said Fagin. "Because usually combative conversations are my version of foreplay."

I was thankful to all the gods with names that it was

dark in my grandmother's driveway. "You need to learn some new foreplay," I told Fagin.

He reached out and squeezed my hand. "I've got you to teach me, haven't I?"

"Yeah. Don't bank on it, Agent."

Bryson rolled his eyes at me when I slipped into the backseat of the Mustang.

"What?" I hissed at him.

"You," he whispered back. "All moony-eyed over Agent Douche—"

I clapped my hand across Bryson's mouth. "Knock it off, okay?"

Fagin slid in and started the car. "You two having a private conversation? Should I turn on my iPod?"

"It's over now," I said, glaring at Bryson. He glared back and pantomimed a ridiculous kissy face that made him look like a smallmouth bass.

The jail was locked down for the night, and the guard regarded the three of us with an expression that clearly said he wasn't getting paid enough for this shit. Bryson slipped me my badge and ID. "You left this in your room," he explained. "Figured you might need it."

"Going through my underwear again?" I asked him.

"Would, if it didn't feel like going through a bin at the Salvation Army," he shot back without missing a beat.

I gave him a crooked grin. "Good one." I wondered when I'd started to look at Bryson as a friend rather than one of my detectives with slightly obnoxious personal habits.

Probably when I realized he was the only person I could trust in my squad. He might be abrasive, twenty years behind the times, and stare at my ass whenever he thought he could get away with it, but you knew where you stood with Bryson, and that was something I wasn't getting a lot of lately.

"Go on down," said the guard, when we showed our various IDs. He yelled, "Open on Seven," even though there was no one around.

Talon was lying on the bed, her arms behind her head, looking as polished as she had the first time I'd seen her. How dare she look that good after she'd been in jail for two days? Her long burgundy hair was still styled, for Hex's sake. It was patently unfair.

The cell door rolled closed behind me, Will in the cell with me, and Bryson staying outside, hand on the butt of his gun. He didn't like weres, in the same way that I didn't like witches: They made us nervous, in some primal and instinctual way that didn't quite jibe with our civilized forebrain.

"Nice threads," Talon said, sitting up and crossing her arms so that her chest pushed up under her gray DOC jumpsuit. Gray for women, orange for men. If Talon was incarcerated and transferred to a real prison, she'd get pale green.

"Thanks," I said, and then reached out and grabbed her by the neck, digging my fingers into the cordlike tendons on either side of her throat. Talon got out a strangled yelp before I whipped her into a standing position and slammed her into the wall hard enough to rattle mortar loose on our heads.

"What the hell . . . ," Fagin started, but Bryson shook his head.

"Take a knee, Boy Scout. Watch the lieutenant work."

"You're . . . hurting . . . me . . . ," Talon squeaked.

I pressed harder on her windpipe. "Yeah, so I am. You

want to know why?" I phased out my claws a bit and let them prick her throat. "One, because you're a nasty, arrogant little gutterwolf who deserves to learn where she really stands in the pecking order, and two . . ." I pushed harder and Talon lifted up on her tiptoes. She was heavy, like a sack of bricks, but I didn't let my arm shake and didn't let her see the effort expended to hold her there. She had to think I was stronger than her for the dominate to work, physically and willfully. "Because I don't have time to mess around with being nice. Or legal."

"You . . . can't . . . ," she choked.

"Do you really think that Agent Fagin or Detective Bryson is going to tell anyone that I did anything but talk to you? Do you really think that guard out there won't erase the tape of this as soon as I leave?" Speaking of which, I'd have to make sure to steal the security footage before I left. The guard didn't look like he was inclined to go along with my scheme.

Talon didn't know that, though, and I saw the tiny threads of doubt creep across her face, her mouth slackening and her cheeks pinking as she struggled to breathe. Everyone knows the cops in Nocturne City are crooked as a country road, and I wondered what horrible visions of phone books and hands slammed in doors were cascading through her head.

I took my opening, looking her directly in the eye, pushing on her with the will of my were. Dominant, strong, predatory.

Talon should be stronger than me, being part of a pack, but she also didn't know where I stood in the greater order of weres. And she was scared shitless, whereas I was just tired and pissed off. I felt her will weaken against my battering, and then break. A tear slid down her cheek, and she began to shake all over like she was going into shock.

It was an awful thing, a violation, and I let go of her, suddenly not wanting contact. My were snarled in the forefront of my mind, flush with victory, wanting to draw blood to cement Talon's humiliation.

Instead, I put my hand on her chest, pressing her back into the wall again, and said, "How are the Thelemites getting information from my squad?"

Talon was sobbing now, trying to get away from me. I was the dominant were, and I could force her to do anything my will could contain. Dominates are raw, primal, and ugly. I had lived in fear of them for half of my life, before I broke the hold the man who gave me the bite held over me. And now I was doing it to another confused, anchorless woman. I was going to hate myself when this was all over.

"Tell me," I snarled. "I know you worked with Grace Hartley. I know she's one of them. *Tell me now.*"

"Barrow Park," Talon shouted. "They meet in Barrow Park under the Saint Michael statue! That's all I know!"

Barrow Park was a few miles from the Plaza, far enough that the informant wouldn't run into anyone they knew. The Saint Michael statue occupied a remote corner, home mostly to bums looking for a place to sleep or hustlers looking for privacy.

"Good girl," I said, stepping out of her space. "You straighten up and fly right, hear? Crime doesn't pay, et cetera."

"Bitch," Talon hissed under her breath. "Do you know what my pack will do to me when I can't use a dominate?"

"Oh, I wouldn't worry about that," I said, turning my

back so she wouldn't see the look on my face. "I have a feeling you're going to be locked away from your pack for a long, long time."

Will saw my expression and banged on the bars. "Open Seven, please!"

He took me by the shoulder and guided me out of the cell. "Hold it together, Luna. Just until we get out of here. Walk."

"Make sure you get the tape," I said, dully. "Don't want anyone finding out we were here."

"David," Will said. "Do you mind? I'm going to give Luna a hand." He guided me through a door and into bright fluorescent lights, which blurred under the tears that had started.

"Shit," I said, swiping at my face with the back of my hand. "Shit. That could have gone better."

Fagin put his hands on my shoulders. "What's wrong with you? What happened in there?"

"I . . . I . . ." I took a long, deep breath, getting my heart back to a normal rhythm. "I broke her will. She's defenseless now if she meets another pack were."

"You did what you had to do," Fagin said. "It always comes down to who's the better predator, and that was you, Luna."

"I don't see it that way!" I screamed, shoving him away. "You don't know what it was like to feel someone's will pressing down on me, taking away everything that was *me*, making me nothing."

Memories of Joshua Mackelroy flooded up, the night he gave me the bite, and then later, when I'd met him again and he'd used his dominate to nearly beat me to death. The crushing feeling of his will on top of my own.

And I'd done that to Talon.

"Luna."

I came back to myself, aware that I'd slid down one green-tiled wall, next to a row of urinals. I blinked at Fagin. "Is this the men's room?"

"It was closer. Get up." He pulled me to my feet, holding me at arm's length. "I've seen you," he said. "You're a good cop. I know you only did what you had to do. You are *not* like whoever it is you're thinking of."

"I didn't think," I said numbly. "I don't think, and I hurt people and all I can do is regret it."

Will pulled me into his arms. "That's not just you, Luna. That's me. That's everyone."

I let myself rest against him for a moment and shut my eyes. "Everything is falling apart," I whispered. "The case, my team, my career."

"So what do you do?" Will said. He lifted my chin with his finger and looked into my eyes. "You pick up the pieces and you keep going."

"I just want it to be easy," I sighed. "I feel like I'm fighting until I break, and for what? So someone can sell me out to the witches and the department can shut my squad down? I've never had it easy, Will. It's not fucking fair."

"Of course it's not," he said. "But you'll manage it, because you're strong. You're one of the strongest people I've ever met."

Will slid his hand to the side of my face, and leaned in before I could pull myself together and stop him. Once his lips touched mine, I didn't particularly want to. He didn't hold any of the hesitation Lucas did, just an intense, needful embrace, like he was starving and I was the cure. I wrapped my arms around him and one of Will's hands went into my hair, pulling me flush against him. I floated, letting my hands dig into his back and pretending there was no reason why we shouldn't be together.

Will started to guide me toward the bank of sinks, his free hand feeling for the buttons of my shirt, and with the cold touch of his fingers on my stomach I dropped back into the real world, hard. "Stop. This would never work, Will."

"How do you know until we try?" He was breathing harder than I'd ever seen, and his pale face was flushed with color.

"I know. Believe me." I stepped back, and ran water into the sink to splash on my face. "Now I'm going to walk out, have Bryson take me home, and you and I will forget this ever happened."

Will gave me one of his darkling smiles, full of promise. "I don't think I can do that. Are you honestly saying you can?"

I looked at myself in the mirror, Will a shadow behind me. "I have to," I said. "It's complicated, Will."

"Complicated I can do," he said.

I shook my head. "I can't do this right now." I put my hand on the door. "Will . . . it's just . . . Right place, wrong time."

"Whatever helps you sleep at night," he said.

Twenty-three

"You're quiet," Bryson said the next morning as he shoveled scrambled eggs onto his plate. "You want some breakfast?"

"No," I said. I was back in work clothes, and I fidgeted with the onyx cuff links on my tailored tuxedo shirt.

"You want a stiff drink?" Bryson said, sprinkling cheese over his eggs, dousing them with ketchup, and shoving the entire mess into his mouth.

"No!" I snapped. "I just want to focus." The plan Bryson and I had decided on was a simple one: I would receive a fax from the "Commissioner"—that would be Fagin—telling me that I had to move the heartstone out of the evidence locker due to complications with Hartley's search warrant. I'd fax an order back that the thing be moved via the old bunker tunnel under the Plaza, at a specified time, to the central crime lab in the morgue building.

Fagin, Bryson, and I would be in the tunnel waiting at the specified time when the crooked cop showed up, ostensibly to shoot us in the heads and take the heartstone back for their Thelemite masters.

"What if a bunch of those Thelema witches show up?"

Bryson said, finishing his eggs and starting in on his hash browns and bacon.

"That's not going to happen," I said, more to reassure myself.

Bryson snorted. "Encouraging. You been honing those psychic powers, Wilder?"

"Look, David, you want the truth? This is my last resort and if it doesn't go off, we're screwed. And we'll probably be dead. Is that enough honesty for you?"

He swallowed his bacon. "Plenty. Now I've lost my appetite."

After our abortive breakfast, we drove into the lot at the Plaza, and I sat in Bryson's Taurus, counting down the minutes until I could follow him in. It had to look like we didn't arrive together.

I let seventeen minutes go by, watching the Halloween decorations flap in the wind and trying to keep my palms from sweating as the tension ratcheted up inside me.

Tonight was supposed to be a night of imaginary demons and ghouls meant to frighten away the real thing. Only Will, David, and I would have to look into the eyes of something really monstrous, someone who'd eaten out the heart of the SCS.

I got out of the car and walked across the lot, trying to ignore the chill in the air. Soon there would be a frost, a scrim of sheen on everything to hide the deadness underneath. The elevator made its groaning way to the basement just like every other day, and I took a deep breath as the doors rolled open.

"Lieutenant." Norris gave me his usual tight-lipped grimace. "Welcome back. Your messages have been forwarded to your extension."

"Thank you," I murmured, brushing past him. I had

myself on lockdown now, smiling and nodding and doing everything that I should be doing. I located Bryson at the coffee machine, out of the corner of my eye, and he didn't look back at me.

"Hey, Luna!" I jumped as someone clapped me on the shoulder. *Way to go, Wilder. Acting just as normal as can be.*

"Hey yourself, Javier. What's up?"

"We've been working the case," he said with a shrug. "Hitting a lot of dead ends. How about you, jefe? You find a new place to live? Any evidence on who set the fire?"

"Everything is moving forward," I said.

"Okay, well . . . you need anything, you just call me, all right? No one messes with my LT." He gave me a friendly punch on the shoulder and went back to his desk. Andy looked up at his arrival and waved at me.

Gods, what would I do if Zacharias or Javier walked out of that tunnel tonight? It had to be someone else. My instincts weren't that bad.

My eyes drifted to Kelly, hunched over the fax machine, poking and cursing. Kelly, who could move without scent or sound, who always looked at me like I was a steak and he was a Doberman.

I checked my watch. Almost ten, when Will had said he would send the fax. Kelly was just standing there, like a block of unfriendly granite.

"Hunter." I came to his side, tapping him on the arm. "Problem?"

"Goddamn paper jam," he muttered. "I was trying to send an expense report to HR."

"Good luck getting blood from that stone," I said. "I'm expecting a message . . . would you mind trying later?"

He glared down at me. "I guess you take priority, huh?"

"That's correct, Kelly."

"The paper is still jammed," he grunted, surly. I was starting to sweat under his gaze. Could he see the nerves, the deception coiled in my guts? What *was* Hunter Kelly, besides a bad cop who might be a hell of a lot worse than I'd imagined?

"Here." Annemarie shouldered her way to the fax machine with a fresh sheaf of paper. "You just have to reach up in there and pull the jam out. Good to have you back, ma'am."

"How are you holding up, Annemarie?" I asked as she reloaded the fax with paper. Five to ten. *Get out of the way, Annemarie.*

"Just fine, ma'am, and yourself?"

"All right," I said. "You get an appointment to talk to the counselor yet?"

"Sure did. I see her next week."

"Good," I said. "Take it easy." The fax whirred to life, a blocked number. Smart. I waited for the printout and then took it over to Bryson.

"David, a word?"

He goggled at me, and then got up. I walked him out of the bullpen, but still in full visibility of everyone. "Just play along," I said, bending close to his ear. "I want to make sure the mole knows this is important."

I read the fax aloud, standing up straight and projecting to the cheap seats. Sometimes it's not about subtlety—it's about the mark thinking that they're smarter than you. " 'This is to inform your staff that the item seized in reference to the Hartley case, numbered three-two-three-four-four-oh, must be removed from your storage facility no later than close of business today and remanded to the central crime laboratory.' "

"That thing will be a bitch to move," Bryson said, equally loud.

"We'll take it through the tunnel," I said. "No use trying to get it onto the elevator again."

I put the fax in Bryson's hand. "I have a meeting to go to."

He gave me a salute and walked back to his desk, laying the fax conspicuously in his in-box. Bryson was less of a screwup than his pink tie and yellow shirt would lead a person to believe. Now I had to leave, and find a way to fill the next eight hours.

"Have a nice day," Norris told me on the way out. I flipped a hand at him, trying to look unconcerned.

My last stop was Pete's office, and I came in through the rear door, the one that led to the hallway and the restrooms. "Pete," I said.

He leapt up from his rolling stool, scattering DNA scans all over the floor. "Hex me, Lieutenant. Why are you sneaking around here?"

"I have my reasons," I said.

"Would those be more of the reasons I'm not supposed to know about?"

"They would indeed, Pete. Now, tonight after shift change I need you to lock up the heartstone and make sure it's well hidden. Put it in with those storage bins we confiscated from the weekend Satanists. And if anyone asks you, it was moved to the central lab."

Pete raised his eyebrows. "After this, I better get to know what these wacky schemes are about. The suspense is killing me."

"You will," I promised him, in a manner that rang hollow even to me.

"Uh-huh," Pete said, picking up his slides. "Believe that when I see it."

I backed out of his office and rode the elevator upward, trying to ignore the sinking feeling in my bones. It didn't go away.

That day, I drifted from place to place. I bought a paper and looked at ads for condos, none of which I could afford even on my new salary. I ate lunch in the Devere Diner, with the insane notion that it might be the last time I got to enjoy their bacon cheeseburgers.

Mostly, I found a bench on the waterfront, near a crumbling warehouse and another crumbling warehouse that had been turned into a crackhouse, and thought. I thought about the SCS mole, about Lucas, about Will.

What to do about the pair of them? Lucas was completely wrong for me, a fugitive, a killer when he had to be. But he was loyal. He was who he said he was, and none other. Will had four hundred years of baggage, and he was just like me—abrasive, cocksure, and couldn't censor himself to save his life.

Neither of them were what I should be thinking of. I drove the LTD through the fading light, gobs of children straggling along the sidewalk in their too-large costumes, clutching bags of candy. A few adults in costume shepherded them, and the clubs along Cannery were open early, dry ice sending swirls of fog into the street to be stained gold and red in the last remnants of sunlight.

I parked at the morgue, passed through the metal detector, and took the elevator down to the service level.

Fagin was waiting for me, leaning against the wall, an

unlit cigarette between his lips. "I used to be cool, you know," he said. "The fifties, the sixties, especially the seventies. Chain-smoking cops were very popular in the seventies."

I took the cigarette from between his lips and tucked it into the breast pocket of his suit, next to his white handkerchief. "Thanks for that trip down memory lane. You still in to help me with this?"

"Can't do anything else," Fagin said. "We're close to the Maiden. I'm close to dying. I can put up with you a little bit longer if you can put up with me."

"I suddenly feel so much better about not making out with you in the men's room."

A smile ghosted his face. "Then I'm glad I stuck around. Your peace of mind is important to me, doll."

The fire exit banged open and Bryson appeared, holding a police-issue shotgun. "I was the last one in the squad room," he said. "And I snuck out through the emergency door. We ready to lock and load?"

"I think you're ready enough for all three of us, cowboy," Fagin said, doing a cursory check of his sidearm before sliding it back into his shoulder holster.

I checked the clip in my Sig. Full, as usual, with a bullet chambered. I stuck it back in its holster with the safety off and unstrapped my holdout weapon from my ankle, checked the cylinders of the .38, and snapped them back into place.

We descended the stairs to the tunnel in silence, like three pallbearers in a medieval funeral, lowering themselves into the catacombs to spend the requisite time with the dead.

The lights were controlled by a master breaker on the

morgue side, and I threw it, bathing the three of us in the red glow of emergency spots.

"Yup," Bryson said, racking the shotgun. "I was right. I'm in one of the seven hells."

I shushed him. "Wait by the door, David, in case they make a run for it. Will and I will wait a little further down." I paced a few dozen feet down the tunnel and knocked the lock off the storage cage. I stepped into the shadows, positioning myself behind a pallet of K rations that had probably been sitting there since before I was born.

Will stood next to me in the dark, slightly behind and to the right so that I cleared his field of fire. I listened to him breathe, steady as if he were sitting in a movie theater.

"It's been twenty minutes," he said. "Where the hell are they?"

"Relax," I murmured. "They want to make sure we're actually moving the stone."

"And if they've figured out we're not?"

"Has anyone ever told you that you're a big fat pessimist, Fagin?"

"I'm not—" he started, but my ears picked up the faraway sound of footsteps on concrete.

"Shut up. Someone's here."

A figure came toward us in the murky light, sticking to the shadows along the far wall. They walked with a measured step, toe-heel, trying their best to be quiet. A click, and a thin beam illuminated the tunnel from a police-issue penlight.

The figure moved past us, their heart and breath speeding up as their light caught nothing but bare walls, rusted pipes, and old prohibitions against smoking in the bomb shelter.

I pulled my Sig off my waist, the trigger guard cold against my finger. The figure in the tunnel stopped moving, and let out a frustrated sigh.

"Looking for something?" I said, and raised the gun.

The figure let out a shriek and spun around, the light dancing crazily off the walls. A slice of shadow and bright illuminated a pale, slender face and a coil of red hair. "Lieutenant Wilder?" said Annemarie. "Agent Fagin? What . . . what are y'all doing down here?"

All of the air stole out of my lungs, and my gun dipped a fraction. "It was you," I whispered.

"Me what?" Annemarie said. Under the red light, her eyes were wide and black, a sick parody of daemon eyes.

"You're the one who tried to have Luna killed," Fagin said at my shoulder. "You're down here looking for the heartstone. Now that you have all of your answers, I've got a question for you: Where is the Maiden?"

Annemarie backed away from us, shaking her head. "I don't know what you're talking about, ma'am, but you've got it wrong. I heard voices down here and I saw the light was out, so I came down to have a look. That's all. . . ."

Bryson stepped away from his concealment in the shadow of the morgue exit and put the shotgun to Annemarie's neck. "Far enough, Annie."

She flinched, and dropped her gaze to the floor. Her hands slowly came up, the right traveling away from her waist. From her gun.

"You shot Brad Morgan," I said. "Before he could tell me what he knew. You told the Thelemites where I lived. And you were going to try and shoot your way out of here."

Sickness and vertigo crashed over me like a wave. This wasn't like finding out Kelly or Norris or someone I would have pegged as dirty was passing information out of the squad. I'd eaten lunches with Annemarie. We'd talked about our ex-boyfriends. Laughed together. She'd smiled into my face and the whole time she'd been trying to get me killed.

Annemarie's jaw set, her hands like small pink birds in the dim light. "So what if I was?"

"Hex it, Annemarie, I was your *friend*!" I bellowed. "Why would you do this? Money?"

She laughed, her thin shoulders shaking. "Luna, you're bein' a little bit pedestrian here, don't you think? Why would I risk a good job for *money*?"

"Then what?" Fagin said, calm and still as a tree, his gun barrel never wavering. I wished I could be so calm.

"That's really none of your business," Annemarie said.

"You came into my squad and poisoned it," I said. "So help me, if you don't tell me why, I will send you to prison in the general population, and I will tell everyone from the warden to the prettiest prison bitch in the joint that you used to be a cop. You won't last a week."

Annemarie flinched. Fagin tightened his firing stance. "I think you'd better tell her, Detective Marceaux."

"Thelema can be learned," said Annemarie. "The sisters instruct me and I help them out." She met my eyes, and there was something in her face that I had never seen before, a blurring of the features, something that my were recognized as off from normal. I'd seen the same thing in hard-core tweakers, and religious fanatics. It was desire, so bright it burned from the inside out.

"I don't understand," I said. My lips felt numb, and my words echoed from a long way off. *Annemarie. Annemarie sold me out.*

"They have so many things to teach me," Annemarie

said. "Workings, wonders to show me, curses for those that seek to harm me. Blood doesn't matter . . . just will."

"You cursed me?" Anger poured from my hindbrain, that kind of cold, clinical rage that precedes the phase. My monster wanted out, wanted its chance at the woman in front of me. "Well, I got news for you, Annemarie—whatever those tattooed nutcases told you, you have to have the blood to be a witch. Fact of biology. Oh, and you couldn't curse a turnip, you two-faced, incompetent, sneaky little magick-whore."

I was yelling by the time I finished, and I felt my eyes and teeth begin to phase as the were fed on my rage like carrion. Bryson flinched, and Fagin took a step away from me, but Annemarie was placid.

"The Maiden provides," she said. "She's forever and eternal, and I will be touched by her." Her hand dipped, and it all happened inside of a second. "And now I'm going to make her proud of me."

"Gun!" I bellowed, as Annemarie swung her arm back and knocked Bryson in the face. He discharged a shotgun round into the ceiling and cement dust fell like snow.

Annemarie drew her pistol and I heard the fall of the firing pin at the same time I realized that I was just standing there, a target big as a house.

The H & K boomed, the muzzle flash bright as the sun in the dim tunnel, and Fagin slammed into me, knocking me into the mesh of the storage cage and then to the ground. He grunted and jerked, and the hot, wet scent of blood filled my nostrils.

"Shit," Fagin said.

"You hit?" I grunted from under him.

"Not bad," he said, voice wound tight with pain. "Missed my heart."

"Huh. Didn't know you had one."

Annemarie turned on Bryson, taking a firing stance. Bryson scrambled to his feet, his nose gushing blood. He'd never get the shotgun up in time—

"Annemarie!" I shouted. I wriggled out from under Fagin and got up to one knee.

"Make another movement and I'm going to put two in his head," she said. "Somehow, I don't think the world at large will mourn the passing of David Bryson." Her hands tightened on the butt of her pistol. "But you-all might."

"Jesus, Annie," Bryson said. He was quivering all over, sweat radiating in rank waves from his body, mingled with pure base fear. Bryson thought he was going to die. "Is this really worth it? Really? You don't want to kill me."

"Actually, I do," she said. "You're easily the most irritating man I've ever met."

I plucked at the leg of my slacks, drawing it up, praying to anyone listening that Annemarie wouldn't notice.

"Please," Bryson said, in a small voice. "I'm sorry."

"Not as sorry as you're gonna be when they deliver you to the gates of Hell," Annemarie said. "You three dead will be just what my sisters need, and they'll have to take me in."

"You," I said to her, "are one deluded bitch."

Annemarie whipped her head around, snarling at me in fury, "I told you to be quiet!"

I closed my hand around my holdout pistol and pulled it free, shooting upward, three taps. The .38 made a boom in the closed space, echoes rolling like we were caught in a summer storm.

Annemarie wavered, staggered, her gun arm hanging uselessly at her side. "You shot me," she said, matter-of-factly, eyes clouding. "Why'd you go and do a thing like that?"

She collapsed, her legs buckling like a cheap skyscraper in an earthquake.

Bryson ran his hand down his face, palm coming away with a sheen of sweat. "Hex me. *Hex* me. I am so beyond too old for this shit it's not even funny."

"Check on Will," I ordered, tucking the .38 back into its holster. I got up, my own joints stiff as if I'd been out in the cold, and knelt by Annemarie.

One of my hollow-point rounds had torn into her shoulder, ripped the ligaments under the shoulder blade clean out, and her arm twitched involuntarily, the body's feeble attempt to say, *I am not dead.*

The second round had gone wide, tearing a gash in her sleeve but little more. She choked, and I saw where the third bullet had gone. "Oh, gods," I whispered.

There was a dark island of blood on Annemarie's crisp shirt, just below her rib cage, the entrance wound lost amid the slow creep of black, vital blood from her abdomen.

"Gut-shot," Annemarie sighed. "Hell of a way to go, ma'am."

I tore off my jacket and pressed it against the wound, but she swatted me away. "I don't want it. I did my job. You leave me alone." Her eyelids fluttered with the beginning of shock. "The Maiden provides. She opens the gates for all of us to walk in paradise."

"You are so stupid," I whispered. "You threw your life away for nothing, Annemarie. *Nothing.* You don't have the blood, and you'll never have magick. Why do any of this? Why come after *me*?"

"You know more . . ." Fluid bubbled in her chest, and she gasped in pain. "You know more than you think you do, ma'am. My sisters fear what you might see."

I took her by the shoulders and lifted her face close to mine, the dribble of blood from between her lips a tattoo on her skin in the red light. "What do you mean, Annemarie? For everything Hexed and holy, stop the riddles and just tell me."

"It wasn't for nothing, ma'am," she whispered, her eyes showing white, fading. "My death . . . I kept you down here . . . long enough. I gave my sisters time."

My fingers tightening as her breathing slowed, I shook her. "They're not your sisters. They used you. Tell me what they're doing, Annemarie!"

"Open the gate . . ." Her voice was barely anything, now. It could have been a ghost on my shoulder. "Open the gate and walk in paradise. . . ."

Her body gave a little jerk under my hands, and then she was gone, limp and still.

Will crouched next to me, blood droplets on his snowy shirt. "I hate to be the insensitive one here, but what do you think she meant by *I kept you down here long enough*?"

My ears picked up noise from the SCS end of the tunnel, and I stood, scooping up my Sig from the floor as I ran. "I think we're gonna find out in short order."

Bryson, Will, and I crested the stairs and I bolted through the empty office, toward the direction of the sound. It was screaming, a hopeless, droning sort of screaming without any sense behind it.

Pete lay on the floor outside the evidence locker, clawing at his face and arms, screaming, his eyes rolled back into his head. "Pete!" I grabbed him, holding his arms down at his sides. A working crackled around his skin, the same flat, cold Thelemite magick that I couldn't Path.

"Get them away from me!" Pete shrieked. "Get them off!"

"Stop it!" I shouted as he thrashed. There was no turning him back from what the Thelemites had made him see, at least not with my voice and my hands alone.

"Luna, he's gonna check himself out," Bryson said, standing well back from Pete's convulsions. "He's like a goddamn hooked fish."

"Crap," I hissed. "Crap, crap, crap." When I had broken Grace Hartley's circle I'd touched the physical working, the earth that gave the binding shape. This working was on a living person, coursing through Pete's blood. . . .

I fumbled my folding knife out of my pocket. "I am so sorry," I told Pete, and then drove it into his shoulder, the soft spot under the collarbone. Blood blossomed at the spot and I clapped my hand onto it, willing the magick worked into Pete's blood to come to me.

The first wave hit me, made me fang out and double over as the pangs of the phase hit. Will stepped in. "Luna . . ."

Cold and smooth, like mercury on my senses, the magick flowed. I felt myself begin to phase, the twinge in my lower back and the cracking of my joints that accompanies the shift from woman to wolf. I snarled at Will, "You might wanna back off."

I held the phase back, fought as hard against it as I ever could, but I did not push the magick away. Pete's life depended on it.

He stopped convulsing with a gasp, finally, and then groaned. "What . . . Did someone stab me?" He sat up, pressing a hand over his knife wound. "Seven hells, that hurts."

I floated for a time, feeling my limbs twitch as the magick ran through my nerves with no outlet, and then Fagin was over me, cupping my face in his hands, pulling my eyelids back, checking my pulse. "Come on, doll. Don't you go napping on me."

"Just Pathed," I muttered. "Not dead."

Fagin helped me sit up. "Take her easy. We're fine. We're all fine."

"I'm not fine," Pete said. "I'm stabbed!"

"Man up, lab rat," Fagin said. "Your lieutenant just saved your life." He helped me up, brushing his suit pants off. "The Thelemites got you pretty good. What did they want?"

Bryson grabbed a rag out of Pete's office and applied pressure to Pete's shoulder.

"I don't know," Pete sighed. "It was that Hartley woman and two I didn't recognize, and one of them hit me with a working and before I knew it . . ." He shuddered. "Cockroaches. All over me. I hate cockroaches."

"You're all right now," I said, rubbing my forehead. The were retreated, leaving me sore as if I'd just run five miles at top speed. "Bryson, call a bus for Pete and let's figure out what they were trying to do."

"Luna." Will stood at the door of the locker, his face drawn. "Pete may be fine, but the rest of us may not be."

I stood up and looked into the locker, hoping that I wouldn't see the gap in between the neatly labeled containers on the floor, knowing I was going to anyway, and feeling a sick drop in my stomach. The gap was there, only a little dust to show something had ever filled the space.

The heartstone was gone.

Twenty-four

The aftermath of trauma is always slow-moving, cold, nothing like you expect. I called the team back in, plus an IA investigator and CSU team to deal with Annemarie's body. I couldn't look at the blood-speckled sheet when the EMTs carried her up the stairs from the tunnel. There was nothing left of her now, just bloody bones.

Another set of EMTs checked out Pete and declared his need for a hospital and stitches. I let him go.

It was quiet then, just me, my detectives, and Will. They were all looking at me like I had the answers. All I had was a headache and a sick, empty hole in my guts.

"I know we've lost someone," I said. "And you're probably all feeling . . ." *Annemarie's eyes, staring up at nothing. Annemarie's smile, as she drew her gun to kill me.*

"This wasn't supposed to happen," I started again. "We were supposed to be a team, and Annemarie broke that trust. I shot her. It's not how things are supposed to go, but here we are." I looked up at their faces. They ranged from grim, Kelly, to sorrowful, Zacharias, and every range in between.

"I need your help, guys," I said. I wanted to put my head down on my desk and sob, but I didn't let my voice break. "We've got a real situation here. If we don't close this case, the commissioner is going to shut us down."

A rush of murmurs broke out and I held up my hands. "I know. I should have told you. But now all that matters is that you're my team and I need help. We still have a city to look after and right now things are going badly. I know that you feel betrayed. I know that you just want to go home or go get drunk or hug your cat, but I need you to stick with me a while longer. I need us to be a squad for one more night."

Silence, for a long minute. I waited for them to walk out, which was exactly what I deserved after the cluster-fuck of today.

Batista stepped forward. "For a start, Lieutenant, how about you fill us in on what's going on?"

"Thank you," I said, giving Batista a grateful nod. "I'm sorry I had to keep all of you in the dark, but it had to happen."

"Doesn't matter, ma'am," said Zacharias. "But you be straight with us from now on. I don't think that's too much to ask."

"Fair enough," I said, feeling a tiny bloom of hope grow. "Here's the deal: There's a sect of witches who have gotten hold of our heartstone, and that's bad news for us."

Zacharias stuck his hand up. I rolled my eyes. "You don't have to ask permission, Andy."

"To what purpose, ma'am?" He shrugged. "They've got the stone—so what?"

"It's a huge amplifier," Fagin said. "If they channeled a working around it . . ."

"What working?" said Kelly. He stood at the back of the group and his eyes kept darting toward the door.

Open the gate, Annemarie had whispered to me. *Open*

the gate and walk in paradise. It had seemed crazy at the time, in the heat of the moment. Just the ramblings of a fanatic who believed her own bullshit.

Now, it didn't seem quite so crazy. "A devil's doorway," I said. Kelly started like I'd poked him with a pin.

"Devil's doorways aren't big enough or lasting enough to do any damage," he said. Will and I both swiveled to look at him, along with the rest of the detectives.

"And you know this *how*?" I demanded, crossing my arms.

"I'm a warlock," Kelly said, plainly. When we all just stared at him, he added, "A witch versed in battle magick?" He glared at Zacharias, Bryson, and Batista like he wished he was working painful spells on them that moment.

"Anybody got a problem with that?" I asked.

"Explains why you're such a cheerful bastard," Bryson said.

Kelly just glowered. "A devil's doorway is a tiny fray in the space between," he said. "Big enough for a single body or maybe two to slip through."

"Or three," I said, thinking of the selkies.

"Okay, stop me if I'm off the course here," said Bryson. "But if this heartstone amplifies a working, wouldn't it make a devil's doorway that's, you know, unusually large?"

"You can't rip the fabric of the realms," said Kelly. "It's not the same as magick on our side. You can just push it aside for a second, like a waterfall. For a rip, something would have to come through and wound it, tear it apart. . . ."

Something else Annemarie had said to me, that I'd put down to the last words of somebody who wasn't too stable to begin with, lit up my mind. I dug into Bryson's desk and drew out a city map, grabbing a marker from his pen holder and drawing an X over Garden Hill Cemetery, the place where Lucas and I had seen Wiskachee, the hunger god riding Lucas's body, reborn, tearing himself out of the aether and nearly taking me with him.

I drew a line out from the X, a line that cut across downtown Nocturne, through the block where Mikado was located, through Milton Manners's shop, and out to sea, only a few miles from the beach at my cottage.

"There is a tear," I said. "When Lucas and I caught up with Wiskachee, his corporeal body died, but the tear he used to come through didn't." I stabbed the marker on the line. "That's how they've been bringing things through in such numbers. That's what they need the heartstone for. There's something big coming. Too big for their will alone."

"I'll be damned," Kelly said, stroking his chin.

"You think it wouldn't work?" I snapped, perhaps defensively.

"No," Kelly rumbled. "Just kind of wish I'd thought of it."

"I'm going to ignore how creepy you are for the moment," I said. "Our number-one priority should be finding these Thelemites and—"

The phone in my office shrilled, and I ignored it, but it kept ringing. I stalked over and snatched it up. "What? What is it?"

"Luna? It's Captain Delahunt."

I paused at the voice of my old SWAT commander over the line. "What's going on, Captain?"

"Turn on your TV," he said. "Channel One."

I fumbled for the remote and snapped on the small set sitting on the file cabinet in the bullpen. We didn't have

HDTV with fiber-optic integrated like most task forces. We were lucky to have cable.

NC-1, the local news channel, was showing a shaky cam view of downtown, shot from a helicopter. "As you can see," the anchor faded in, "the destruction is widespread, and SWAT is on the scene attempting to contain the threat." Smoke was rising in a thin plume, and ruptured water mains sprayed high into the air. In the low light, an enormous shape moved through the ramshackle buildings of Waterfront, leaving a wake of broken brick and smashed cars as it loped along on legs like trees. "It's unknown at this time whether this is an act of terrorism or a supernatural occurrence . . . ," the reporter droned on. "But the creature who appeared on the thirteen-hundred block of Cannery Street this Halloween evening seems unstoppable."

"What the fuck is that?" Bryson said.

"Captain," I said into the phone. "What the fuck is it?"

"We were hoping you could tell us," he said. "This thing just showed up, out of nowhere, and started doing a Hulk number on five square blocks. Rapid response is in the shit, Lieutenant. The SCS needs to step in here. You're supposed to be equipped to deal with the freaks of nature."

I looked back at the screen, in time to watch it fuzz and blur as the thing flung a car bumper at the news chopper.

"We're rolling," I said to Delahunt. "Okay," I said, hanging up the phone. "Batista, Kelly, Bryson. You're with Will and me. We're going to go down to Waterfront and back up SWAT."

"What about me?" Andy said, with a long face.

"You stay here and figure out where the Thelemites

took the heartstone," I said. "Dig into property records, financials, whatever you have to." I checked the clip on my Sig and chambered a fresh round. "As soon as we deal with this critter, we're going to bust them and hopefully ruin their day."

I didn't say the second part aloud: that we'd bust them and make the world safe for puppies and rainbows only if that thing rampaging through Waterfront wasn't exactly where the Thelemites wanted us to be, to meet some manner of a horrible death trap.

As I was jogging after Fagin to his car, my BlackBerry rang. "What?" I snapped, sure it was Andy with yet another inane question.

"Luna, have you seen what's going on?" Lucas's voice was low, controlled, but I could hear the fear creeping in.

"We're headed there now," I said, glancing at Will. He started the car without comment, but I knew he was listening. It's what I'd be doing.

"I need to see you," said Lucas. "Something's off about this whole thing. Daemon creatures, that codex, Cerberus. It's bad mojo in the city tonight, Luna."

I slid into the passenger seat of Will's car. I'd been so careful to keep them apart, so guilt-ridden over the whole thing.

I had enough guilt to push me down into the earth. I put the BlackBerry back to my ear. I was through with the angstful high-school crap. "Meet me at the scene," I said to Lucas. "Thirteen-hundred block, Cannery Street."

If my team could deal with rogue witches trying to pull something through a temporal rift, I sure hoped they could deal with me seeing a wanted man.

Will downshifted, taking the curve on Cannery with a squeal of rubber as I hung up. "Who was that?"

"Lucas Kennuka," I said, looking ahead toward the plumes of smoke and steam rising through the night. We had to be over the line of the tear now and I realized that I could feel it, a chill on my skin, raw power seeping into the air like a chemical leak. If I didn't know better I'd put it down to edginess, tension over my job stress, but it was magick, trailing its fingers along the back of my neck.

"The guy who shot me," Will said, tightening his hands on the steering wheel. We were coming up on the police cordon, the familiar carnival of red and blue on the tops of patrol cars turning the street into a grotesque parody of the parties going on in the nearby clubs.

"Yes," I said. "The very same."

"I don't like that, Luna," Will said, nudging his door open. I got out of the Mustang and looked at him across the roof.

"If this thing is as bad as the selkies and the basilisks or, hells forbid, that daemon, we're going to need his help. Whatever wounded man-pride you're nursing—get over it." I marched over to the cordon and flashed my shield at the nearest uniform.

He waved me on. "Captain Delahunt's over there, Lieutenant," he said. "Never thought I'd see a day when I was happy the freak squad showed up."

"Your comments are appreciated," I said, making sure to give him a bump with my shoulder as I crossed the scene to the captain.

"It's in the alleys, back in those tenements," he said, pointing. A loud roar floated back from the skeletal brick buildings, rattling what little glass remained in their windows. "We tried flashbangs, tear gas, plain old M4 rounds, but nothing's denting it, and it's getting pissed."

"You three, hang back with SWAT," I told Batista, Bryson, and Kelly. "Will and I will go get a look."

"I can help," Kelly said. "Give me some time and I can work an offensive spell to contain it." He pulled out a shaving kit, and drew out a caster and a piece of chalk, going to one knee. Delahunt and the uniforms regarded all of us as if we'd sprouted secondary, shrunken heads.

Kelly looked to me, hesitating. He was waiting to see if I'd take his side. Could I really afford the fallout if his spell failed? Workings that went wrong would be a hundred times worse than the thing down the alley.

Another shattering roar rocked me. Then again, I could be wrong. "Do it, and make it fast," I said. "We need to get it locked down before it does any more damage."

Kelly complied, and started drawing on the pavement. "There's just one thing, LT."

How did I know that I wasn't going to like this? "Spit it out, Kelly."

"Someone has to drive it toward my working. Get it close enough for the binding marks to grab hold."

Will looked at me. "I'm game," he said.

"Oh no," I said. "You don't get to run in there by yourself and play the hero."

"I can't die," he said, stripping off his jacket. "You can. It's not even worth talking about."

I grabbed Will by the tie and yanked his face level with mine. "If you want any sort of shot with me, Fagin, you can cut out the white-knight bull crap right now. If we don't stop this thing, there's going to be a lot of dead people for our trouble. I'm not going to sit on my ass and hope for the best, Will. I'm out in front, and you'd better just get used to it now, or leave me alone."

"Lieutenant?" the same surly uniform shouted to me from the cordon.

I saw Lucas's thin form standing behind the tape. "Let him through," I called. "He's with us."

Lucas ambled over, obviously nervous with so many police around. Fortunately, with the ruckus from up ahead, no one was paying one skinny Wendigo the slightest bit of attention.

"I'll go with you," Lucas said. "What's the move?"

"Get it close enough to Kelly so he can take it down," I said, not looking at him. I was looking at Will. His face hardened, as some internal battle played out. I knew what my response to such a challenge would be—I'd walk away, do it on my own.

I didn't want Will to walk away, I realized. I wanted him here.

"Please," I said. "We . . . I . . . need you here."

Lucas made a soft sound in the back of his throat. I prayed that he'd understand.

Will tightened his fists, and then lowered his hands consciously, like he'd wrestled something huge back under control. "Fine," he said. "Let's go say hello to this thing."

Lucas walked toward the sounds without a word, and I walked abreast of him, Will slightly behind. Lucas's face was like a thundercloud threatening to burst into a storm, but at least they were both with me. Which was good. Because much as it hurt to admit, right then I needed the both of them.

Lucas and Will followed me into the maze of alleys, away from the cacophony of light, into the dark.

Twenty-five

Wreckage strewed my path, as if something had simply forced its way through the alley, something twice the size of anything that fit.

Great. That made me feel a lot better about being down here with just Will, Lucas, and my were to keep us alive.

A shadow loomed ahead of us, offset by the small fires that had sprung up as downed wires and ruptured gas lines colluded. It was hunched over, a mighty puffing sound emanating from it.

"If that is a dragon," said Lucas, "you can count me the hell out. I didn't sign up for any *Lord of the Rings* shit."

"If it's a dragon? Do you even listen to yourself?" Will said. "Dragons are like vampires—they don't exist."

"Both of you shut up!" I hissed. The corner of the alley was close, the thing just beyond the bend. A crunch and a shriek of metal reached my ears.

I pressed myself against the slimy brick of the alley wall and crept forward, the mottled back of the thing sliding into view. It was at least fifteen feet tall, crouched over a metal trash bin, snuffling. It appeared to be chewing on pieces of the bin. It also appeared to have teeth the size of my forearm.

"What *is* that?" Lucas whispered. He was close enough that I could feel the cool air coming off him.

"I have no idea," I said, watching the thing stand to its full height on dumpy, bowed legs. It was wearing a tattered skirt that appeared to be made out of awning cloth, but otherwise its gray-green skin gleamed in the firelight. A thick face with close-set black eyes swung from side to side and flat nostrils scented the air. A pair of teeth pushed over its lips, yellowed and pitted but still big enough to turn me into a crudité.

Lucas let out a breath beside me. "I haven't had a lot of experience with critters from the netherworld, but that thing is a gods-damned troll."

The troll whipped its head toward us and let out a roar that shook the ground under my feet. Then it picked up the remains of the Dumpster and flung it toward Lucas and me.

"I concur. Move!" I shouted, pulling him back around the corner. The twisted metal sailed past and went through the wall opposite with a crunch that sounded like a hundred bones breaking.

"All right," Lucas said, shifting with a snap of moisture against my cheek. "No more chances."

I realized belatedly that we were one intrepid adventurer short. "Where's Will?"

Lucas flowed back and forth, his pure silver eyes tracking over the alley. "Gone."

"*Dammit,*" I growled. "Will!"

The troll lumbered closer, and looked down at us, its chest heaving. It rumbled something that sounded like rocks cracking together, pointing a finger the size of my thigh at me.

"We don't want to hurt you," I said. "We just need you to leave, preferably with the rest of the block intact."

The troll reflected for a moment, picking an entire chicken carcass out from between two granite-colored molars, and then it shook its head with a roar, jabbing its finger at me and spouting more invective. I may not speak troll, but I can tell when I'm being cursed at.

"Hey!" I shouted. "Hey, settle down!"

The troll reared back and its massive fist came sweeping down. It passed through Lucas's misty limbs but grazed me, throwing me backward onto my ass.

From my lopsided vantage, I spied Will, clambering up a half-ruined fire escape behind the troll. "Don't do it," I murmured, as I lay there trying to get my air back.

Will stepped out into the air, falling straight down and latching onto the troll's back, grabbing the few wisps of moss-colored hair still riding its lumpy skull.

The troll screamed, lashing and twirling like a ride in a nightmare carnival. Will held on grimly. "Go!" he yelled. "I've got it!"

"Idiot," Lucas hissed, his Wendigo voice sinister and scraping at my ear. I tended to agree with him.

"Let go, Fagin!" I yelled. "You're just pissing it off!"

Will didn't have a choice a moment later—the troll reached back and with remarkable accuracy plucked Fagin from its neck and sent him sailing through the third-story window of the nearby tenement building. There was a sick body-meets-brick thud, and then silence.

"We split up," I told Lucas, looking at the troll, which had a distinctly annoyed gleam in its beady eyes. "We circle through the back alleys and bring it to the cordon."

"Fine," Lucas said, and leapt up, landing a good ten

feet away, bounding off the walls and the ground as if he weighed less than the air. The troll followed him, trying to bat at Lucas like he was milkweed.

"Ugly!" I shouted at it, waving my arms. It grunted and turned on me. "That's right," I said, hoping I sounded encouraging. "You want to chase something, don'tcha, big fella? Well, come on. Fetch."

I took off running, pouring all of my strength into the sprint. Down twisting alleys, overhung with disused wires, filled up with garbage and the detritus of lives lived in poverty, past abandoned tenements with doors like mouths and windows like blind eyes, skidding and turning until I'd lost count, always winding back toward the cordon, and Kelly.

The troll kept behind me, the narrow spaces between the abandoned buildings giving it trouble. I heard crashing and the screech of rebar as I rounded what should be the last corner, and almost smacked into a solid brick wall.

"Hex me," I said, the words coming out soft and meek. There was no exit from this end of the block, just more tenements, marching in their endless slumped line down Cannery Street until they terminated at the water.

The troll came lumbering, jabbering at me in its earsplitting language.

"Buddy, I wish I could help you; I really do," I said. I kept myself on the balls of my feet, watching the ungainly hands that could crush a compact car.

The troll picked up a dislodged bathtub and flung it at me, and I dropped, rolling to the side as ceramic shards split the air where my head had been.

"This is in no way productive!" I yelled at it. "I am not a Whac-A-Mole game!"

It let out a loud chuffing, covering me in breath that smelled like the inside of a bar bathroom after St. Patrick's Day, and bared its teeth.

Great. At least it thought I was funny.

I ducked another volley of debris from the troll, trying to find a way out of the gods-damned blind alley. There was none. The walls around me were smooth and windowless, and the troll blocked my only potential exit.

I had my Sig; maybe I could just shoot and scare it off. Its hide, though, looked like it would bounce normal bullets right off, and potentially back into me. I drew anyway, drawing down on a spot between the troll's eyes.

"Back off of me," I warned it. "I'll use this."

The troll's face crumpled in rage and it let out a bellow, charging straight for me. The ground jumped and I felt myself fall, one round discharging and impacting with the troll's shoulder.

I was right—a small dimple appeared in its skin, and that was it. It slapped at itself like it had been stung by a bee, and then ran at me again.

Crap. I was going to be a grease spot on the wall in three more seconds. I could try to get out of the way, risk being trampled underfoot . . .

The troll raised its fists and gave a war cry, high-pitched and earsplitting. Watching it bear down on me like a runaway Sherman tank, I got an idea that most days I would classify as *insane* and even now seemed a little improbable.

I stayed rooted to the spot as the troll closed the distance—three steps, two steps, one. As it barreled forward, lowering its shoulder and lunging at me, I went low and to the side, curling myself into a ball, covering my head and my vital bits.

The troll windmilled, trying to stop, skidded on the wet pavement, and went crashing through the alley wall, raining plaster and insulation around it. It fell, tangled in wire and pipe like a huntsman's net, screaming in fury.

I sprang up from my crouch. The troll was facedown and I planted one foot in the crook of its knee, the second on where its kidneys would be, and my last step on its neck, before I jumped down in front of its smushed-up face and took off running again, through trailing plastic and moldy furniture and the wrecked walls of the old tenement.

A stitch was developing in my side, from the running and the adrenaline, and the were howled in my head, begging to be let free to dance with the biggest predator it had ever encountered.

I saw the front door, half off its hinges, leading me out onto Cannery a few blocks down from the cordon. I practically fell through it as the earth began to shake again, the troll in hot pursuit. It was a tough bastard—I had to give it that.

A spotlight from the SWAT helicopter picked me up and I kept running, because my life depended on it. The troll burst through the front of the tenement and out onto the sidewalk, yelling and gesticulating.

"Kelly!" I screamed. "It's coming!"

The cordon was a hundred yards away, seventy, thirty. I saw Kelly standing in the center of an intricate chalk drawing, unlike the working circles I was familiar with. Power shimmered around him and the circle grew three dimensions, an extension of his power.

He was yelling something at me, which turned out to be, "Get out of the way!" I cut right, rolling over the hood of a squad car and landing hard on my shoulder, as the troll powered down on Kelly.

Kelly raised his hands and the troll stopped dead as the tendrils of the working flowed outward, wrapping the troll like a spider wraps a bug. It wavered for a moment, and then fell over with a crash, eyes rolling up in its head. Kelly stayed where he was, the lines of power from his working snapping and dancing as he manipulated them to tighten even further around the troll's prone figure.

I stood up, the adrenaline running out of me. Now I just hurt. Everywhere.

"What do you suggest?" Captain Delahunt said, as his team trained their M4 rifles on the troll.

"Tranquilizers," I said. "Lots of them."

The troll was groaning, mumbling to itself. It almost sounded like it was saying, "Stupid, stupid, stupid," which is probably exactly what I would have said, were I in its position.

Kelly firmed up the trailing ends of his working and then lowered his hands, a few beads of sweat gleaming on his forehead. "It'll hold for now."

"You did good," I said, clapping him on the shoulder. Bryson and Batista were watching the troll warily, but with the excitement of small boys looking at race cars.

"That is the biggest goddamn thing I've ever seen walking under its own power," Bryson said. "It would make a hell of a linebacker."

Batista just shook his head. "What did it want, Lieutenant?"

"I don't know," I said, looking at the troll. It was quivering now, with cold or fear. Seeing it so humbled, I felt sort of bad for it. I would have felt worse if it hadn't tried to eat me, though.

Bryson pointed. "Looks like your boyfriends came through okay."

Lucas and Will appeared from out of the wreckage, Will limping heavily and Lucas looking like he always did, with only a few streaks of dust to indicate he'd been anywhere near Trollapalooza.

I jogged over to them, slowing to a walk when pain stabbed me hard in the side. Lucas's stare was fixed on the troll. "What will you do with Big Ugly?"

I pursed my lips at the troll. "We can't leave it here."

"Kill it," said Will without hesitation. "It's dangerous."

"Will, it was terrified and hungry. I'm not killing it for doing what comes naturally. If it came to that I'd have to kill *you*."

"Nah, that's extreme," said Lucas. "Maybe one of those shock collars and a couple of training classes for the agent here."

"Kid, you do *not* want to start down that road with me," Fagin warned.

"Good gods, will the two of you knock it off?" I demanded. "You're worse than tigers in the zoo. The female of the species is not impressed."

I left them and went to Kelly. "Thank you," I said, hesitantly.

He shrugged. "It's what I was trained to do."

"So, any opinion on what happens to it?"

Kelly looked at the troll, its chest rising and falling fast with panic. "Nope," he said.

I pressed my fingers into the point between my eyes. "Can we get it out of here, for starters? I think there's been enough of a scene for one night."

"I can go with it and keep the binding in place," Kelly said. "But it won't hold forever. It's going to get loose again, sooner or later."

"All right," I said. "For now, we need some open space

where it can't wreck anything, and something for it to eat. The rest . . ." The rest I would figure out after we'd gotten the heartstone back and stopped the devil's doorway from tearing a wound in the fabric that held my city together.

"Barrow Park," Kelly said. "Big, mostly empty at night. We could take it there until you figure out a permanent solution." The way he said "you" conveyed clearly that the troll was my problem.

"Can you handle it?" I said to Kelly. Get him on my side by giving him the big manly job.

"Sure," Kelly said. "I'll get it over there in one piece and make sure it doesn't chow down on any more of our fine citizens. Ma'am."

"Kelly," I said, as he stepped away, the bindings curling back from him and clustering around the troll.

He stopped. "You got something to say to me, Lieutenant?"

"I was wrong about you," I said. "I thought some things of you that you didn't deserve, and I'm sorry for that."

He snorted. "Hell, ma'am, I knew I wasn't your favorite. Don't have to get sentimental."

"You could have mentioned you were a warlock instead of being a son of a bitch," I admitted.

That earned a tiny smile. "I'll remember that."

"Do. Good luck, Detective."

"And you, ma'am."

I walked back to Will, who was on his phone, and Lucas, who was standing and glaring at every cop in sight.

"It's that squirrelly Zacharias kid," Will said, handing his phone to me. "Says he can't get through to you. Sounds upset, like someone just stole his lunch money."

I felt in my pockets. I'd lost my BlackBerry during the troll fight. "One thing after another," I muttered.

"Luna?" Andy said. "Luna, is that you?"

"I'm here, Andy. Since when are we on a first-name basis, anyway?"

"I've been thinking," he said in a rush. "The heart-stone is massive and how would they get it out of the building?"

"Magick?" I suggested.

"But why call that much attention to themselves?" Andy sounded pained. "I think . . . I think the heartstone didn't go anywhere," he said. "It's a holiday and the building is deserted. Floors and floors to disappear in. I don't think the heartstone got any further than the elevator."

Leave it to the egghead to point out the obvious. It was so simple, I was pissed off that I hadn't thought of it.

"Luna?"

"That's not bad, Andy," I whispered.

"Luna, I—" He cut off.

"Andy?" I said. "Andy, are you all right?"

There was a hiss of static on the line and a new voice spoke. "If you want to see Detective Zacharias in one piece, then you and your team stay far away from the Justice Plaza until dawn."

I knew those clipped tones, that snooty delivery. "If you've hurt Andy, I'm going to fucking rip you to shreds, Grace," I growled into the phone.

"You stay away," she said again. "Otherwise, dear Andy is going to be one of those poor unfortunates so overcome with despair that they fling themselves from high places. Do we understand one another?"

My heart was beating so hard I felt it would break my sternum. Not Andy. Andy was innocent. He was a by-stander, collateral damage.

"No deal," I said.

Grace sucked in a breath. "You're playing a very inadvisable game with your detective's life, Miss Wilder."

"You have something I want," I said. "And I have something you want."

A moment of silence. I willed Hartley not to hang up on me. "I'm listening," she said finally.

"The codex that I took from your little group of live nude cultists," I said. "I mean, losing that thing has got to suck. No way to call more critters to do your bidding, no way to control Cerberus . . . what's a good Thelemite to do?"

"I suppose you want a bargain," she cut me off.

"You get the codex back, and I get Andy," I said. "Simple."

"It had better be," said Hartley. "No tricks and no cleverness from you, because I know that you are capable of it. You're outclassed, Detective. We are on the rooftop of the Plaza. Come alone." The call clicked off and I slowly lowered the phone from my ear.

Outclassed? "Worst thing you could have said to me," I murmured, and handed the phone back to Will.

He scanned my face, his brows drawing together. "What happened?"

"They have Andy," I said, numb. Fatigue had hit me, shock, and everything else that comes with a heaping of trauma.

"Who's Andy?" said Lucas.

"He's my friend," I said. "He trusted me. Now he's in harm's way. I have to go get him."

"You don't have to be a hero," said Lucas, taking my shoulders. "It's not your job."

"I know," I said. "But taking care of my detectives is my job. Dealing with supernatural threats is my job. And making sure that these Thelemite bitches don't open a devil's doorway is most *definitely* my fucking job."

Lucas sighed, and moved his hands off of me. "I wish you didn't feel that way, sometimes."

"But I do," I said. I gestured to Fagin.

Lucas stepped away from me, his eyes silver in the sheen of the scene lights. "You do," he agreed, finally. "I understand, Luna. Will I see you around sometime?"

"Not if I see you first," I said, and turned to Will. "Let's go. I'm done fucking around with these people."

Twenty-six

Sunny opened her door before I had a chance to knock. "I saw the news," she said. "Was that thing really a . . . ?"

"Troll?" I said. "Yeah. Big, fugly, smelled like a tide flat at high noon."

Sunny wrinkled her nose. "Ew."

"But we've got a bigger problem now," I said. "I need the codex back."

Her face closed up, got cagey. "Why?"

"I just need it, Sunflower! Go get it!"

"I will not, not until you tell me why you want it."

"Look," I gritted. "You said yourself that it's practically worthless."

"In the right hands, Luna, anything can be a weapon. It's still dangerous enough. You *saw* the Thelemites summon a daemon with it."

"Yes, and now they're holding one of my friends hostage unless I give it back, so get your ass in gear, Sunny, and get it!" I shouted.

Will laid a hand on my shoulder and I growled at him, "Back off."

"Maybe we should think this over," he said. "Do you

really want to chance Hartley getting her hands on this thing again?"

"It's not a question of negotiation," I said. "They're going to kill Andy unless I bring it to them, so that's what we're going to do."

"I don't like it," said Fagin. "You're giving them exactly what they want, and the Maiden gets more daemons on her side, and it'll go hard for us when we try and take them down."

"Will, this isn't your decision!" I threw up my hands. "I made my choice!"

"I'm going to have to stop you," he said, almost regretful. "This can't happen."

"It can," Sunny said. She went to the bookcase and took down the battered ledger, tucked between a road atlas and a Greek cookbook. "My cousin isn't going to let someone die for the greater good, Agent Fagin. If you think she will, you don't know her at all."

"All due respect," he said, "you don't know what we're dealing with. You're a sheltered little caster witch."

"All due respect," Sunny shot back, her eyes hot, "but you ever condescend to me like that again and you'll spend the rest of your life thinking you're a pretty princess."

"This isn't up for debate," I told Will. "You can either come with me or walk away. I'm going to get Andy out of there."

He paced away from me, paced back, spots of color on his cheeks.

"Which is it?" I asked quietly. Sunny stood at my shoulder and I felt prickles along the back of my neck.

"You're too damn stubborn for your own good," Will said finally.

I lifted a shoulder. "Not news to me."

He went to the window and looked down at the ocean, moon-sheened, hitting the rocks far below. "I've waited too long for this," he sighed. "I'm tired, Luna. I just want it to end."

"Me, too," I said. "With everyone alive."

"You have to know that's not how the Maiden will let it go," he said.

"She's not *letting* me do anything," I said. "I take my own path. Now if you're through having a tantrum, come on. We're wasting time."

Will banged out the door without another word. I made to follow him, but Sunny caught me.

"What will you do when they have the codex?"

I ran a hand over my face. "I have no Hexed idea, Sunny."

She grabbed her jacket off the hook. "Then I'm going to come with you."

"It's too—," I started, but she cut me off.

"Don't tell me it's too dangerous, because I know that's BS. How can it be more dangerous than Alistair Duncan, than that state's attorney who was making doppelgängers with blood magick, than Wiskachee? I was there for all of that, Luna, and if you want any hope of keeping that devil's doorway shut you're going to need my help. So just take it, and stop trying to soothe your pride, okay?"

"All right," I agreed. "But you hang back and stay with Will. Enough people I care about have been hurt over this."

Sunny squeezed my hand. "I won't be. I'm with you."

At least one of us had faith. As Will drove us back to the city, the knots in my gut grew tighter, and larger. The Thelemites had odds overwhelmingly on their side, and I was walking into what had to be a trap, willingly.

Memories flew on fleet wings across my vision—Wiskachee, Lucas's twisted face as his possessed mind fought with his soul, the awful, overwhelming tide of power that flowed from the rift between realms.

What could *I* do to stop such power? Pathing it would kill me, fry my brain like an egg inside my skull. Allowing the doorway to open would mean the end of my life as I knew it, and most of the city overrun. And stopping it would probably get me killed, too, if I even knew how.

This was my job, I thought. This was what, ultimately, I was built for. I was the front line between the people of my city and the things that scurried through the dark, showing their eyes and teeth, waiting for the campfires to go out.

I caught a flash of gold out of the corner of my eye, but when I whipped my gaze in the direction, it was gone, a brightly lit jack-o'-lantern on the front steps of someone's town house the only light.

"You okay?" said Will.

"No," I said. "Park here."

Will pulled into the load zone at the front of the Plaza, and I got out. I felt like I was moving through a dream, all of my limbs weighted and weightless in the same moment, like I was floating a few inches off the ground. Before, when I'd gone toward things like this, I was resolute, fired with rage and righteousness, determined.

Now, I just wanted to turn away and let someone else be the hero, just once. But I walked anyway, after I told Sunny and Will, "Stay in the lobby and wait for me. They told me to come alone."

I mounted the steps, the gray granite edifice of the Plaza glaring down at me, the black hollows of the relief carvings of valkyries and mortals along the face of the building swirling like snakes. The handle of the brass doors was cold under my hand, and I stepped into the marble lobby that I so rarely walked through, preferring to come through the service entrance where things were smaller and human.

The great scales worked into the floor were surrounded with Latin, designed to soothe or intimidate, depending on if you were guilty or innocent: *Vero justicia argo.* In truth, justice lies.

It would be nice if things were that simple.

There was one elevator working, brass-bound and ornate like the rest of the public part of the Plaza, and I called it. Sunny didn't look happy to be stuck with Will, but she waited all the same.

"We'll give you five minutes," he said. "And then we're coming up after you, hostage or no."

I just nodded. I'd be dead in two, if Hartley didn't like what she saw, and this wouldn't be about poor Andy anymore.

I felt like I should at least say something to Sunny, about how I wished I'd been a better cousin, mended the fences with Grandma, teased her less growing up—even though the part about Grandma would be a bald-faced lie—something for her to hold on to if I indeed didn't make it back with all of our parts attached, but the doors rolled shut before I could say anything at all.

The drop of gravity as the ancient elevator began its slow progress upward made me flinch. I was on edge, swore I could feel and smell the stale air passing over my face.

I've had a few bad moments before—the first man I ever shot lying on his filthy bathroom floor, the overwhelming magick of Alistair Duncan, standing breathless at the crest of the Siren Bay Bridge, prepared to jump to keep a blood witch from blowing most of the city to kingdom come.

I'd had dozens of moments when my life was at risk on the job, and a handful when I knew death was there, standing next to me just out of my line of sight, watching and waiting.

But I'd never had the real certainty before that I was going to die. The were wouldn't let it in—it would fight and survive even when the human in me had long given up.

The were was quiet now, and I felt alone as I ever had. I looked at my distorted face in the walls of the elevator, rippled and monochrome in the brass, and then shrieked as a second pair of eyes flamed to life behind me.

"You're not wrong, Insoli. You face death," Asmodeus purred. *"Your bone and your blood know this even if your mind refuses to admit the darkness of the truth."*

"Leave me alone," I snarled. "I don't want any more daemons. I've had enough."

"If you go to the sisters of Thelema with your empty hands and raging heart you will not emerge," Asmodeus said. *"The magick of the Maiden cannot be funneled or undone. You have no protection."*

I knew that, of course, but far be it from me to admit that a daemon was right about anything.

"Let me guess," I said instead. "You're here to offer me another deal."

"Far from a deal, Insoli. You and I already have business that will be attendant in the future. What I am offering you is a choice between flinging your body onto your sword and turning the blade on your enemy."

I turned and looked at him, the gold halo around his smooth too-perfect features flickering under the fluorescent bulbs in the elevator car. We were passing through the fifteenth floor, the small red *R* of the roof creeping closer on the dial.

Asmodeus pulled back his full lips in a smile, his pure black eyes never wavering. *"You are thinking about my offer. I can see it."*

"I don't need to owe you anything else," I told him. "I'd rather the Thelemites killed me."

"You lie, Insoli, and poorly."

"I'd have to repay you," I said, jabbing a finger at him. He felt like a static shock, like a disturbance of air.

"You would have to allow me to work through you, Insoli. I have no love for those who reach into my realm without permission. It is a harsh place, hot and dry and full of stinging wind, but it is my own and the few inhabitants my charges." He twitched his lion's tail irritably. *"After the Descent, so few left . . . and now these humans presume to tear my only home to pieces. It cannot be allowed."*

"And if I let you . . . work through me . . . what would I have to do?" I said. "Spill my blood? Sacrifice a memory, or something worse?" The elevator slowed, the brakes groaning.

Asmodeus reached out and laid a hand on my shoulder, and I made a heroic effort not to flinch away. His touch spread cold through me, like snow on bare skin. Like drowning in cold water. *"If you require my aid, Insoli . . . all you would have to do is speak my name."*

The doors rolled back with a *ping* of the bell, and I was alone, on the rooftop.

I shook off the vestiges of the daemon's touch and put his words out of my mind. They lied. Daemons could be good or evil or anywhere in between, but they all lied.

They all seduced, needing the feed of human emotion to sustain them. It was why the first caster witches had banished them to a shadow place, caused the Descent, and rid the blood witches of their avatars, to keep the great rising black power that they offered out of human hands.

It wouldn't come to that. I'd get Andy and get the hell out of there, and Nocturne City could throw a couple of heavily armored squads of SWAT at the Thelemites.

And SWAT would be decimated, because Hartley and her sisters were too powerful. They'd die screaming, eight widows made in one night.

"We were beginning to think you wouldn't come," Grace Hartley said. Speak of the devil. She and six other Thelemites were arrayed at the far end of the roof, the heartstone at their center. It gleamed and threw off deep blue-purple sparks in the low glow of the emergency lights strung up along the roof.

I calculated that with both of my weapons I probably didn't have enough bullets, and I sure as hell didn't have enough time to get them all down before someone slapped me with a working.

"Let's see your weapons," said Hartley, as if she could read my mind. Maybe she could. Damn witches.

"Let's see Andy," I countered, my voice surprisingly strong over the sound of the rooftop wind.

"We'll get to that," Hartley said, as if I were a small child demanding ice cream. "Guns on the ground. Now. Or you can forget about any negotiation."

I unstrapped my holdout and threw it, and took out the Sig and laid it down gently, feeling a pang of regret even though guns were next to useless right then.

Hartley watched me with bright eyes, her lips curling up. "Good. Now the codex."

"Demanding bitch, aren't you?" I said. "No wonder your husband left you."

"He didn't leave," she said pleasantly. "I killed him and fed him to a scavenger, a carrion hound from the Realm." The way she said it, I sensed the capital *R*. It's always a bad sign when the fanatics start tossing around the proper nouns.

"Ah," I said. "So you've been at this for a while, then? Testing devil's doorways? Calling creatures?" When in doubt, get them talking.

"I have been Thelemite my entire life," Hartley said. "I have existed upon the grace of the Maiden. She took me to her bosom, raised me as her own after my talents obliterated my own parents. Helped me care for poor Milton."

"Up until you had a harpy slaughter him," I said, drawing out the codex and holding it up. "You have some screwy priorities, lady." I tossed the codex to the gravel. "There you go. Now give me my detective."

Hartley sighed, as if I were being intractable. "Get that odious little man and let him go."

A Thelemite woman grabbed Andy from behind the HVAC unit. His hands were cuffed with his own handcuffs and his face was streaked with moisture.

"Lieutenant!" He gave a huge shudder. "They made me call; they made me bring you here—"

"Oh, shut up," said Hartley crossly, and Andy's voice cut out, his mouth working uselessly. "I never met such a man for idle talk," she said.

The Thelemite shoved Andy at me and I caught him. His face was purpled with panic.

"Andy. Andy!" I gave him a hard shake. "I need you to listen, now. Go down the elevator and go to Agent Fagin and my cousin. They're waiting for you. Run, now!"

Andy took off running, panting in fear, and I pointed at the codex. "A deal's a deal. Are we done here?"

Grace favored me with a thin smile. "You upheld your end admirably. You have honor that is hard to find in such a time as this." She bent and scooped up my Sig. "However, I don't think you stupid. You must know we can't leave you alive."

I expected posturing, magick being flung, Hartley declaiming her grand plan to me. Crazies usually love the sound of their own voice. But Hartley said nothing else, merely flicked the safety off of my SIG, aimed, and pulled the trigger.

Really, it happened inside of a second. Even with my reflexes, I had no chance of avoiding the bullet, and it slammed into me with the force of a truck, blood misting into my eyes and my left side shredded with pain. I saw the hole, with remarkable clarity, smaller than I'd expected, just above my heart.

Then I swayed and fell, my cheek cut on the gravel that covered the rooftop. I could hear my heart in my ears, a small rhythm that grew fainter with each *thud-thud.*

"That's that," Grace said, turning her back on me and tossing the Sig away from her like it was an unsavory magazine she'd discovered under someone's mattress.

She'd shot me. I'd expected arrogance, because witches were almost always arrogant, thinking they could use their power against me because I was something weaker. But someone with as much juice behind her as a Thelemite didn't need arrogance.

I'd been wrong. And now I was lying there bleeding to death because of it. *Nice work, Wilder. Your finest hour.*

Grace strode back to the heartstone. From my skewed vantage, the Thelemites appeared terrifying and asymmetrical, purple-veiled creatures that floated around the gathering power of the stone.

"Begin," Hartley said crisply, and the women joined hands. There was no chanting this time, nothing except the rush of magick that swept over the rooftop like a hurricane and coalesced at the heartstone. The Thelemites dropped hands and Grace snapped her fingers.

Were my five minutes up? Would Will and Sunny be coming, to walk into the same mistake I had?

"Come forward, child," Hartley said. "Don't dawdle. Who knows what sort of wild plans that policewoman made to bring the truth-and-justice cavalry down on our heads."

The veiled figure stepped out of the circle and laid her hands across the heartstone. "I don't know about this."

"The Maiden commands it," Grace snapped. "You are her vessel, blood of my blood. Now stop your whining and take her into you!"

Sophia pushed back her veil, her pale hair spilling around her face. "Mom, I don't want to."

Grace's face curled itself into a fearsome glare. "Young woman, you are blessed. Touch the stone and receive the Maiden!"

"I'm scared," Sophia protested. "This has all gone so wrong, Mom. . . . The cops know about Annemarie, she's dead, and that troll you sent out didn't stop them from coming here and finding us! This isn't going to work."

"This city is going to be a paradise," Grace gritted. "A place where all those reviled can walk in the sun. Open your eyes, Sophia—that cop is dead and she could do nothing even when she was alive."

I wasn't dead yet, but I stayed still, waiting for my legs to start working again. My blood was warming the gravel under me, hot and overpoweringly dense, a smell that stuck to my throat and nostrils.

"It's not going to work," Sophia said again. "You think the devil's doorway will let those *things* through and everything will be a paradise? They and all of us with the blood just live side by side with plain humans? It doesn't *work* that way, Mom! Human beings are afraid of us."

Grace slapped her across the face. "I led the sisterhood my entire life, waiting for the Maiden to return from her eternal walk. She chose *you*." She grabbed her daughter by the neck. "Hold her arms." Three Thelemites, plus Grace, forced Sophia's cheek against the heartstone.

"I am opening a gate to paradise," Grace whispered. "This city, a haven from humanity, from pain and from fear for the sisters and brothers of the blood. No one will stop me, Sophia, most especially not my own daughter."

Sophia's skin touched the heartstone and she gave a scream. A great flare of power sprang up, a column of light that blinded me. I shut my eyes, feeling the slow eddy of my last minutes of life pull me under.

"Maiden, we offer you a vessel," said Grace, and I felt the Thelemite's magick focus through the heartstone. It was like a knife in the brain—so huge and obliterating that a human mind couldn't comprehend. The heartstone ripped through the layers of energy in the air, drinking it all in and transmitting back something that covered all of us in blackness.

"I offer you my only child, the flesh begot of my loyal flesh," Grace said. "She receives you into her and carries you in her heart for all days."

"So it will be," the Thelemites echoed.

Sophia gave one last agonized gurgle, and then she

went still, her pale torso sprawled across the heartstone. Still for a long moment, like a broken doll, I watched her stare at nothing. Grace touched her forehead, reverent. "Come to me," she whispered.

Sophia jerked and gave a gasp. She shook herself, like she was just waking up after a long night, and blinked at the world through new eyes, blue and dancing with fire.

"Grace," she intoned, and reached out to stroke Hartley's cheek.

Grace let out a joyful sob, like we were at a wedding instead of the end of the world. "Maiden. I serve you always."

"Your vessel is so fragile," said the Maiden. "Could you not have found one of stronger constitution?"

Grace dipped her head. "Forgive me. In our new city, you will have your pick of any vessel you wish."

The Maiden gave her a cagey smile. "You have never given something for nothing, my child. What is your price for returning me to my flesh?"

"A doorway," said Grace. "A way through the woods for all those who suffer as we have suffered, alone and in the dark. We offer you the power from the hunger god and the fealty of Thelema for all time, in our new city, of those who are one and the same, free of human influence."

The Maiden tilted her head at me, and I swore she smiled. "This notion pleases me. You will have your doorway."

She placed her hands on the heartstone, her movements jerky. She reminded me of Lucas when Wiskachee had been riding shotgun—not quite real. Sophia was gone, I knew in that moment. Only the Maiden remained.

I shut my eyes as the power spiked, and hot wind blew

sand and rock into my face. Touching the other realm was like putting my hand in a fire, the absolute, searing agony that nothing could stop.

I opened my eyes again as the Thelemites cried out. The air around us shimmered, power struggling to manifest, and then it was sucked backward into the heartstone with a sonic boom as the air filled the space. The Maiden threw her head back, running her hands down her body, writhing in ecstasy. "It's done."

As the Thelemites bowed in reverence, I saw it. The devil's doorway was a simple thing, an arch of dark against darkness, faint white smoke wavering at the outline.

The sound was the worst thing—a high, constant shrieking of wind over barren plains, cries and snarls from the inhabitants, and a faint, sharp whispering against my mind that felt the same as when Asmodeus spoke to me. The language of daemons.

How many existed beyond that tear, the opening in the rift Wiskachee had made?

A bird's cry split the night, and three winged creatures erupted out of the doorway, bare breasts and wild hair and talons all taking to the sky. Harpies, like the ones that Hartley had sent after her brother.

Next came things with the heavy heads of bulls and the scarred bodies of men, their horns dripping with blood, and a parade of oil-skinned, yellow-eyed creatures maybe three feet tall, all tooth and claw. They came for me, chattering, and I was reminded of the carrion hounds that had eaten Hartley's husband.

The devil's doorway was open, and things that should stay in nightmares were walking. I could do nothing. I was dying, plain and simple. It was colder and more painful than I'd imagined it, and a lot less dignified.

I opened my mouth and used the little bit of energy I had left to say the name. I didn't debate it, didn't let myself think what sin I might be committing. I just knew that I couldn't die, not yet.

I spoke the name aloud. "Asmodeus . . ."

Gold closed over my vision, light that made my eyes water. It was a child's fantasy of Heaven, the light lifting me up and on to my eternal reward.

"I knew you would call me, Insoli," Asmodeus said, and my dizziness disappeared and my vision cleared.

Asmodeus wasn't visible, but I could feel him, in the blood in my veins and in the air I was breathing and in the squeeze as my muscles knit and the bullet in my lung landed on the gravel with a *clink*, darkened with my blood.

"Don't get too excited," I said. "It wasn't my first choice."

"Close the devil's doorway, Insoli," Asmodeus whispered. *"Trap the maker in her own machine."*

"Could you be any less helpful?" I wondered, making it to my knees. A harpy shrieked and bore down on me, claws swiping at my shoulder. My shirt tore, but the wounds knit, fading to scars with pink edges before my eyes.

Asmodeus gave a low chuckle. *"I can indeed withdraw my aid if it is not required."*

"Don't be a smart-ass," I said. I felt light, lighter than air, and the rush was addictive—it was a hit running wild through me, a clean, pure high that would never drop me down. I felt a small shiver of panic underneath the euphoria, but I shoved it down.

The feeling lasted until I came up against one of the bull-headed creatures. He bellowed at me and then lowered his head and charged. I jumped out of the way, but one of his horns still snagged my side and he threw his head back. I rocketed toward the HVAC unit and slammed into it, leaving a Luna-sized dent in the top.

Two Thelemites came to me, their diaphanous costumes managing to look more like the shrouds of the dead than ritual wear. "Guess she's not dead," one said.

The other looked toward the parade of inhumans spilling through the devil's doorway—horses with glowing red eyes and hooves of iron, great green-skinned hounds with yellow teeth, hags who tore at their hair and shrieked so loudly that I felt my eardrums start to bleed. The sky above us cracked with lightning as a pair of winged, skeletal creatures took flight, stirring the clouds to a boil.

"Wait for it," she said. They smiled at me, the thin mean little smiles of children torturing animals.

"Get up, Insoli," Asmodeus hissed at me.

"Would it kill you to use my name?" I grunted. I pulled myself out of the wreckage of the HVAC. My side stung, but the flow of Asmodeus's magick through me faded it away to nothing.

A mob of the tiny, toothy yellow things ran at me, their red tongues lolling from their mouths like a herd of creepy, animated dolls. I braced myself for their onslaught, determined that I'd fling every last one of them back through the devil's doorway, even if they chewed me to the bone.

Cold swept over me, different from the wind or the magick of the Thelemites, and I saw a misty silver shape fly into the cluster of imps, spilling them like bowling pins.

Lucas swirled to a stop next to me, his teeth bared. "Stay away," he snarled. The imps scattered, chittering their disapproval.

"Lucas?" I said. I felt disconnected, like I was watching it all on film, even my hand as it reached out for the incorporeal bits of his body.

"Luna," he said, and then really looked at me. His eyes flickered and he began to shift back in alarm. "Luna, what have you done? What's inside you?"

An explosive sound came from the direction of the elevators, fists hitting metal, and the door flew open, discharging a muscular red-tattooed creature with bulging eyes, teeth like a walrus, and curling ram horns.

The tattoos were familiar. "Akira?" I said.

"Not just me," he rumbled. Kelly came out of the elevator, followed by Will and Sunny, Mac, Bryson, and Batista. A crowd of people I didn't recognize were behind them. A few were Wendigo, like Lucas; many more were witches, their workings crackling around them like they'd drawn the lightning down. Some had scales or feathers, claws and fangs, or four feet instead of two. They all, to a man, looked angry as hell.

"What did you do?" I echoed Lucas's question.

"Not me," said Lucas. "Your cousin. She called on the *oni* and he called his friends. It's their city, too."

A second wave of silver mist and teeth flowed over the edge of the roof, a trio of Wendigo alighting. Lucas gave me a crooked grin. "Those guys are mine."

Bryson cocked his arm back and pistol-whipped a harpy as she dove for him. Sunny drew down power and created a shimmering bubble of light magick in front of the ragtag cavalry, the Thelemite's magick bouncing off it with a shower of sparks. Kelly got out his chalk and cleared away the gravel, drawing workings that spun and danced out like blades, cutting down a swath of the imps and knocking one of the minotaurs off its feet.

Batista and Mac both had an M4 and they opened fire

on the hags, silencing them mid-shriek. Will fought his way over to me, grabbing me by the arm. "Where's the Maiden?"

"We're not finished here," said Lucas. "Luna's done something to herself."

He shifted back to human as his brethren howled past, falling on the great green hound and drinking its heart blood down. Lucas just stared into my eyes. I tried to tell him that everything would be fine, but it was so hard to look at him and see his human face. Asmodeus's vision showed me the crimson, shrieking hunger behind it and I had to look away.

"Luna," he whispered. "You're not . . . you've changed."

I'm sorry, I wanted to say.

"Don't be foolish, Luna," Asmodeus said. *"He would cut you down and drink my essence where we stand. Wendigo hunger. That is all."*

His words made a certain amount of sense. Should they? I couldn't tell any longer.

Will dragged me away from Lucas. "Hate to say it, but you're going to have to play this touching breakup scene later."

"Luna . . . ," Lucas started, his face crumpled and desperate, but one of the harpies fell on him and he shifted back to mist, turning and sinking his talons into her chest.

Bryson was taking fists and gun to anything that got close to him. Mac and Batista were reloading. Kelly and Sunny were flinging workings like they'd engaged in a desperate rooftop battle with spawn of a hell portal dozens of times.

The Thelemites were scattered, and Akira picked up one and bit down on her middle. Blood covered the rooftop now, black, red, green, and anywhere in between.

It didn't matter. Will was taking me, and we were going to find the Maiden, the keeper of the doorway. Through my new eyes, Will was terrible and mighty—a halo of pure white fire around his head and blood trailing from black hollows that were his eyes. A great thorn twisted in his chest, where his heart should be, an old wound that spread black tendrils into the energy around him, binding his life so close and tight that it could never escape.

The curse, when I looked at it, was beautiful in the way that a blade is beautiful, or the fiery aftermath of a bomb is brilliant.

"It was the greatest thing I ever did." Sophia stepped in front of me, Grace next to her. Her eyes were pure white, clouded with the form riding her body. "Ensnaring him for eternity, in his greed."

Will slowed to a stop, his jaw slackening. "I've been looking for you for such a long time."

The Maiden ran her hands over her brand-new virgin body. Around us, the sounds of the battle faded as her power rose. "And now that you've found me, William, what course do you propose we take?"

Will drew his weapon. "I'm going to send you back to the seventh hell. Where you belong."

The Maiden threw her head back and laughed. "How long have you been practicing those words, William?"

Will stepped forward and pressed the gun into her forehead.

This wasn't right. Asmodeus watched dispassionately, but I grabbed Will's arm. "No. There's still a person in there."

"The quality of mercy is usually wasted," said the Maiden. She still smiled. "It makes you weak. Human."

"If you shoot her, she'll just find a new host," I said. "That's how she's stayed alive all of this time, Will." I tightened my grip as he struggled to raise the gun again. "Your curse can't be broken with another death."

Will shook his head. "Four hundred years, and I'm not losing the chance to end it."

"This isn't an end," I said. "She'll turn you into a murderer and you'll live with it forever."

"Let him go, Luna. Let him run wild. He will make it much easier for you."

"Shut up," I hissed. Will and the Maiden both looked at me askance.

"You can't imagine how I suffered for you," Will said, raising his pistol again. "All of the years, all of the days, death after death . . ."

"William." The Maiden reached out and stroked his cheek. "I didn't do a thing to you. You brought it on yourself—your lust and your petty need for power. You and you alone are the bearer of the curse. I taught you a lesson, at the most."

"You'll pay," Will ground out. "You'll die, and I'll die, and you'll roast on a spit."

"Will." I leaned close to him. Could I get the gun away from him? Not in time. Not fast enough to keep Sophia from getting a head shot. "She's just playing with you. She's not worth it." I slid my grip down to his wrist, touched his skin. "You're not a murderer, Will."

He gave an all-over shudder, and lowered the gun. "Is she right?" he ground out. "Is there no way to break it?"

The Maiden spread her arms. "The same way it has always been, William. End my life. But I am without end. It seems you have a quandary."

Will sagged, and I saw his knees give out. He sat down

on the gravel and pressed his hands over his face. "I have to die," he whispered. "It must end . . . nothing is without an end."

"Just me," said the Maiden. "I am eternal, as my new city is eternal."

Grace touched her shoulder and she hissed at her, power lashing out and drawing a line of blood across Hartley's face. "You presume?"

"I am merely suggesting a retreat," said Hartley. "The violence is growing worse and I fear for your safety."

"I fear for yours, if you continue speaking," the Maiden said. Hartley backed away, and the Maiden looked over the rooftop. "You'll excuse me," she said. "But the doorway will bring the daemon wanderers through, and I cannot have this reception waiting. Either call your people off or I will make sure they end up as broken dolls on the sidewalk below."

I stepped in front of Will, blocking her advance toward him with my body. "I got a better idea—how about you go Hex yourself and I shut the doorway, or your mother over there can identify your body."

"She is not my mother," said the Maiden. "She's nothing to me. I am ageless and—"

"You're eternal. I got it the first time," I snarled, as she took another step toward me.

"Don't you want to join me? Be one of my fold? I can arrange that, you know. All you have to do is die."

She raised her hands and I saw the energy crackle off the heartstone and fly to her. The working formed, coalesced, and flew toward me. I braced myself for the impact, but instead I felt my Path energy spring to life and take the magick in, like grabbing a naked wire with my bare hands.

In the back of my mind, Asmodeus smiled. The Maiden lowered her hands. "Impossible."

I flexed my fingers, my claws growing sharp and black with the influx of energy. "Apparently not."

She backed away from me. "What *are* you?"

My own voice surprised me. *"I am the Wanderer."*

The Maiden's eyes widened. "Not possible . . . ," she quavered.

Asmodeus spoke through me again. I was frozen inside my own head and I didn't like it one bit. *"I am the protector of the space between."*

"You are lost to all," the Maiden cried. "And I have my own daemon to keep as a pet. You don't frighten me." She spread her hands and I felt a vibration through the aether, like a dog whistle made of power.

This wasn't good.

"If you're not frightened," Asmodeus whispered, *"then you should be. You are old, but your days are dust compared to mine. I am the Wanderer, and you have trespassed in my tracks."*

"And I do not care," said the Maiden. She pointed over my shoulder and I turned under Asmodeus's power. I fought, but it didn't do any good—I was riding shotgun. He was in control.

Will let out a choked sound, and pointed toward the edge of the roof. Cerberus was slithering toward us, his hound heads flinging spittle and his teeth gleaming sharp as steel blades.

"Crap," I squeaked, in my own voice.

Cerberus drew up, and his triplet nostrils flared as he scented me. *"Skin-changer?"* he said, the three voices screeching discordantly. *"You are changed. . . ."*

"This is not your world," Asmodeus said.

Cerberus snarled, his lips drawing back over those teeth, like I was watching some nightmarish mirror. *"You and I share no friendship, Wanderer."*

"Nevertheless, I will send you back to where you belong," Asmodeus said, sounding smug.

I felt his control of my body slip just a bit, as he focused on Cerberus. I was not going to be ripped apart because of a demonic pissing contest. I forced the words out, my own voice, and it echoed inside my brain like a hammer against my skull.

"She called you a pet, Cerberus."

Cerberus looked at the Maiden with one of his heads. "Lies," she said. Too quickly. "I let you out. . . . I'm on your side!"

"The skin-changer speaks the truth," Asmodeus said, back in the driver's seat. *"She would set you on her enemies and leash you with her favor."*

Cerberus let out a howl that vibrated my teeth. *"No one is my master! I am the hound of the seven hells! I guard the gateway!"*

He lowered his heads and advanced on the Maiden, and her eyes went wide.

"I can't die," she said. It was meant as a threat, but it came out like a protest.

"No," said the daemon. *"But you can suffer."* Cerberus leapt, caught her between his jaws, and shook the body like a doll. The Maiden let out a scream and I saw through Asmodeus's eyes the bruise-purple curls of aura around Sophia's body retreat and gather into an orb above her corpse as her own life force ran out.

Her body fell back to the gravel, blood spattering her face. Her torso and legs were nearly at right angles, the center of her a bloody mess.

"No one is my master," Cerberus said with a satisfied chuckle. He was larger than when the Thelemites had called him, and more intelligence gleamed in his six eyes than I was comfortable with.

"We have to do something about him," I said.

"The heartstone, Insoli," Asmodeus whispered.

"There's no way I can destroy that thing," I said. "It's a freaking *rock*."

"If you do not destroy the focus, the devil's doorway will rip a hole in the aether large enough to swallow most of this city."

I looked toward the doorway. It was getting bigger. The Maiden's control was gone, and she drifted above the fray. The doorway was lifting the gravel around it, beginning to pull from our world into the daemon realm.

"Let me take charge, Insoli," Asmodeus said. *"I know what to do."*

I took a halting step toward the heartstone, against my will. "No," I said. I stopped us by folding one leg and sitting down hard.

"No?" Asmodeus sounded incredulous. *"This is the bargain you struck. My power flows freely in you and I am in control until the doorway is shut."*

I was up again, and moving toward the heartstone. "No!" I said, louder.

Darkness slipped over my vision, and I saw Asmodeus's eyes, glowing with fury. What would something like him do with the power of the heartstone, if he touched it? Become whole, like Cerberus? Open something a thousand times larger and worse than the devil's doorway?

"You are not in control, Luna," he hissed at me. Gone was the conciliatory tone. *"I am the guardian and I will have the stone. What reason have you that I cannot?"*

I grabbed my penknife from my pocket, a small gesture that required minimal effort. Every inch of movement was torture as we fought over control of my body.

"Because I don't trust you," I whispered, and plunged the knife into my thigh.

The pain made everything snap clear for a moment—my limbs came back, along with hot white pain, and my vision cleared into human, the spectral wisps of energy around the people and creatures on the rooftop blowing away. Even Cerberus looked marginally less terrifying.

"Oh, Insoli," Asmodeus growled. *"This is a fight you are going to lose. You are one against me. Less than nothing."*

"I may be nothing to you," I snarled. "But I'm not alone." I got up and staggered toward the heartstone, under my own power. All of the wounds I'd sustained started to hurt again, shoulder and side and chest.

I fell against the heartstone, shoving it with all of my strength. It budged maybe an inch across the gravel. Asmodeus laughed.

"No one is going to help you, Insoli. You have nothing."

I pushed again, gaining another inch. The thing weighed close to five hundred pounds, fatted with magick, and my strength was fading. My wounds were bleeding in earnest now, from the strain. I felt Asmodeus's energy running out of me.

"If you wish to be alone, Insoli . . . so be it," he whispered. *"The next time that I see you, it will not be as an ally. I promise you."*

There was a flicker of warmth in my chest, a flash of gold behind my eyes, and then he was gone. I was alone, next to the heartstone, bleeding and dying.

Just like I'd started.

I pushed again, black dots swimming in front of my eyes, and I jumped when a second body joined me, sending the stone flying.

Will looked at me. "Jesus Christ. You need a hospital."

"The doorway," I gasped in return. "Send it through."

"The Maiden is dead," Will said flatly. "Gone. This thing could be my last chance."

"Will." I put my hand on his chest, leaving a smear of blood. "For once, could you stop fucking thinking about yourself?"

He gave me a one-sided smile. "You really are stubborn, you know that?" He put his hands next to mine and we shoved. A moment later someone else came running and Sunny joined in, her small hands white-knuckled against the rock. There was a kiss of cool moisture on my bloody face and Lucas was there, shifted, his prodigious strength enough to lift the stone and send it flying.

It caught the edge of the sucking void the doorway had become and then with a *thud* of displaced air it vanished through the devil's doorway.

A shriek went up, from the doorway, as it began to close, funneling energy through a tiny space. The creatures on the roof turned their heads, and then they began to run, or fly—fleeing from the doorway any way they could.

"Down!" Sunny shouted in my ear, yanking at me. "It's going to discharge the working's energy!"

The only thing that didn't get clear in time was Cerberus, feeding on Sophia's body. His small arms scrabbled at the gravel, his mouths opened in a scream, as the doorway stripped the flesh from his tail, pulling him backward through a space half the size of his bloated body.

Cerberus let out a howl that chilled me, rattled me to

the core. It was the sound of a doomsday hound, the sort of thing that would ferry you to the seven gates of the seven hells.

Then, with a low wet sucking sound, he disappeared through the doorway, silenced.

It was the size of my fist now, discharging magick in white-purple sparks visible to the naked eye.

As the devil's doorway shut for good, I saw the Maiden, her formless dark mass of a soul against the bright white of the door. I think she screamed before it pulled her down, but I couldn't be sure.

In another few seconds, she was gone, and there was a blast of hot air, like wind from a forbidden place reaching your skin. The devil's doorway closed, leaving nothing but the scent of charred magick in the air.

Satisfied that the world wasn't going to end in the next few minutes, I put my forehead down in the gravel and passed out.

Twenty-seven

Waking up in the ICU is like waking up in some Kubrick-esque version of Hell—I could see nothing but white ceiling, white light, white tile walls, the sheen of an oxygen mask covering my face, and felt the foreign steel sting of multiple IVs in my hand and arms.

"Hello?" I tried, and my voice came out a breathy whisper. How long had I been out? I tried sitting up and found that the swath of bandages around my chest and middle made that pretty much impossible.

I lifted my mask away from my face, and that triggered some kind of alarm, along with a nurse.

"Lieutenant, you need to keep that on," she scolded.

"I can breathe the air just fine, thanks," I said. There was a commotion outside the swinging steel doors and then Will and Sunny came in. The nurse tried to shoo them back.

"I need to fix Miss Wilder's oxygen."

Sunny gave me a huge hug, which started a fireworks display of agony behind my eyes. "Ow," I managed, feebly.

"I'm sorry," she said. "But you've been unconscious . . . the doctors thought you might have lost too much blood. . . ."

"You had two major wounds, a gunshot and that stick you gave yourself," Will recited.

"There are *no visitors*," the nurse said sternly. "You can come back when organized visiting hours start. Leave, now."

She fiddled with my IV and I felt the cotton wool slipping down over my consciousness again. I tried to tell Sunny I'd see her later, but I fell asleep and didn't really wake up again for another two days.

They moved me out of the ICU and into a regular room, and then a few days later the doctors pronounced that I could go home. I think they were just glad to get rid of me. I don't like hospitals, don't like being poked and prodded when I knew I'd heal, if they just left me alone. I got a little surly toward the end.

I called Sunny to give me a ride, but as I was dialing, Will came into my room.

He looked over my sling, the bandages still covering the gunshot wound, and probably the generally hermitlike appearance I'd cultivated during my stay—pale corpsey skin, tangled hair, deep half-moons under my eyes. I hadn't slept much in the hospital. I kept dreaming about Asmodeus.

The next time that I see you, it will not be as an ally. I promise you.

"You can say it—I look like hell."

"Actually, I was gonna say you looked pretty good for someone who beat down a daemon and shut a devil's doorway."

"You're a liar, but thanks anyway." I picked up the clothes that I'd come in with, folded into a paper hospital sack. They were torn and bloody, and they carried the smell of daemon. I stuffed them into the trash can in the corner of the room.

"Feel like giving me a ride home in your Compensationmobile?" I said to Will.

He didn't smile. "The Maiden is gone," he said finally.

Crap. "I know, Will, and I'm sorry, but she was trying to turn my city into some kind of magick Utopia by dint of killing all the humans with a daemon army—" I had a litany of excuses, but Will stopped me.

"It's not your fault, Luna. It's mine. She was absolutely right. I got myself cursed and I got obsessed."

"Just a little," I agreed, cautiously. I still had enough morphine in me to throw caution to the wind.

"Someday, I'll find her," Will said. "And someday, she'll have to release me from the curse, but . . ." He took a step closer and took my hand, the one that wasn't bound up in a sling. "I'm fine if that someday isn't today."

"Will . . . ," I started.

"I need to live," he said. "I spent a lot of time looking to die, and that's not living. I like you, Luna. You're the same as me. I've never really met anyone like you."

He leaned in, our foreheads touching, so that we could share breath. "I know that I've been a real ass, but maybe we could give this a shot." He kissed me, gently, and when I didn't respond he looked at me, searching for what would make it right. "Please. At least give me a chance to try."

"Will," I said, gently disengaging from him and picking up the phone again. I hit redial. "I'm glad that you had this epiphany, but it doesn't mean I'm comfortable around you. You scare me a little, if you want the truth."

"I can change," he said. "Please. . . ."

"Stop."

On the other end of the phone Sunny said, "Hello?"

"Hang on, Sun." I cradled the phone and looked at Will. He was everything the romantic stories talked about—blond, handsome, cursed, tragic. And enough like me, with enough of the same demons inside, that I didn't know if I could ever sit still with him.

"I'm not saying no," I told him. "But I need some time. You need to give me that if we're even going to start to have a chance, all right?"

Will slipped his sunglasses on and gave me a crooked smile. "Anything worth having is worth waiting for, right?"

"Something like that," I agreed. "See you around, Will."

"Don't be a stranger, doll."

He walked out, into the sunlight, and I stayed where I was, waiting to go home.

Bryson looked almost mortally offended when I told him I was moving out. "No offense, David," I said, "but if I have to spend one more week in that little room I'm going to go insane."

"It's Uncle Henry, isn't it?" he said. "He's been bothering you. He always went for the brunettes. That's why Aunt Louise put rat poison in his blintzes."

"David, your house is not haunted. It's just very small, and very frilly. I am not small and not frilly. You see the problem."

"Yeah," he sighed. "I ain't exactly a fan, but if Aunt Louise ever gets out of the home she'll kill me for changing stuff."

I had another week of sick leave, more than enough

time to find an apartment if I didn't care too much about exactly where or how many of my neighbors were crack-heads.

"Thanks, David. Really. It's been fun, but it's time I got my own place like a big girl."

I climbed the kitchen stairs, still a little slow from the beating I'd taken on the roof. I was healed, a few scars, nothing that I couldn't handle, but I still remembered that sickening sensation of not being in control of my own body, and the second I did the room would start to spin.

I ignored it, swallowed it down, and started to pack my few new things I'd acquired since my cottage burned down.

Someone knocked on the front door and after a moment of raised voices Bryson thumped up the stairs. "Luna, you won't freakin' believe who just showed up on the stoop."

I followed him down and found Lucas standing in the living room, looking at family photos like he belonged there.

"Should I arrest him?" Bryson said hopefully.

Lucas looked at me. "It's up to her."

"David, I think we can forget about this, don't you? He did save my life." Again. I kept quiet about that part.

Grumbling, Bryson retreated to the kitchen.

"I should be long gone," said Lucas. "Police are still looking for me. I should be out in the woods laying low."

"Then why aren't you?" I asked.

Lucas met my eyes. "Because you're here."

I held up my hands. "No. I can't do this again. It would never work: You're a wanted fugitive, a Wendigo, plus—"

"Luna, shut up," he said, closing his mouth over mine. I let Lucas kiss me, because our monsters responded to each other and I don't know that I could have stopped even if I wanted to.

"I'm willing to stay for you," he said. "Just think about it." He went to the door and walked out without another word, leaving me standing there flushed and mightily conflicted.

Lucas was another man with a beast in him, someone with a bad past and a future that wasn't too bright, either. But he called to me and I responded in spite of myself, and he was loyal, strong, enticing, because you knew when you looked into his dancing dark eyes that there would never be a dull moment.

I ran after him, out onto the front lawn, knocking over one of Bryson's creepy gnomes.

"Lucas!"

He turned back. His hair was like a raven's wing in the late sun, blue-black and shiny, the rest of him a long lanky shadow. He came back to me, standing on the other side of Bryson's fence. "Yes, Luna?"

"I can't," I said. "I want to—you're everything I want, really. But you're not safe, Lucas. I chase after the dangerous ones, the ones with monsters in their blood, and look where it's gotten me."

"You seem fine to me," he said, reaching for my face.

I caught his hand and squeezed it. "But I'm not. I'm a mess, Lucas. I careen from one bad choice to the next. I need something that's orderly." I shut my eyes. "I want you, but I need something that's safe."

"Fagin," he said, without any prompting, dead and flat like he was talking about the weather.

"I don't know," I said. "I just know that it can't work with us. And I am sorry."

Lucas shoved his hands into his pockets, his posture

like his strings had been cut, but he still managed to give me one of those crooked, promising smiles. "You're making a mistake, Luna."

I opened my mouth to protest that on the contrary, I was displaying sense for probably the first time in my adult life, but he shook his head. "I understand why you're doing it." He leaned over the fence and gave me a kiss on the cheek. "You ever change your mind, and decide that safe isn't what you need . . ."

I gave him a hard hug, the chain mesh pressing into my belly. "Thank you for saving my life, Lucas."

He returned it, and it felt so good to just be touched with no expectation that I held on to him. "It was a life worth saving," he whispered in my ear.

When I let him go, he smiled again. "You take care of yourself, Luna."

I laughed, because it was just funny. With cults, curses, and now a city full of citizens of the daemon realm, how likely was that? Still, anything was possible.

I returned Lucas's smile. "I'll try my best."

Epilogue

My new apartment had leaky pipes, a loud steam radiator, and a closet that wasn't nearly large enough for my imaginary replacement collection of vintage, but it was five minutes from the Justice Plaza and no one was dealing smack or running prostitutes in the immediate vicinity. I left it in the morning and came home at night, just ghosting through.

After I'd come back to work there had been a further two weeks of review that kept me away from the SCS—the IA hearing on Annemarie's shooting, the commissioner's review of my squad, questions upon endless questions about that night on the roof. I answered as quickly as I could and didn't provide a lot of details.

I went to two funerals during those two weeks, Sophia Hartley's and Annemarie's. Sophia had a crowd—even her mother got a pass from the judge hearing her murder case to attend, flanked by two U.S. Marshals. Grace Hartley looked tired and wrung out, all of the energy run out of her. They kept her so doped that she couldn't even cast a simple working, so I'd heard from Bryson, and she didn't even look at her daughter's coffin when it was lowered into the ground.

Will Fagin and I were the only attendees at Annemarie's

service. After the priest finished the ceremony, Fagin went and put a white rose on top of the coffin.

"I didn't bring anything," I said.

"Well, she did try to shoot you, and curse you," he said. "I think you get a pass on that one."

"Stupid girl," I said, more to Annemarie than anyone. "She really thought the Thelemites were going to take her in."

"Bad magick always attracts the lost lambs," Will said. "By the way, whatever happened to that troll?"

"You want to see?"

He shrugged. "I took the city tram from my office. You got a car?"

I spun my new set of keys around my fingers. "Do I ever."

The car had been the only thing on the lot that I could afford and that ran decently. It wasn't the Fairlane, but it had its ugly, ratchety charms.

"'71 Nova SS," Will said, running his hands over the primer-colored fender. The rest of the car was pea-green, except for the passenger door, which was blue. The Nova had something of an identity crisis.

"Glad you approve," I said to Will.

"Man, I tell you," he said, climbing in. "I had one of these back in the day. Good times in that car. There was a girl, Cheryl Lynn . . ."

"You want to get some dinner?" I said as the car rumbled to life.

Will blinked at me. "Right now?"

"No, stupid, it's one in the afternoon." I angled us toward the port of Nocturne City but took the disused access road just before the gates. "I mean some other time, in the future. Dinner."

Will cocked his head. "What happened to you not knowing what you wanted?"

"That was then," I said. "This is dinner."

"Hell, doll, I'll *make* you dinner," he said.

I held up a hand. "Let's not get carried away. Three dates, like a real couple, and then we'll see about that."

"Three dates," Will agreed. He looked out at the rotting wharf in the shadow of the supports for the Siren Bay Bridge. "Where the Hex are we, body-dump central?"

"Be quiet," I said. "It sleeps during the day."

I got out of the car and took the slimy, rotting steps down to the sliver of sand under the bridge. The troll was curled up against the cement, snoring softly. The boundaries that Kelly and Sunny had worked manifested as graffiti marks along the pylons and the wharf, and the troll was bound on the other side by the sea.

"It eats garbage," I said, pointing to the flotsam drifting past in the current. "It has shelter, and they like the shadows and the damp. It can never go home, but . . . it's happy here, I think."

Will shook his head at me. "Why, Luna Wilder. I never knew you had a soft side."

"There's a lot of things you don't know about me," I said, getting back into the car. Will chuckled.

"A troll under the bridge."

"And a werewolf in the police and a cursed immortal in the ATF field office."

"It's a hell of a town," Will said, as we drove away.

"Yeah," I said. "But I kind of like it that way."

I dropped Will off after settling on Thursday for our date. That gave me enough time to find something to wear and not long enough to start freaking out and second-guessing myself. Will Fagin was a lot of things, but above all he was different. And that was what I needed, even more than stability or safety or anything else. The city had changed, and I had changed, and I was willing, with this new me, to give Will a shot.

I took the elevator down to the SCS offices, still open for business. Sure, we were still working out of a bomb shelter and didn't have a coffee machine, but at least we weren't all jobless, either. Once you save the city from a rift to another realm, the commissioner is inclined to be generous.

I could still feel the rift if I walked across the right part of the building, just a cold little breath on the back of my neck. I wondered what else was on the other side, just waiting for their chance to slip through.

"Lieutenant." Norris handed me a stack of folders when I reached his desk. "All of the case reports collected while you were absent." His face was screwed up, way off normal. It took me a second to realize this was Norris's version of a smile.

"Thanks," I said, trying not to reveal how freaked out I was. I paused at the bullpen. Except for Annemarie's empty desk, it was a normal day. Pete was in his lab with his headphones on, Bryson was eating a meatball sub at his desk and cursing every time he dropped sauce down his shirt. Batista was writing up a witness statement and Kelly was glaring at his computer, in what I'd come to recognize as his normal expression.

Andy Zacharias jumped up when he saw me and came over. I'd been sure we'd lose Andy after what happened on the roof, to a safe desk job or a private security firm.

But he got himself patched up and came back to work,

and never said a word about what had happened. I hoped that he was at least talking to his shrink. He had that shadowed, haunted look about him that I knew all too well. I'd been in that jumping-at-shadows spot, and it was no place to be.

"Why don't you let me take those, ma'am. You don't need to be burdened so soon after you've come back."

I patted him on the shoulder. "Thanks, Andy, but this is my job."

He gave me a nod, like he understood. "You let me know if you need anything, ma'am. Anything at all. I owe you."

"Andy, you don't owe me a thing. You're my detective. We look out for each other."

I saw a little bit of the tension in his face drain away at that. "I never thanked you, ma'am."

"Your continued presence on the squad is more than enough," I said. "Now go bother someone else, Andy." I made a little shooing motion. He surprised me with a grin.

"You got it, ma'am."

I gave my squad—my squad, and no one else's—one last look and then unlocked my office.

I had work to do.

Read on for a preview of Caitlin Kittredge's next Nocturne City novel

Demon Bound

Coming soon from St. Martin's Paperbacks

When you're a cop, you learn fast that any attempt at a nice evening out can and will be spoiled by a dead body.

The restaurant was Macpherson's, an upscale steakhouse with medium-rare walls and décor made of antlers, and my dining partner was Agent Will Fagin, Bureau of Alcohol, Tobacco, and Firearms. More than just my dining partner, really . . . I guessed that William Fagin was, after six months of steady dating, my boyfriend.

I don't do well with the boyfriend/girlfriend designation, but we went out on too many dates to be friends with benefits and stayed in too often to be friends, period.

Will smiled at me over his porterhouse. He had a great smile. Great everything, if you wanted to quantify it—forty years ago he would have been staring back at me from a movie-house poster. Thick blond hair, dancing black eyes, a long skinny frame that belied strength and manly prowess and all of that stuff that women supposedly swoon over in a boyfriend.

"I get something on my face?" he asked, running a hand along his mouth.

"No," I said. "Sorry."

Will's eyes gleamed. "You were staring at me like you're thinking hard. That never bodes well for me."

"I was just thinking about what this is," I said, gesturing with my napkin at the table, the near-empty wineglasses, and the remains of my New York strip, the crumbs in the bread basket. Will held up his hand.

"Say no more. That *what is this* talk never ends in anything except me sleeping on a sofa, so I'm going to ask for the check and we're going to head back to your apartment and have great sex until we forget about this conversation."

I laughed, pulling Will's hand down and covering it with mine. "If you let me finish, I was going to say that for me, this is good. It's the first time it's been good—calm—since I was in high school, and I like it. Gods, you're neurotic sometimes."

Will turned my hand over, running his thumb along my palm. "The offer to go back to your apartment still stands, Lieutenant Wilder."

I was about to tell him that that sounded like a fine idea when my BlackBerry chirped from inside my purse. As the lieutenant in charge of the Supernatural Crime Squad for the Nocturne City Police Department, I was never really *off* call. The brass liked me to show up at crime scenes, wave to the news cameras, prove to the plain humans of Nocturne City that their pet werewolf detective was on the job.

"Hold that thought," I told Fagin, praying it would just be a text message from my cousin Sunny and not an emergency call.

My luck is never that good. *Code 187, Pier 16, Port of Nocturne*, the message read. It came from Javier Batista, one of my detectives who had started picking up overtime and doing night shifts a few days a week.

"What's the word?" Fagin said, forkful of steak poised halfway to his mouth.

"Homicide down at the port," I said. "Batista wants me at the scene."

Will shrugged. "It happens. Don't take all night, doll." He leaned across the table and kissed my cheek, then turned around and called for our check. One of the benefits of having a man who has the same job you do—he may not like it, but he can't very well complain about the odd hours and the rushing off and the constant low background noise of the job in your everyday life. Yet another check in the plus column for Will.

I was already jogging out of the restaurant when he pulled out his credit card to pay. I got my 1971 Chevy Nova out of hock from the valet, who looked at the car like it personally offended him when it rumbled up at the curb. He did not receive a tip. My baby might not be pretty, but it had a decent amount of power under the hood and the roomy, boxy interior that I favored for things like changing out of a couture dress into jeans and a blouse in the front seat.

I kicked off my Chanel pumps—vintage, like most designer clothes worth wearing—and slipped on a pair of motorcycle boots that I kept on the passenger seat. Another thing you learn fast as a cop—have a change of clothes handy. You never know what will get spattered on you at a crime scene. I pulled around the corner into the alley, wriggled into a pair of battered jeans that had seen more than one washing to take blood, fingerprint ink, or plain grime out of them already, and a plain black blouse.

I was a lieutenant now—torn T-shirts and leather jackets were a thing of the past. Sadly. Wardrobe change accomplished, I put the Nova in gear and drove.

The Port of Nocturne is a sagging, rusting collection of warehouses, piers, and cargo containers stacked like a futuristic labyrinth along the broad main avenue that stretches like a skeletal finger into the dark water of Siren Bay.

I rumbled up to the gate, flashing my bronze shield at the gatehouse guard. He waved me on. "Your people are down at Pier 16. Hell of a thing."

Well, wasn't he a ray of sunshine. I drove through the stacks of cargo containers, the sodium lights spitting in the light mist rolling off Siren Bay. It was mid-March, that dank, chill time when even sunny California hunkers down and hibernates until spring. Nocturne City, poking out into the Pacific, felt the chill more than most.

Batista's unmarked car and a pair of patrol units were at the entrance to the pier, and a small cluster of officers milled around, staring at something in the water.

I reached over and grabbed my tub of Vapo-Rub out of the glove compartment. As a werewolf, I have the heightened sense of smell to go with the temper, the strength, and the once-a-month bloodlust, and floaters never smell all that great even if you're a plain human.

"LT," Batista called to me, waving me over. I met him at the edge of the pier. Batista looked tired, rings under his eyes and his normally tanned and healthy face sallow. "It's a bad one. My wife is gonna kill me when I don't come home at six."

"How's Marisol?" I asked. His wife was the reason he was working nights.

"Pregnant," he said. "Morning sickness, and I'm still pulling double shifts to pay for the kid's nursery, and his college fund, and God knows what else."

I patted him on the shoulder. "I'll make sure you clock out on time, Javier."

"I appreciate it, *jefe*." He gestured to the water. "She's caught up against the pilings. I called the ME and he's en route, but it's definitely a homicide."

"And the SCS caught this how?"

"One of the first responders, Natchez, says he recognizes her. Says she's a were."

Freaking fantastic. "All right," I said, taking out my pen light and walking to the edge. The water was black and oil-slick, the weak lighting catching the detritus and spills floating on the surface.

The girl's face floated up at me on the gentle swell of the waves, caught just below the surface of the water. She had pale hair that drifted in the current like sea life, wide staring eyes, and an open mouth, everything pale and bleached by her time underwater.

I saw a gaping stab wound in her sternum, dark against the translucent skin. It was ugly and broad, nothing clean or surgical about it. The girl was wearing a black miniskirt, mesh top, and bra. Club clothes. She'd been having a good time somewhere, and ended up here, suspended in the filthy water of the port.

"Call the rest of the team, will you, Javier?" I said, standing up from my crouch. "Once we get her out of the bay, I want this wrapped up quick."

"Sure thing, LT," he said, pulling out his cell phone. The rest of the detectives in the SCS wouldn't be happy about getting rousted out of bed, but a dead were-girl warranted it. Were-packs are territorial and hostile on a good day, and when one of their number is killed, they close ranks faster than a bunch of bad cops facing an IA investigation.

I walked over to the knot of uniforms and found Officer Natchez, tall as a beanpole and curly-haired. "You told Detective Batista you recognized the victim?"

"Yes, ma'am," he said. "I worked private security before I joined the force and her family hired me for a few events." He pushed a hand through his hair. "This is pretty awful. She was a nice kid."

"And this nice kid's name would be?"

"The family name is Dubois. The girl was named . . . Lila or Lisa or something. I'm sorry, ma'am. I can't recall."

Dubois didn't ring any immediate alarm bells as badass pack members, but at least we didn't have to faff around with dental records or DNA for an identification. Unless Natchez was wrong, which was entirely possible, judging from his shellshocked expression.

"This your first floater?" I said gently. He nodded.

"We don't catch much worse than junkie ODs or bar fights, ma'am. I was going off shift and I heard the call."

"Take a break," I said. "I'm sure my detectives and the CSU team could use some coffee."

"Okay," he said, and got into his patrol car, backing away from the pier. It's all about delegating at the crime scene—an officer who's losing his shit is worse than worthless for actual police work. Plus, everyone needs coffee.

"Sawbones is here," Batista said. "And I've called in."

"Great," I said absently. I was watching the second car behind the ME's black city Lincoln. It was a pale green hybrid, the sort of thing that Will—and me, too, I freely admit—would have dismissed as a "chick car." Sure enough, a chick was driving it, and she got out from behind the wheel in a swirl of *Columbo*-esque tan trenchcoat.

"Lieutenant Wilder?" she called. I sized her up as she came over. Brown hair, carrying about twenty over her ideal weight, flattering, flaw-minimizing pantsuit, makeup that was way too good for this time of night.

"Help you with something?" I said.

"I'm Detective Lane, with Special Victims," she said. "You can call me Natalie, though. I don't like that whole formality deal . . . it wastes time that a squad could spend doing actual police work."

I cocked my eyebrow at her. "Right. Good to know. Was there something you wanted?"

"Oh, yes, actually. I got the call that there was a minor homicide."

"I appreciate you coming down," I said, perfunctorily, "but we've got it under control."

"If the victim is under eighteen that makes it SVU jurisdiction," she said. "The rules are in place for a very specific reason, mostly to prevent cross-contamination of sensitive investigations . . ."

"Detective Lane." I held up my hands. "I appreciate that your captain yelled at you and made you drive down here, but the dead girl is a were. That makes it an SCS case."

"Actually," she said. "It was Deputy Chief Beck. Your boss? He requested someone from Special Victims liaise this case to cover all of the bases."

I shut my eyes for a second, praying for self-control. Beck never did a thing with the SCS unless he was haranguing me for something he figured I'd done the wrong way. He preferred to cozy up to the lieutenants and captains in Vice and Narcotics, who were men and didn't turn fuzzy on the full moon.

I hated the guy, but if he'd set this perky soccer mom with a badge on me, there wasn't much I could do except act bitchy and complain a lot.

"All right," I snapped, since complaining never did anything for me. "If I'm stuck with you, hang back and don't expect a warm, friendly group hug from the rest of my squad."

Lane—sorry, *Natalie*—blinked. I got the feeling she was used to her sweet round face and perky demeanor making people nice and cooperative. "I . . . all right. You're the ranking officer."

"What do you know. You can recite protocol." I was probably being nastier than I strictly had to be, but I resented Chief Beck sending some white-bread kiddie cop to babysit me. I was good at my job—two years on the street, five in Homicide, and nearly a year heading up the SCS.

Ignoring for the moment the suspensions, write-ups, and general chaos that had categorized my time as a detective, I went to meet Bart Kronen, the night-shift medical examiner.

"Only the good die young," he greeted me. "I'll wait for CSU to take a few scene photos and then we'll get her out of the water."

The techs showed up in short order and once they'd documented the scene, Kronen laid out a body bag and then got one of the patrol officers to lend him a rope from his prowler car.

"A bit of help, if you please," he said to the scene at large. No one moved, so I came over.

"We will attempt to slip the rope around her torso to avoid unnecessary damage to the skin," he said. We laid down on our stomachs, the girl's face staring back at us.

The rope looped around her skinny torso, and Kronen drew it tight. "Pull, Lieutenant Wilder. If you please." We got to our feet and drew the girl up and out of the dark water. Even waterlogged as she was, she weighed barely enough to strain my arms.

I'm stronger than a human, but even Kronen only gave a slight wheeze as we lowered her into the body bag. He crouched, unzipping his portable kit. Lane crowded at my shoulder.

"Poor girl. She can't be more than seventeen." She bent down to examine the body and Kronen cleared his throat loudly. I reached out and pulled Lane back by the shoulder of her coat.

"Let the doc work. Save the Oprah moment for later."

"Cause of death appears to be mutilation to the left upper chest," Kronen said. "She most likely bled out, accounting for the lack of lividity in her skin."

He took a pair of tweezers and plucked at the edges of the wound. The top layer of skin sloughed off, with a sound like wet paper bunching. Lane's face lost color and she let out a small, choked sound. Kronen had the grace to pretend not to notice. "By the condition of her dermis, I would estimate that she's been in the water at least twelve hours. Time of death will be difficult to fix because of the condition of the body."

He probed the wound further, and his forehead furrowed. "Hmm. That's odd."

"What?" I said. Kronen finding things "odd" was never good. After twenty years as a Nocturne City ME, he was about as hard to rattle as an android would be.

"Her heart," he said. "It appears to be missing."

"You mean it's hacked up?" Lane said. "That wound looks pretty severe. Maybe she got impaled on something."

"No," Kronen said. "Her ribs have been cracked. Her heart is not damaged. Her heart is gone."

I cocked my head. "*Gone?*" Just when you think you've seen everything.